# DREAM MASTER

## COLIN MARTIN

DIAMOND MEDIA PRESS CO.
1-304-460-1427
https://www.diamondmediapressco.com/

Copyright © **2022**

By **Colin Martin**

**ISBN Paperback: 978-1-954368-51-4**

*'Within his mind, a dream to dread;*
*Appear will the demon, fiery red.*
*Rider of the night, cloaked body and head;*
*Shadowed creatures, behind him tread.*
*Commands are given, speech unsaid;*
*Kill the dreamer, he must be dead.'*

# Personal Acknowledgements

### Vickie

Thank you for your positive feedback after being the very first person to read the first eight chapters of the original manuscript… you're a dearly missed friend.

### Sinéad

Thank you for your help in editing Part One of the story…your comments regarding my use of grammar, prose, dialogue and description have been so helpful.

# PART ONE

# ONE

FROM A BLANKET OF DARK cloud, rain poured upon a shadowy landscape. Distant heathland weaved its way through hills, where solitude and lifeless trees stood like statues, anchored within the earth. Shallow valleys cradled drifting fog banks that rose slowly, resembling limbless ghosts, gliding across the land. Far left, a truncated hillside formed a cliff, disclosing a dense coniferous forest. Parting the forest, a narrow country road twisted to a gradual slope and meandered into darkness.

From the sky echoed a fading storm, flashing sheets of light and bellowing distant thunder. Between the abating rumbles, rain could be heard hitting the ground.

Suddenly, from the road a flash of light shone onto bordering pines and the trees glistened with wetness. Headlamp beams from a car moved rapidly across the trees, creating eerie figures swaying in the fierce wind. The beams progressed simultaneously from tree to tree and then a silhouette advanced, climbing a twisted incline. The car cut the sound of pouring rain, bellowing a surge of mechanical power as it ascended the road. Treacherously, the car turned and sped about a corner, spraying a stream of rainwater from a puddle to the roadside. Slowing slightly, the car then reached a level and straight road. With headlights shining on the drenched road ahead, the car accelerated.

Inside, a stern faced driver erratically steered the vehicle, veering violently and tearing the car about corners. The car was being pushed to its limits and the driver looked as if he had no time to live. His fate was nearing... only a glance away...

At the roadside the car scathed the hedgerow, sheathing foliage and demolishing limbs from overhanging trees. Broken twigs and severed leaves hurled upon the car bonnet and windscreen, along with pelting raindrops. Rapidly, the screen wipers thrashed the cascading water and debris from the windscreen as the driver, a man in his late forties, looked terrorised. Somehow this adherent trailed the driver's every move, scrutinizing his every activity, suppressing his mind and soul, and torturing him like some impassable nightmare. Was he to escape and survive, or would this evil strike swiftly? Conclusively the driver was determined to eliminate this nightmare that haunted him and destroy this horror tormenting his soul.

Eventually the driver became delirious, hysterically talking to himself; his forehead soaked with sweat. As turmoil prevailed, his driving became erratic and dangerous, but somehow he kept the vehicle upon the road. He glanced into the offside wing mirror hoping to be reassured that nothing was following. However, the nightmare grew worse as his imagination became reality.

Shadowed within the mirror galloped a dark stallion with eyes glowing red, its thunderous hooves speeding the animal closer to the vehicle. Mounted upon the stallion, the rider was enshrouded in a black cloak, the body hidden and head obscured by a thick, dark veil. As the powerful animal sped ever faster, the rider's heavy veil thrashed and folded in the wind, until suddenly it fell.

Unmasked, the head revealed a human skull but framed with spiralling ram's horns and a face forged from hell itself. The skeletal face turned and glared with piercing red eyes, manifesting torment into the driver's very soul. The villainous rider jolted the reins again and it sped nearer within the mirror. The driver swerved from side to side hoping to stop the adherent advancing anymore. Suddenly, the mirror was blank, showing only an empty dark road behind. Yet he could still hear hooves, louder and louder.

There it was. His adherent could now be seen in the nearside mirror and so he panicked. With a desperate laugh, he turned to the roadside, slicing the evil into the hedgerow. The driver swiftly gazed into the mirror as he veered away from the roadside. Suddenly, the rider and its creature had vanished. The driver was puzzled. Had he defeated his evil adherent? He laughed hysterically before rectifying his directions for the road ahead.

For a short time the driver decelerated and drove about the glistening road with ease, but progressively the fear returned. Decisively, he realised time was short and valuable, so again, the accelerator pedal reached the floor. A mighty strength pulled on the front wheels and the tyres screeched upon the drenched road, spraying fine jets of water. The car sped down into a shallow valley where the road widened and trees dispersed to scatter the undulating heathland. The car raced down the straight road leaving behind an odour of burnt oil and a dissipating cloud of exhaust fumes. Now and then, the car's brake lights flickered and the noise from the distant car faded. Slowly the sound of pelting rain returned and the landscape became gloomy and lifeless once again.

The car approached a junction where a side lane veered towards the right, cutting vertically up a steep hillside. The driver pulled down to a lower gear and swerved right. The car strained against the incline, the headlight beams shimmering bordering trees and the wet road that climbed ahead. Towering the hilltop stood a large white building, its roof pronounced with an enormous glass dome framed of dark metal. Tall coniferous trees obscured lower structures and the whole building was lifeless and dark.

The sound of the nearing car advanced toward the building and the headlights appeared, flickering upon the walls of the structure. The car speedily reached a bend and the driver swerved the vehicle. Suddenly the car turned and skidded slightly. The front wheels turned, losing grip upon the road and the car sped down a short descent. It reached a small car park layered with loose grit. Sharply, the wheels turned and the footbrake reached the floor. The abrupt skid impaled a pair of lines into the grit as loose chippings fired into the air, hitting the car's underside and the front entrance of the building. As the weight of the car halted, the driver was suddenly lunged forward and then pulled back into his seat.

Briskly the driver opened the car door and it swung heavily, screeching upon its hinges. The man clambered out from the vehicle and stood tall in the pouring rain. The refreshing droplets of water revitalized his senses and for a moment he hesitated, staring obliviously at the building. He shook his head, wiping water from his eyes and pulling his hair back with his fingers. Quickly the rain soaked his rumpled clothes as he heard it hammer loudly upon the car.

He ran toward the entrance of the building and slumped heavily against the door. Leaning against the thick dark glass of the door, he tested the lock, but to his disappointment it was locked. Aggressively, he pulled the handle and with the side of his fist he slammed the glass. Under a whisper the man swore, and then searched about the front of the building.

Turning a corner he noticed a window, small but capable of accepting his body. Regretfully the window was closed, but assertively the man advanced toward it, trampling through undergrowth and bushes. He looked through the drenched window into a dark and shadowy room, and then examined the window frame. Inside, a latch arm locked the window securely.

With an ear-piercing smash the window shattered into fragments. The man looked about him brushing debris from his jacket, his elbow throbbing. Eagerly he began to rub it, massaging the joint. Trying to ignore the pain, he reached inside the window, probing carefully between jagged blades of glass, and slowly he lifted the latch arm. The window swung open and loose fragments of glass fell as the frame hit the inside wall. He waited, expecting the sound of voices and the switch of lights. Awkwardly, he lifted his legs and thrust them through the window slot, kicking bits of remaining glass. Nervously, he threw himself into the darkness. His leg caught on something and he slipped. With a thud his body hurtled upon the floor and he rolled across fragmented glass. The man halted and turned upon his stomach in pain. Anxiously, he looked about the room, wondering if the building was occupied. Recapturing his senses, gingerly he stood tall and inspected the room, staring angrily into the darkness.

Bordered with pictures, a shadow of a door stood ajar. From the opening, a strip of light extended across the floor and glittered upon scattered glass particles. Slowly he approached the door and peered through the gap, gradually opening it to reveal an illuminated hallway, which extended to the front entrance. Headlamps from the outside car ejected light upon the walls of the narrow corridor, illuminating pictures and surrounding furniture. Cautiously, he closed the door behind and advanced to the front entrance. He progressed slowly to a nearby door. Tugging at the handle, he found it tightly locked and advanced to the next. The next door opened exposing a large, tall room. As the heavy door swung slowly inward, a beam of light shone across the expanse of floor. The silhouette of the man advanced into the dark room.

The capacious floor was naked of furniture, but decorated with tiles resembling a chessboard. The surrounding walls were entirely stocked with books and various other literatures. As the man stood erect upon the centre of the floor he hesitated, searching the room with aching eyes. For a time, he scrutinized shelves about the walls, and then looked upward, toward the ceiling. Arching extensively overhead, a rigid foundation of glass revealed the nefarious sky. For a second the room illuminated with a brilliance of light and then a clap of thunder echoed in the distance.

For a moment the man felt a malicious evil sensation, and he shivered as his mind played tricks with the shadows. Attempting to calm himself he examined the books above, which circled below the glass construction. Suddenly, he recognized a piece of literature and with frenzy erected a nearby stepladder, testing its sturdiness. After some reluctance, he began to climb. At the top he took the volume of literature and sorted briskly through the pages. He cursed and swore, but then turned to one of the rear pages. Drawn crudely was a sketch of a pendant, with markings like runic symbols and other engraved patterns. As he reached into his damp coat pocket and pulled out an edifice of glittering metal, he began to read the handwriting surrounding the sketch. It was skimpy and hardly legible but with amazement the necklace he held resembled that in the book. Speedily he returned to reading.

From behind his head, through the glass and into the ominous night, clouds swiftly gathered then coiled into a swirling mass. The assemblage of clouds turned bloody in colour and a tempest developed. A cyclone of cloud descended to the ground and reached the hills and forestry in the distance. Abruptly a flare of deep red light shot through the cyclone, to the ground.

The man turned suddenly to view the landscape about him. To his satisfaction the surrounding land and weather was all as he expected. The cyclone of cloud had disappeared. As echoes of thunder rumbled in the distant sky, the monotonous drone of rainfall battered upon the glass and rivers of water ran down the panes of glass. As the man read anxiously through the literature, a ball of scarlet light flared and darkened in the distance. For a moment the light faded, but then a ball of fire sped toward the building. The colossal mass of fire twisted and entwined forming a perplexing image. As the assemblage of fire continually reformed, bursts of glittering flames exploded and dispersed, dissipating into the night. The ball of conflagration advanced quickly through the distant trees and progressed toward the building. For a moment the fireball poised, hovering in the nearby woodland. Suddenly the infernal mass unravelled into a malicious demonic face. Two enormous hands expanded forward and the gruesome phantasmal creature advanced ferociously upon the glass dome. From within the glass foundation the demon's head flared with nebulous heat and the fallacious beast rose towering ever taller over the dome. The head of the demon was crowned with spiralling horns and centred below, a face of indescribable horror intensified such a hellish glare. The gaping mouth exposed a bloodied tunnel of death and misery. As the fiery image moved, the detail blurred then reformed.

Suddenly the man shivered cold and looked toward the sky. As he stood aghast in unbelievable terror, an enormous fiery hand covered the dome and blazing white sparks began to hit the glass structure. At first the structure shook with intense vibration, but then with an explosion, the glass shattered and flew to the floor of the library.

Countless blades of glass assailed the man and within a second a multitude of glass blades pierced his body. Acute fragments of glass sliced into his face, chest and legs, erupting streams of blood. The man screamed, but his ears could not hear his own deafening cry. As his voice dissolved, his visibility melted into blackness and his balance became uncontrollable. With an overwhelming weakness in his legs, the man wobbled upon the ladder. As he stumbled about, the room was darkening and the pain became extreme. For a moment the ladder withheld his weight and erratic movements, but as his sensitivity darkened and his stability crumbled, the ladder toppled and he fell.

Suddenly, he hit the floor and was rendered into a haunting unconsciousness. The book and pendant flew across the room and bounced upon the floor. Face up and near the contorted body, the book's pages flickered over and settled. The pendant skidded across the floor and hit a wall, where it lay upturned. Fragments of glass fell upon the distorted body as pools of blood expanded across the floor.

From above, the demon's forefinger pointed towards the library floor and a flash of fire discharged from a lengthy talon. A spark ruptured the book and the pages ignited with bursts of smoke. The demon's hand contracted into its fiery body and gradually the beast's face decayed into a vague image. As the demon reversed into the distance, it contorted into an entwining ball of fire, and within seconds it had dissolved within the distant woodland, leaving nothing but a thick mist. Suddenly, a flash of scarlet light hurtled to the sky through the distant tempest and all went quiet.

Inside the library, the book burned to a smouldering mass and the man lay twisted, motionless and silent. Rain percolated through the demolished glass dome as a vicious wind howled about the rooftop.

# TWO

THROUGH A NARROW GAP BETWEEN curtains, dim light shone from a neighbouring street lamp into a shadowy bedroom adorned with antiquated furniture. Objects stood shadowed in corners, shaded between a murky light and the darkness. Apart from the harmonious and melodic ticking of an old wall clock, the room was silent.

Sprawled upon a large bed, within the darkest corner of the room, lay a motionless body, asleep and silent. Some bedclothes wrapped the body tightly, but some overhung the floor. Upon the wall opposite the window hung a large circular mirror, framed with tarnished brass. The shadows reflected in the mirror made the object resemble a mysterious dark void.

Suddenly the body upon the bed twitched, became aroused, and turned over. The eyes of a man opened and looked upon the ceiling, his face stern and distressed. He turned again, closing his aching eyes. He fumbled with the bedclothes to bring comfort, but this proved useless. Some tormenting fear agitated him and he cursed his thoughts and actions. Opening his eyes again, he searched the room and noticed the foreboding darkness reflected by the mirror. Suddenly, as he watched, a mist assembled within the mirror and swirled like a whirlpool. As it formed more densely, it poured from the mirror and onto the floor. Within seconds, a layer of mist had formed above the floor and started to advance towards the bed.

Bewildered, he sat up, rubbed his eyes and looked closer upon the creeping mist. As a cold breeze circled the room, the mist glowed brighter and from that he wondered if he was not dreaming. As the young man pulled himself from beneath the bed sheets, he looked upon a floor now engulfed with mist. Abruptly, the bed jolted and lifted a little, before turning somewhat. Bewildered the man decided to jump from the bed, but in return a power hit him, catapulting him back upon the bed and against the headboard. Unsure of what would happen next, he knelt firmly, grasping the bed post. However, the bed then began to toss about as if it was upon a stormy sea. Steadily, the bed rose higher and jolted more vigorously.

Swiftly from within the shadows of the mirror, the mist expanded and formed a glowing vortex. Within seconds, the man looked now, not at his room, but at a tunnel of revolving mist. About him the mist spun faster, and he suddenly realised he was being drawn into the tunnel. The man held onto the bed frame and hid his head within the pillow until he heard screams bellowing his name. He looked up and recognised faces formulated within the whirling mist; somehow these were plagued by misery and torment. As the bed started to accelerate down the tunnel, the faces span, circling him, calling for help and reassurance. Once again the man buried his head within the pillows, wishing the nightmare would stop, but felt the bed begin to spin. Suddenly, the man lost grip from the bed post and he was thrown into the swirling mist.

Wet and covered with soft debris, the man found himself upon firm ground. For a moment he lay dazed until his eyes could focus upon the surroundings. He pulled himself up from a woodland floor, coated in mud and leaves. The frosted floor glistened and his warm breath exhaled into mist as he shivered, feeling the cold upon the wet of his pyjamas. Although confused and sore, his sense of fear returned and warned him to flee. He looked about himself searching for routes to escape. Escape to where, he thought? And then he thought he saw something in the trees, something watching him. Although his body shuddered and he felt his heart racing, he shot to his feet and ran.

Awkwardly, his feet trod upon the uneven floor. Numerous times his strength crumbled and he fell, but quickly he crawled back to his feet and continued. His hands and face stung as they were scratched by tree branches and shrubbery. The cold was intense and his feet throbbed although covered with thick socks. Pausing momentarily, he glanced behind him. The scenery seemed to be scrutinizing him – the shadowy trees, the bushes... the distant darkness. Suddenly everything about him felt evil and the eerie silence became intolerable. With clothes torn and muddied, he again began to run until his foot became snared in the bracken below and he fell. Rolling upon the cold earth his mind became faint and eventually his consciousness escaped him.

Awakened by an abrupt halt, he hit a wall. For a moment his senses faded, but gradually his eyes focused from a blur. Above him stood arching trees, standing like towering statues that branched out arms to conceal the sky. Through the branches was a dark and clear sky, littered with small clouds that concealed several stars. Nearby, a bright moon was almost full, its cold face grinning at the fool below him. The man turned upon his stomach and pulled himself to his feet. Over a collapsed wall he could see an old churchyard with shadowed gravestones and lifeless trees. Towering to the left, he noticed a church, dark and silent. As he began to walk alongside the wall, the detail of the church became more noticeable. Finally he stopped, watching as an old iron gate swung slowly upon its hinges. Pushing the gate aside, he hesitated and then glanced over his shoulder. Feeling his sense of fear return, he decided to head for the church.

In the distance something moved – undistinguishable, but it stirred within bushes. For a split second, an ear-piercing tone shot between his ears as from the depths of the woodland a cloud of smoke developed. Grasping all the energy left within his body he decided to run toward the church.

With a great surge of power he burst the church doors open, but collapsed upon the church isle and was left sprawled upon the tiled floor. He hesitated for a while, studying the church interior and then sat up, searching beyond the church doors. However, before he could stand tall and stretch his aching limbs, his heart raced again as he heard the sound of distant hooves. Somehow he recognised this deathly gallop; when or where he did not know, but knew it was positively evil.

He raced down the aisle towards an altar, where he found a broken crucifix, along with a spilt goblet of wine. He stopped and so did the gallop of hooves. For a number of seconds all was silent and he searched the church, squinting in the darkness for an exit. He fumbled to an arching alcove that revealed a wooden door. He stopped, looked about it, and then gradually opened it; turning its ringed metal handle. Below him lay steps and a dark tunnel. Descending the steps, he scrambled through the darkness and followed it. For once the tunnel straightened and led to an open gate. He pawed his way up a small embankment and found himself in a graveyard, one at the rear of the church. For a time, confusion overwhelmed him, and he walked among the gravestones wiping his face of dirt. His lacerated hands stung, as too did his face. Tired and muddled, he began to feel weak and tormented. Somehow, he recognised this church and its graveyard but could not recall any memories. He passed grave after grave, rubbing his hands to warm them from the cold air. Noticing one particular grave, he stopped and unwillingly looked upon the gravestone, reading the inscription. Memories flooded his mind as he saw himself as a child again. Decayed, but legible, the inscription was that of his father's name. He knelt upon the overgrown earth, looking upon the grave with emotion. For a while he felt sorrowful, but warmed by memories.

Abruptly, the still night became wild and a freezing wind howled through the tree-tops. As he looked upward, clouds developed and raced across the sky. As the moonlight disappeared, a fierce wind blew him off balance and onto the grave. With vigorous power the earth below him moved and started to disintegrate. He sat back in astonishment and then attempted to stand. The earth moved again and he felt he was being toyed with. The ground moved once more, crumbling away until a hole was exposed. Suddenly the whole area collapsed. He fell, rolled, and then hit something. Lying upon his side, he tried to focus on his surroundings. Shaking dirt from his face, he noticed that this grave had no coffin, no high walls, but a long dark passageway. It was very narrow and stood several feet high, and in the distance he could see the silhouette of something. He looked up and attempted to climb out, but his feet slid upon the crumbling earth and he fell back. In pain and anger he rose to his feet, and then crawled down the passageway. Feeling claustrophobic, he became frightened and wanted to turn back, but he could not get out.

Fumbling through the passageway, he approached a wooden door, pacing gingerly nearer, stopping and hesitating. Before him, and within the shadows, stood an old wooden door held shut by thick steel chains, secured together by a large rusty padlock. As he knelt, wiping dirt from his face and hands, he noticed a large key upon the earth. Unexpectedly, his body jolted – agitated by a sudden hammering sound that pounded the door from the other side. Moving and tightening, the chains reverberated and pulled powerfully upon the padlock. Suddenly, all went quiet and for a time his ears rang. As the eerie silence returned, he felt a cold, evil spirit around him. Tormented and freezing, his limbs became petrified, but then he remembered; the key. He threw himself to the floor and grasped it between thumb and forefinger, but strangely his hand froze and it flew from his hand and into the padlock. The man trembled, totally transfixed in terror as the key turned slowly in the lock. The padlock snapped open and the chains broke free, disentangling the door in frantic speed. With a hefty clatter they hit the floor. For a moment the door stood ajar, and then opened, revealing a menacing darkness.

For some time he lay terrified, but then crawled to his feet. Gradually his curiosity overwhelmed him and he advanced towards the opening. He paused and cautiously looked inside. Although he could not see beyond the foreboding darkness, he smelt an acrid odour that stung his eyes and scathed his throat. From above a clatter of chains resounded and he looked up. Towering above him was a tunnel to the sky that resembled the inside of a chimney. Confused but curious, he reached further in to the opening. From above came the resonance of disentangling chains and a falling object. Quickly the man withdrew from the door and stumbled backward upon the floor in horror.

As the clashing of chains halted, he heard a loud cracking of bone. Beyond the opening, swinging between the darkness and light, hung a body, its face horribly contorted and splattered with blood, the head pulled from the shoulders. A thick chain cut deeply into the neck and the body turned, hitting the inside of the tunnel. The sunken eyes of a man had turned up into their sockets and the lips were purple and dry, the mouth puffed shut.

Crazed with terror, Carl awoke, nerves trembling, sweat saturating his body. For a moment his heart pounded, his body frenzied with heat. Gradually, he realised that again he had been subjected to another terrible nightmare. Although wrapped within the bedclothes, as his nerves calmed, he became cold and faint. For a moment his thoughts escaped him and his sight was blurred. Moving beneath the bedclothes his senses returned, but so did images of the nightmare. He pulled back the bedclothes and glanced at the window. As a breeze stirred the heavy curtains, outside he could see that the night was dank, but the sky dark and clear. Deciding not to turn over, he shuddered, remembering that the mirror was behind him. For some reason he was truly frightened, scared of the mirror in his own bedroom. He gazed upon his digital clock radio. The time shone 01.08. Reaching for his bed-lamp, the room illuminated. Carl felt relieved as the images of the nightmare diminished into thoughts of work, of the articles almost completed for his editor. For a few minutes he lay with the lamp shining bright, but felt tiredness overwhelm him. As he reached to switch it off, his body also felt peculiarly drained of energy. Eventually his thoughts melted into a haze and he fell asleep.

Carl flinched and woke to the shrill of a telephone. Suddenly there was silence, and then it rang again. He sat up in dismay and rubbed his eyes. The sound bawled again. Still half asleep, Carl slid to the side of the bed and turned on the lamp. Lifting the handset he answered, but his acknowledgement was quickly interrupted.

'Carl?' a voice called. Without awaiting a reply the sharp voice continued.

'It's Mike! Hey, I expected you to be up by now. You'd better get your arse in gear; work's a bit earlier today.' The voice gabbled on, 'Err; yes, we've got to go somewhere, the boss just phoned. Looks like another busy Monday, eh?' the voice stopped for breath. 'No office this morning, we're off south near the Mendip Hills.' Another pause lasted a couple of seconds. 'Actually err; it's near the town…' he paused as if reading. 'Shipham,' he announced.

Carl acknowledged that he was listening and became more coherent, 'Where?'

'I'm not sure; the boss said it'll be on an attachment.' The voice continued, 'Oh hell, looks like we'll have to go to the office anyway. Besides,' the voice chuckled with laughter, 'I'm not sure of the bloody way, but you'll drive, won't you?'

Carl agreed; his work-mate was a very indecisive character and although Carl was curious of their assignment, he asked no questions. Carl replied.

'I'll pick you up. Give us half an hour or so. Be there about seven-thirty.'

He hardly heard Mike acknowledge the arrangement, and then the phone went silent. Carl replaced the handset, got dressed and turned off his bed-lamp.

Outside the window he could see the morning was dark, and heavy rainfall battered a quiet street. Strangely the birds were silent, as too was the usual distantly barking dog. The glistening street was littered with puddles and leaves, rolled along as a powerful wind circled about the buildings. Reluctantly Carl turned to wash and get dressed.

In the kitchen, Carl could hear the rain lashing loudly upon the back window as a bush tapped its branches at the ledge. After gulping down some strong coffee and stale biscuits, Carl snatched his briefcase and proceeded outside to his car. After locking the front door of his flat, he ran to his car and rushed inside. The side street was lifeless and dark, but a violent wind swayed the treetops above. The rain battered hard upon the windscreen of the car, and for a moment Carl shivered. With a turn of the ignition key the car pounced into action. Carl flicked on the headlights and turned the car out into the road. Within seconds the car had sped down the street expelling grey whirls of smoke, before disappearing around a corner.

The car weaved its way through bumpy side streets, thrashing rain to the pavement and illuminating buildings. As Carl reached the main road, early morning people were rushing about their duties trying desperately not to get wet. The main road was a smoother drive, but delays were inevitable when travelling to the other side of town. Mike lived with his parents in the outskirts of Bristol and thought of him as ambitious, but irresponsible and ignorant. Although Carl found Mike good company, especially when meeting people, for this reason Carl usually found himself left out of conversation.

As Carl's thoughts of past meetings and friends busied his mind, he reached Mike's street. Number forty-six, or the Red Ashes as it was known, stood elegant and tall in the street. Approaching the house, Carl noticed all was dark, except the hall and kitchen lights which shone dimly. Carl parked the car at the roadside and hooted the horn. All was quiet apart from the hammering rain and the noise of the car engine. Suddenly, the front door of Mike's house flew open and a silhouette appeared, followed by another. The first figure was clumsy and bundled with valuables. The second figure stopped in the doorway, leaning lightly on the door. As the light from the hallway darkened, Carl could see Mike clambering toward the car. Closing the porch door and slowly retreating in to the house walked a silhouette of a slim body, clothed in thin cloth. Carl watched as the sensuous body of a girl turned and closed the front door. Suddenly, his concentration was broken by the opening of the passenger door. Before entering the car, Mike threw in some articles.

'Don't know about you but this job's hell for travelling; all these things to carry? It's a bloody nuisance.' Mike's voice broke a moment while he comforted himself in the front seat. 'Well, that's all my stuff. All we need now is this rain to stop. What a scream… probably some boring lecture to report about.' He paused and then announced, 'That's it! Okay mate, let's head for the office.'

Carl kept quiet for most of the journey, listening to Mike's extraordinary night before and some of the girls he had seen. Mike's face was blushed and his blonde hair glimmered from city lights. His eyes were wide with excitement as he told Carl about a party he attended over the weekend. As Carl drove through the city, he changed the subject; work proved to be the strongest discussion. Within a quarter of an hour they had reached Palmer House, a multi-story office in which they worked, along with several other companies. However, Haigh and Reece covered two floors, but they worked on the second floor. The best thing Carl liked about the building was its reception area – the artistic design and clever use of space.

Carl drove into the open car park and raced to a favourite spot. Carl and Mike grabbed their belongings and ran toward the building, sheltering for a minute under the overhead walkway. By the doorway, they tidied themselves before sauntering themselves toward the reception desk. The room had a low ceiling, decorated with spotlights that were fixed at angles, lighting pictures and surrounding walls. The reception desk was long and spacious, arched like a crescent moon. At this time the receptionist had not yet arrived and the only other occupant was a security guard, who was searching through his keys as he fumbled with the doors of a lift. Above him stood a spiral staircase, of which ascended several floors. Below, a beautifully lit water fountain cascaded vibrant colours onto enshrouding foliage. They advanced toward the lift where the security guard acknowledged them. Inside the lift, Mike pressed for the second floor. Within seconds, the doors silently opened and Mike shifted quickly out, nervous of the mechanical enclosure. Carl followed in a much leisurely pace.

After walking through several corridors and open plan offices, they reached the office where they worked. Mike, burdened with articles, sorted them as Carl flicked on lights and switches. The dark of the office lit up and electrical equipment began to hum. From within a corner Carl keyed with a computer terminal and a nearby printer shot into action. Mike sorted through paperwork from his belongings and walked over to join Carl.

'Hey, these instructions are good, eh?' Mike announced. 'No directions,' he paused for a second. 'Oh, yes of course, *he* said there should be an attachment!'

'Look on the other machine, Mike.' Carl said, pointing 'The large one, over there!' Mike took the sheet of paper from the other printer and walked back toward Carl.

'Jesus! Look at this, its miles away!' Mike shouted after looking at the paper in hand. 'Here it is… Shipham, that town I said?'

Obviously Carl realised that Mike had thought it was nearer home – his local geography had never been a strong point. After a few minutes busying themselves with the computer equipment, they made their way to the car.

It was a long drive in the darkness of the late autumn morning and the rain had not stopped for a minute. With the printed map at hand, Mike tried his best navigating, but his conversation overwhelmed him. Nattering continually, he was aggravating Carl, who found the route hard enough to pursue. However, Carl's concentration became more focused on driving as he ignored his friend's conversation. As they crossed Clifton Bridge and joined a major road south, the dark clouds had separated and the morning sun was rising slowly in the east. After crossing the river Yeo and passing through the town of Church Hill, Carl found he could race through the countryside. Towards Shipham, the roads were narrow and twisted about the landscape, weaving between lifeless trees and overgrown shrubbery. Distant meadows exposed furrows as the first arrival of sunlight expanded across them – however, the woodlands and valleys of the landscape were dark and placid.

According to what Carl had seen of the map and after noticing the landmarks nearby, they were close to their destination. Carl advanced the car up a twisted incline and continued down a widening road. Towering upon a hilltop, he could see Centridge House, one of the oldest manors in southern England. It stood profound like a lighthouse; tall and bright in the morning light.

Carl turned right at a junction and sped the car up a lane until they could see the top of the building above the trees. As they approached the building, the trees dispersed, revealing a gritted drive and parking area. The car lifted and then bounced as it entered the parking area; stones hitting the car's underside. Carl steered toward several other parked vehicles and found a convenient spot. Obviously this incident had already aroused much curiosity and one vehicle parked outside the entrance was surrounded by police barrier tape. As they sorted through their valuables and stepped out of the car, Carl and Mike noticed a dark sports car shoot in front of them. As they collected their valuables, they stood aghast as the sports car door swung open, revealing a young blonde woman dressed in a loose fawn blouse and a tight, short black skirt. Her long bronzed legs tightened as she got out of the vehicle and reached over toward the passenger seat. As she stood tall, she slung a small bag over her shoulder and lifted a dark case. Carl and Mike glanced at one other before watching her walk quickly to the entrance of the building.

Shortly they followed her to join a crowd gathered inside a central room of the building. Noticing that the room resembled a small library, Carl's eyes were distracted from looking upward and around, to a flash of light. Another flash flared from a camera, as the girl operating it hovered about a corpse sprawled upon the floor. Repeatedly, the camera flashed as several uniformed gentlemen stood secretly talking in one corner. Carl and Mike advanced further into the room, walking slowly towards the body sprawled upon the floor.

'Excuse me, gents, but this is no exhibition for the public. I'll have to ask you to leave'

Carl turned and saw a policeman, leaning with arms folded, against the doorway. He stood tall and walked toward them as Mike turned and announced.

'We're reporting on this incident for Haigh and Reece, Bristol.'

Mike searched his pocket and eventually revealed a business card.

'Both of you?' the constable questioned.

'Yes, of course!' Mike snapped, thinking the question ridiculous.

After Mike confirmed their identity, they proceeded toward a body, which a group of men were covering with a white sheet, after examining it.

'An accident; it is high up here but I've never heard of lightning hitting any buildings in this area before.' A grey-haired elderly man announced, kneeling beside the body. 'What I can't understand is why he broke in just to get a *book*. There's nothing stolen... well, there's nothing in his pockets, except that sketchy map.'

Mike noticed the remains of an open book upon the floor nearby.

'How come the book is burnt?' Mike questioned.

The elderly man turned his head quickly and stood up. He approached Mike and looked at him, his sharp blue eyes widening. His face was plump and rounded, his eyebrows curled with white hairs and his nose long and wide.

'And what concern is it of yours?' he replied, looking at the constable to reveal their identity.

'Reporters Sir,' a distant voice announced.

'We haven't got time for this lot. They're all the same, nosey buggers.'

The chief constable scowled at Mike and walked toward another gentleman, also clothed in a suit and overcoat. Mike heard them converse quietly, occasionally looking over their shoulders at him.

Carl looked upon the girl's actions and body movement, as for a moment she broke concentration and stared at him. However, she seemed disaffected from the others, alone in her work, now photographing the room and its contents. Carl wandered astray for a while and looked at the shelves encircling the room above. Then he looked toward the ceiling where a shattered glass dome arched overhead. He looked toward Mike, who was kneeling beside the body, talking to another man. Tired, Carl rubbed his eyes and yawned. Focusing his eyes against the floor, he noticed a sheet of broken glass covering a small metal object. He turned toward the crowd to find all engaged in conversation, except the constable at the door, who watched the girl mess with her camera. Slowly, he paced toward the object. Kicking aside the glass, he placed his foot over the object and snatched it whilst pretending to tie his shoe laces. As he stood tall, Carl secretly placed it in the breast pocket of his coat as the constable at the door shouted.

'Watch it!'

'Sorry!' Carl apologised, 'There's glass everywhere. I didn't see it. Better watch my step!'

Carl continued to wander about the room, pretending to look interested, but secretly wanted to look at the object he had found. However, he realised he must help Mike report on the incident and so walked slowly toward him, trying not to disrupt his conversation with a policeman.

'Can't say what he was doing here, but in the position that he's lying, looks as though when lightning struck the dome, the glass struck his body and he fell. It accounts for the awful loss of blood.' The young doctor continued, 'His neck is also broken. There's internal bruising around the base of the cranium. You can see it clearly from this angle.'

As inquisition overcame Mike's manners, he questioned the doctor further.

'How long has he been dead?'

'I would say about… well…since about midnight.'

Carl caught a glimpse of the corpse as the doctor stood up and replaced the sheet. Suddenly Carl froze. Mike turned to his colleague, seeing him stare nervously upon the corpse. Although he only saw it for a few seconds, Carl recognised the face of the corpse.

'What the hell's wrong with you?' Mike demanded, and then looked closer at his partner. 'You okay Carl? You're white as a ghost!'

Carl did not answer for a time and then muttered a few undistinguishable words.

'It can't be… Not him…' His voice groaned hoarse and other words were but a breath. Mike repeatedly asked his friend if he was all right and escorted him towards the hallway.

'Can't be? Can it?' Carl croaked, turning to approach the corpse. Mike struggled, trying to restrain his friend from uncovering the body, but eventually pushed him toward the hallway.

'Son, you'll have to leave if you can't compose yourself,' the constable announced, stepping towards them. Mike reassured the constable that his colleague was fine and that they were about to leave anyhow. Whilst Mike talked to the constable, Carl pulled away from his friend and walked toward a nearby statue. Slowly, Carl pulled the object he had found from his coat pocket and began examining it. Suddenly, Mike approached and shouted.

'What's the fuck got into you, eh?'

'Nothing... nothing,' Carl snapped, hiding the object from his friend. Mike stood quietly for a while, looking occasionally into the library, then back at his colleague. As Mike started moaning, muttering sentences about not gathering enough information, Carl secretly replaced the object within his coat pocket and swiftly passed his friend, slapping him on his arm as he paced to the entrance.

'Come on then! There's nothing here but an accident.'

Mike followed in bewilderment, pausing to take a last glimpse of the scene and that of the girl, clipping her case together.

'We've got all we need. There's other work to catch upon,' Carl explained leaving the building.

'What about photos?' Mike questioned, but Carl did not hear him.

Outside, a fresh morning breeze calmed Carl's nerves, although his thoughts still oppressed him. Mike swung his arm about his friend and smiled.

'Something bothering you, mate? Don't you want to talk about it?' Carl looked at the wide grin that stretched across Mike's face, his eyes now sympathetic and glimmering light blue from the morning sunlight. Behind them clicked the sound of high heels. The girl brushed past them closely and proceeded to her sports car, long hair thrashing in the wind. Mike called out as she opened the car door.

'Hey! Excuse me, but…' he stuttered the last words as she turned to face him. She brushed the hair from her eyes and pulled it back over her shoulder. As Mike continued to question her about her interest here, she walked slowly towards them. From behind his friend, Carl poised, watching the girl inquisitively. As she explained apathetically her assignment for a local paper, her voice was soft and Carl found her presence irresistible. Her face was small, her skin tinted bronze and unblemished, apart from several freckles on her nose. Her dark brown eyes sparkled in the sunlight as her shaggy hair fell over them. Mike found conversation awkward as she was disinterested, looking about, excusing herself.

'I've got things to do, lads,' she said, 'They want these pictures desperately.'

Mike burst into voice as she turned and paced swiftly to her vehicle.

'Hey, look! Haven't I seen you before…somewhere in…?' Mike was cut off as she exclaimed.

'There are a lot of you I've bumped into; all the same. Do anything for a piece of the action… boring… overworked journalists.'

Mike replied laughing, 'Hey, all the girls I've overworked with haven't complained!'

She smiled mischievously, before descending into her car.

'What's your name?' Carl demanded, 'Surely there's no harm in telling us that!'

Carl stood pondering for a response as she drove past.

'It's no concern of yours,' she laughed, changing gear. Within seconds the two were left in a cloud of smoke and her car was speeding down the country lane.

Behind them, the police assembled outside the entrance of the building, talking and examining the open door of the deserted car. Mike moved over to a policeman he had previously found helpful, to discover more about the vehicle. Apparently the car was abandoned as soon as it was parked. The engine would still be running, if they had not switched it off. Also, Mike learned that a window had been forced at the side of the building. Mike scratched notes on his pad and stopped recording the interview on his Dictaphone. After placing them in his sports bag, he took a last look at the scene whilst Carl drove his car to the exit of the car park.

Soon they were back on the road, swiftly driving through the countryside. As they reached the outskirts of Bristol it was nearing lunchtime and so they searched for a spot to eat. On the left of the road, obscured by large evergreen trees, stood a small public house enshrouded by shrubs and ivy. Carl found the car park small, but managed to park without difficulty. They left their valuables in the car and proceeded to the entrance, where above them hung a banner of the pub. With an accompanying picture, it advertised – The Falcon's Head. As usual, Mike was the first to enter, and found a small but quaint front lounge. Although almost empty, a few characters were conversing secretly by the bar and a couple of elderly gentlemen looked suspiciously at them from a corner. As they pondered, inspecting the room, a deep voice announced.

'Can I help you, gents? What would you like to drink?'

Mike cleared his throat and then ordered two drinks. Carl forced himself into the conversation and asked about lunches. The barman disclosed that they provided a small food menu and presented a menu-card.

'Please give us about ten minutes to serve lunches. Ham salad is on special as it's not been popular, what with the weather.' He poured their drinks, exchanged money and excused himself to a nearby room. Deciding where to sit, Carl and Mike stood hovering for a moment. Eventually, Carl sat near a window shaded by heavy dark curtains which gave the room a hazy scarlet shade. The furniture was antiquated but firm and comfortable – the air soft and warm. They sat for some time discussing their menu choices, and the incident they had investigated earlier. A young dark-haired girl approached, holding a pen and note-pad.

'Excuse me, but are you the gents wishing to order lunch?'

Mike agreed and announced their choices.

'Here's your order number. It'll take about ten minutes,' the girl said, smiling.

Like many girls, Mike found something about her incredibly attractive and joked with Carl about her as she disappeared into the kitchen.

It was several minutes later when they were served, and although they were deep in conversation, they had finished their drinks. They ate and drank a little more until early afternoon, then decided to leave.

The afternoon weather had become quite pleasant, with warm sunlight shining for long intervals between the dissipating clouds. Towards Bristol the traffic became congested, and it took a good half hour to reach Palmer House. Again Carl and Mike made their way to the second floor office, where people were assembled, wrapped in heated discussion. Sitting at Carl's desk, in one corner, the Editor and Sales Director were listening to the network of discussion. Quietly Carl and Mike walked in hoping to listen in on the discussion, trying to find out whether they were involved. Suddenly the debate ceased and everyone turned to look at them. The Editor and Director sat up and then slowly walked out the office, continuing their own private conversation. Carl and Mike approached cautiously, and understood after listening to the conversation that the Editor had been pressured to speed up publication.

'What's happening?' Mike questioned with concern.

A small plump, dark-haired man replied.

'Apparently, it's us. We're not up to scratch with stories. By the time we get them drafted, our competitors already have their articles in the newspapers, magazines, even the advertising.'

Pete was one of those guys everyone found easy to get on with – harmless and self-conscious of being overweight. Suddenly, a tall character cut his way into the conversation.

'If it wasn't for *you* two being given stories to bugger up then we'd be okay... That's countless times I've known you two to be behind, rushing work. Two idle bummers if you ask me!'

Carl snapped a response.

'If we wanted your opinion, we'd ask for one!'

David sternly looked at them and hesitated.

'Ask me for one, would you? I bet you would!' he announced, and then retreated to his desk, sitting back with a document in hand.

For some hours the usual talkative atmosphere in the office was calmed, but remained busy. As Mike followed up their reporting of the incident, Carl sorted previous articles for publishing, adding some final touches. Carl had committed himself to many stories and lately the work had been piling up. Carl decided that this week he would work harder in order to finish two articles for a national magazine, one for a local newspaper and several others that he had been inspired to publish.

Engrossed in word processing and using publishing software, Carl hardly noticed how the afternoon fled. Carl worked profoundly upon the equipment and admired the agility, the labyrinth of design techniques. The new computer software and machinery had revolutionised the production of publications in efficiency and neatness. Compared to his earlier days with the company, the job was now more technical and professional. He fully enjoyed the literal work but left his friend to his best ability – talking to people. He had helped Mike get the job in corporate journalism, and sure enough, Mike adapted quickly to the oral work.

As Carl worked late into the afternoon, his thoughts drifted occasionally to that of earlier days at study class, and memories that could never disappear. As Carl's thoughts of the article he was typing were clouded by the memory of one Christmas where he and Mike had won Story of the Month, a voice interrupted.

'Are you going to be long? We're going for a quick drink in town. Coming?'

Carl closed his eyes tight and opened them to look up. Mike stood poised over his shoulder, looking at the screen of the computer terminal.

'No, I'm going to stay 'til late. This story's a long one – lots of research and history to cover... Sorry, see you tomorrow?' Carl asserted.

'Alright, mate. See you over the weekend then, eh? When all that's done?' Mike said, tapping the computer screen.

'Yes, that'll be fine. There'll be no pressure then.'

Carl heard voices behind him fade away as Mike left with Pete and a few others. Shortly after, Carl found himself in the office accompanied by only a few other members of staff, who were printing documents, faxing articles, phoning clients and generally busy with paperwork. The Editor was, as usual, working late and on the phone, whilst gliding his way through articles for publication.

It was about a quarter to nine when Carl finally escaped the seizure of his work and began to pack away documentation. After switching off his terminal and gathering his belongings, he proceeded to the lift. He eventually realised that late at night it was inoperative – the stairs being the only alternative.

It was not until he had settled himself in the cold dampness of his car that he shuddered with the thoughts of the incident that morning and the nightmare that had preceded it. He started the car and drove through town, trying to forget the vivid resemblance of the man in his dream and that of the one found dead at Centridge House. Near to his flat, Carl's thoughts were broken as he passed a café he had frequently visited. Thinking the cold night air may clear his thoughts, he decided to park the car near home and walk to it. As he bundled belongings into his car and locked the door, the thought of a hot meal soothed his nerves.

With clearer skies, the night air was now freezing and fog had descended into the outskirts of town. As he walked anxiously toward the café, he turned down an alley enclosed by high redbrick walls. He stopped and looked sternly into the darkness that lay between the houses. Abruptly, a shriek pierced the silence and then faded, along with the shadow of a cat from which it had come. Discouraged but hungry, Carl wrapped his coat about him and walked speedily down the gritty path, into the shadows between the buildings. After walking twenty yards the alley opened into a narrow street, where opposite was a park. Light here was scarce and the blackness of the park looked ominous as a chilling wind rustled the trees and bushes.

Carl turned quickly toward the lights of the café and then shivered as loud footsteps advanced toward him. In the dimness of the alley behind him, he could see but faint shadows, and then suddenly something cold and hard hit his neck. Shortly after, a blow to his stomach rendered pain throughout his body and his sight blurred. With another blow against his legs, he lost balance and collapsed. Through the pain and numbness he felt his pockets being searched and his watch removed.

As he rolled upon the frozen pavement and curled into a ball, his stomach convulsed. Carl's eyes rolled uncontrollably, viewing nothing but shadows. Gradually, his sight became cloaked in darkness, and consciousness escaped him.

# THREE

CARL AWOKE WITH BRIGHT DAYLIGHT shining powerfully into his eyes. A strong clinical odour filled his nostrils as he rubbed his eyes, accustoming them to the light. He turned his head and lifted it from the hard pillow to look about him. He found his body covered with heavy sheets and blankets. As he searched the room, he saw other beds surrounding him and so realised he was in a hospital. Other patients were sitting up in bed, busying themselves; eating, drinking, reading, and some were in conversation.

Carl pulled his body to sit up and although most of the pain had disappeared, the soreness continually hurt. He levered his body further to sit against the headboard and looked about the ward at patients, some staring curiously back at him. Carl had never felt so discomforted, not knowing what to do, but lie perplexed by his accident.

His grievous thoughts were interrupted by a young nurse, who spoke slowly and politely. Unfortunately, in his dismay, Carl misheard her questioning but nodded in pretence and wriggled to comfort his aching limbs. As he felt the feverish heat from his body cool from his sweat, his senses steadily returned. However, as the nurse interrupted him again, Carl felt himself growing increasingly weary and drowsy. Although a couple of nearby patients stared at him, the kindness of the nurse comforted him and gradually he felt less distressed. She asked the usual questions of how he felt and if he had any continual discomforts to report. For a while she pondered, awaiting a reply and then continued, asking if he wanted any refreshments. Carl agreed and found courage to ask what had happened to him. While he drank a cold orange juice, the nurse explained of how he was found unconscious last night by a man walking his dog. As she busied herself at his bedside, tidying his bedclothes, the nurse explained how he had to be sedated during the night. She suggested that he must have taken some time to react to the trauma of the attack.

'You're lucky to escape with just cuts and bruises... One guy who was attacked in the early hours? Well, I hear he was...' The nurse cut her sentence short, her face anxious.

'No...' Carl cleared his throat, trying to explain, 'It's not the attack... I have bad dreams... Terrible headaches... I wake up sweating...'

'Anyone would, with the nasty knock you took on the back of your neck,' she replied, refilling a water jug.

'No, it's the dream... I had another terrible dream, but this one felt different... as though I was the executioner.'

'Executioner?' the nurse asked with concern.

'Well, it's hard to remember... Like most dreams I suppose, but there was a man awaiting execution.'

'Where?' the nurse asked, regretfully thinking her patient not so innocent as originally thought.

'I'm not sure... a small dingy village shrouded in dense fog and half lit, as if twilight. It was so small but it had one of those wooden platforms like a guillotine...'

'A guillotine?' the nurse asked, interrupting.

'Yes and...' Carl paused to search his memory, looking distressfully at the ceiling. 'The man was dragged up a wooden staircase... to a platform where *he* stood...'

'Where, *who* stood?' The nurse questioned.

'A cloaked and masked figure... all in black...' Carl's speech became hoarse, slow and loud. 'The man screamed as... his blade came down on the man's neck and all went silent... and then the mist... the darkness...'

Carl's eyes widened in fear and he became agitated. The nurse leaned over, hearing nothing but riddles and tried to settle him, asking for assistance. Soon she was accompanied by another nurse asking if he needed a sedative, but shortly Carl became overwhelmingly tired and sank into a haunted sleep.

It was noon when Carl awoke; the hospital ward was almost empty. Although distressed by his aching limbs, he pulled himself to the edge of the bed and stood up. At first his legs were uncontrollable, but after walking a few paces he regained his foothold. From outside the ward and in a small room, Carl found a table surrounded by chairs, and in one corner a television bawled out adverts. The room was empty except for an elderly man dressed in a striped robe, who sat in an armchair watching the television.

Suddenly, a voice called Carl's name and footsteps ran behind him. He turned around to face a small nurse who repeatedly asked him questions. After a short discussion, Carl agreed to take a shower while his clothes were cleaned and agreed for the doctor to see him. Whilst showering he felt discomforted, distraught how his body was badly bruised and that several cuts were sore. After gingerly drying himself he got dressed in a hospital robe and preceded to the room with the television. Finding his mudded coat and shoes on an armchair, he removed them and sat looking for other belongings.

'They've probably gone to the cleaners,' a voice announced.

Carl looked up to see the elderly man he saw earlier, watching the television. Although the man looked engrossed in the programme, he noticed him quickly squint at him and then back at the television. Now and then Carl heard the man murmur words and cough, as if to sprout an opinion about a rape discussion programme. Nervously, the elderly man's face twitched and shook, his cheeks covered with bristles, his nose long with hairs curling out. His narrow face was engulfed in untidy grey hair that weaved about his eyes and neck. Wriggling deeper into his armchair, the man glanced at Carl and grinned before focusing again on the television. For a minute or two Carl considered starting a conversation with the man, but was reluctant. Then he noticed the man become discomforted by the views expressed in the television programme. Carl cleared his throat and announced, giving his opinion.

'Too much promotion and freedom of sexually explicit material today, don't you think?' Carl awaited a response, and then continued. 'Okay, well people should be able to express their emotion and love to others, but today the world's turning daft. Friends are people you love but not sexual lovers. Emotions are driven by the same engine, but are released by different gears, and it's these that determine...'

Abruptly, Carl was interrupted by a loud cough and the man shouted.

'It's the way of an evil heart... to corrupt mankind by the things he pleasures by. They will be replaced by the corrupt mind of the beast that lives in all.'

The elderly man leaned forward, pointing at Carl and shaking his head. 'All this promiscuity proves it! It was allforetold centuries ago. They could see this rising after *he* could be unbound. The beast himself would try and revenge… using mankind to find a way to avenge.' The old man's voice was abruptly interrupted as he coughed. Carl sat bemused by the old man's reaction and focused upon the television screen, occasionally peering at the man gulping water from a glass.

'Believe me, all of this is the start of an evil corruption of civilisation, and not one of the holiest will be able to –' Abruptly the small nurse interrupted the old man.

'What are you preaching about now then, eh? Nice to see you've eaten your breakfast this morning.' The elderly man groaned and began to talk in riddles as the nurse calmed him, saying that the doctor was coming to see him.

'You too!' the nurse exclaimed, looking at Carl. 'As long as there are no complications, I should think you can collect your things and go home.'

The nurse tidied about the table and removed cups and plates that lay there. After she finished tidying the room, she disappeared into the ward. The elderly man murmured and coughed as adverts replaced the television programme. Carl found himself distressed as some pain had returned in his stomach. Uninterested in watching television he wanted to move but realised that his body needed rest, and so he sat back trying to find comfort in the armchair.

It was about half an hour before the doctor arrived to examine Carl. Within a small cubical, Carl answered the usual questions as the doctor examined his bruising and lacerations. As he attended to Carl's injuries, the doctor expressed short and sharp advisory dialogue.

'There's nothing serious, young man. I take it you've had that scar for some time?'

'Oh, that… an old childhood injury…' Carl said, slowly covering his left forearm with his hand.

'You've been quite lucky really, but if you incur any problems such as hallucinations, sickness, fainting… funny dreams?' The doctor grinned and pulled off his spectacles. 'No seriously, do see your doctor if complications arise.'

'And work?' Carl exclaimed.

'Mainly office work, isn't it? Well, have plenty of rest until the weekend. You should be fine to return on Monday'.

After a short discussion with the nurse, the doctor handed Carl a prescription of painkillers and arranged for his dismissal.

As the doctor struggled with examining the elderly man in the next cubical, the nurse agreed to phone Carl's work and explain the situation. He requested that she contact Mike, so that his best friend could sort things out quietly, as well as pick him up. Otherwise, Carl would need to order a taxi and pay for it at home. He only ever carried a limited amount of money, but that had been stolen. Luckily that day the Director and Editor were both out, and Mike agreed to pick Carl up from the hospital. Pretending a magazine client had agreed to be interviewed, Mike hoped his little idea would cover up Carl's accident.

Carl waited impatiently in the foyer of the hospital and was glad to see Mike when he arrived. Although the nurse insisted he had some hot soup before leaving, his sore body was vulnerable to the cold air. Mike was amazed by Carl's affection toward him as they met and headed toward the hospital car park. Apparently Mike had borrowed his girlfriend's car to get to work, as Carl did not answer his phone that morning. Although Mike could see his friend was tired and distressed, he could not help but ask what had happened. Slowly, Carl explained as much as he could remember, but became stressed when thinking about what his assailant may have stolen. Awkwardly he searched his pockets, but found nothing but the paper towel and prescription he had been given at the hospital. As Mike drove through town, Carl found it difficult to think, and excused himself from talking as his headache intensified. Mike decisively drove to his house to leave Carl in the capable hands of his girlfriend. Oblivious to the discussions around him, Carl heard nothing but droning voices after he was put to bed. After failing to listen to a conversation in the hallway, Carl faded into a sleep.

Carl awoke to a soft voice and a shrug on his shoulder. It was Mike's girlfriend, Rachael.

'It's nearly five, Carl!' Rachael repeated, looking into Carl's face, 'Mike will be home soon. Do you want anything for tea?'

Carl groaned and then turned on his side to face Rachael.

'Yes, okay! I'll have something soon.'

'What, then?' Rachael inquired.

'Anything… whatever you're having,' Carl replied sluggishly.

Alright, I'll do you the same as Mike. Come down when you're ready!'

Carl rolled back upon his stomach, still sore, wandering if he could eat anything. He could feel the coldness of the room upon his face and wriggled deeper into the warmth of the bed.

From a distance, Carl could see the city lights shimmering from the heat of the traffic. Above, the night sky was clear and cold. Bordering the city lay the open countryside, dark and lifeless. Obscuring the lower trunks of trees lay a dense fog, glowing as it moved in a calm breeze. Gradually it started moving and then crept speedily along meadows and through woodland, until it reached the outskirts of a nearby housing estate. It hesitated for a moment and then glowed before flowing like a wide river along the street. At frantic speed, the blanket of mist widened, covering several streets, and then from the dark woodland a tall bank of fog poured upon the housing estate. Menacingly, it covered streets, cars and buildings, and then raced in toward town.

Carl glanced back over his shoulder. That terrible sense of fear had returned. His body tingled and became cold. The room was calm, but dark and eerie. Carl exhaled with a sigh of relief, and then turned to face the open window. Pouring in from the window ledge, a mist covered the floor and spread wildly. It engulfed Carl's feet and raced past them, filling the room. He span around to see the room filled with a thick, swirling mist. As the air grew cold, he froze and saw shadows moving within the mist, slowly becoming more recognisable. Three pairs of hefty boots paced heavily upon the floor and soon Carl could see three men, two of whom were clothed in uniform, the other in a robe and crowned with a grey curly wig. As they looked at him through the swirling mist, their faces were distorted and angry. Carl's voice went unheard as he shouted at a tall figure, it slouched as if to collapse. As a large book dropped from the figure's hand and struck the floor, the room filled with blue streaks and from every corner, enormous ghostly figures flew at the men. Progressively, the ghostly figures developed into ghastly phantasmal snakes that spat and hissed, showing large, venomous fangs. Each time they flew passed the men, the mystical snakes inflicted a noxious bite upon the men's faces. Quickly, the room was deafened with cries of pain as the men stumbled about, their faces slashed and bleeding. Objects smashed and furniture crumbled as the evil voices from the creatures shrieked. Within minutes, all three figures collapsed and the snakes spat viciously as they circled the room.

Carl! Carl! Hey, wake up! What about your tea?'

Carl awoke in a second and sat up with eyes glazed and wide.

His heart was pounding and his body burned with frenzied heat.

'Hey! What the hell's the matter?'

Carl stared at Mike with fear in his eyes, back arched stiff, his face beaded with sweat.

'Carl?' Mike became concerned and held Carl's shoulder with his hand.

'It's okay, now. What is it? Did you have a bad dream again?'

Carl calmed and his breathing eased, but his voice was hoarse.

'Not a dream… a bloody nightmare… another one, so vivid.'

Mike could see his friend was distressed and shaking.

'Maybe it's the accident…? Something to do with what happened to you last night. People say it sometimes has that effect.' Carl turned to face his friend and replied.

'No, Mike! I've had dreams like this before, but these are so real. Remember when I went to boarding school after my father died? I dreamt that night, after my Aunt took me… I thought I'd never have dreams as real as those again.'

'It's all imagination, mate. Loosing someone close…? You've told me about your past, but…' Mike was interrupted.

'Come on, lads. Dinner's getting cold, and besides, John's here. He's got a lot to say about your work.'

Carl found Mike's house redecorated, and the old fashioned style living room was impressive. The dark wood beams expanded across the ceiling to flush in with the fireplace and windows. He walked through into the dining room and found John and Mike eating at a table. Through into the kitchen, he could see that Rachael was cooking.

'Carl's here, Rachael!' Mike called, food spilling from his mouth. John looked up at Mike, and then at Carl.

'Hey, Pal, are you alright? I heard what happened; my lips are sealed. It's in the paper, but don't worry, you're not famous yet. No names are mentioned.' John paused, swallowing the remains of his sandwich, and then continued. 'Not like this one here!' As he pointed to an article, Mike took a glimpse and John continued. 'This poor bastard stood no chance! Pissing around on a building site? It's not very clever, you know… trying to steal metal and stuff. Guess he needed cash after being in prison.' As John gulped at a mug of tea and sat back, he read aloud some of the article.

'Here it is! Listen… *Police were completely baffled today by how a local man, an ex-jailbird, was found decapitated. A building site supervisor, who discovered the body early this morning, remarked that he had never seen such a brutal accident. Members of the public are advised to stay clear of all our building sites, especially glass and piled sheets of metal.*' John paused, and then added his own words. 'How grim is this job getting? Only the other week I reported a similar case, but this time a guy was found hanged. They said it was suicide, but it didn't explain the fucking state of the poor guy!'

'Do you mind?' Rachael shouted as she entered the room.

'Sorry…' John said softly, but raised his voice, 'Hey, you girls are just as bad! I've heard them down the Woodman swearing and going a game.'

'For your information, I am not one of *those* girls!' Rachael snapped.

'That's not what *Mike* says; a right little raver, I've heard,' John said winking at Mike.

'Stop shit-stirring will you, John?' Mike exclaimed, 'Carl's had a bad enough experience. I'm sure he doesn't want to hear all about that! We have to deal with that every day at work. I'd like to remind you, we're not there now.' Mike silenced the argument and noticed Carl looking at the paper from where John had placed it.

Carl picked up the paper and folded it out as Rachael placed a hot meal in front of him. Mike argued quietly at John as he muttered sarcastic words about Carl's disposition. Carl took more interest in the article, but found it hard to read.

'Bloody shut up will you!'

Whilst all three looked at Carl in astonishment, they noticed Carl's face become white and his eyes widen.

Carl threw the paper back on the table and ran upstairs. Mike looked at Rachael who, like John, was totally bemused. Mike met Carl as he ran downstairs, clinging on to his trench coat and staring at a hall clock. Quickly, Mike obstructed his friend at the foot of the staircase and grabbed his arm.

'Look, Carl, I don't know what the fuck's got into you, but I'm not playing sympathetic anymore. Go back and have something to eat, Rachael's done extra for you!'

Carl halted and looked at Mike clenching his arm.

'I've got to check something out. You won't understand but it's important. You're not stopping me!'

As Carl broke free from his friend's grip and raced out the front door, Mike turned and shouted. 'Wait! Where the hell are you going? Can't I help?'

Mike could do nothing but watch Carl race up the dark street, totally bemused by his friend's strange act. Returning to the dining room, Mike was questioned by Rachael about Carl's oddity, but all he could do was examine the paper story that Carl had previously read.

At the top of Stepperton Hill, Carl rested to regain his breath. He could feel his heart pounding and his legs quivering like jelly. In the distance and on the edge of town shone the lights from a police station. As Carl shivered uncontrollably, he noticed a fog bank retreat slowly into nearby woodland, where it strangely disappeared. Sweating, but cold and with lungs still hurting, he raced down the hillside toward the edge of town. In the distance and on the right of a gradual incline, Carl could see the police station. It stood shadowed against the dark woodland behind. Approaching the old building, he found it to be strangely quiet. Carl halted and looked at the police sign shining dimly above. What was he doing here? He could get into more trouble than it was worth. Confused and troubled, he progressed along the driveway and reached the entrance. He turned left, and then right, hesitating; his thoughts playing with him as he exhaled into the cold air. Decisively, he stepped inside and gingerly walked from the lobby toward the enquiry desk. Although covered with paperwork and writing utensils, the small desk was unoccupied. Carl pressed against a bell push and from a distance the silence was broken. Carl waited. The silence was uncanny. Eagerly he stood pondering over the desk. Suddenly, Carl heard a smash and he flinched as something rolled, as if along the floor. Petrified, Carl froze until the noise stopped.

He crept toward a door beside the desk and peered through the frosted glass. Slowly he opened the door enough for him to peer in.

The room was littered with folders, paper and office utensils, untidily scattered everywhere. The furniture was up turned, articles broken, and twisted within the rumble, Carl noticed the body of a policeman, silent and still. Sprawled against a desk was another body, clenching a broken lamp. Looking further into the room, Carl saw another body, lying in a doorway. Carl entered, curious but nervous. As he approached the nearest body, his feet crushed the litter scattering the floor. The constable's face was pale; his mouth foamed with saliva, eyes and expression frozen. His neck and face were swollen where numerous long, triangular marks had cut his skin. His clothes were lacerated; each tear exposing skin from where blood had run and dried. Cautiously, Carl examined the room and found that the other body was similarly lacerated. However, after hearing a car pass by outside, Carl's interests diverted and he began to search the room, frantically looking in draws, cabinets and on shelves. Across the room and inside a glass cabinet were objects cased in small, thick plastic bags. Carl approached the cabinet.

Abruptly, a phone rang from behind him. It silenced with an echo, and then it bawled again. Unsure what to do, Carl remained motionless until it stopped ringing. In the silence that followed, Carl heard a groaning noise and approached the room from where it had come. Crawling through the doorway was the third body that Carl had noticed before. He advanced toward the man and stepped over him into a shadowy room.

'Please…! Help?' the man murmured, 'the call button… please?'

Carl found himself in a dilemma and angrily searched the room, squinting in the darkness. Looking for a light switch on the walls, he noticed a sturdy, long torch and reached to a shelf for it. He heard the man groan again as he played with the torch, eventually finding the switch. A powerful beam of light circled the room as Carl examined all about him. At first he noticed several glass cabinets, all locked and containing many different articles. Most enclosed jewellery, watches, knives, keys, all sealed in plastic bags. One cabinet held a revolver and a shotgun. Then he saw it, lying amongst the other jewellery – the pendant; the one he had found at the library yesterday morning. He swung the torch to smash the glass and retrieve it, but suddenly below him, the man grabbed his ankle. Awkwardly Carl fell back against the cabinets, breaking a lot of them with his body. At first, he stumbled against the cabinets until the man lost grip of his ankle, but then Carl fell. Slouched in a corner, Carl could see the struggling policeman reach underneath a desk and towards a big red button. Crawling to his feet, Carl crouched over the man and pressed the button. As it blinked on and off, Carl hesitated, hearing a nearby whirring sound. Leaning against the desk, he focused the torch on the cabinets, but took a while to relocate the pendant. Stepping toward the cabinets, Carl announced, 'Sorry pal, but this is important! Help will be here soon.'

Carefully with the torch, Carl broke the surrounding glass and reached between the blades to snatch the pendant. From a distance, Carl could hear the noise of approaching sirens and looked about him, searching for an escape. Within the other room Carl could see a back door and so hastened toward it. With his elbow, he pressed against the safety bar and the backdoor swung open. Carl jumped and then turned, pushing himself against the door to close it. Leaning against the door, Carl searched the surrounding woodland, the sound of approaching sirens nearby. Carl poised for a second, and then headed for the nearest trees. As fast as his legs could carry him, he ran toward the trees and slumbered against the nearest. For a moment, Carl rested to look back at the building. At the front of the building, he could see the blue of flashing lights as suddenly there was a screech of brakes. Heading into the woodland, Carl began to run up an incline, entwining his way through the trees, disappearing into the darkness.

From a clearing near the hilltop, Carl could see policemen scurrying about their cars, scouring the grounds of the station with torches. He crouched, watching the distant lights and shadows in the darkness. Kneeling, Carl searched his pockets to find the pendant. Quickly, he removed it from the thick, clear plastic bag, dropped the packaging and examined it before placing it into his inside breast pocket.

Carl stood tall and took a last look at the distant scene below before zipping up his breast pocket. He thought of how the events of the past few days had been terrible, first the man in the library, the man in the newspaper, and now, three police officers all brutally murdered. Watching the action below, he shuddered in the cold of the night and so decided to make his way home. Heading through the woodland and across the farm to the park, a shortcut would take less than twenty minutes.

As he approached his street, Carl found it deserted. His car had been covered by twigs and leaves from overhead trees, and his apartment appeared dark and eerie. Using a spare key hidden in the canopy above the front door, Carl entered his apartment. At first his apartment was cold, but with heating on as he changed clothes, it soon became warm. After a snack, he sat in front of his television, partnered with a glass of whisky as a night-cap. However, the late night programme he was watching became interrupted by a newsflash concerning the attack at the local police station. Carl watched with interest and learned that the police were confounded by the attack on the station, and could not decipher a motive. Early investigations could only indicate that it was related to a cult gang using poisonous snakes to steal jewellery or weapons. Although all three policemen were identified in the newsflash, Carl was not told if all three had died.

# FOUR

CARL AWOKE TO THE SOUND of a dog barking. Daylight proved too powerful to be early morning, so Carl realised it must be late. Once dressed, he looked out of his bedroom window to find the street outside occupied by several people; one man painting the front of his house, a young girl walking her dog, and his neighbour, an elderly woman, returning home with some shopping.

Noticing the time was nine-forty, Carl began to panic as if late for work, but realised that the doctor had told him to rest at home for at least a day. However, as he was restless and found reading impossible, he finally decided to visit work. At least he could explain about his attack and maybe apologise to Mike for his actions last night. As he pictured the menacing images from the previous night, Carl's thoughts deviated to that of his stolen wallet and car keys. Regrettably, he did not have time to find them at the police station, but realised he kept a spare set of keys in a kitchen draw. The only remaining task was to persuade security to let him in to the office.

The second floor of Palmer House was busy; staff poised at terminals, desks piled with papers and folders. The whole office was a continuous noise; phones ringing, people talking, the rustle of paper, as well as clicking keyboards and the sound of the printers. Carl walked through the office, snaking his way between desks and cabinets until he slowly approached Mike. Carl stopped, hearing Mike swear as he was trying to replace a printer cartridge. Carl stood for a moment, to watch

Mike curse as he tampered with the printer. A wide grin stretched across Carl's face as his friend turned to see him. Mike's face relaxed and the furrows that lined his forehead disappeared. He placed the cartridge down on the desk and stepped to face Carl.

'Can you mend this bloody thing? I'm sick to death that every time I want to use it, it's not working properly.'

Mike was just about to continue moaning when Carl stepped forward, leaned over the device and started examining it.

'Haven't you managed to familiarise yourself with these yet... after all these weeks?' Carl's voice ended with a bit of laughter.

'Oh, it's okay for *you* to laugh! You were here when the maintenance guy showed everybody how to use them!' Mike lowered his voice, slightly stuttering. 'I... I was...'

'On holiday, soaking up the sun and flirting with some young girl?' Carl replied, taking the ribbon from Mike's hand.

Within a minute, Carl had replaced the ribbon and told Mike to print his work. Printing some articles, Mike showed Carl the stories he was working on, but as usual the conversation diverted to their personal life. Mike peered over his terminal screen at Carl who was settling down to work. Carl told him that he had explained to the editor that, although he had been advised to rest by the doctor, he needed to get his work up to date. Besides, it would help keep his mind occupied. As their conversation continued, Mike started to question Carl's behaviour and why he left so quickly last night. However, Carl refused to provide answers and proclaimed that it was personal. Fortunately for Carl,

Mike changed the topic, as he did on regular occasions.

'Hey, Carl! What about the weekend? I forgot to tell you!'

'Tell me what?' Carl replied.

'There's a party in line for the weekend. Saturday night. Friends of Rachael's... well, more a friend of a friend, if you know what I mean.'

'Where's this, then?' Carl asked, somewhat uninterested.

'Don't know exactly, but it's somewhere near the river.' Mike paused to think. 'Anyhow, Rachael will take us. She knows where it is.'

Carl's voice grew sheepish.

'I'm not sure I can make it.'

'Why not?' Mike demanded.

Carl paused, searching for an excuse, knowing he just wanted to be alone for a while.

'Well, it's just not my scene... I'm –'

Mike cut Carl short of sentence.

'Your problem is getting laid. It's about time you put yourself about a bit. You know, *mix*!'

Carl's face contorted with anger.

'Look, just because I don't sleep around with loads of girls when I'm already engaged, doesn't mean I'm a bore!'

Mike ignored Carl's reply and stared at his terminal screen, whispering.

'You just haven't got it like most guys. I don't know why I bother. It's like trying to get blood from a stone!'

Carl's face grew distressed once Mike's voice silenced. Suddenly, Carl exclaimed softly, 'I'm sorry, Mike, but after the past few days, I just haven't been myself.'

'If you weren't such a drag, I might have somebody interesting to go out and have a drink with,' Mike snapped.

Carl became stressed. 'Just don't understand, do you? No compassion. Don't give a shit about my accident. You know it's still here... in my head... in my bloody, bruised body.' Carl drew breath. 'To put it honestly... *yes*, maybe I'm not up to it anymore. You'll end up feeling sorry for your poor excuse of a friend, making excuses. It's just...'

Mike stood up and reached for Carl's shoulder, patting it gently.

'Sorry Carl. We're at work, aren't we? I'm always snappy at work. You, above all else, should know that. Maybe I should have asked you later.' Mike sat at his desk, leaning forward, his chin in his hands. 'I wasn't thinking straight. Just thought it would help you forget all the stuff that's been going on. Maybe forget the accident. Even some of those erotic dreams you keep having.'

Carl managed a smile and the conversation eventually diverted to the work that needed to be finished. Carl had not reported on any stories of late and after finalising his own, helped Mike tidy up his articles. Somehow, together Carl and Mike's work was both innovative and remarkable; the comparison between two opposing and individualistic minds. That was the idea of the editor and it proved successful; these two friends combined work was always good for sales. On many occasions Carl and Mike had spent time with the director, their articles outselling the rest because magazine publishers were pleased with artistic designs as well as the reported hard facts.

Mike and Carl spent the rest of the day working on articles for evening newspapers. These proved to be the hardest as they needed to be done quickly. Mike was working on a regular feature for a local newspaper concerning school sport activities, and although he had documented the facts and figures, his untidy work needed the hands of an artist. That is where Carl's design skills came in. To keep Carl busy, Mike transferred documents he had been working on to Carl, who found it a challenge to rearrange their appearance and design to make the article more presentable. As Carl knew, he may someday require Mike to return the favour.

During the day Pete interrupted them, asking Carl how he was and how the work was progressing. He acted like a curious schoolboy, pestering everyone, stealing ideas and storylines; but on the whole, most people got on with him. The office sometimes became a school playground when David annoyed individuals, especially Pete. Few other staff conversed during the day as they concentrated on their publications. Two girls, Lisa and Debbie, worked together on areas the men disliked; fashion, music and local entertainment being their main focus. On the second floor office alone, there were nine clerks allocated to pairs or working independently, all reliant on attitude, experience and team work. The editor was responsible for staff management, but it was the directors who dealt with the promotion and sale of publications. As the time crawled its way towards four, Mike agreed to talk to Carl about things another time, as he could see his friend was tired. Maybe the work had helped Carl forget about the remorseful incidents he had witnessed, but the painkillers he had taken regularly were making him drowsy. Therefore, Carl returned home after excusing himself from attending a meal with other staff at a local restaurant.

Throughout the rest of the week, Carl managed to regain a foothold in his work, and although apprehensive to see police officers, he was glad that they only visited in order to return his wallet and keys. Luckily, the security pass inside his wallet identified him and where he worked. However, as the police stated, any money or cards stolen would need to be declared within a number of days. As he focused of the same repetitive duties, his bad memories became a blur. However, Carl's sleep was still troubled by undecipherable dreams. Once he had fallen asleep at work, as haunting dreams continued to interrupt his night sleep. Mike had noticed his friend's drowsiness in the week and that something was affecting him, making him lethargic and incredibly irritable. Mike wanted to ask why he ran off that night. Had the attack affected his friend more than he realised? It was unlike Carl to hide secrets, as Mike saw his friend as intelligent, artistically gifted, but most of all *rational*. Over the past few days, Carl had looked oppressed and would distract himself from meaningful conversations. He did become weary, and without his work and the company of friends, Carl felt he would become secluded. Strangely, however, the peace of isolation was soothing, although he felt awful sometimes when alone in his flat. Still, he was determined to remove the recent haunting memories and the recollection of the attack; now that the weekend was almost here, he convinced himself that he would be alright.

# FIVE

CARL ENTERED LAST AND CLOSED the door behind him. He followed Mike and Rachael into a hallway and found the air clouded with the odour of cigarette smoke and alcohol. A small, plump girl greeted Rachael, stopping them for a moment for their coats. She peered at Carl and Mike, and then looked back at Rachael whilst placing their coats over a nearby balustrade.

'Which of these fine guys is yours?' she asked.

Rachael swung her arms around Mike and replied, 'This hunk here!'

Before the girl could ask and looked at Carl, Rachael exclaimed.

'This is Carl. He's a friend of Mike's,' she paused, and then announced stepping forward, 'he works with him.'

Carl acknowledged her with a smile and timidly crept behind the three as they turned into a large living room. Suddenly, Carl's ears were deafened by the sound of loud music as a voice shouted to lower the volume.

Carl looked about him, noticing individuals, drinking, smoking, some laughing and stumbling over others. Whilst he observed the people around him, Mike, Rachael and the girl had walked to the other side of the room. Carl became agitated and started scratching his cheek, running his fingers through his hair. He noticed a couple of girls who he found quite attractive, but they were huddled amongst other men. Continuing his inspection of faces, he hoped to notice someone he might possibly know. Disappointingly, there was only Mike and Rachael he knew, and they were talking over the other side of the room. Decisively, he turned to make his way towards the couple he knew, but stopped abruptly. Waving her hand to Mike and Rachael, Carl noticed the plump girl directing them in to another room. From a crowd obscuring the kitchen, a slim blonde girl appeared, struggling her way through the people blocking her path. Carl's heart raced, his nerves twitched; his body frenzied with heat. As the girl wriggled her way through the crowd, Carl studied her face. Moving his eyes to admire her figure, he noticed how a tightly stretched cotton dress revealed her thighs. Carl froze, questioning himself about who he recognised. Or was it? As the plump girl searched the room and pointed toward Carl, the blonde girl began talking to Mike and Rachael. Suddenly, Mike waved him over, but he hesitated as he began to sweat. Nervously, he stepped toward them, gradually hearing their conversation.

'This is Carl. He works with me, as you'll probably remember.' Mike paused then clicked his fingers, holding Rachael tighter. 'But of course you should know that. You saw us at the library… where was it, now?'

A soft voice replied.

'Centridge House,' she said, clearing her throat, 'the old library near Shipham. You were the two guys reporting about the accident, weren't you?'

'Yes, and you're?' Mike asked, awaiting a name, but then continued, 'the photographer… the girl in the sports car!'

She smiled and then viewed each of them in turn, her hand reaching to shake theirs.

'My name is Sarah, Sarah Layton.' She shook each of their hands in turn, 'It's my twenty-third birthday and being that my parents are away for weeks, I thought I'd have a party of some sort.' She paused, thinking. 'I haven't had one since my twenty-first and that's one I can't really remember, you know.' She laughed, rolling her eyes and then changed the conversation. 'Carol's introduced Mike… I knew Rachael had a fiancé, but I've never seen you before. Who's this?' She reached her hand toward Carl and he almost shuddered at the sight of it. As usual Mike introduced Carl before he could present himself.

'This is Carl, a friend since college; we studied journalism and several other things.' Mike continued, winking his eye, 'He's a good friend, but a bit shy.'

Carl shrugged Mike's hand from his shoulder, annoyed that he was trying to embarrass him again. Sarah's soft and delicate hand grasped Carl's, and he managed a smile through his suppressed timidity. As Mike hugged Rachael he talked to Sarah, her eyes focusing frequently on Carl. He blushed and turned away, pretending to watch the people in the room; most drinking, some others smoking. Carl stood silent, not knowing what to say. How would he start a conversation? Suddenly, Sarah brushed past him and with determination he stopped her, trying to hide his inhibitions.

'It's turning out to be quite a crowd. Are you expecting any more?'

'Yes, a few, but not many more. I don't want too many people in here. However, I think a lot of these may leave early; clubbing, I think.' She glanced at her small wrist-watch and began to move away, 'Excuse me, I must speak to someone.'

Sarah walked over to a couple of girls spreading food on a corner table. The food looked as if it had already been ravaged earlier. She mingled within the crowd near the window and slowly others joined her, collecting sandwiches, cakes, crisps and other food. Gradually, the music became soft, as a rock ballad played from the speakers fixed upon the walls. Slowly, Carl felt his nerves begin to calm, as he liked this record – it brought back some good memories. He saw Sarah's head pop up from the crowd as she moved to the music player. He raised an eyebrow and smiled, but his concentration was broken as a girl flung her arms about him and kissed him on the cheek.

'Didn't see you before... was you here earlier? Are you one of Paul's mates?'

Carl gazed down into the eyes of a short girl, her face round with flushed cheeks, her hair straight and dark, reaching below her shoulders. Carl wafted the smell of vodka as her breath exhaled into his face. As she looked at him blearily, her eyes grew large without blinking.

'No. I'm sorry, I don't know Paul,' Carl said, searching the room for his friend. Mike only laughed at Carl's predicament, as he was pulled into a doorway by Rachael.

'You want to have a drink, don't you, boy?' she messed with her hair and stuck her hand in a handbag, pulling out a packet of cigarettes, 'or a fag?

Carl agreed and levered one from the packet. Before he could place it between his lips, the girl had a lighter flaring in front of his face. He reached forward and the flame lit the cigarette. At first the smoke stung his eyes and scathed his throat, but then he felt a little giddy. He had not had one for several days and it had some effect.

As Mike and Rachael had disappeared from the room, Carl found himself in the hands of this girl. As he listened to her slurry speech, he managed to decipher that her name was Katie. She had already been warned about smoking in the house, but hid her cigarette from view when her host walked by. Carl therefore decided to dowse his cigarette in a nearby empty beer can whilst she walked to the corner table. At the table she littered a plate of food and poured Carl a drink, then encouraged him to sit with her. He ate and drank, answering questions that Katie and other people nearby asked. For a while he was uneasy with his company and showed no real interest in their conversation, but by ten o'clock he had drunk some lager and several glasses of a whisky and cola. Soon he found himself talking amongst strangers, with Katie now and then secretly groping his thigh. However, he was distracted from the crowd by Sarah, who wandered about the room, refilling glasses and the food table.

It was well after ten o'clock by the time the crowd around him had left the party and Carl found himself accompanied by only a few others. The remaining guests were slouched upon the sofa, leaving the room spacious. Carl had crawled into a nearby armchair, hoping to steady his mind from the effects of alcohol. Although his recent feelings of oppression had left, they were now replaced with tiredness.

'How about a game, Carl, there is seven of us left?'

Carl's stupor was interrupted by Mike's outburst. He looked up to see Mike holding a deck of playing cards and leaning over him. Mike nudged his shoulder and asked.

'You okay, Mate?'

'Just a bit tired,' Carl replied, rubbing his eyes.

'Come on, then, I've got just the thing to wake you up. We'll have a laugh. We're playing poker in the dining room.' Mike helped Carl up and they walked into the dining room to find all but Sarah seated around a large, polished table. Sarah was messing about in the kitchen, washing plates and glasses. Carl sat at the table and comforted himself. Mike sat beside him after calling Sarah to join them. She entered and announced whilst approaching the table.

'I'm not really partial to cards. Are you playing, Rachael?'

'Yes, I'll have a go. Mike's talked me into it,' Rachael replied. She nudged Mike and he pushed her back, laughing. Carl's eyes followed Sarah as she made her way to the table and sat beside a couple opposite. Mike dealt, and as the game began, Carl studied everyone. At first he watched Mike and Rachael look secretly at each other's cards. The couple beside Sarah played quietly. The other player sitting beside Carl was a spectacled, dark-haired librarian – apparently, an old school friend of Sarah's.

The game continued for half an hour, but slowly the girls became disinterested, uttering sarcastic words about the game and laughing. Suddenly the girl next to Carl questioned aloud, 'Have any of you heard about tarot cards? They're like these but used differently. I've got some in my bag if you want to see?'

Mike snapped a response to ridicule her.

'You don't believe in that, do you? It's all a load of crap!'

'Don't talk to Liz like that. What do you know about it anyway?' Rachael argued. Mike replied, defending his case.

'I know that it's all hogwash about reading stars and fortunetelling… it's just a gimmick. It's to get people like her to buy the stuff. It's all about making money. Some girls at work do it. Surprises me how many idiots buy the crap!'

Liz stared at him before she stood up and threw her cards on the table. Moving from her chair, she insisted on leaving, as it was getting late.

'It's only half eleven, Liz!' Sarah said, glaring at Mike with annoyance, 'Please don't go! I thought you were going to stay the night?'

'I was, but, well, I've got to travel into Birmingham tomorrow and I could do with a good night sleep.'

Sarah stood tall and exclaimed.

'Look, if you're interested in that stuff, I've got an old set of tarot cards you can have. They were my Gran's, I think.'

Mike whispered under his breath, 'Looks like we have another ludicrous believer.'

Rachael silenced him and snapped, 'Are you satisfied, now? You've ruined the game!'

'Didn't think you were *that* interested in playing anyway,' he replied sarcastically.

'Sometimes you really piss me off. God knows why I'm with such a pig-headed arsehole.' Rachael said, folding her arms.

69

Carl sat quietly picking at his cards, and noticed that the couple opposite had become irritable. As Sarah and Liz walked out of the room, Carl heard Sarah say,

'I remember now. You've just jogged my memory. I'm sure my Gran had one of those board games circled with letters and numbers! What's it called?'

Liz replied, a tone of surprise in her voice. 'You mean an Ouija board.'

'Yes, if that's what it's called?'

Their voices faded into the hallway, and were overpowered by an argument between Mike and Rachael.

'Mike! Mike!' Sarah's voice called from the hallway. 'Will you get something down from the loft for Liz? As you've ruined the card game, it's the least you can do.'

Mike cut his argument with Rachael and proceeded to the hallway, followed closely by Carl. Entering the hallway, Carl found Mike standing with Sarah and Liz at the foot of the stairs.

'What is it I've got to get then?' Mike questioned.

'It's an old, large, green and purple coloured box, about A3 size. It's got old writing on it, I think.' Sarah stated.

'What's in it?' Mike questioned.

'Just something… an old game,' Sarah replied.

'I'll know just what to look for, then!' Mike stated, with a hint of sarcasm.

'It's an Ouija board, okay! Just fetch it, would you?' Liz asked.

'I'm not touching one of those fucking things!' Mike snapped, cutting her sentence short.

'I thought you didn't believe in all that crap,' Liz snapped with aggression.

'I don't, but I've heard they bring bad luck. Last thing I need… more bad luck!'

'Look, will you get it or not?' Sarah demanded.

'I'll get it!' Carl announced, forcing himself through the gathering. He climbed a few steps, and then turned to ask. 'Where is the loft? How do I get up there?'

Mike returned to the living room to be interrogated by Rachael about what was happening. Carl and Sarah climbed the stairs, followed shortly by Liz, who exclaimed she didn't want to be too much trouble. At the top of the stairs, Carl stopped and stared into one of the bedrooms. Sarah bumped into him and searched his face. She followed his eyes into her room and at first she seemed annoyed, but after continuing along the landing, she smiled mischievously whilst biting her fingernail.

It took a few minutes to unhook the loft door and pull down the loft ladder. Carl climbed gingerly up and at the top shouted.

'Where's the light switch?'

Sarah scratched her head.

'Oh! I think it's blown… you'll need a torch!' Sarah answered, searching her room. Shortly after, she returned and tested a torch she had found in her room. She hated the dark and since a blackout a few years before, she kept one at hand. Watching her smooth face and innocent eyes looking up at him, Carl paused, overwhelmed by her beauty. She stretched out her arm to hand him the torch, but Carl hesitated.

'What's the matter?' Sarah questioned, 'Are you scared?'

'Of course not…' Carl replied, taking the torch from her fingers.

The loft was quite high, but he could not stand tall, and so decided to crawl on all fours. The beam shone powerfully about the darkness, revealing dust, cobwebs, and pieces of old furniture, which lay scattered precariously. It took a while to find the box lying submerged between some books and a set of old curtains. He pulled it free and brushed it with his hand. The dust swept the air and made him sneeze. It was a heavy, hardened box, square and coloured green and dirty blue. Ornate inscriptions stretched over the front, but it was difficult with the torch to make out any instructions or illustrations. It was heavy in his left hand, as he needed his right hand to steady himself, whilst holding the torch. Directing the torch to the entrance, he could see Sarah's head peering through, her eyes shining beautifully in the torchlight, her hair glimmering as she moved it from her face. He clambered back to the door and knelt before descending. His foot searched for the ladder step. Carl felt a hand grip his ankle and guide his foot to the step. He clambered down with the box tucked against his chest and then felt a hand press his thigh. Excited by the manoeuvre, he looked down. As he descended, Sarah's hand moved over his jeans, his buttocks and then up to his waist.

'Can you manage?' he heard her ask.

'Yes… I'm okay now!' His left foot reached the floor and he gasped, before stating, 'It's a bit of a crawl up there!'

'I know, my father often moaned about going up there. I thought sometimes there was a monster, but that's when I was a little girl.'

Carl smiled and handed the box to Sarah.

'Here it is, Liz! God, it's heavy… I haven't seen this for years. My Gran told us not to mess about with, until…' she silenced, thinking, 'well, until my mother would tell us stories about it.'

'I just wanted to see what one was like, really,' Liz said. 'You know I've seen them mentioned in the magazines. They're hard to get now.' She paused searching Sarah's face and then gazed at the box. 'It looks like an old one. Has it always been your Gran's?'

'It was my Gran who gave it to us. She died shortly after my Grandfather. I guess my mother never got over that… the two dying… within months of each other.'

Realising memories were flooding Sarah's mind, Liz plodded downstairs, weighted with the box upon her chest. Sarah and Carl followed her, after securing the loft ladder.

The weight of the box eventually became too much for Liz to hold, and she clumsily dropped it on the dining table. Before Carl and Sarah could offer any assistance, Liz had struggled to slide off the lid. Inside was a square made of wood, more than an inch thick and decorated with carvings and entwining artwork. At the centre was a round mirror surrounded by ornate letters and numbers. Engraved in opposite corners were the words YES and NON; carved in each corner below was a sun and moon. Beside the wooden square was a rolled up piece of paper. Yet the thing that Liz found interesting was a triangular piece of wood supported by three balls of glass at each end. At the centre of the triangle was a circle of glass that reflected the mirror below. Liz had seen drawings and some photos of these, but this one was so different; old, and with more detailed artwork. Curious, she enquired.

'I'd like to know where your Gran got this from, or exactly how old it is?'

'Like I said,' Sarah replied, 'it was given to my mother when I was a little girl, just before my Gran passed away.'

For a moment, they looked at it quietly whilst Liz ran her fingers over the carvings and the glass of the mirror. Carl joined them, trying to show a keen interest in their discussion, thinking it might help him get to know Sarah better. Leaning closer to see the open box he had fetched, Carl became distracted by Sarah's curvaceous figure, especially as she changed stance.

'Well, let's give it a go then. I'm game for a laugh!' Mike announced, striding into the room.

'You've got to take these things seriously or they won't work!' Liz affirmed.

'She's right, you know,' Peter said, holding Karen in his arms as they stepped into the room. Eventually all seven were now scattered about the dining room, looking at the object in the box.

'I'm not sure I want to have a go,' Carl stated, 'I have enough bad luck as it is, and...' he paused.

'And what?' Sarah asked.

'Yes, and what? Why not? It's only a stupid game. Nothing will happen. It never does!' Mike added.

Carl stood silent for a moment, all faces looking at his half lit face.

'Mike knows,' Carl said quietly.

'Knows about what?' Mike questioned.

'The dreams I have.' Carl found his throat dry and hard to swallow.

'Well, those don't make any difference. Everybody has dreams, don't they?' Mike proclaimed.

'Well if he doesn't want to have a go, fair enough. He can sit out.' Sarah said sympathetically and then continued, 'Anyhow, how come *you* want to have a go if nothing is going to happen?'

'I suppose I've been proven wrong before,' Mike said, grabbing the box, 'but not many times… and definitely not on this occasion. We'll play it without him. I've always wanted a go with one of these… just to prove that they don't work.'

'You've got to believe that you can force the planchette to move with your mind, otherwise it won't work!' Liz stated.

'It'll move, alright, if you push hard enough,' Mike replied cynically.

'You've got to let it move by a force… a spiritual force that each player gives out,' Liz argued.

'We'll use some sort of force,' Mike joked, but saw Liz becoming angry, 'okay, I'm sorry, I'll do what you say.' Liz had influenced Mike to be courteous. It was either that, or Rachael had threatened him. 'Come on then, what do you have to do? Don't you just have to put your finger on this and wait?' he questioned, sitting himself at the table.

The rest of the group sat down, Rachael beside Mike, Peter and Karen, and the two girls next to them. As Carl slowly backed away, he noticed that one seat was empty – the one beside Sarah. Carl watched as Liz tried to decipher the instructions and read them aloud. He sipped at a glass of water and leaned against a bookcase, watching Liz have trouble with reading the instructions. The condition of the paper did not help and so Sarah informed her to skip the introductory text. Liz read aloud and all followed her instructions, each lightly touching the triangular object.

'With all participants touching the planchette with thumb and fore-finger, move the planchette to the sun, and then the moon and spell out the alphabet... A...B...C...' They all read aloud each letter in turn and at first Carl found it amusing, but then for a moment he felt a shiver run through his body. Concerned with a sudden dizziness, his thoughts became serious, thinking something bad might happen.

'All forces of good, able, or concerned, please at this hour, help us in our quest for knowledge to...' Liz paused, having difficulty reading, 'to speak with those who have departed. Our friends, our loved ones, all we now miss dearly,' Liz continued, sincerity in her voice, 'talk amongst us against the glass, scratch your words upon our reflections and speak to us. Your letters, your words, your messages...'

As she paused, Carl grew cold and stared about the room. He stood shaded between the darkness from the kitchen and the light from the living room. However, it was not the shadows that were daunting, but somehow this event itself; or was it just his imagination getting the better of him again? He stood for minutes, watching them, their eyes searching each other, and then down at the object upon the mirror. A couple of silent minutes passed, and then Liz read more instructions from the paper. Another five minutes passed until the silence was broken.

'We're doing something wrong,' Liz announced, 'Maybe there's something else, something I haven't followed correctly from the instructions.'

'I knew it wouldn't work,' Mike whispered.

A nudge from Rachael's elbow hit his ribs as she asserted, 'Give her time, you fool.'

'Well, those instructions *are* hard to decipher Liz,' Sarah stated.

As they both scrutinised the ragged instructions again, Mike grew bored.

'You can count me out. This is stupid. I knew it was a waste of time. See, I told you so!'

'Give it chance, Mike!' Peter announced, 'Like she says, she's probably reading the instructions wrong. Maybe it needs a certain number of people.'

'Well, you can count me out. I'm going to watch that late night film I noticed in the paper,' Mike said, standing up, looking at those about the table. He scrutinised the board and noticed something.

'What's that?' Mike questioned.

'What's what?' Liz became frustrated as she thought he was playing her along.

Mike pointed at a hole in the board and stuck his finger in it. He scraped his nail against the bottom, finding it soft, not at all like wood.

'Candle wax… you've got to have a candle in there!' Mike announced, as he retreated into the living room to switch on the television.

Sarah searched the cupboards for an appropriately sized candle and picked some matches from the sideboard. They positioned the candle within the hole, and soon it was a light and flickering upon the dining room.

'Okay then, let's give it another go,' Sarah called, and saw Carl looking sadly out of the window.

'Going to have a go?'

Carl stood oblivious to Sarah's question.

'Carl! Are you going to join us now?'

This time he turned and said quietly, 'Do you think I should?'

'Yes, why not?' Sarah said, 'We've already lost one player. You can sit here!' She pointed to the seat next to her, and Liz beckoned him to participate.

'They say that disbelieving people or those with no genuine interest won't get any results.'

After some persuasion, Carl agreed and sat beside Sarah. She winked her eye at him as if to say thank you. He smiled and thought how he would love to date her someday, to sit with her at home in front of the fire, hugging, kissing... His thoughts were broken.

'Place your finger here, Carl.' Sarah said, taking his right hand and separating his fore-finger from the rest. She placed his finger against the planchette and then replaced her own.

'All forces of good, able, or concerned, please at this hour...' Liz re-read the inscription from the instructions and read further than before. 'We close our eyes, we concentrate and release our thoughts... we share our souls...'

At that, they all concentrated, eyes closed. Liz wanted to prove Mike wrong, to reach some deceased soul and speak to it, while he could only watch in anticipation. The couple were thinking of each other; their marriage and the possibility of raising a family. Sarah thought of her mother, her Gran and Granddad, of when she was a little girl. Rachael was angry with how appalling Mike's manners were, especially after she had asked if Mike and Carl could come to the party. Carl's thoughts were of nothing but the girl beside him. She was beautiful.

As their thoughts continued and hands twitched, their fingers ached and Liz read more inscriptions. Several minutes passed, but there was nothing but silence. Then the candle flickered as they felt a cold draft pass by. Carl's stomach heaved and his vision blurred as he opened his eyes. A pain shot from his groin through his chest and up to his neck. He almost winced as the pain was that he had in the hospital. Images from his past nightmares all of a sudden returned, flashing through his mind. Sweat beaded his forehead, and yet, he felt cold, almost shivering.

Abruptly, the planchette moved. Only an inch at first, but as pain ran through Carl's body, it moved again, and again, jerking an inch to and fro. Sarah and Liz's eyes shot open simultaneously, followed by Peter and Karen's. They looked upon the planchette, bewildered to see it moving freely – like a skate on ice. Half a minute passed before it slowed down, and then Liz cleared her throat, finding the courage to ask a question. As the silence was broken, Rachael's eyes shot open.

'Is there a force here… a soul in this room… one strong enough… one powerful enough to talk with us?'

The planchette circled upon the mirror and everyone looked perplexed, wondering who was moving it. Carl trembled, nerves shaking and skin perspiring. He was the only one now with his eyes closed, not hearing the words Liz said slowly and quietly.

'Can you hear my question? Listen. Please, listen carefully…' Liz gazed upon the tattered instructions and remembered what she had read earlier. 'Are you in light or darkness… can you see light… can you see only darkness?'

The planchette moved and cut her in mid-sentence. At first it wavered in a circular motion, but then quickly slid to the moon carving.

'You are in darkness?' Liz questioned.

The triangular figure shot toward the carving of YES.

'Can you read our thoughts? Which of us is of concern to you?'

It moved again and slid toward the NON carving, and then moved slowly to the YES carving. It hovered between them and then stopped at YES. Quickly it shot to the centre of the mirror and halted. For a moment it did not move and then shot from one side to the other, gliding fast upon the mirror. It moved and in turn stopped beside the letters; d… a… n… g… e… r…

'Danger?' Liz questioned.

The planchette moved speedily to YES.

'What danger?' Liz enquired, 'who are you… can you help?'

The object circled erratically and then spelt out, h… e… l…p… l… e… s… s… It paused in the centre of the mirror and then spelt, e… v… i… l… and shot to the moon carving. A minute passed before Liz broke the silence, inquisitive and excited.

'Who are you? Please, spell your name…'

The reply was NON.

'Why not?' Liz queried.

The planchette quivered and shook upon the mirror, then spelt out erratically, s… h… a… d… o… w… A moment passed and then the object moved about the letters, b… l… i… n… d… Finally, after a momentary pause, the planchette spelt out the letters, h… e… l… p…

Carl's eyes opened wide, glazed in a menacing stare. Suddenly, the room swirled with a mist and a large image developed. He shook with cold and saw his hands before him, clambering through mud, his fingers tearing at the earth. Instead of touching the planchette, they scratched at stones and grit. As he felt himself stand tall, he looked about him. He was small… a boy.

Before him was a narrow road, bordered with walls and winding through darkness and mist. He glimpsed behind, to notice eerie woodland, enshrouded in banks of fog. He looked below to find himself standing upon a bridge – a humpback bridge. Somehow he recognised this place, but for that moment it evaded him. He heard a distant rumble of thunder and then it grew louder, gradually nearing. As terror grasped his heart, for that second he thought it would stop beating. It was not the sound of nearing thunder, but a sound he had heard from his nightmares. Thundering hooves galloped somewhere in the distant landscape, and it grew louder. He stared about him and thought of running in the opposite direction to hide in the foggy woodland, but he froze. He looked above the trees into a dark and murky sky. Suddenly a ball of red light, like an exploding firework, flared and then darkened in the distance. It reappeared and grew bigger as if moving toward him. The ball of fire folded and twisted, reforming, and through it all, he could see a hideous face – a portrait of demonic evil.

It was then that he ran from the road to the side of the bridge to look in all directions. From the woodland, the ball of fire sped toward him, expelling mist. In the distance and along the road, he could see a dark shadow of a horse and rider, cloaked from head to foot. As the figure thundered toward him, the rider's black cloak thrashed and folded in the wind.

Carl clawed his way down the riverside, and then stopped to notice the menacing blackness of the river. Above, the sound of thunderous hooves stopped and then paced upon the bridge. Suddenly, all went quiet as Carl stared into the river from beneath the bridge. Within seconds of looking into the water, a whirlpool had developed and Carl felt himself slip. Thrusting his arms above the surface he tried to grasp air, but the water was heavy. Within the blackness of the thickening water, he could see the faces of dead people;

wailing about him as their grim, rotting faces infested a pain into his body. All he could do was to thrash out at them and send them flying back into the darkness. The blackness of the water was like tar and he was sinking… struggling to breathe… *drowning…*

As he sprang to his feet, Carl's finger retracted from the planchette and his arms shot in the air. The table shook and the planchette flew from the board. The candle glowed large and blue before it blew out. As a freezing cold entered the room, the mirror of the Ouija board cracked. Carl stood tall, his arms now at his sides and his eyes glazed and open wide. The five shot to their feet as Carl's body convulsed and his head turned erratically. His arms began fighting; clawing the air, and then his body arched and he flew backward, stumbling over the chair. Falling near the entrance of the living room, he thrashed his hands in the air.

Peter and the four girls stood up, astounded by Carl's outbreak. For a minute they could do nothing but watch him lash out, scratching at the air, his eyes glazed white in the dimness of the room. Hearing the noise, Mike entered the room and almost stumbled over Carl's frenzied body, horrified at what he witnessed. As Mike opened the living room door, he could see Carl's face from light flooding the room. Carl's eyes were fixed, his face contorted with agony, his body convulsing as his limbs thrashed sporadically.

'What the fuck's happened?' Mike shouted, hearing his friend growl like an animal.

Liz stuttered, her voice trembling.

'He's freaked out! The whole bloody place is *freezing*!'

'What the hell you done to him… he's gone wild!' Mike responded angrily.

'It's… it's the board… the game… it shattered… something's here!' Sarah shouted horror in her voice.

'Something's here, alright… a fucking crazed Carl!' Mike shouted.

'Calm him down, for God's sake!' Peter cried.

'I'm not touching him, look at his eyes… he's fucking possessed!' Mike yelled, 'you've done something to him… he's had too much drink… that bloody game's gone to his head! I told you not to fuck about with that stupid game…'

'We've not touched him! He just went like that all of a sudden,' Peter exclaimed.

'Bollocks!' Mike shouted. 'You've done something! Shit, I've never seen him like this before… maybe it's the accident!'

'Accident?' Sarah shouted.

'Yes, that bastard who beat him up last week!'

Their argument grew intense, and so did Carl's spasmodic attack, his limbs bouncing off the floor and door, head thrashing from side to side, and then he began wheezing, gasping as if drowning. The girls ran to Peter and Mike followed them, before all being huddled together in a crowd, watching the rolling body of Carl thrash upon the carpet.

As the water dispersed, Carl could see the underside of the overhead bridge, and suddenly faces appeared, looking down at him through a dissipating mist. Through the mist he could see the dining room and Mike's face staring anxiously. For a moment, Carl's eyes searched the room and fixated upon the ceiling, but then all went dark. Suddenly, a blood-red tunnel expanded to the ceiling and he was being sucked into a growing vortex. Flashes of scarlet light blinded Carl as he tried to pull himself up. The agony that possessed him was uncontrollable, but he felt a power from within his body overcome it and he stumbled to his feet.

Crouched against each other, the two boys and the girls watched Carl fall about, trying to stand. Then he managed to stand tall, his arms stretched out wide above his head, bellowing a cry of pain.

'No…'

Suddenly Carl's voice changed into a deathly growl.

'You can't fight it… it's too strong…'

Carl relaxed, but his body remained erect. His head drooped, sweat rolling over his face. The devilish voice announced again from his lips.

'I'm alive…'

Carl's voice croaked normal.

85

'No…I deny it!'

Carl's head faced upward, his eyes glistening with tears. Suddenly his body shot backward, as if hit by a thunderous punch. With unnatural power, Carl's flimsy body flew across the room and crashed through the patio doors, onto the lawn outside. Liz screamed. Mike swore.

'Holy shit! What the fuck?'

Mike raced to the shattered doors and glanced through the opening, followed by Sarah and Peter. They stood, shocked and quiet, as they looked upon Carl's motionless body, sprawled upon the centre of the lawn.

'Phone for a fucking ambulance!' Mike shouted.

Peter ran into the living room and dialled the emergency number. The girls stood frozen as Mike carefully opened the shattered patio doors. He paced carefully toward Carl's body; his face frowned, tears swelling in his eyes. There lay his friend, unconscious, battered and bruised, but breathing. Mike crouched beside him and searched his face, trying not to touch him, although he was deeply concerned. Carl's eyes were open, but stared oblivious into the night. Mike felt the cold autumn air grasp him and he shivered, his nerves trembling.

As the sound of sirens neared, flashes of blue light flickered upon the living room walls and Peter ran toward the front of the house, accompanied shortly after by the girls.

From within the house, Mike heard voices and the movement of heavy feet. Two men appeared in the doorway of the patio and stopped, their eyes searching the garden. Mike glanced back at his friend and then back at the house. The men were dressed in luminous yellow jackets and heavily burdened with equipment. Suddenly, Sarah advanced toward Mike and the two men followed.

'What's happened to him, lad?' One paramedic questioned, crouching beside Mike.

'He's had a fall… an accident! He crashed through the patio doors… stupid, but… is he going to be okay?' Mike asked, standing tall.

One of the men examined Carl and messed within a bag he was carrying. He took out several items of equipment and turned Carl over, checking his breathing, eyes and neck. As the man checked Carl over, the crowd watched attentively from the patio doors. Karen turned and smothered her face within Peter's chest, and Mike joined the group, his distressed face watching the ambulance men hasten about his friend's body.

Eventually, Carl's flimsy and unconscious body was placed gently into a wheelchair and carried across the lawn into the house. He was wheeled through the living room and out of the hall on to the driveway. As the ambulance men wheeled him toward the back of the waiting vehicle, one man turned and requested. 'It would be best if one or two of you could come along. We need identification, and besides… I think he'll need a friend.'

Outside on the driveway, the group stared at one another. Mike stepped forward, then glimpsed back at his audience. They looked at him before Sarah joined and said. 'Look after the house, Liz! You can sleep here and leave in the morning for Birmingham. I'll be back as soon as I can.'

Liz nodded and followed the others to the front of the house. Mike assisted the ambulance men in lifting Carl into the back of the ambulance. Mike and Sarah climbed into the ambulance as one man jumped out. He closed the doors and then ran to the front of the vehicle. He climbed into the driver's seat, and shortly after, started the engine. At first only the lights flashed brightly blue, but within seconds a siren bawled noisily as the ambulance sped off down the narrow street. Peter, Karen, Rachael and Liz stood silent for a moment, watching as the ambulance disappeared into the distance. Gradually the sound of the siren faded and they turned to enter the house, each person silent but busied with thoughts.

# SIX

CARL'S UNCONSCIOUS BODY WAS HURRIED through the white corridors of the hospital. Mike and Sarah accompanied the two ambulance men and nurse, weaving their way speedily through the building; the nurse attending to Carl as they travelled.

The wetness that bathed Carl's face roused him, and his eyes flickered open. Above him, he could see a white ceiling racing by with powerful lights that blurred his vision. For a while Carl felt his senses return and he could feel the movement of the bed as it jolted sideways, carrying him to an emergency ward. Even though he lay awake and witnessed the activity that raced before him, he felt paralysed and only could move his eyes to see the faces of friends peering at him from above. Increasingly he became uncontrollably cold and felt his body shivering, although his skin felt like it was burning. Abruptly the bed halted and the face of the nurse searched his. The image of her face dissolved as he felt his body convulse with the pain. As he felt his consciousness melt away, a great fear gripped his heart, making it pound faster in his chest. Something was playing with him as if he was still a part of a nightmare, rendering him unstable, as if any moment he could fall. Distressed, as he could not move, Carl's anxiety intensified and his fear escalated. Tears stung his eyes and his vision was cloaked by blackness. Carl took a last controlled inhale and held it for a few seconds. Then he cried out, his throat burning.

'Mike! Help me… Stop me from falling…'

Mike rushed to assist his friend, brushing away the nurse that was close to the bedside. Mike stared anxiously into Carl's eyes and although they were open, they rolled about not focusing, not recognising him. Mike shouted his friend's name before taking his heads in his hands.

'I've got you… I'm holding on to you, Carl… You can't fall now!'

Suddenly, Carl felt the soft, warm skin upon his cheek and the hands that grasped his shoulders. Hearing the cries from his friend's voice, he felt himself fighting, his will, his love and emotions extinguishing the fire that raged inside. Carl's hand shot into the air from the bedside and searched the blackness. Suddenly it connected with something warm and smooth. As another hand caressed his, he could feel his pain subside, leaving his body with just a bitter ache.

Carl's eyes closed and reopened in the split of a second. This time they were still, and then moved about controllably. Beside him, Carl could see the concerned and distressed face of Sarah, her hand clenching his.

'Mike!' she called, 'he's awake… I mean he's… he can see me!'

Mike released his grasp upon his friend's shoulders and their heads separated. Carl saw Mike stand back and look at Sarah, before staring back at him. Mike stood silent for a moment and then crouched forward, his face inches from his friend.

'You alright now, pal? For a second we thought we'd lost you!'

'I hurt… the pain… but I can't move…what's happened?' Carl's voice croaked; he cleared his throat, 'Where am I?'

'You're going to be fine, mate. Just stay in there and you'll be fine,' Mike responded.

'What happened?' Carl asked.

'Nothing much… maybe you had a little too much to drink. I think that attack affected you worse than you thought. Fucking bastard… hope they catch him.' Mike's voice grew angry, but his eyes swelled with tears of concern as he noticed the cuts that littered Carl's face.

'No, he's dead… killed,' Carl announced.

'Killed?' Mike questioned but was unheard.

'I ruined it… I've ruined everything,' Carl sobbed. 'Have I done anything… anything bad?' he asked, trying to sit up, his voice releasing the pain that shot through his back. He cried out before slumping back upon the bed. Mike and Sarah looked at one another, enough for Carl to realise that something *had* happened. Carl's hand grasped Sarah's harder, and her other hand covered his as she looked hard into Mike's face.

'What happened? Will someone… tell me?' Carl cried. Mike and Sarah stood silent. 'Tell me… how come I'm cut? Look, there's blood on me!'

'Help him, please!' Sarah demanded.

'What can I do?' Mike replied quietly.

'You're his friend… I hardly know him. You've helped him to come round. Help him again… he's in agony!' Sarah exclaimed.

'Well, don't back off… he needs as much attention as possible,' Mike whispered.

'Well, you do it… he's your friend... you can help him. I don't like to see him like this.'

Carl lay sore and drowsy, but could hear Mike and Sarah's argument loudening. Feeling withdrawn and saddened that any chance with Sarah had finished, he began to cry irrepressibly. Somehow the soft touch of her hands suppressed the pain, but now the pain grew worse, returning to how it was before. Carl felt Sarah's hands release his as she turned away to finish her argument with Mike. As his senses dissolved, Carl again was plunged into darkness, into the dark where images twisted and haunted him. Then, as a deathly face raced toward him, Carl felt the worst pain yet.

Mike and Sarah stopped in the middle of their argument to see Carl's body twist and jerk erratically. As they rushed toward him, his body arched backward and rose several inches from the bed. After a few seconds, Carl's body relaxed and he slumped back upon the bed, his face contorted with pain. Mike raced toward a nearby wall to hit a bell push and shouted.

'Nurse, nurse, come quickly!'

A nurse raced into the ward as Carl's body dropped upon the bed, motionless and twisted. Mike and Sarah paced backward from the bed as the nurse was joined by a doctor. Mike rushed forward only to be stopped. The room sprang into action, as more medics hastened about the bed, rushing equipment and instruments to assist the doctor. For a number of seconds the doctor checked Carl's condition, shining a torch into his eyes, checking his breathing, but most importantly reacting to the fact that his heart had stopped beating. As medical equipment was placed around the bed, the doctor tore open Carl's blood-stained shirt, placed two wired discs upon his chest, and shouted.

'One thousand... Two thousand... Three... Clear... On!'

Carl's body jerked and a mask then covered his mouth. Mike and Sarah could hardly see Carl's body through the crowd.

'One thousand... Two thousand... Three... Clear... On!' the doctor repeated.

After several minutes of commotion the crowd dispersed; a nurse turned to Sarah and Mike.

'His heart failed and then so did his breathing. We've tried resuscitation, but as you can see, he's not reacted to it. We can't do any more...' she continued after taking a long breath, 'I'm sorry... he's given up on us.'

Mike raced towards the bed, and then stopped abruptly. Poised over Carl's face, he stood silent, tears swelling his eyes. As he took Carl's head in a powerful embrace, the nurse pulled on his arm, beckoning him to retreat. Sarah followed, grasping the nurse and commanded. 'This is our friend. We want to stay with him for a while.' Sarah's eyes now were also spilling tears, 'Please... he was his best friend...'

She pulled away from the nurse and turned to grasp Carl's hand, which hung lifeless over the bed. She clenched it tightly as emotion overwhelmed her. This reminded her of her Gran's passing and her memories returned. Tears now filled her eyes as she stood silent, watching Mike hold his friend's body and cry out. The nurse retreated to the corner of the room, her eyes also swelling with emotion.

'Why… why has this happened? If I only knew… he doesn't deserve to leave us like this. He's too young…'

There followed a daunt silence.

'I loved you, Carl! You'll always be my best friend. I'll remember you when others won't…' Mike cried.

'I liked him too, Mike,' Sarah blubbered. 'In fact, I was just getting to like him a lot. Strange, but, I couldn't tell him… he seemed so soft-hearted.' Sarah spoke softly as she approached, noticing the lines of tears down Mike's face as he turned to face her.

'I can't believe this has happened. All he needed was a girlfriend… someone to love him. You know…' Mike paused, memories flooding his mind. 'I tried so hard to help him fulfil what he wanted… but… but he was so strange, in his own kind of way.'

As Sarah listened to Mike's distressed voice, she felt an electric shock shoot from her hand that held Carl's and up her arm. Abruptly, Carl's hand twitched and she screamed. Mike turned, releasing his grip upon his friend. He looked at Sarah, to see her eyes staring madly at her hand. Suddenly, Mike felt warmth upon the side of his face as a deep groan bellowed from Carl's throat. He turned to face Carl, totally transfixed by the event. Coughing and trembling, Carl's face changed from silvery white to a deepening pink. His body convulsed and jerked about, but Mike held him tight, tears now pouring from his eyes.

'It's a fucking miracle… you tough, stubborn bastard…' Mike shouted, tightening his grip around his friend. 'You got me going for a minute!'

Sarah felt Carl's cold hand close around hers and grip her even more tightly. She could not believe he was alive. From the doorway the nurse and doctor entered, intrigued by all of the shouting and commotion. For a moment they stood aghast, amazed that Carl's once lifeless body was now coughing, breathing… *alive* again.

They rushed in and paused beside Mike, watching for a moment. Crowding Carl's bedside again, the nurse and doctor gathered medical equipment and instruments, examining him several times. The nurse placed an oxygen mask over Carl's face and the doctor noted the readings from nearby instruments. As the nurse cushioned Carl's body, his coughing had stopped and his breathing eased. Testing Carl's pulse again, the doctor turned to Mike and Sarah with a puzzled scowl.

'His heart failed to respond… it's a miracle he recovered. Those last few minutes… he must have been in shock. The treatment must have been delayed… but why? What made him recover?'

# SEVEN

It was into the hours of early morning before Rachael drove Mike and Sarah home. Mike's thoughts whilst he was driven back to the house were that of Carl – remembering his face beset with anger and pain. He said little on the journey back as he felt guilty in leaving his friend alone at the hospital. It was Rachael who started a conversation about the accident and questioned Carl's condition whilst driving. Sarah explained all that had happened in the hospital, but like the others, Rachael became puzzled by Carl's miraculous recovery.

Mike got out of the car and stood silent, listening to the two girls talking inside. His breath exhaled into the coldness of a night as a calm breeze brushed his face. His mind disbanded from listening and he stood thinking, overwhelmingly tired and distressed. His thoughts were broken by the sound of car doors shutting. The car's lights and engine had been switched off and the two girls walked steadily toward the house, continuing their conversation. Suddenly Rachael turned and stepped a few paces towards Mike.

'Coming in, then? I hope you're not thinking of stopping out here all night!' She paused, and then realising his grief, continued in a more sympathetic tone, 'He'll be alright... we're just going to clean up and have a cup of tea, then... we'll get back home. At least we've no work tomorrow.'

Mike stepped forward and said nothing, but then followed them into the house. It was Sarah who had persuaded Mike to help in tidying the house. Whilst he moved furniture and covered the patio window with a large sheet of polythene, the girls cleared the party litter and washed up. It took about half an hour to make the living room and dining room respectable again and the girls, who had finished first, sat down waiting for the kettle to boil.

Mike entered the living room to find Sarah and Rachael talking quietly whilst sipping mugs of tea. The room was enclosed in darkness, apart from the area where the gas-fire flickered light upon the nearby furniture. Mike sat down quietly in a nearby armchair and looked angrily in to the fireplace.

'Finished… everything okay? Will that covering hold up?' Rachael questioned.

Mike acknowledged and leaned forward, staring at a mug of tea upon a coffee table.

'It's yours,' Sarah announced, 'Thank you for helping out. I would never have been able to cover those patio doors… doubt it'll hold out the cold, but I'll get someone to look at it. It's going to cost a bit.' She paused and then realised, 'Shit… forgot about my parents.'

Mike took the mug of tea; the hot liquid stung his throat as he drank. For a long moment the room was silent, all thinking their own thoughts.

'I'm a bit new to all that's happened tonight,' Sarah whispered and then paused, thinking.

'Aren't we all?' Rachael exclaimed, looking at Mike. 'Maybe the drink went to his head... probably had too much. I don't know. I hardly know him, really.'

'I thought you knew him since... well... I thought he had been a friend of Mike's for years?' Sarah questioned.

Mike sat quiet, allowing his fiancée to answer Sarah's questions.

'Carl's been a friend of Mike for years before I met him. I only meet him at Mike's work or when there were lots of us – you know, in the pub, or something like. When we went out... the three of us that is... he always sat quiet. I suppose he felt a bit awkward, but he's never had a girl, has he?' Rachael turned to face Mike, her face glowing from the flicker of the fire.

Mike leaned forward, placing his mug on the coffee table, his blonde hair falling across his forehead.

'Not to that I know of.' Mike cleared his throat. 'He's never been out with a girl properly since I've known him. I've tried... I've tied to set him up... Somehow he finds it more difficult to talk to girls. Yet he always talks about...' Mike explained, before being cut short.

'I take it he's a virgin, then.' Sarah assumed.

'Why, you interested?' Rachael asked, with a hint of sarcasm.

'Don't take the piss! If you could have seen him at the hospital, you would have tried to help anyway you could have. He looked so in pain.' Sarah answered.

Rachael's expression changed; the silence revealing her guilt.

'I've never seen him that bad before… not just the pain, but… but something was different.' Mike's voice grew cold.

'His voice… No, not his, but it came from him. The one we heard before he smashed through the…'

Sarah was cut short as Rachael exclaimed.

'Possession… it's like those films you see, people getting overtaken by the devil… ghouls… ghosts and things.'

Mike's temper flared. He could not bear to have his friend's personality be ridiculed, especially by his fiancée.

'You didn't fucking see him, did you? What the hell do you know about it? You had to make sure Liz got back.' Mike shouted, before calming his voice. 'Waiting around for ages in that bloody hospital for a lift… what took you?'

'Oh, thanks for the lift by the way! Is this the same way you thank Carl for carting you around? Treat him with contempt as well, do you? Bet you don't argue and moan at him. You always defend him,' Rachael disputed, turning to face Sarah. 'He's caused many arguments between us… wanting to go with him all the while. Why doesn't he find other friends, new friends? Can't he accept that we are supposed to be getting married and living together?'

'It's you that starts arguments. Besides, you've never liked him,' Mike stated, and then paused, thinking. 'He respects you, even though you interfere with our friendship. At least with him I don't get the petty sarcasm, mood swings… these bloody arguments… why do I bother?'

'Why don't you go to bed with your mate then, and you'll have the best of both worlds!' Rachael whined.

Mike stood tall and walked into the darkness of the dining room, muttering, 'Why don't I... teach you a lesson, bitch!'

Rachael felt her blood boiling and then she erupted into tears. Sarah sat nearer to Rachael to comfort her, taking her hands from her face and explaining.

'Look! We've all had a terrible night and we're all tired. I know it's hard to prioritise between a partner and friends, but Mike's just stressed out. If you had seen Carl at the hospital... watching all of the staff examining him, holding him down and then his body being electrified. His body... poor Carl must have been in terrible pain.' She paused, holding Rachael's hands tight. 'Mike's face when he thought he had lost him... It's too much for anyone to take.' Sarah stopped, a shiver running up her spine.

Mike turned and faced the firelight in the doorway, exposing only a portion of his body and face.

'It's shaken all of us up!' Sarah continued, 'How about Peter and Karen? How about Liz? What did they think?'

Rachael gasped a response through her tears and sobbed.

'Liz thought it all her fault... if we hadn't played with that stupid game, things would be alright.'

'Liz believes in all that supernatural crap anyway!' Mike announced, 'It was my fault. I asked him to come. It was me who persuaded him to come tonight, although he told me at work he was not up to it. That bastard who beat him up... he must have damaged his head. After tonight, God only knows what he'll end up like.'

Mike rubbed his forehead vigorously and turned away. Rachael lifted her head and looked toward Mike, squinting as she could not see him properly in the darkness. Then she looked at Sarah, her smooth face glowing against the fire light, her eyes sorrowful and watery.

'It was the game, wasn't it, Sarah? Things like that are true, aren't they?'

'Who knows, but that's the first time I've seen anyone get a response through an Ouija-board. The stuff that was said... it was all quite menacing. It seemed that whomever we were in contact with was positively frightened... as if someone or something was preventing them from talking.' Sarah continued, 'I didn't believe in all that. I was sceptical... like anyone else, I suppose... but after tonight, a lot has to be explained.'

Rachael's rational thoughts were returning, and her anger and tears escaped her.

'There's *some* rational explanation, and it's not one to do with bloody devils and ghosts. If you ask me, poor Carl hadn't fully recovered from the attack.' Mike calmly finished the conversation and changed the subject. 'Look, babe, I think it's time to go... all of this will seem clearer in the morning. With no work, we'll visit Carl and see how he is, eh?'

Sarah ushered her visitors outside and stood talking quietly on the driveway for a while, before Rachael and Mike retreated to the car. Sarah announced that living without her parents for a week would be lonesome and so hoped that Liz would stay for company that night. However, Sarah explained that the incident had frightened Liz and therefore she had returned home. As the early hours of the morning had become cold, Sarah was relieved to say her goodbyes and return to the warmth of the house. However, oppressed by memories of what had happened earlier that night, she paced gingerly about the house.

After checking all of the doors were locked, she stood for a minute pondering over the polythene sheet that covered the patio door. However, after realising she could do nothing much else to secure it, she decided to go to bed.

At the bottom of the staircase, Sarah picked up a coat that had fallen from the balustrade, from where it had originally hung. As she slowly ascended the stairs, she rummaged through its pockets but found nothing. Upstairs whilst entering her bedroom, she noticed the inside pocket was sealed and decided to unzip it. Surely it would be the only way to identify to whom it belonged. Although her bedroom lamp was dim, it gave her sufficient visibility to notice an object slide out with a chain attached. As it fell into the palm of her hand, she grasped the chain and held the object up against the light. Ornate and moulded tightly to its chain, a pendant was centred with a dark and polished stone. Although tarnished, the metal that encircled the stone was engraved with symbols of which Sarah could not decipher. Totally bemused by the object, she dropped the coat on to her sun-bed and placed the pendant on top of her dressing table, thinking that someone at the party will no doubt ring to claim it.

Once undressed, she paced about her bedroom, a thin laced pair of knickers revealing the darkness between her legs and a skimpy silk shirt hiding her bra. She crouched and picked up several items from the floor, placing them neatly in other places. Through the opening between her curtains, she noticed powerful moonlight shining against the window ledge. Curious, she turned off her bedroom lamp and noticed a narrow beam of moonlight stretch across the carpet. Concerned about leaving on her lamp, she decided that the moonlight would light the room sufficiently for her to sleep untroubled. Settled with the outcome, she opened the curtains a little more, before sliding under the bedclothes.

# EIGHT

FROM A WINDOW A PALE light flooded a room, shadowing figures against a wall. Outside, the night sky was dark and clear. Inside, the room was silent.

A groan broke the silence as bedclothes moved upon a bed. Submerged within the depths of a soft pillow, but unveiled by a quilt, was the head of a girl. Her face was small, round and surrounded by long, curly blonde hair. Suddenly the girl's eyes opened and her legs closed together under the sheets. She opened her eyes again, but this time they showed anxiety. For a while she lay scared, glaring at the window, expecting something horrible to happen. Although cold, she felt her body perspiring, her heart beating fast; she shuddered. Her heart almost stopped as she noticed the outside of the window become blocked by a swirling, thick mist. As it wavered, it thickened and the room became frozen with biting cold. She was in the safety of her own home, yet for some reason she was frightened, scared to even move. Quickly she searched the room and then looked back at the window, hearing a noise scrape against the outside wall. The sound neared and she suddenly realised something was climbing the house. As the mist parted and swirled aside, she felt her teeth ache and her blood run cold. Hovering in front of the window outside, a shadow was at first undistinguishable. It was not until it floated inches from the glass that the girl felt terror stiffen her body. Poised outside the window was Carl, his eyes nervously searching the room until they stopped to focus on her. She shuddered and crouched, sitting up against her headboard. She could hear groans, calls for help, asking her to open the window and let him in. She stared, bewildered at how he could be there, holding onto the wall outside. Carl called again, shedding tears, beckoning to come in.

Nervous, Sarah pulled back the sheets, slid from the bed and stood in the pale light. She started shivering as she felt the cold embrace her and penetrate the warmth between her legs. Indecisively she began to walk slowly toward the window, her naked skin gleaming and her underwear brilliant white.

Carl's eyes looked anxiously upon her and he called again. Suddenly she stopped a yard from the window, but he called again. Wrapping her arms about her chest, she stared at his face, thinking something was wrong. Abruptly, her thoughts were broken as Carl's grip from the wall outside broke and he toppled back. Sarah ran toward the window and pulled at the latch. The window swung inward and hit the inside wall. As she reached her arms out to grasp him, his body fell back, his grip broke and he fell through the mist, to the ground below. Hearing a thud, she leaned over the window-ledge and looked downward through the mist as it reassembled.

It was one of the most hideous and venomous creations of evil that shot up through the mist toward her. Between its outstretched, scaly arms was a face constructed from the depths of hell to resemble a lizard. Jagged teeth snapped and saliva spat as its jaw retracted whilst its distorted face revealed a menacing large eye, the other only a gouged hollow. Within a second the creature flew up at her before its grim, malicious face melted into darkness.

Carl could only see blackness until his eyes focused properly. Staring upon a moonlit ceiling, he felt his skin perspiring, his body trembling, but most of all he felt his heart racing. Once again his body felt as it did after every nightmare, but this time his arms and legs ached. Tormented by the nightmare, he sat up, hoping to eradicate the images that flashed within his thoughts. To his discomfort, however, it was instability that sent him falling back upon his pillow and unfortunately, this time the nightmare images persisted; the man swinging from the darkness into the light, his neck stretched tight, and then the man being decapitated; ghostly snakes biting at the shadows of men; the closing of the cloaked figure upon the black stallion and the fireball above the trees; the rotting faces swirling about him in the darkness; and now, this hellish lizard pouncing up at Sarah.

Sarah? Carl thought she may be in danger. But it was just another bad dream. Or was it? He sat up and shook his head. He could not let his thoughts agonise him anymore. Determined to revitalise his senses and ignore the pain that distraught his body, he fought against the visions that haunted him. Pivoting his weight upon his arms and stretching forward, his stomach convulsed and he coughed, but found the visions disappearing.

It was the clinical odours that Carl first noticed, and then he saw the room, hardly twelve foot square, empty walls painted white like the ceiling, a door and a window. Beside the bed was a metal drawer and arching overhead was a stand holding a bag of clear liquid, of which ran through a thin and transparent pipe.

Gradually, Carl became cold and started shivering. His thoughts wavered as he struggled to remember his recent experience. He slumped back against the hard bed and stared at the ceiling, trying to regain strength. For minutes he lay oblivious, feeling nothing but a tingling sensation. What had happened? How long had he been here? It was so hard to remember. It was his recollection of Mike's voice that assembled his memories together – the game, the party, the week… the nightmares. Suddenly, he became cold again, and a shiver ran down his spine. He lay perplexed for a minute and then glanced through the window into the night sky.

As the headlights of vehicles moved through the city streets, a shimmer of light brightened the orange glow of the nearby surroundings. As his vision accustomed to the shadowy room, Carl could make out the overhead lights of a car park. In the distance, the city was dark, the landscape lit only by moonlight. Again, he realised that he was in hospital. Above the city lights and in the dark sky was the moon, full and gleaming bright. Carl looked at it for some time, but as his eyes grew weary, he pictured a grinning face. Slowly, as tiredness overwhelmed him, the moon quivered and developed into a smiling face with rounded cheek bones. Slowly the image reminded him of the girl he had met that night. For a moment, he pictured Sarah's face smiling at him and felt the touch of her hand. However, as he recalled the past events, he eventually remembered the recreation of her in his dream, and what happened in the last part of it.

Gradually the image of Sarah's face disappeared as the face of the moon turned dim and then reformed into an image of a skull, its dark eye sockets glaring down at him. For a moment Carl's blood ran cold and his body froze. It was then that he realised that all that had happened was somehow related to his dreams. Or was it? His head ached as he pondered over the questions whirling about his thoughts. Why was Sarah in the dream? Why was he in it – at the window looking in? He brushed aside the questions, thinking dreams were nothing but confusion. His dreams always puzzled him, but now was he making something of them? Or were they just a subject of his vivid imagination?

For a while he lay perplexed, and then stared to see the moon was normal. However, one thing was certain; he could not just wait around as if all was normal. Could what had happened to other people, happen to Sarah? He thought of his chance in warning her, or was it already too late? What if all of this was just coincidence – what would he say when he got to her?

Ignoring the pain and instability of his body, Carl slid out of bed and stood nervously upon a cold floor, to find he was dressed in a nightgown. In haste he searched about the room to find his socks, shoes and jeans. From a nearby chair he retrieved them to quickly get dressed. Pushing the gown inside his jeans, he stumbled toward the door. Slumped against the wall, for a moment he had to regain his balance – his legs were not just tired, but sore. He tried the door and opened it slowly. For yards ahead he saw a dim corridor and at the end was a big, brightly lit desk. He closed the door behind and tiptoed swiftly down the corridor, looking around to avoid people. He stopped, crouching in a doorway, as two women dressed in white gowns walked by and talked on their way down the corridor. After noticing the women disappear into a room on the right, Carl carefully moved again.

He paced his way through corridors avoiding people, and within a couple of minutes he had reached the hospital entrance. It was busied with patients: some walking about, some being pushed in wheelchairs, and by the entrance a nurse was handing two security guards hot drinks. Realising that the security men would be difficult to pass, Carl moved about the edges of the room, trying his best to stay out of sight. A couple of yards away and draped over a chair, Carl noticed a doctor's coat. Quickly he raced past and grabbed it before disappearing behind a couch in the waiting area. Carl rose to his feet with the white coat buttoned, his fingers combing back his hair. He began to pace quickly towards the entrance and, noticing that the security men had turned their backs on him, he scuttled closer toward the entrance. Abruptly, he froze as one security man turned after hearing a patient behind him cry hysterically. Carl reached into the pockets of the doctor's coat and, fingering about he recognised a pen, a small torch and then some sort of cloth. Grabbing the cloth, he pulled it out to see it was a handkerchief. Shrugging his shoulders and pulling his collar high, he walked swiftly towards the entrance. Covering his face, Carl pretended to blow his nose and had almost reached the entrance doors before he heard a call.

'Goodnight, doc... finished early tonight?'

Carl shuddered before turning to see a black security man, squinting at him through the light. With the handkerchief still smothering his face, Carl nodded and then pretended to sneeze before hurrying toward the entrance. The black security man nudged his companion, and then they stared at Carl as he dropped something. They stood perplexed for a second, and then raced toward the entrance to pick up the identification badge.

Outside, Carl felt relieved and made his way speedily towards the car park. He turned suddenly, hearing voices shouting from behind. Noticing the two security men hurrying toward him, Carl began to run. With weakness in his legs, Carl could hardly run and his balance crumbled to send him sprawled upon the tarmac. Speedily he crawled to his feet and ran again until he reached the road. The men behind seemed almost upon him, yet his legs felt like lead. He reached the road and ran across blindly. Suddenly he tripped and rolled upon the ground. Stumbling, his vision blurred, he rose to his feet. Hearing the security men calling him, he then ran in the opposite direction.

A flicker of light blinded Carl's vision as he heard a screech of brakes. Jumping aside to avoid the oncoming car, he spun toward the ground. He rolled over as a scream pierced his ears. He stumbled about and crawled, pulling his weight until he could stand. He heard voices and although his vision was blurred, he noticed shadows approach – people running toward him. He turned from the noises and ran as steadily as he could. He could feel his lungs burning for air and the pain in his legs was agonising. With the freezing air, however, his senses became clearer and he stopped to catch his breath. He opened his eyes wider after rubbing them and noticed blood on his knuckles. Although the distance behind him was noised with shouting, the street ahead was dark and clear. Carl continued stepping along the streets and away from the voices, gradually regaining his directions.

It was not long before he reached the river. Washing his face at a shallow bank, he remembered that Sarah lived not far from here – only a mile across a field into a small housing estate. Although his mind faded occasionally with pain, he felt reassured when he reached the woodland and field near her house. He climbed a stile and stumbled into a moonlit field of which expanded to the dark shadows of a distant housing estate. The field seemed to be miles long, but he ran on, knowing every second was vital.

Eventually Carl reached the edge of the field and fought his way into the woodland that led toward the housing estate. He stopped to catch his breath, the cold air freezing his mouth and throat. It was then that he noticed that a strange glowing mist had covered the field and was on the edge of the woodland. He frowned, puzzled that a mist would be lingering on such a cold and clear night – it was so densely compact. Suddenly as he remembered the mist in his dream, a great fear ran through his body. Frantically he continued searching from one house to another, looking into the gardens, through fences, over walls – anything in hope to reach a house that resembled Sarah's.

He stopped to look once again into the woodland. Now he was convinced that it was not just a dream or coincidence. Nearing every second, folding its way through the trees and engulfing all in its path, was the mist, glowing bluish green and wavering for intervals before spreading quickly through the trees. Carl ran again, searching the gardens – looking for Sarah's house. He knew roughly where it was, but that was from the drive by road. Oppressed by his thoughts, he turned once more to face the woodland. Swirling yards from him the mist wavered, as if it was awaiting his next move. Again he ran; the mist following him. He ran as fast as his feet could carry him, but now the mist was almost upon him, standing above him like a wave ready to engulf him any moment.

Carl stumbled, pain shooting through his legs. Leaning against a nearby tree, he looked swiftly about him and noticed a garden with a pool. The lawn that surrounded it led to a patio door covered in thick polythene. By the time he recognised the house and garden, the mist was swirling about him. It had now reached the garden and was almost upon the house. Carl fought with the hedgerow that bordered the garden from the woodland and felt his hands being pricked. He scrambled through the hedge as much as possible before diving into the garden. He looked up toward the house after rolling upon the lawn and noticed a dim light shining from an upstairs window, whilst before, the house had been completely dark.

Carl rose to his feet. Shivering but determined, he raced across the lawn and leaped crashing through the polythene, and felt it wrap around him as he rolled across the floor. He turned upon his back and sat up, pulling away the polythene. Although in pain, he got to his feet and crept through the house.

Sarah was already awake to hear her bedroom door handle turn, and then suddenly all was quiet. A knock sounded against the bedroom door and she rolled over to look, still half asleep. The room was dim with only a hazy light filtering through a dense fog from the window. Everything else was quiet and still except for a scarlet light glowing from her dressing table. She pulled the sheets from her and slid out of the bed, standing in the dim light. She hesitated, realising she was alone, thinking what if a burglar had got in? But burglars do not knock. She turned on her bed-lamp and called, asking who was out there.

'It's me! Can I come in? I've got something... Carl's got something to tell you!'

Sarah replied, puzzled at his presence, noticing her clock displayed nearly three in the morning.

'What are you doing here this time of the morning? You were in hospital. What is it?'

'Let me in, girl, and I'll tell you! It's important,' the voice at the door became hoarse with a tone of desperation.

Sarah stepped slowly toward the door and then stopped, noticing something glow from her dressing table.

'Come on, it's urgent! You need to trust me!' the voice called again, disrupting her hesitancy.

Sarah stepped closer to the door and slowly unlocked it.

'I don't usually lock it, but... well tonight... being alone and all.'

The door slowly opened as Sarah stepped back, forgetting she was half dressed.

Standing within the darkness of the landing, Sarah could see the silhouette of a man, dressed head to toe in a gown. She retreated back toward her bed, rubbing her eyes as they had become hazy and the silhouette stepped slowly into the bedroom. In the dimness of the bedroom, she could only make out his pale face and hard staring eyes. Sarah grabbed her bathrobe and pulled it around her as she sat upon the bed. Carl stepped nearer until he stood tall above her, his eyes glaring upon hers.

'Stand, girl. I have a lot to tell you… things that have been and are to be.'

Sarah stood up, perplexed at his presence and by the way he talked. His skin was not as she expected – cut and bruised or beaded with sweat, but glazed like a porcelain doll. She rubbed her eyes to clear her vision and parted the shaggy blonde hair from her face. Carl's hand cupped her chin and rubbed her cheek. The other felt its way from her shoulder to her waist. At first she felt discomforted and wanted to pull away, but for some reason she felt drawn to him. She moved out of the moonlight and again noticed the mist swirling outside her window. Peering back at him, she asked. 'What is it, Carl? What's so important? You've not just come back here to tell me that you love me, have you?' She paused, and then continued. 'I'm too tired… besides… you should be resting, back in hospital.'

Sarah felt his touch stretch down between her legs and grasp her skin, rendering coldness between her legs.

'Hey! What the hell do you think you're doing? It's not *that* what you said you came for!' she demanded. 'Tell me what the hell is –'

Sarah felt her rage build and pulled away from his grip. As she pulled herself from him, she turned her head away and glanced by accident at her wardrobe mirror. Reflected in the mirror and standing before her was one of the most gruesome creations of evil. As she screamed, it turned its head to face the mirror. Sarah stood, petrified, now seeing a hideous, scaly lizard standing upright like a human. It's horrible face quivered and contorted as its eye sockets widened and a jaw retracted, revealing razor sharp teeth. As it shook spiralling horns upon its head, saliva dripped from its mouth and it bellowed a deep laugh.

Sarah turned away from the reflection and looked at what was truly holding her. What was an imitation of Carl was now a body reformed into a hellish creature. Its scaly hands gripped her tighter and she could hardly move. Her heart jumped as the creature bellowed in a deep voice.

'You're a lively one, aren't you? And such a pretty one, too!'

Its savage face grinned at her as one eye focused – the other just a gouged, lifeless hollow. Suddenly she felt its scaly dry hand slide down to her neck and grip her throat. She heard him bellowing words, but her mind was slipping and her vision clouding. No matter how much she pushed with her arms, all she could do was struggle.

'Where is it? Where is the call-stone?' the creature demanded, its voice loud and menacing. 'What have you done with the warlock's stone?'

Sarah's vision was darkening and her strength weakening. She could not fight much longer, as the creature's grip was tightening and soon she feared she would pass out.

Suddenly, Sarah felt the pressure on her throat ease as she fell to the ground and rolled upon the carpet. For a while she could see nothing, but as she sat up and coughed, her blurred eyesight became clear. Arching above her, and staring madly at a figure in the doorway, was the creature.

At first she could not see what was happening, but as the figure by the door moved slowly into the light, she could see Carl – his face bruised and lacerated, his clothes muddied, spotted in blood. The creature turned and looked down at Sarah, her wide eyes gazing up at it. It now stood with wings flapping and was searching the room. Carl leapt from the doorway and toward the dresser after realising the creature had noticed the pendant. The creature sprang to the air also, and was faster. Carl reached for the pendant but the creature's hand grasped his wrist, its sharp talons scratching down his arm. Carl's eyes swelled with tears, but he neglected the pain and clenched his free hand into a fist. He swung at the beast, punching into its jaw. Its head jolted and its eye rolled, but the creature hardly flinched. However, the vital seconds gave Carl enough time to grab the pendant.

Noticing the pendant had gone, the creature raged, its mouth opening wide and disclosing razor sharp teeth. Its grip clenched Carl's wrist tighter, but he swung again whilst holding the pendant. This time the creature's grip slackened and Carl managed to pull his wrist free. The creature stumbled backward, stood upright and shook its head, its eye rolling and blinking. Carl had no time in studying the creature or to think where in hell it had come from. His sole intention was to protect Sarah and to do that, he needed to destroy it.

Feeling a strange power overcome him, Carl ran forward and leapt to the air, his foot stretched out before him. Soon he came crashing down upon the bedroom floor after hitting the creature's face. Carl crawled upright to see the creature lying, sprawled in a corner. He looked at Sarah crouching beside the bed, staring at him and then at the creature. She raised herself, clenching the bedclothes and then raced for the door. He would have leapt after her, but as she reached the door, she screamed and retreated back into the room.

Carl froze, undecided as to what to do. He looked at the motionless creature and then stood up. Decisively, he made for the door and raced into the darkness of the landing. As he looked down into the darkness of the stairway, he could see several streaks of blue mist sliding up the stairs. Firstly there were only three, but then two more appeared, and within seconds they were accompanied by three more. The first three streaks had already reformed from the condensing mist into ghostlike snakes.

Carl's heart froze. He had seen these phantasmal creatures before – surely they were the ones in his dream. He raced back into the room, closed the door and locked it. Sarah was about to join him but he pulled her to the bedside. As they watched the door, they could hear the snakes hissing and spitting as blue light glowed from under the door.

As Carl heard something move behind him, the room flickered into darkness and then lit up again. He turned to see the creature standing, looking at the bed-lamp it had just knocked over. Carl reached for the nearest instrument that could harm the creature and grabbed a tall wooden ornament. He was about to stand and assail the creature with his weapon but saw it slide a knife-like boomerang from behind. Carl stooped as the boomerang flew past the bed, about the room and back into the creature's hand. The creature took flight but collided with bedroom furniture and so poised itself by the door. Within a second of throwing the weapon again, Carl flung the ornament at the creature, pushed Sarah to the ground and dived on top of her. The ornament hit the creature's stomach and its busied wings stopped flapping. Suddenly, a bellowing cry echoed the room and so the couple looked up and over the bed. Embedded into the creature's shoulder was the weapon. The creature grasped the boomerang and pulled the weapon from its wound and laughed.

'You'll have to do better than to try your luck! My pets will finish this little game.' The creature's eye glared at them as he unlocked the door and announced, 'They cannot be harmed like flesh and bone.'

As the creature rolled its hand around the doorknob, the room flickered again, from light to darkness and back to light. Eventually the room was plunged into darkness.

'Sarah... Sarah!' Carl called, 'Turn on the light... find something to light the room... I can't see!'

In the dim of the moonlight, Carl could just make out the silhouette of Sarah as she crawled to the side of the room. She stopped by a cupboard to desperately search for the torch she knew was there. Suddenly, she realised it had been left in the kitchen after Mike had covered the patio doors.

'Shit! He's opening the door...' Carl shouted.

The door swung open and at first there was nothing but a strange blue glow on the carpet. Then, with slow and silent movement, a half transparent snake wriggled into the room, snapping its venomous mouth. Seconds after, several others followed, slithering slowly through the air. The creature stood back, clenching its hands together as its eye gazed madly into the darkness. Carl noticed the snakes reach the expanse of moonlight across the floor. As he leapt across the bed and flung himself to the floor, he heard them hiss and snap their mouths. They changed direction and were almost upon him.

Abruptly, the room lit with bright blue light as Sarah found the switch to her sun-bed. Carl hit the floor and rolled over as one snake flew at him. He felt his arm impede something but grasped the pendant hard. He looked up dazed and frightened, his eyes searching for Sarah. He called her as he threw the pendant. She failed to catch Carl's throw and the pendant slid upon the sun-bed. As the scarlet glow from the pendant's stone disappeared, so did the hellish creatures. As the snakes dissolved into misty streaks, the creature decomposed, diminishing into a ghostly skeleton. Within seconds the creature and its dominions had vanished. For a long moment, the room was silent but left with an acrid odour of burnt flesh. Carl and Sarah sat bemused, staring about the room and then focused upon the pendant – its metal glittered in the bright light, but its stone dark. Carl crawled toward the sun-bed and reached for the pendant.

'No, Carl! Don't take it! Leave it there!' Sarah cried, her voice croaking.

'The sun-bed destroyed them?' Carl mused, his speech heavy.

Sarah shivered and stared, thinking. 'I don't know. Maybe it's the light... the light from the sunlamps.'

Carl stumbled and crawled to his feet. With the last ounce of strength, he pulled Sarah up and held her arm.

'I came as fast...' Carl paused, 'It all sounds crazy, but tonight...' He drew breath, but felt increasingly nauseous, 'they're all connected... piecing everything together... but what I am missing? Why?' Carl felt heavy and his legs gave from under him. 'Why...'

Sarah caught him as he collapsed and sat him up the best she could, propping his head up with her hand.

'Nothing happens like this... only when...' Carl's voice became sluggish and his head dropped.

'When what? What was that? Have you seen that thing before?' Sarah questioned nervously, her eyes wide, her mind still comprehending what had just happened in her own house.

She pulled Carl up to steady him, but he dropped on the bed, his eyes rolling, and his mind dizzy.

'No... no but, they are always there... in the dreams,' Carl answered, delirious, and then continued, 'I would wake and it would be gone. Just a nightmare... a strange and horrible nightmare...'

Sarah stood for a minute, watching Carl press his forehead and rub his eyes. It was too bewildering; her thoughts sprang from one to another. As she calmed, her thinking cleared but she shivered, her legs and arms cold. She looked at herself in the mirror, at her near naked body, perplexed by such an unreal event. But then she remembered the cold, powerful hand that grasped her throat. She shuddered and looked at Carl, his face distressed and angry.

'Carl, you need help, you're bleeding. You really need to go to the hospital,' Sarah said, sitting down beside him on the bed.

'No. I can't. I came from there... to stop it happening,' Carl answered, holding his hands over his eyes, 'They must be stopped. The dreams must stop. What else has been done? How many have died already?'

Sarah looked sorrowful upon the man before her, his eyes releasing lines of tears, his voice agonised. She stroked his forehead and his hand covered hers.

'You've not done anything,' Sarah said softly. 'No-one's been killed. It's just the nightmares that make you think you have.'

'No!' Carl contested, 'It's been since childhood. Waking from nightmares in the hours of darkness... sweating, heart thumping... scared; so scared. In a way I've become accustomed to them, but I never knew... never knew what they meant or what they did!'

Sarah leaned closer, her hair falling over her eyes. Carl's eyes opened slightly as her head shadowed the light.

'Every dream you have... it makes things happen. Like tonight?' Sarah questioned.

'Yes, it happens. I must believe it now, however much it sounds ridiculous,' he cried.

'You dreamed of me?'

'Yes!'

'You've dreamed of others?'

'Yes!'

'Then why does it happen? Have you witnessed the dreams you've had?'

'No! I've never been there when… I've never realised that…'

'So, why now? How did you know this… that they were coming… and why for me? Was it the Ouija board?'

'I don't know. Please… my head… I'm so tired… please just leave me…'

Sarah watched Carl turn on his side as she stood. She looked around the room and frowned. She shuddered as she visualised the creatures that were in her own room. What would she have done if Carl had not come? She glanced back at him. He lay motionless and silent upon the bed. All that had happened seemed so ridiculous and unbelievable, yet she had second thoughts in turning off the sun-bed.

Sarah's attention now focused on Carl, as he was too exhausted to go to hospital and was by now in a deep sleep. Although Sarah had undressed children and babies in her earlier days of baby-sitting, Carl's body was limp and heavy. It took her quite some time to undress him before placing him under the sheets. For a while she looked at him before retreating to the bathroom to soak a flannel in cold water. Carl awoke after feeling his face bathed. He groaned and moved his aching body under the sheets trying to find comfort, but again, conscious escaped him.

Carl awoke again, not knowing how long he had been asleep, but noticed the landing light was still on and from a distance; he could hear a tap running. Through his dry and tired eyes, Carl squinted at the room. The moonlight had now disappeared and the only light came from between the half open door. He looked about him, his thoughts troubled by pain. Slowly his thoughts dissolved as the need for rest overwhelmed him.

Carl awoke again and turned upon the cold bed, his body bruised and aching, his hands and face sore. He rolled upon his back and slowly stretched his legs. His eyes were blurred and so he closed them, but felt something stirring beneath the sheets and by his feet. Gradually, he felt warmth reach his legs and the caress of silky skin brush the hairs on his legs. He twitched, his nerves still trembling, but then relaxed. He opened his eyes and squinted down toward his feet. Appearing from under the sheets, a foot above his thighs poised Sarah: her face and shoulders bear, silky bright in the shadowy light. Her legs opened wider so her buttocks could rest upon his knees. She crouched forward and laid her hands upon his waist, steadily moving them up and down his body. She made no noise and Carl asked no questions, but just groaned pleasurably. The hands continued as her legs wiggled to gain more comfort.

Carl felt bleary, but stretched even more, his limp penis growing with uncontrollable excitement. Sarah's hands reached between his legs and she pressed against his hardened testicles, fingering with his hair. His erected organ disappeared with her soft and gentle hands and as she pulled back the skin, she noticed how the tip glistened. Suddenly she stopped and Carl exhaled a deep breath. For a moment Carl felt cold return over him, but then felt a moist tip run from the base upwards. Slowly, sticky warmth enveloped the tip and slid down. Saliva leaked from Sarah's mouth and ran to his testicles as she moved her head up and down. Carl felt senses arouse within his groin and he felt the excitement was climaxing. He felt weary, but Sarah motioned continually with more speed.

Carl sat up, his eyes wide with excitement. Kneeling over his legs was Sarah, her head quickly lowering and lifting. The sheets had fallen from her waist and were resting on the back of her legs. Her body shone dim against the half-light and her smooth limbs flexed and contracted. Carl pivoted his weight with his right arm back and took Sarah's head with the other. As he messed with her shaggy long hair, she stopped to look up. Her guilt turned into a mesmeric smile and Carl was absorbed. Carl moved her head to meet his and as they rearranged their legs, their tongues entwined and their breath was loud and heavy. Soon they were both kneeling upright, bodies embraced, hands kneading each other.

Sarah moved toward Carl and he ran his hands down her back, sliding until he reached the round of her buttocks. As he took her with his hands and lifted her gently, she groaned and broke their kiss. She swung her arms about his neck and her legs about his waist, crossing them behind him. Carl lifted her more and arched back in balance. Soon he could feel her groin against his penis. Although drained after his ordeal Carl grew powerful and as he probed, Sarah embraced him, her breasts flat against his chest. As he slowly lowered her, her breath exhaled loudly onto the back of his neck. She leaned back, realising his tip was inside her. Sarah exhaled again, a deep surge of breath closing her lungs. Carl motioned her buttocks, riding her body upon him. Suddenly he leaned forward and together they collapsed upon the bed.

Resting between her legs and on top of her, Carl gripped the bed and continued the motion. Sarah felt the heat within her peaking as he penetrated her more. She felt muscular twinges within her stomach and thighs, but Carl could not last any longer. With a last thrust, the excitement erupted and both lay over the bed, bodies embraced and mouths panting.

Carl lay motionless for some time, his organ still inside her. Sarah could feel a frenzied heat burn from within, and yet she shivered. Carl did not want to move and although his body was heavy, Sarah was content to let him warm her. She was overwhelmed with the passion and wanted more, pressing her hands upon Carl's buttocks, feeling his organ still in her. For minutes they lay upon the bed, locked together, and for a moment Sarah kissed the lacerations on Carl's face. The bedroom lay still until the bodies separated, shining silky in the darkness. Then they moved together again as sheets were flung over them.

Rain started to pelt hard against the outside window and a vicious wind howled about the alleyways and rooftops. Sarah held Carl tightly, comforted by his presence.

'I became scared… I couldn't be on my own,' Sarah said softly, 'I'm proud of you coming to help me… I was right… I know you really do care…'

'I felt that there was something… something between us… you know me… what I am…' Carl replied.

'Yes, you're alone and needing… you're compassionate, but cold.'

'No, not cold… just need someone to believe in me… someone to love.'

# NINE

THEIR CONVERSATION CONTINUED WITH THE difficulty it began with. The silence was occasionally broken by short, futile questions during their walk to the park from Sarah's house. The reluctance of developing a conversation was prominent, but it was cold. Were they both perplexed and frightened, or was it the blustery air that restrained their voices from speaking? Carl and Sarah were silent for the first hundred yards along the twisted entrance to the park, their mouths muffled with scarves and their collars pulled high. At first both minds were too busy with personal thoughts to manage any discussion.

Carl was angry with himself, submitting questions against the only short memories he had of his father, picturing the image of his mother, and then his memories of school. How stupid he was as a child. He was a powerful but somehow quiet, half-witted and irrelevant member of the class. As he knew well, this was due to the work he did for his father. At barely ten years old he remembered his one and only parent busied with communion and the church he loved, whilst Carl looked after their little home. The job he hated most was chopping logs and stacking them in the wood-hut. The memories were now hindering his mind as the pain did his body. Trying to accept that something evil was overpowering him was difficult. Now it was Sunday morning, and tomorrow was work. But how was he to concentrate on his work? Should he revisit the hospital, as Sarah advised?

What had he being doing at work? On what stories had he been working? His thoughts were severed as a soft voice announced.

'Where did that thing come from, Carl? Things like that shouldn't exist, should they?' Sarah questioned, a breath releasing the words with strength, her eyes searching the floor. 'I'd say it was all just imagination… a hallucination, but…'

'It happened, Sarah,' Carl replied, cutting himself off from his thoughts and the sadness that surrounded them, 'It's like waking from a dream, but only to have been in it… and with someone else.'

He was about to continue when Sarah stopped and pulled him back, looking up into his eyes. Somehow her feelings were oppressed. She hardly knew the tall, dark-headed man who walked with her. It was as though she had been cornered in a strange room surrounded by evil, and the man before her was the culprit. He had caused the hideous creature that could have killed her. On that thought she was fighting with her emotions and feeling the gap between herself and Carl widening. She wanted to help him, but her fears told her to escape this relationship. As she glared up into Carl's eyes, she noticed water swelling around them and realised he too was upset. She wanted to comfort him, but stood her ground. She did not want to be snared by evil again. Yet it was she who enticed him to make love, to have sex last night. Sarah's defences collapsed as she realised how Carl had come for her. He put himself in as much, if not more, danger than her. But how long had Carl been through all of this before she had met him? Her mind ached with the onslaught of too many questions. Tears burst from her eyes and she reached forward, swinging her arms about Carl's waist, feeling warmth from inside his coat.

'Please help me forget all that happened… the creature… the snakes… that evil cold that filled the room…' Sarah's voice grew taut with fear. She tightened her grip on him and he looked down at her as she laid her head upon his chest. He stroked her blonde hair and cupped her chin within the palm of his hand.

Lifting her head, he said, 'Don't cry. You've got to be strong. It's me who's weak.' As he released a sigh, his breath exhaled into a ball of mist. 'I've been through a lot lately. Don't ask me why, but… it's all menacing. I've seen people dead… killed by those things.'

'Like the one that –' Carl cut Sarah short of sentence.

'Yes, like the creature that attacked us.' Carl then paused, thinking. 'I've dreamt things… things at first I didn't understand. Maybe I still don't, but… now… now I'm beginning to understand.'

Carl noticed an elderly woman pass them by and so pulled away from Sarah's grip. Sarah turned to face the woman also, but she looked away, pretending to have not seen them and called her dog. Carl turned, took Sarah's hands and hugged her. As he set pace along the path, he released a burst of air from his lungs and sighed.

At a leisurely pace they walked upon the frosted gravel paths of the park, but slowed down towards the grass verges that ran alongside the lake. The cold wind bowed the treetops and whistled through the branches, making a sound like children crying in the distance. Sarah stopped to look at ducklings that followed their mother, paddling hard against the rough water to keep up with their mother. Sarah looked at Carl's face and searched his eyes. He frowned as if she was to ask a question. A thin smile stretched across Sarah's face before asking, 'Tell me about you. How can these dreams come true? How can this all be possible?'

Carl stopped abruptly, the pain still tormenting the muscles of his body. He looked into nearby misty water of the lake. Sarah knew he was thinking and so she waited. Finally his eyes fixed upon hers again, but the cold air troubled his throat and he began coughing. Bending forward, he coughed again, his face flushed. Sarah held him and guided him to a nearby bench, where she helped him to sit. She knelt before him and took his head in her hands, cushioning his coughing movements. Carl's throat eased and he looked up, his eyes bloodshot.

'You ok now?' Sarah questioned, 'shall we go back home… back to my house? I'll fix you some soup. It'll soothe your throat.'

'No. I'm ok now. It's just the cold air,' Carl reassured.

'Maybe you need to go inside… in the warmth.'

'No. I like it out here. It's peaceful. It clears my head. It will clear my throat.' He leaned forward, his face inches from Sarah's, 'Besides… I want to stay with you. You're the only one who has seen things happen. Even if we both deny it, you're the only one who would believe me about all that's happened.'

There was a moment of silence before he whispered.

'You've asked me about myself. Mike says it's a boring sob story.'

'What does Mike know? He's not lived your life for you, has he?' she exclaimed.

'Well, a good part of it.' Carl said, turning his head aside.

'What do you mean?' she asked.

'Mike's been a friend since I finished school and went to college, years ago. He was the first person to help me find a different lifestyle – a change from staying in and studying, watching the same old favourites on TV. He showed me how to socialise – how to talk to people. I suppose that's why I leave him to talk to people on our jobs. Its art work I love, designing things, creating things, using my imagination. You know what I mean.'

Sarah's face stared vacantly, but then a smile spread across it, her brown eyes open wide with anticipation. Her interest beckoned him to continue, and for the first time, he thought someone was actually interested in him. He questioned that maybe Sarah was just being sympathetic towards him, but if so, her company soothed the pain and loneliness.

'Only it was hard to live as a child in boarding school, especially after my friend died – such a horrible death. It was the man that killed him and *he* was jailed for it!'

All this was too much for Sarah to comprehend, and she cut him short, seating herself beside him on the bench.

'Who died? What man?'

'As I said... I had a friend at school before my father died – before I had to go to boarding school. We were close friends. Alex was his name... Alex Guildford. It seems such a long time ago, now.' Carl paused, searching Sarah's face, recalling the memories that he had evaded. All at once memories flooded his mind and a shiver ran up his spine.

'Alex and I always played about my father's churchyard. My father was a priest, and I, he said, was a mistake. Guess it was wrong for a man of the church to have children. Yet, as he told me, I was born before he was fully committed. Maybe that's why he looked at me as adopted.' Carl paused, and then looked straight into Sarah's eyes. 'Do you know? I've not got a picture of him anywhere. I was told that Mother burnt everything. An emotional frenzy, he said she had.' Carl paused momentarily, realising he was changing the course of conversation. 'However, my friend Alex, his death came shortly after we had broken into a large mansion. Apparently, the owner had some prize possession of my father's and being boys, well; I thought I could do him a favour. Should have realised, a man of the cloth like him would regard it immoral. However, he was so obsessed with *his* faith; he thought he could redeem all men of bad character – even men he resented. Of what I can remember, on certain occasions my father would never let us go by his church. One time, Alex and I spied on the church grounds one evening, as we were told not to go near there that night. But as kids do, we witnessed a group of people from the nearby village, circled about Fiddler's Mound – a hillside overlooking the church. It was all a bit weird. It was that night that we found our way into the mansion to find a book my father had described. Anyway, to cut a story short, we liked pranks and my friend got the book. All I can remember is that it was large and hard to carry, as Alex stumbled with it as we ran across the mansion lawns. I went back for him and although Alex had hurt himself, by God did we run for the woods when lights flooded the grounds! How we had the guts to do it I'll never know. When he found out, my father was livid with us but, by God did his face light up when Alex showed him the book!'

Sarah, although confused, was curious.

'Why did your father want the book? Was it his work? Did it belong to the church... a Bible?'

Carl sat quiet, his thoughts buzzing.

'Carl!' Sarah called, raising her voice.

'Shush!' Carl said abruptly; his eyes grew wide as a shiver shot through him. 'Holy shit,' Carl said slowly, 'I knew I'd seen it before.'

'Seen what before? You're scaring me,' Sarah exclaimed.

Carl looked into Sarah's eyes and sat silent for a minute.

'The pendant,' Carl announced, 'the thing the creature was after!'

'What about it?' Sarah became vexed.

'I'm sure it's what Alex stole as well. He showed it to me shortly before he went missing.' Carl slowly continued whilst thinking. 'He said it fell from the same shelf.'

Sarah was muddled and returned to her original question.

'Why was the book so special? Did it belong to the church?'

'No... oh, no... it was something of research... history... that's all I remember.' Carl answered.

'But why did your father want it so badly?' Sarah questioned.

'It was something to do with village history. Somehow the community became divided,' Carl continued. 'Most people in those days were keen church goers and visited the parish frequently. However, some living on the outskirts –

farmers especially – seemed fanatic with following the *Dark-man*, as I called him. Children like me saw straight through him, thinking the man wicked and sinister and so did some of my father's friends.' Carl paused as Sarah moved to gain comfort on the cold park bench.

'There were many arguments, but he was a wealthy man – his mansion passed down through generations. I thought my father resented him as he was just envious – him having all that land. We had to settle for a small house in sight of the church. There was a lot I didn't understand… well, I was a child, and besides…' Carl paused again. 'I was caught in the middle of my father's work, school work and helping to keep home.'

Sarah sat bemused, and then croaked the question she had wanted to ask for some time.

'What happened to your mother?'

As he clenched his hands together, Carl's head dropped and Sarah realised she had touched on a tender subject.

'My mother died giving birth to me. I've seen nothing of her but photographs… old photographs.'

'Didn't anyone tell you what she was like?'

'My father said she was a wonderful woman; kind, loving, but had been physically weak most of her life. He said she was strong minded and gifted, but never mentioned how. Guess there's a lot that only *he* will know, or hid for the sake of his church.' Carl paused, a tear escaping his left eye, 'At the funeral, my Aunt was angry at him… arguing against his mention that her passing was somehow a blessing... maybe what he meant was... she died to give me life?'

'I'm sorry,' Sarah said softly. 'You've never had a mother, then?'

'No.'

'Not even a Gran?'

'Yes, my Grandmother looked after me in my earlier days, but arguments between her and my father made her leave. My father needed me to look after the house and things. A lot for a boy of nine, don't you think?'

Sarah changed the subject, but was curious on one other thing.

'How did your friend die?'

'Alex?'

'Yes, the one that got the book.'

'Well… at first he missed school,' Carl cleared his throat, 'a day, a couple of days and then a whole week. I thought he was just ill and by the time I called for him that weekend; the local police were out in search for him. His parents thought he had run away and argued with me, thinking I knew where he had gone.'

'Did he run away?'

'No, a policeman said his body was found with mutilations, bruising, his…' Carl stopped abruptly, his head dropping.

'His what, Carl? What happened to him?'

'His throat was cut. Well, more like…'

'An animal?' Sarah deduced.

'A psychopathic murderer the police said. At first they related his death to an escaped convict from the south of England, and that's how it was shown in the papers. But it was different.'

'Different? Wasn't it the convict?'

'No, I knew it was the *Dark-man*. But who would believe a boy of nine? I had no proof!'

'Well, I think you blamed yourself for his death, Carl. A wealthy man like that wouldn't kill an innocent boy just because he stole a book... anyhow, how could you have known it was him?' Sarah asked.

'Oh, I knew, alright. Anyway, the bastard was sentenced for it. All the money he had couldn't buy his way out of that one and I confessed our deed to get him sentenced.' Carl paused, looking upon Sarah's face, searching her eyes, trying to forget the past, but Sarah probed further.

'And how did your father die?'

'I'm not sure, but he got trapped within his own church. All I saw were flames bursting out the church windows and villagers racing in the shadows, collecting buckets of water in a desperate attempt to save him. By morning the church was nothing but a charred hollow. The skeleton they found was buried in the churchyard, and the church itself was never restored.'

'How long ago did this happen?' Sarah said, but went unheard.

'I left a month or so after my father's death and my Gran fixed me into boarding school. Life was so different to that of the countryside and I hated it. I never made any friends, really, not until college. That's when I met Mike. It was his friendship that helped me forget the past. He only talks of the future.'

'Does he know of all this?'

'Vaguely… not everything… he doesn't like me talking about it.'

Sarah reached her arm around Carl's shoulder and stared at the side of his face, seeing him troubled. She turned and whilst thinking, stared upon the mist that coated the lake.

'It all sounds disturbing… especially for a young boy,' Sarah said as she rose to her feet, 'Come on. I'll make you something nice back home. A bowl of hot soup should do the trick, eh?'

Carl agreed and walked slowly through the park, holding on to Sarah's hand.

# TEN

IT WAS THE SOUND OF the doorbell that startled Sarah, and she almost dropped the plate she was drying. Carl awoke, his head aching. An empty glass slid from his fingers and rolled across the living room floor. Again the doorbell rang. Carl noticed Sarah race along the hallway and disappear toward the front door. As Carl's mind and eyes were blurry, he could only hear voices – Sarah's he recognised, but there were two more.

'He's in here. Carl? You okay?' Sarah's voice was heard, but Carl's vision took a while to clear. He was still fuzzy.

'It's Mike. I've been everywhere looking for you!'

Carl noticed Sarah standing, poised over a body in front. Mike leaned forward, his blonde hair falling over his eyes, as they searched his face with concern.

'You okay, mate? I've been everywhere; the hospital, your flat, Rachael's house. How come you're here?'

Carl rubbed his eyes and cleared his throat, but his reply was interrupted by Sarah.

'He came to save me from –'

'She was worried about me!' Carl cut in, glaring at Sarah whilst he sat up, 'Anyhow, I needed some company and when she phoned…'

Sarah stood silent; obviously, Carl wanted to cover up what had really happened. Besides, how ridiculous would it sound? Mike looked perplexed, and then smiled as he took a look at both of them.

139

'What have you two been up to then, eh?'

'Just talking,' Carl answered over Sarah, who said.

'Walking... yes, we talked... through the park!'

Again Mike smiled, looking at each of them, and sat down. He looked at Sarah's figure and glanced over her uncovered legs. With only a short, thin nightdress, Mike found her quite sensual. Mike took a deep breath and switched his attention to Carl.

'Well, what have you two being doing all morning? Have you managed to figure out what happened last night, or does it still evade us as to why Carl should break out into such... err... frenzy?' Mike was trying to avoid the word 'fit' as he knew it offended Carl.

'Let's not talk about last night; Carl's obviously been under stress of late, what with those men robbing him.' Rachael stated, entering the room to sit beside Mike. There was a moment of silence until Sarah stepped forward, seating herself on the arm of the chair in which Carl sat.

'Carl said that he awoke after having a dream and was scared, so –'

'So I came here,' Carl interrupted, 'I thought Sarah could help me. Besides, I never apologised.'

'You came here because you knew something was to attack me and it...'

'Thought something was...' Carl snapped, interrupting Sarah. 'It was just the dream I had. I was in a bit of a state and my dreams are a bit vivid, aren't they, Mike?'

'Well, I believe so. That's what you've said,' Mike agreed, but changed the topic. 'Still, it doesn't explain why you weren't released from the hospital.'

Carl froze, realising Mike had looked there for him, thinking maybe he should still be in hospital.

'There must be some confusion, I picked him up early. He did sound very distressed on the phone,' Sarah lied. 'Must be hospitals... I don't like them either.'

'You must be well interested Carl!' Mike grinned to exclaim. 'Getting her phone number on the first night.'

'Shut up, Mike!' Rachael shouted.

'Sarah's number was –' Carl started, before being interrupted again.

'Actually, I phoned the hospital... naturally I was concerned.'

Mike sat back and sunk into the armchair, finding comfort, and then announced.

'So I take it that Sarah's been acting nurse, then. Carl's probably pleased he's got such a gorgeous one at that, too.'

'Don't tease,' Rachael beckoned.

'It's okay, Rachael... he must have a fetish about women in uniform,' Sarah stated, as she retreated into the kitchen.

'Oh, well, maybe, just maybe,' Mike said slowly. 'Well, pal. How do you feel, seriously?'

'Not too bad now. Just ache a lot,' Carl replied.

'I'm not surprised. You had us all worried, the way you fell through the patio... No deep cuts, I hope?' Rachael asked, reaching for the lacerations on his face.

Mike changed the subject as Rachael commented on Carl's bruising as well.

'Argh... yes... Sarah? The polythene, did it stay up?'

Sarah answered, shouting from the kitchen.

'Well, no. It had blown down this morning, but Carl's fixed it. Thanks anyhow.'

'Well, he can't be hurt too bad… doing jobs around the house and all.' Rachael said. 'Just suffering from that attack, I suppose.' She paused, and then continued. 'Did the doctor say what the reasons for your,' she paused again, trying to evade the word, but it slipped out, 'fit?'

Carl was annoyed by the word, finding it humiliating and wriggled in his chair trying to hide his agitation. Mike continued the conversation, as Rachael felt awkward.

'Did they say you were epileptic, or was it just some spasmodic effect from the attack last week? Surely they took that into consideration?'

Carl leaned forward, his head in his hands, kneading his forehead.

'I don't know'

'Well what did the doctor say?'

'I can't remember.'

Mike stood up, turning to his friend.

'Don't know much about it, do you? I'd want to know everything if it were me.'

Carl's hands shot from his face and glared menacingly at the figure above him.

'How can I know anything? Stupid bastard! I didn't have time to read the medical report!'

Mike backed away a couple of steps and looked at Rachael. He frowned, hearing viciousness in Carl's voice, something he'd hardly ever heard before. Carl continued.

'I'm pissed off with all you're questioning. I suppose you want a story for the folk at work tomorrow, something to talk about when I'm not there. Well, I'm going in and I'm going to be okay... okay?'

'For fuck's sake, Carl, I only wanted to know if you're okay!'

'Okay for what, a lift in the morning? Doing your article covers? Stopping you argue with everyone?'

Mike's temperature rose and his face blotched with fury. He turned as if to walk away, and then faced Carl again as if to argue.

'Oh, fuck it! What's the use?' he pointed his finger at Carl and declared, 'There's something wrong with you, mate. Those muggers must have messed up your mind. Either that or your fixation on Sarah has you unnerved. Whichever, you're beginning to piss me off!'

Mike turned and stepped into the hallway, missing Sarah by inches, nearly knocking a tray from her hands.

'I don't know what you've done to him, but I'm not staying. I leave him in *your capable* hands.'

Mike raced to the door and then turned, his eyes squinting.

'I'm sorry Sarah, but I've got better things to do than argue. At least he's in good hands,' he winked and then called, 'come on Rachael; don't want to be at your mother's to long either!'

'But your tea, I've made sandwiches!' Sarah pleaded.

'I'm very sorry, but we've got to get going, if you knew her mom, well...' Rachael patted Sarah's shoulder and smiled stating, 'Keep in touch! Maybe we'll come round in the week, before your parents get back?'

'Yes, that would be nice,' Sarah agreed softly.

Mike reached for the door and swung it open, pausing to face Sarah with a look of sincerity.

'Goodbye. Look after him. Maybe a good night's rest and he'll be okay. Seriously, I think it best if he misses works tomorrow. If you need our works number, phone Rachael.' Pacing out the door he turned once more to see Rachael hug Sarah, 'Once again, I'm sorry. I didn't know you were doing us sandwiches.'

'That's okay. I'll eat them later.' Sarah exclaimed.

Sarah watched the door slam and glanced into the living room. Carl sat poised over the armchair, his breathing restricted by the hands that smothered his face. Sarah walked into the room, placing the tray on a nearby coffee table and knelt before him. She pried the fingers from Carl's face and touched the tears that wet his cheeks. A surge of air exhaled his lungs and he bellowed a cry. He reached forward, enveloping Sarah's neck with his arms and whimpered.

'Please forgive me. I don't want to argue with Mike. I don't want to offend anyone, especially you! You know what's happened, but maybe it's best if no one knows. Best to forget it; like it was all a bad nightmare.'

# ELEVEN

CARL HAD NEVER DRIVEN SO fast and unruly. It was a blessing that most of the morning traffic was dispersed and the roads were relatively clear. He would have been on time if only he could have slept. Although most of the lingering pain in his body had disappeared, his thoughts had plagued him throughout the night – the realism of the nightmares, the events at Sarah's house, his first sex in years – but most of all, the argument with friends. The last thing he wanted was to lose his best friend. The way he spoke to Mike and Rachael was unacceptable. How would Mike react when he got to work? Would he refrain from talking to Carl and hold some sort of grudge? Surely not; they had been friends for such a long time and besides, like all friendships, there had been many ups and downs. It was all too much to withstand. He could only see when he got to work. Carl reassured himself as he reached the building, he would find out when he got there. Anyhow, surely Mike needed him to work on the stories.

Carl paused as the car door swung open, allowing cold, moist air to flood the inside. For a moment all was silent and Carl's mind blurred. Suddenly, the cassette radio bawled again as a new song started. Carl's concentration broke and he frowned, realising he had only turned off the engine and not the ignition. He switched off the stereo and turned to retrieve his briefcase from the backseat. Standing tall, he locked the door and momentarily stared at the windows of the building that towered above. There it was, his place of work, but how would it go? What would Mike say to him? Or would he speak at all? He received some peculiar looks as he made his way through the reception area and up the staircase. Or was he becoming paranoid? He was sure he saw the security guard glance at his watch before looking inquisitively at him. Carl decided to ignore his actions and hurried up the stairway.

Reluctant to enter, Carl hesitated outside the main entrance to the office. Slowly he opened the first set of doors and crept past the company's small reception counter. Fortunately Shirley did not notice him as she had her back to him whilst probing within a filing cabinet. The noise from office activity grew louder as he glided his way through the corridor to the next set of doors. Opening one door slightly, he peered in and searched the room, trying not to be noticed. He recognised Mike and studied him for a while as he fiddled with the rear of his terminal screen. Carl managed a smile as he realised Mike was not the best with hardware devices. However, the recollection of yesterday's argument soon dampened his contentment. Carl slid himself between the doors and closed them quietly behind. Quickly he paced towards his desk, avoiding people and staring over at Mike. Carl was troubled by negative thoughts and could only hope that Mike had forgotten yesterday's quarrel. Suddenly, his concentration was broken and his heart jumped.

'Good for you to come in today, Carl!' a voice shouted from behind him.

Carl span to face his editor's chubby red face, his piercing dark eyes suppressed by heavy eyebrows and half bald head, glimmering against the florescent light. At first Carl was calm and thought the editor was being just sarcastic, but the colour of his face revealed his displeasure.

'I heard about your endeavour last week. It's a pity you didn't pick a fight with someone a bit smaller. However...' he continued, after clearing his throat, 'I suppose it's only an individual incident... one that we hope won't happen again, eh?' He chuckled to himself and then frowned; his body stiff and erect, 'Now then, let's get to work and catch up on what you've missed. That's if you're well enough?' He coughed to clear his throat again before announcing, 'Mr Mackenzie's got a number of assignments that need your attention.'

Carl quietly replied, unsure of how to explain.

'Well... I'm not sure how, ah, whether Mike and I are on level terms. You see, we've had a bit of an argument and I'm not sure... well, we've had differences of –'

'Differences...? Don't be ridiculous! You hang around each other like, like...' the editor coughed as an excuse to find the right words, 'flies around shit!'

'Excuse me, Sir?' Carl's voice croaked with resentment.

'Look, I don't know what happened exactly; your experience with those muggers, and I'm sorry to hear of your misfortune, but –' he exclaimed, and then raised his voice, 'there's a lot to do! There are those stories that you and Mike have been assigned to.' The editor paused, almost turning away, and then questioned. 'Are you are fit to work? You haven't got a doctor's note, have you?'

Carl tried to explain. 'I've come back to catch up on my work, but the explanation I was just about to give would affect that.'

The editor growled and said agitatedly, 'Okay. Let's sort this out.' He pushed Carl aside and searched the room until his eyes found Mike. 'Mr Mackenzie? Mr Mackenzie!' the editor called, and saw Mike standing, already watching their discussion.

'What? I mean, yes, Sir?' Mike called, stepping a few paces forward.

'Are you still working with Carl on assignments? Have you got a problem with him *working* with you?' he questioned.

'What's this?' Mike questioned in return.

'It's a question, young man!' he demanded, then repeated, 'Are you alright to work on assignments with Carl?'

'Yes, but of course? We've always worked together,' Mike answered.

The editor turned to Carl and stared expectantly.

'Well, does that answer your uncertainty? Any other problems I need to know about before you continue to waste my time?' the editor said turning, waiting to leave.

'You,' Carl whispered turning to face his desk, thinking he had walked on.

The editor pulled Carl back by the shoulder and said quietly, 'I'll pretend I didn't hear that! You'd better watch your step, young man.' He continued after a deep breath, 'It's unlike you to answer me back, but no matter how good your work is, or of what *importance* you have here, the directors, like me, won't tolerate insolence.'

Carl moved his shoulder from the editor's grip and walked to his desk, looking back until he had disappeared.

'Arrogant bastard,' Carl muttered to himself, as he noticed Mike peering up at him from his paperwork. Mike stood hesitatingly before approaching Carl.

'What was all that about?'

Carl looked at his hands and softly replied, 'I wasn't sure how you... you would be with me, today. I thought you'd not speak after yesterday.'

Mike raised his hand and explained.

'Look, I'm sorry about what happened yesterday, too. I guess I didn't realise how upset you were from the attack, and besides... I was still angry from an argument with Rachael.' He paused, drew breath and then asked, 'You okay, mate? There's no need to involve *him*. Everyone has differences, but we've all just got to get on with stuff.'

Carl managed a smile and clenched Mike's hand, saying, 'I'm sorry too. I shouldn't have talked to you like that yesterday. I've been a bit of an arsehole.'

Carl straightened Mike's tie and explained.

'Just help me get over, you know, what happened. Need to get back into my work. It'll probably help me get over all the shit that has happened.'

Carl saw Mike's face screwed up in confusion and staring oblivious. Carl reassured.

'Just help me get back into the swing of things!'

Mike patted Carl's shoulder firmly and announced,

'Of course,' he smiled. 'You can start by fixing this bloody thing!' Mike clenched a pile of notes and announced. 'Besides, how the hell do you expect me to finish *these* articles without you?'

It took a good part of an hour for Carl to settle into his paperwork and reorganise particular computer files and publications. By this time Mike had sorted out the problem with his terminal, and with Carl's help, managed to fax finished articles to waiting publishers. Mike had been on the phone to clients practically all morning, and one wanted to lower the commission rate on a weekly regional history publication. Mike's excuse was that public interest in the subject had declined and so the market for the magazine had dropped. However, he had to await a decision, as the editor had discussed terms with this client. It may just have been speculation, but David, another employee, had heard that one of the directors had spoken to this client and agreed on a reduced commission rate. David declared that Mike's research may not be up to scratch, but had recently reassured the client that the publication would still be marketable, but on a monthly basis. Carl and Mike knew that although David was harmless, if there were rumours or inside information, he was the one to know about it and disclose it for a price. This usually resulted in helping him one way or another – either at work, buying a beer, or an invitation to a party.

Near lunch, Carl was immersed in research, using the central database and library facilities to gather new information for a story of Mike's. This was not a job Carl was used to but found it challenging. He preferred artwork and using his desktop publishing skills. Mike himself, although he had worked a late evening, found that he was behind with work. It was David who later disturbed Carl's concentration, and for that he was angry.

'Can't you see I've got loads to do, eh?'

'Yes, mate, but I thought you may be interested in coming to see a certain client of mine.' David paused, fingering his mouth like he always did when thinking.

'What the hell are you on about?' Carl snapped.

'Well, if you're too disinterested and involved in your work, I'll…'

'Yes, alright, you've ruined my concentration anyway. What is it that's so important?' Carl asked sarcastically, swivelling his chair round to face him.

'Well, I need to see a client for which I'm researching a story. Well a client of a client, if you know what I mean. Says he knows you – or was it, knows *of* you? He seemed interested in the conversation.'

'Conversation… conversation concerning what?' Carl demanded.

'You!' David asserted.

'What kind of answer is that?'

'Well, I'm just teasing really.'

Carl gave up playing along with him.

'Well, obviously you've some information to hide… what's the price this time?'

'It's not money I want,' David asserted.

'A beer, a free lunch?' Carl asked sarcastically.

'No, nothing like that.'

'What, then?'

'I need some help with a technical journal, one I'm working on at the moment. It needs certain artwork drafted into it.'

'Well, well…' Carl sat back further into his chair and probed his mouth with his pen. 'The dear know-it-all school boy wants some help with his homework…'

'Just a little, but it's important,' David reassured.

'As important as this person you're about to…'

'Yes. Yes it is… but you haven't agreed.'

'Agreed to what?'

'To the transaction… the homework,' David reiterated sternly.

'Okay! I've nearly finished here, so after lunch I'll see what you want doing. Now, who are you on about?'

David looked about the room and leaned over towards Carl, fingering his chin and mouth.

'I'll agree our little transaction with the editor first, about you helping me later on… and when we can visit.'

'Visit… why, is the guy in hospital?' Carl questioned.

'No,' David said quietly, 'the Wiltshire Rehabilitation Institute.'

'Jail?' Carl shouted.

'No idiot, not quite,' David said, 'Well, maybe it's *like* that, but they're special patients.'

Carl swallowed, and then questioned, 'Who is he?'

David stood tall and, pointing his pen at Carl, exclaimed, 'This case somewhat puzzles me… opened up again after such a long time…and so many contacts just to get one appointment. But it should make a worthy article for criminal publications.' He stopped and then said slowly, 'A substantial profit as well. I wonder how much?'

'How does this man know me?' Carl questioned.

'He reads papers and magazines. He noticed articles written by you, I expect. Besides, your name popped up when….' David paused momentarily and then continued, thinking aloud, 'Funny how he wasn't really interested until

I mentioned that I knew of you… that you worked at Haigh and Reece.' David continued, pretending to be inquisitive, 'Maybe he's a relative?'

Puzzled by David's vague explanation of the client knowing his father, Carl said softly.

'I don't have any family… there's no-one I know of left.'

'Maybe he's a long lost Uncle. After all, they say that mental instability is hereditary,' David stated, laughing.

'Thank you, I'll remember that… maybe I'll reconsider helping you,' Carl replied, annoyed at his sarcasm.

'Awfully sorry, old pal, but I couldn't help myself. That one just slipped out!'

# TWELVE

'Good to see that you guys take it so seriously. Made up, have we?' a voice echoed from beyond the tall, office cabinets. Carl and Mike turned to notice the editor walk briskly past and exit through nearby doors.

'What's he mean… made up?' Mike questioned.

'He's just taking the piss! You know my uncertainty this morning. It was stupid to involve *him*!' Carl replied.

For a few minutes there was silence between them, until Mike exclaimed that Rachael had booked a table at a favourite restaurant and that he didn't want to be late.

'Better get going. Don't want to be in her bad books, again,' Mike said, reaching for his briefcase. 'Mind you, we're not alone… one of her friends is coming.'

'Sarah?' Carl questioned.

'No, some tart from her school days. Hasn't the looks of your friend,' he answered, leaning over Carl's shoulder and looking at his terminal screen. 'Talking of…' Mike paused, 'But what's this?'

Carl noticed Mike pointing to the technical document given to him from David.

'From mister know-it-all,' Carl explained. 'He wants my artistic help, he says.'

'Well, make sure there's something in it for you!' Mike shouted as he pushed open the office doors.

'I'll make sure of that, don't you worry… it's a personal matter,' Carl replied quietly, knowing Mike would not hear him.

Carl pondered on the thought of finally finding out what had happened to his father. He was told things shortly after his father's church had burned down, but he was only a child. He just remembered feeling deeply saddened. The questioning did not come until later. At first, there were too many arguments between his relatives to make sense of anything, never mind the commotion of being thrown from one family to another. It was a wonder he could make sense of what had happened at all.

Between his thoughts, Carl experimented with the software that improved the presentation of David's documents. He tested different graphical elements and pondered on how best to display statistical data. The document itself was uninteresting, as it consisted mainly of large amounts of data, along with analysis figures. However, it was the type of work that Carl enjoyed and was good at – making a dreary article look at least somewhat appealing.

It was almost an hour after Mike had left that Carl's concentration was broken.

'Is that mine?' a voice asked.

Carl looked up and was blinded by a bright reflection from spectacles.

'My, it's looking a lot better than before… all those numbers listed in tables and figures showing their percentage of inclusion,' David exclaimed and continued. 'I like the graphs. Don't they make it easier to compare the percentage of chemical elements?'

Carl muttered some agreement whilst continuing to touch up certain features.

'Almost finished,' Carl muttered. 'Just needs…'

David looked about the room and leaned over Carl's shoulder, fingering his mouth and chin, before asking.

'Has *he* gone?'

'Has who gone?' Carl replied.

'Your so-called, friend.'

'Who, Mike, you mean?'

'Yes, mister blonde and full of himself.'

'That's my friend you're talking about, and I don't like –'

'That case I'm working on,' David cut short Carl's sentence, 'it's brought up some information about your father.'

'My father?' Carl questioned.

'Yes, apparently your father was a reverend from the south of England. Devon, was it?' David questioned, although he knew more than he was letting on. 'A little village some miles from Dartmoor, was it? I believe your father's practice became a little unpopular, until…'

'What makes my father news?' Carl interrupted, questioning angrily.

'Well, it's not too clear. The research is rather unclear when digging up past events. But I believe your father tried to, let's say, *rehabilitate* people… restore their faith as, so to speak,' David said. 'Your father dabbled in what was known then as *soul casting*… a practice closely related to *exorcism*'.

Carl flinched as he said the word, and noticed how David spoke it with a hint of cynicism. It was obvious that David saw Carl's father as some crack-pot, religious fanatic who thought he could cleanse his communion of sinful deeds. Reluctantly Carl beckoned him to continue, although he was beginning to hate this work colleague even more.

'Well, it seems that your father, as crazed as he was about saving the world from evil and so forth, held rituals, ceremonies… you know… all *that* kind of stuff. Mind you, at first he must have had a strong congregation. His followers certainly gave *him* trouble.'

'Him… what do you mean *him*?' Carl asked.

'A scientist, a doctor of psychology… or was it parapsychology?' David questioned himself, before staring at Carl. 'Anyway, throughout England he was one of the most eminent researchers into the Black Art.'

'Black Art… a doctor, you say,' Carl said.

'You've heard of him?' David questioned.

'I think I know the man you're on about,' Carl assured, and then enquired, pretending not to know much, 'but, what can you tell me about him?'

'Well I had some trouble digging out old files, especially from newspapers. The library system is somewhat outdated. Anyway, the guy was clever and a genius at his profession, but sacrificed himself to wayward beliefs.'

Carl had not followed David's explanation and thought of it as somewhat vague.

'Sacrificed? I don't follow.'

'Blimey, no wonder your stories are shit. Have I got to spell it out for you?' David replied sarcastically.

'You may know what your research has come up with, but I can't read your fucking mind. What the hell do you mean, '*he too sacrificed himself?* '.

'Your father,' David assured.

As he disliked David anyway, ridiculing his father enraged him and with temper flaring, Carl stood up.

'What of my father? Are you just trying to wind me up? If you are, you can piss off!'

'My, my… sorry if I've hit a nerve. Never seen you so bad tempered,' David said.

Carl was about to walk off as David reassured, guiding Carl back to his chair.

'Look. Sit down and I'll explain.'

'What's your research got to do with my father?' Carl demanded.

'Well, apparently your father had many confrontations with this man. At first the villagers of the town liked your father. As people would like a clergyman in those days, I suppose.' David paused momentarily, then continued. 'However, in some instances a number of villagers threatened your father, or other people closely befriended. This doctor was accused of blackmailing locals to do deeds for him. But did you know…' he paused, thinking.

'Know *what*, for Christ's sake?' Carl implored.

'There's even a record of attempted murder – against your father, that is,' David revealed. Carl was curious. He did not want to disclose his childhood experience, but conversely, did David's research differ to what he thought was the truth?

159

What had really happened to his father? Although police had learned of the differences between this man and his father, the investigation could not connect this man to his father's death. Surely his conviction came from his alleged killing of Carl's friend. Carl's mind blurred, but he cut into David's unheard conversation.

'This man... this doctor, what of him now; what relevance has it to your work?'

'Well let's say this doctor's conviction cannot be supported anymore. It's that or some parole. There's new evidence, or something like that. I've yet to study the case in its entirety so I saved it. It should be a blast of a story and quite a little money earner, as well.' David paused and pulled a floppy disc from his pocket. 'I'll clear it with the editor, and... now, save that document on here.'

'But I was going to –'

'Please. The time is pressing on. I'm in a bit of a hurry,' David said, cutting Carl short again.

'Does this mean I'll be coming along?' Carl enquired, whilst saving the updated file.

'Coming along?' David questioned, his interests focused only on his updated file.

'To the institute, to see the man who knows...?'

'Oh yes, err... it'll all be sorted,' David cut short Carl's reply. 'I'll clear it with the editor in the morning. Just be in normal time. No hurry. Ah, that's it... great!' he said retrieving the floppy disc from the drive. As he turned away, Carl pulled back his arm and said.

'I've worked all afternoon on your stuff. I want some information tomorrow.'

David pulled back his arm and said, walking briskly away, 'Have I ever let you down?'

'Well, at least you can tell me the man's name?' Carl shouted.

'Doctor Joseph Kieran Schroeck,' David announced slowly, whilst reading his notes and pacing backward.

Carl leapt from his chair as his curiosity overwhelmed him. As he caught up with David, he announced.

'Err; you'd better check those files! My drive's been playing up!'

'The files you've just saved, the ones on here?' he asked, holding the disc aloft.

'Yes,' Carl replied.

As David leaned over his desk, Carl pretended to take interest in a nearby photograph.

'Where's this?' Carl questioned.

'Tenby, Wales,' David replied.

'Nice there, is it?'

'Yes, very.'

Whilst pretending to be interested in the photograph, Carl noticed the sequence of keys David had pressed to log into his terminal. As he busied himself, testing the files saved on the disc, Carl fitted the sequence of keys to a word.

'Look, they're fine. They're all fine!' David asserted.

'Well, I thought it best to check. Don't want all that good work wasted, do we?' Carl replied.

It was just after David had left the office when Carl considered whether to check out the files on his colleague's computer. However, it was getting late and Carl was exhausted. The headache was returning and he felt nauseous again. Maybe he should have taken the day off, as the doctor advised. But at least he had sorted things out with Mike. He had also finished off a good number of articles, and tomorrow he would have a day away from the office, even if it *was* with David.

Although he had gulped down nearly all of a small bottle of cola, Carl was again feeling tired. Why was he walking around a superstore instead of directly going home? But he remembered. This purchase would be, without doubt, an essential one. As he knelt, squinting tiredly at some low shelves, he noticed an item that would be satisfactory. He almost jumped out of his skin as a young boy appeared, arms outstretched and his face covered in a mask.

'Zombie… zombie got him!'

'Stop it! You've frightened the poor man. Now come on!' the boy's mother shouted, pulling him away.

Carl felt his heart race for a moment, his body perspiring. Watching the boy being escorted down the aisle, Carl became faint. As the boy looked back at him, his image blurred and Carl felt a tingling sensation in his ears. It was as if the high-pitch sound of a flute was resonating in his ears. Carl shook his head and pulled himself to his feet. Trying to ignore his giddiness, he grabbed the article and walked unsteadily towards the payment kiosk. For a moment he felt nauseous again, but his dilemma was broken by the voice of the store assistant. After being questioned, he reassured the girl that he was okay and hurried with his payment.

Outside, Carl felt a lot better. The cold, early evening air revitalised his senses and, with another gulp of cola, he was ready to drive home.

Trying to unlock his front door, Carl heard the sound of his telephone ringing from inside. Whilst trying to hold his briefcase and shopping, he fumbled with the key. By the time he had entered his flat, however, the phone had stopped ringing. He stopped in his panic and after closing the door, started to put items away. He placed his briefcase on the sofa, put his shopping on a nearby coffee table and retreated to the kitchen for some refreshment. He had just managed to make himself a cup of tea when the phone rang again. Quickly, he placed his cup on the coffee table and answered the call.

'Carl, thank God I got through…'

He hardly had chance to recognise it was Sarah before she exclaimed, her voice distressed, 'It's gone, the pendant, it's gone!'

'It's okay Sarah, it's okay!' Carl reassured.

'What? It's missing and if it's not under my sunbed,' she cried, 'that thing… that creature will come back!'

'It's okay!' Carl reiterated, opening his briefcase and retrieving the pendant, 'It's here. I have it.'

'But you'll be in danger… that thing?' Sarah cried.

'That *thing* won't be returning for this,' he said, rotating the pendant by its chain against the light. 'I've got something like what you have.'

From a shopping bag, Carl pulled out a ultra-violet sun-lamp and started to unpack it.

# PART TWO

# THIRTEEN

IT RESEMBLED A STATELY HOME, more than some institute for the criminally insane. The narrow, winding road that led to a gritted parking space was littered with dry, autumn leaves that snapped as they were driven over. Eventually David reached the parking area and decided to pull alongside another car that was under the shelter of trees. The cold of early morning had being replaced by warmer air and by now it was beginning to rain. After grabbing his briefcase, David ran toward the building's entrance.

As he uncovered his head from the shelter of his coat, David received some peculiar looks from people; in what he derived was a waiting area. Wiping the wetness from his hands and face, he straightened his overcoat and cleaned his briefcase before searching for some assistance. As he edged along a nearby wall, it was difficult to avoid the staring eyes of people seated and then one man coughed as if to get his attention. David looked up whilst cleaning his glasses and noticed a man pointing.

'Around the corner,' the man said, 'all visitors have to check in at reception.'

He acknowledged the man's advice and proceeded around a corner to a high, circular reception desk, where an elderly lady sat typing with half-moon glasses poised on the end of her nose. David thought how ridiculous the grey roots looked after her feeble attempt of hair colouring had failed, when she announced stridently.

'Can I help you, young man?'

'Yes, err…' he replied slowly whilst trying to reveal his company card. 'I'm from Haigh and Reece with an appointment to see…' David again paused to retrieve notes from his coat pocket, and then announced, 'a Doctor Joseph Schroeck'.

'Have you a confirmation letter?' the woman said, removing her spectacles.

'It's amongst those notes, somewhere?' he said, whilst trying to remove his coat.

'I'll have a look shall I?' she exclaimed with a hint of cynicism.

After removing the letter from a crumpled envelope, the lady checked his name in the diary of appointments and said slowly.

'So you are?'

'David… David Hedrick!' he stated, again showing her his company card.

'Ah, yes… okay. Please be seated and read these guidelines,' the lady said, handing him a form.

David edged over to the nearest seat available, which fortunately happened to be some distance from staring faces. After sorting himself out and folding his damp overcoat over a chair, he decided to dispense a drink from a nearby vending machine. Although he did not like coffee, for some reason it would not dispense tea and he did not want to waste his money. He thought it revolting as he drank the bitter liquid, but needed something to soothe his dry throat.

His reading of the institute regulations were subdued by his thoughts of meeting a murderer; or was he? Surely, the reason that David was asked to report on this case was to help acquit this doctor. Surely, he was a man of reading; a well-educated and an astute man like himself. The reason why he chose this case was because of his background in law, but surely it was time to move on; all those years sacrificed at university could never be rewarded in this role. He needed a break; a big story that would land him into a better job.

'Mr Hedrick? David Hedrick?'

David's thoughts were interrupted by the receptionist as she called aloud his name. After he stood tall, grabbed his briefcase and headed toward the reception desk, she directed him through a pair of tall, white doors and to another room down a corridor. Unnoticed on his way, David was accompanied by two men dressed in white clothing and acknowledged by security badges. After following him into the room, the security men searched his clothes and belongings, whilst voicing their actions. David opened his briefcase after one man demanded to examine its contents. Quickly frisking through his files and folders, David explained that there was nothing but his paperwork. The men stated that any documents to be signed are to be passed using a metal drawer integrated between rooms. Once again they asked him if he had read the regulations and after nodding, David was escorted down another white corridor, bricked heavily with white painted breeze blocks. It was obvious that this part of the building was some modern extension; customised cells were sealed with heavy red doors and there was no carpet or furniture. At the end of the corridor David was led into a small room, where after turning to ask about toilet facilities, had the door shut on him.

As he placed his briefcase upon a small table, he noticed the room was attached to another by a waist-high wall and above that was a thick, transparent glass. As he looked around the edges and top, he noticed a pattern of holes through the glass.

'It enables the sound to travel my dear boy... it sounds like a fish tank... and looks like one for that matter,' a deep voice said slowly from the other side of the glass.

At first David did not see the man seated in the other room; he was obscured by light reflected on the glass. However, after the voice requested him to sit in the chair provided, David could see a mature man, tall and slim. He had quite a long face, with dark-hair combed back, although many strands had turned grey. This aging feature was also apparent in his moustache and beard as some facial hair had turned grey. As the man stared at him through the glass, the thing that unnerved David the most was the man's dark, piercing eyes and eyebrows. As he appeared from out of the shadows of the room, David noticed he was dressed mainly in black; a suit that had been worn somewhat, with patches stitched about the elbows. His tie was worn loosely with waves of gold stitching glittering against a dark red material. Although his shirt was white, it had lines of dirt about the collar. David predicted this came from the man's frequent action of fingering and scratching his neck.

'So your work colleague chose not to come?' the doctor enquired.

David cleared his throat whilst opening his briefcase.

'I'm afraid not, the...' David paused pretending to be busy with his notes from his briefcase. 'My work colleague did want to come, but I guess he had other commitments. Anyhow, I've got most of the paperwork regarding your case, but if I can have a little more detail regarding–'

'What's his name again?' the doctor asked, cutting David short of sentence.

'My work colleague... the one you said you know?' David asked.

'Yes, my dear friend, the one of the *Aston* family,' he said, regretfully having to explain himself again.

'You mean Carl,' David said. 'Like I said he had other commitments.'

'I thought our little meetings were based on trust. You disclose details of improper justice and proceedings on an innocent man and get him acquitted whilst reporting a commendable story. I thought you wanted to aspire as a top journalist?' the doctor enquired.

'Yes, of course I do.'

'Then don't *lie* to me boy!' the doctor shouted, 'I want to know if it is *him*!'

'Well, he was certainly interested when I talked of you, but... well actually... our editor doesn't allow us to report on cases that involve personal matters, or for personal gain. It can lead to bias or inappropriate behaviour.'

The doctor groaned.

'Anyhow, more importantly... this story,' David announced before clearing his throat. 'I've drafted up your story, including a lot about the false conviction and how you said you were set up.'

'Is all *that* from those files you had?' the doctor stated, cutting David short of sentence. 'All that deficient information from those computer files?'

'Yes, well most of it,' David replied.

'It won't get you that job, you know. You need particular information about things. Past events that are unknown; stones unturned, you may say.'

'Well tell me more. If it's going to get you acquitted, why wait?'

'Do you think I've mutated myself into some obedient pet not to get out of here any faster? That *good behaviour* I've earned hasn't come with your help; it ensures the security of my wealth… my house,' the doctor asserted.

'Fine, well maybe *Carl* could take up your story. I'm sure that his incompetence would keep you in here for years; he knows nothing about law.' David said as he stood. 'You've gave me nothing *new* to go on. I need something to help your case, but all you seem to be interested in, is my *work* colleague?'

The doctor realised that his visitor was losing patience with him and so changed the conversation.

'Have you the papers that support my last statement?' the doctor asked.

'Yes, sorry, I forgot. You better sign those before I go,' David said.

David fingered through several folders within his briefcase and retrieved documents attached by a paper-clip. Before he could remember the instructions given by the security men, the doctor was poised over the metal drawer that slid between rooms. David placed the documents in the drawer and slid the mechanism toward the doctor. Unexpectedly the drawer was pushed back.

'What now?' David questioned.

'Please, I have no ink pen, only blunt pencils,' the doctor exclaimed.

David went to grab a ball-point pen from his inside pocket, when the doctor noticed a fountain-pen within David's briefcase.

'I prefer to use that one, if you don't mind. I prefer to use ink; real ink that is. Calligraphy used to be one of my hobbies,' the doctor said pointing to the pen.

'But this was a gift,' David said holding it aloft. 'Mind you, it hardly has any ink left in it.'

'Let me try,' the doctor asserted.

David hesitated to look at the documents in the drawer.

'It's a gift, but does it work?' the doctor remarked. 'At home I have ones jewelled, with gold and silver and they work, or used to.'

The doctor noticed how David's face took a sudden interest in his words and related David's curiosity to his wealth. At first he hesitated, but seeing that the doctor was to continue, he placed the pen inside the drawer.

David watched the doctor practice with his fountain-pen before voicing some instructions.

'Try the small lever; it sucks and pumps ink into the pen's reservoir.'

'How quaint,' the doctor answered. 'This would come in *very* handy'.

After several attempts, the nib filled with enough ink for the doctor to sign the paperwork from the drawer. After removing the paper-clip, he began to scrutinise the documents, sorting through them page by page. However squinting at David, his thoughts were focused on other intentions.

'You know of my wealth?' the doctor stated, flicking through the documents. 'At least you have confirmation to guarantee my visits to my mansion and ensure that it is secure and operational on my release. I have many artefacts that someone of your intelligence may find interesting. And not just expensive pens either.' The doctor chuckled before continuing, 'I'm sure there would be *some* antique back home that would interest you.'

At that point the doctor placed the documents neatly within the drawer and pushed them toward David.

'But my pen?' David asked, thinking the doctor had forgotten to return it.

'I'm sure there's *something* of interest you could have, especially if you could also do me a little favour; only a small one that is.'

'Why should I listen to *you*? How can you promise things in here?' David snapped.

'Well once our little task is done, I'll explain enough to get me out of here and reward you with that prodigious story. Oh...' the doctor paused, leaning closer toward the glass; rolling David's pen in his fingers. 'And you'll have enough to buy hundreds of gold pens.'

'I should only concentrate on the case and besides,' David stood up trying to distract his thoughts from the wealth of his client, 'it's all but *words*.'

'Would you be interested if I told you my little favour involved getting one up on your friend *Carl*?' the doctor questioned.

'Carl?' David asserted.

'Yes, your colleague,' the doctor replied, scratching his neck again. 'See, that is why I asked about him. He has *something* of mine; something old and precious.'

'What is it?' David questioned, but the doctor continued.

'Listen carefully. All you need to do is take it from him and hide it where he lives – *somewhere* that only you and I know. Then when I get out... I can claim what's rightfully mine.'

'What is it for Christ sake?' David snapped, 'Why hide it at his own home?'

The doctor ignored his questioning, realising he had something else to add.

'But never have it on you after –'

Abruptly their conversation was interrupted by the entrance of a security guard.

'Mr Hedrick? Mr Hedrick, I'm afraid your allotted time is now up,' the security guard said, gesturing him toward the door.

'Use your initiative my *friend* and you'll get that top story,' the doctor announced standing over the drawer mechanism, 'but don't forget *your* documents'.

David turned after closing his briefcase, but then realised the documents were still in the drawer. He snatched the documents and slid back the mechanism.

'But my…' David's voice was stifled by the doctor's loud voice.

'You have *everything* there, my boy. *Everything* you need. Just remember our little agreement.'

At that moment, the security guard ushered David from the room and slammed the door loudly before locking it. As he was ushered through the corridor again he overheard the conversation of a nurse, who stood in front of large white doors.

'Yes, I'll check them again, but Mr Schroeck hasn't done it for some time.'

'Well maybe that's why he's getting a bit violent,' a voice replied.

'The doctor's never been violent with me… but maybe his had his pipe by then,' the nurse stated.

'Look, just give him his medication and check his arms again.'

David could not help but ask the nurse about her conversation. After he clarified that the doctor was a client, the nurse quietly disclosed to him that the doctor had been having violent outbursts, but had never physically attacked anyone. She stated of how the doctor had been put in solitary confinement for personal reasons. After being accused of killing an innocent child, even if it was many years ago, David realised how his would be necessary. However, maybe he would get the facts from the doctor and report the story that would acquit him; more importantly, the doctor would be hugely grateful and reward him with *something* of great value. David realised his thoughts were distracting him from what he wanted to know, so he questioned the nurse again.

'Excuse me, you were asked to check his arms, what for?'

'Cuts,' the nurse stated directly.

'Cuts?' David questioned.

'Yes, we believe he is subjective to self-harm. He draws blood from his forearms. At first he seems to have violent outbursts and talks riddles, but calms after a few minutes or so...'

'Cuts...' David repeated, 'from knives and forks...'

'Oh no, he's not allowed sharp objects. We can't stop this self-sedative disposition, but we certainly don't condone it. He refuses to take most medicine, but likes his pipe though. Has special tobacco from Trinidad, Tobago, or somewhere like that... anyhow, I'm sorry, but I must press on, I've got other stuff to do!'

Never mind how interesting the nurse's explanation may have been, the words that stuck in David's mind, was 'sharp objects'. Indeed, the fountain-pen did have a sharp point and so did the unreturned paper-clip. Then again, David thought, how many other sharp objects could be in his room after all this time.

It was not until David bundled his belongings quickly into the car that his documents spread across the seat. Although the rain was now falling hard and percolating through the open door, David froze for a moment. Hidden between the pages handed back to him from the doctor, was a drawing; crudely etched in thick pencil, but that of a locket. No, it looked more like a charm, or was it a pendant?

# FOURTEEN

NOTICING THAT DAVID'S CAR WAS not parked in its usual spot, Carl became anxious and raced his way up the stairway to the office. Using his briefcase to force the door open, he stumbled in, almost knocking over Lisa and Debbie who were carrying cups of coffee. After their bitter remarks, he quickly apologised and raced over to the part of the office where David worked. Seeing David's desk vacant, Carl paced briskly to the next section of the open office where Alex had just taken off his coat.

'Hey, Simmons, where is *he*?' Carl questioned angrily.

'The *name* is Alex,' he replied, pushing out his hand to stop Carl's advance. 'And *who* are you on about?'

'David of course,' Carl announced. 'He was *supposed* to be taking me to see a client this morning!'

'A client, eh; looks like his gone without you.'

'Have you seen him this morning? Has he definitely gone?' Carl asked.

'No, I don't know, I've only just got here,' Alex answered. 'What's with all the fuss, anyhow?'

'Look, he said he'd pick me up first thing, but he's not here,' Carl explained. 'Has he already gone?'

'Like I said, if you'd *listen*, I've only just got in,' Alex reiterated, but then noticed a green light on David's terminal screen. 'He *must* have been in, he's terminal screen is on. He must have logged in earlier and forgot to switch it off.'

'Bastard, he's gone without me!' Carl said, slamming his fist against his briefcase.

Carl moved swiftly to David's desk and hit a key on his computer keyboard. As the terminal lit up with a login screen, Carl swore again, but stopped to glare at the screen.

'Don't let the boss hear you swearing in the office,' Alex said, 'and get away from his desk; you know how protective he is about his work!'

Carl ignored his comments and whispered, calling Alex a creep.

'What's with all the commotion?' a voice questioned, approaching Carl from behind.

'He's gone without me!' Carl announced, realising Mike had placed his hand on his shoulder. However, before Carl could explain the situation to his friend, Alex interrupted.

'What's with you going with David anyhow, it's not your forte – you can't go visiting *anybody*. Appointments have to be cleared. Anyhow, you'll be out of your depth. Stick to those simple stories. I'm *surprised* you were allowed to report on that murder at the old library!'

'Murder?' Carl questioned quietly.

'He means that lightening accident; the one where we first saw Sarah,' Mike said, before directing his voice loudly at Alex. 'What do you mean, *murder*? It was an accident!'

'Was it? I don't know. According to David it wasn't!'

After hearing loud voices from within his office, the Editor approached and questioned what all the commotion was about. Above Carl's whinging, Alex explained.

'Looks as though Mr Hedrick has left early Sir; apparently he was *supposed* to take Mr Aston to see a client.'

'Well he never mentioned anything to me, and I was here at eight,' the Editor announced, 'although I'm thinking of changing things around here a bit.'

'Has he gone then, Sir; David that is? Did you see him this morning?' Carl asked.

'Yes, unlike you lot, he was here bright and early!'

'So he never said anything about taking me along with him to see a client of his?'

'No,' the Editor replied, 'what's it of your concern anyhow?'

'Well, you see Sir, this client of David's knew a lot about my father, and I thought–'

'Sorry, no!' Carl was abruptly interrupted by the Editor. 'You know company policy. We don't allocate stories to colleagues for personal gain or relative interest.'

'But this man may know a lot?' But again Carl's sentence was cut short by the Editor.

'In fact, I'm thinking of putting people on different stories. Learn new areas, deal with different clients; work with different colleagues. Besides, someone has got to cover bloody holidays. Holidays this *time* of year, I ask you?' He paused, then after taking breath announced. 'We need to publish faster; maybe get into mainstream newspapers. Trouble with you lot, your too slow. And the complaints are rising again; supposed to report facts, not bullshit waffle.'

Unusually Mike stood quiet, but witnessed a different character come from his friend.

'What do you mean? It's all bullshit anyhow! You've added stuff to my stories just to sell them! They're not *attractive*, not marketable, and nowhere near profitable enough. It's all about the *sales*, not the facts!'

'I don't like your tone Mr Aston and I would advise you to calm down,' the Editor said slowly, noticing the two girls peer at them from over their terminals. 'Mr Mackenzie would you please calm your colleague down, whilst I refrain from saying something I may regret.' The Editor leaned forward and staring at Carl said, 'We may be short on holiday cover, but I suggest you take some leave; I think that attack has struck a bad nerve, wouldn't you agree?'

Mike pulled Carl aside and voiced to the Editor that he would calm his friend down over a coffee in the canteen. As the Editor walked back to his office, Carl noticed a large grin expand across Alex's face, before he stuck out his tongue.

'You don't think I'm working with you two, do you? Lazy buggers!'

Carl reacted, trying to get at him, but Mike pulled him away, holding the collar of his coat.

'Carl, what the hell are you doing?' Mike questioned, ushering his friend to his desk. 'Have a go at those *dorks* if you must, but not the Editor?'

Seated at their desks, Carl explained to Mike how he had worked on David's documents all afternoon just to get a chance to meet his client. Maybe David was hiding information from him, as this man did have some bad dealings with his father when he was a child. Although he did not explain everything, Carl recalled the memories of his father and those of which were related to this Dark-man. Carl communicated how he wanted to find out the true cause of his father's death and, although Mike listened attentively, he could not help but realise his friend's personality had changed. As Carl disclosed his real interest in visiting David's client, he could not help but notice his resentment and frustration. Yes, he knew Carl had always been protective of his father, as losing his mother at birth must have been devastating, but the anguish he released against this man was unprecedented. He could not support Carl's hatred against this man – a man he hardly knew. Carl avoided the story about his friend and the deed they did against this man, although Mike may have heard it before. Mike, although showing concern, wanted to change the conversation and so copied some documents to a floppy disc that he wanted Carl to present in his own decorative way.

For a couple of hours Mike's plan worked, but as he left, sarcastic comments voiced from Alex aroused Carl's aggression again. Mike insisted that his friend's reporting skills were not inadequate and that his computer skills were superior to anyone's; why else would David ask for help? However, Mike paused in his appraisal; thinking how his friend behaved irregular at the old library that morning. Although Carl was only a couple of years older, Mike thought his friend more mature and level-headed; especially for a twenty-six year old. As he grabbed the floppy disc from his friend, Carl started barraging him with new developments in desktop publishing and the release of a software package he had seen. This was all too much for Mike and so he persuaded his friend to join him for coffee in the office canteen.

At first this scheme seemed a good idea; the environment of dining with employees from different companies changed Carl's persona. The coffee again was distasteful, but the broken cookies were fresh and a bargain at the discounted price for a bag. However, Mike made the mistake of voicing his concern about his friend's earlier retort with the Editor. He felt that Carl's outburst could fuel the Editor's excuse to assign them with colleagues that they despised. He knew fore well that neither of them would be put with Lisa or Debbie, as they covered each other's holiday in turn, and to work alongside a condescending and surly character like David was unimaginable, never mind his younger accomplice. Carl however, did not listen to Mike's advice and babbled on about how he wanted to get one over on David; how he would get the information himself from the files David had on this client. At first Mike thought he was jesting, but as Carl disclosed his intention to use David's password, Mike raged in disagreement. Mike himself, was nowhere near the world's most honourable man, but this activity was against company policy and Carl could get cautioned; most probably sacked. It was so unlike Carl to contemplate such a deed. For some reason he was besotted with this client; the man that knew his father. Mike could not listen to the intentions that his friend whispered, never mind assisting in his plan, and so saying that he was to meet Rachael for lunch, Mike stormed out from the building.

Carl worked alone for the rest of the afternoon, and although he chose particular articles that required interesting design skills, he could not concentrate; the thought of David having hidden information about his father. He convinced himself that soon he would try and see if the password worked; if he could try and browse his computer files.

By now he had waited until the afternoon and knowing that the Editor and Sales Director had gone, it was just a matter of observing who was left. Mike had not returned and had no intention to. Both David and Alex had gone to see clients, and Pete was as usual, chatting to the two girls; pretending to take an interest in articles on fashion, shopping habits and their 'old mother' recipes on baking. Carl had overheard their conversation on his trip to the drinks machine to get a coffee; his real excuse was clearly to scan the office and observe who was about. Also, it was an opportunity to ask Pete if he would let him know when David came back.

Timidly, Carl crept over to the open-office plan where Alex and David worked. With their desks being partitioned, Carl needed to ensure he had a lookout; where he could observe people, without been seen himself. Cautiously, he hit the keyboard of David's computer and the screen sprang into action. Using the log-in screen, Carl attempted entering the word that he had observed the day before, but several times it was rejected. He was certain of David's username; this was simply his employee number, but what about the password? Then he remembered, as he was about to ask David about the year he went to Tenby, David hit two numerical keys along the top of the keyboard. Was this the year he went to Tenby? But it was mandatory to change passwords at least every twelve months. Then Carl thought, maybe the password was the word and the current year. Carl entered what he thought was correct, but again it was rejected. Realising David's keyboard had a green light on the top-right; Carl hit the *CAPS LOCK* and entered *RAINMAKER89*. Suddenly, the screen flashed, menus appeared and Carl was in.

He had spent nearly five minutes scouring David's documents and folders, before noticing a folder entitled Dr J. K. Schroeck. Inside, Carl browsed several different documents; letters, appointments, case studies, a conviction order as well as some old photographs that had been scanned. Although Carl was curious of everything in this folder, it was a court attendance letter that intrigued him, as it was near the end of October; next week in fact. Also, he noticed a document requesting visits to the Wiltshire Rehabilitation Institute, as well as a scanned, letter-headed document, in reply. After taking a quick view of the office, Carl swiped a blank floppy disc from his desk and returned to David's computer. Swiftly he inserted the disc into the floppy drive.

Although most of the files had been transferred, it was the folder of scanned photographs that filled the disc to its maximum capacity. The computer requested that another disc should be inserted in order to copy the remaining files. It was then, that Carl heard voices. Carl panicked and started cancelling all copying. He heard Pete ask David aloud about where he had been all day, and from that Carl became desperate. Quickly Carl rebooted David's computer, but had to wait for the floppy disc to stop revolving. As soon as the drive stopped and its light darkened, Carl snatched the floppy disc from the drive and raced toward his desk. By this time David had already stumbled upon him.

'Where is everybody this afternoon?' David asked, 'What's that you've got in your hand?'

Carl opened his right hand slowly after passing the disc to his left hand, from behind him. The floppy disc then found its way into his pocket.

'And the other?' David enquired.

'What do you think this is a schoolyard?' Carl announced, raising both hands in the air. 'I don't have to answer to you; especially someone who promises one thing and does another!'

'Argh, your trip to see my client, well…'

'So you didn't bother to ask the Editor, then – or even leave a message?' Carl interrupted.

'Well, actually, if you need to know, they have very tight security procedures; only one visitor is allowed at any one time!'

'Is that so? Guess I won't get anything on my father then?' Carl enquired with sarcasm. 'And after all that work I did yesterday afternoon, for *you*!'

'Look, I'm sorry that you put a lot of effort in on my behalf,' David said, placing his briefcase down on his desk. 'I tell you what, once I'm finished here, I'll print off what files I have on your father and pop them round to you later.'

Carl stood silent; he was baffled. Firstly, he was wondering whether David would notice that his computer had been tampered with. Secondly, David was being usually pleasant; maybe he was hiding something or he had found out something from his client. He watched as David logged in and started browsing files and folders on his computer. David turned, noticing Carl watch him closely.

'What's the problem? I said, I'll print them off!'

Carl was stumped and paused to ask.

'But you don't know where I live, do you?'

'Of course I do; you invited me to a party at your flat last year, or were it the year before?'

'Oh yes, *that* party. What a laugh.' Carl voiced sarcastically, turning away. As he walked slowly towards his desk, Carl looked repeatedly back at David to see if he had suspected anything. He stopped and peered down, taking the disc from his pocket, thinking he did not need a visit off David after all. He froze as a voice shouted.

'What number is it, your flat?'

Carl turned to see David leaning over the office partition.

'Number sixty-three,' Carl shouted and then muttered quietly, 'not that I need your stuff now.'

Smiling, Carl placed the disc back into his pocket, and then returned to his desk.

# FIFTEEN

THINKING THAT IT WAS JUST another day at work tomorrow, Carl poured another measure of whisky into his glass. However, it was not just the thought of work that distraught him; he had been having quite some discomfort from his injuries. The painkillers helped during the day, but without having a drink or two at night, he would lie awake, shifting beneath the bedclothes to find relief. Also, there were a number of other things that were troubling him; his confrontation with the Editor, arguments with Mike, Sarah's feelings towards him, David's dishonesty, but most of all – this man who opposed his father. This unease had surely brought on the strange, short dreams he had been having about his past, but the whisky helped; it mellowed his worry and prevented the intensity of his dreams. Nevertheless, it was work tomorrow, so he splashed a little water into the glass.

It was then that he heard the doorbell. He realised that David had proposed to bring round those printed case files, but then again, why would he keep that promise; especially after the fiasco this morning. Carl had the disc, but only having a computer at work he could not view files, never mind print them off. He did not manage to copy all the photographs, but maybe David had them. He may also have additional information about his client. The doorbell rang again. Putting down the water jug, Carl glanced at his suitcase before going to answer the door.

'I thought you'd never answer,' David said, turning from observing the garden. He squinted at Carl, blinded by the bright light bulb that hung from the hallway ceiling. 'I have those documents; they're mainly photographs. I considered sliding them through the letter box, but,' David paused momentarily, 'well, better if I explain. Besides, I haven't seen your place since that house-warming party.'

Carl considered whether he should just take the documents, but David had kept his promise and for some reason, he was being remarkably friendly, so Carl stepped aside and quietly invited him in.

'It's gone exceptionally cold for this time of year, don't you think? I'll go through these things in a minute,' David said, tapping a cardboard folder, 'but you've done wonders with this place. Argh yes, I remember it now.'

Carl followed him past the kitchen and into the lounge.

'Still got that old dresser; the one with that antique mirror?' David asked, his spectacles shining bright from reflected light.

'Why yes, it's still in the bedroom. Funny you should mention that!' Carl replied.

'Why's that? It's such an antique. Have it priced up, if you want; depends on its condition.'

'It's been giving me strange nightmares about my past!' Carl explained, lifting his glass from the table. 'Fancy a drink? I've got a beer in the fridge.'

'I don't drink; don't you remember that? Anyhow, I'm driving.'

'Argh yes sorry, a cup of tea then eh?' Carl enquired.

'Yes, but at first I'd like to have a look…'

Entering the bedroom, David could not believe his luck. He thought he may have to make up stories in order to search the flat, but there it was – the pendant. Why it lay under a sun-lamp he did not know, but it positively matched the drawing he was given. Amongst other items shadowed on the top of the cabinet was a large pebble, but then realised it was a paperweight thermometer.

'Sugar… milk?' Carl shouted from the kitchen, but then heard a commotion.

Racing into his bedroom, Carl noticed David sprawled across the floor, trying to sit up.

'Sorry, think I'll forget trying to look at that dresser; must have stepped on something!' David said, pulling himself up. He noticed his folder on the floor and bent down to pick it up, 'There's your culprit. I must have stepped on it!' he said, pointing at the paperweight thermometer. Straightening his coat with the cardboard folder in one hand, he handed Carl the paperweight with the other. 'Want to watch where you put stuff. Never mind, accidents happen, think I'm okay! Better give that antique a miss. Let's go over this stuff instead, eh?'

Carl watched David shuffle his way into the centre of the lounge, before straightening his coat and spectacles. Noticing Carl's glass of whisky, David chuckled to him and said.

'Thought you didn't drink week days; don't touch the stuff myself!'

As he sat down on the edge of an armchair, Carl walked round to join him. Slowly, David pushed the glass of whisky along the coffee table with his folder, but as it began to topple, he withdrew and the documents fell from the folder. Carl grabbed the glass and seeing the documents scatter the floor, stepped over to collect them. As Carl knelt down to collect them, David rummaged in his coat pocket. Whilst Carl assembled the documents together, David quickly looked down at the object he had put in his coat pocket. Entwined by a metal necklace, he could not observe the object properly, but surely it was the pendant. As David looked up and saw Carl in the light, he could not help but notice the bruising around his face and that his hands and wrists were lacerated. His thoughts of how Carl must have taken quite a beating were interrupted.

'You're not usually this clumsy,' Carl proclaimed, placing the documents neatly on the coffee table, 'in fact, you're more finicky than me.'

'Sorry, I'm not used to visiting people.'

'Like your clients you mean,' Carl said with hint of sarcasm. 'Surely you're used to following formalities; especially medical institutes, or places like that.'

'Oh well, that's different. I suppose your right to be angry about visiting this doctor, but as I said, they would only allow me to visit; only one person at any one time.'

'Is that so,' Carl said, taking a mouthful from his glass. 'You didn't say that yesterday evening. Surely you'd know all *this* before your visit.'

Carl felt himself becoming tired, slurring words, and churlish against his visitor. Yes, he was angry, but maybe David had new information about his client; information that concerned his father.

'So, what have you got? Does this doctor know of me?' Carl asked.

'Well there's some photographs here, old photographs of this doctor. I believe your father's in one. He was a clergyman wasn't he; a man of the cloth as so to speak?'

'Yes, he was a priest with responsibilities to his parish.'

'Well, according to the history in the case files I've gathered, your father had disliked this doctor for years. He accused him of practising devil worship, or something like that, but he could not prove it. Even your father's followers couldn't get sufficient evidence, until–'

'Until what?' Carl questioned, leaning forward to examine the documents.

'A young boy was murdered many years ago. At first it was blamed on an escaped prisoner, but enough evidence was found to convict this doctor. Stupid of how a man of such intellect would let the police search the grounds of his wealthy mansion, only to be reprimanded with concealing the murder weapon. Well, it was found on the mansion grounds; in a greenhouse I believe. It could have been that the criminal got spooked when he tried to hide it. Come to think, the doctor did like that angle.'

David paused, thinking of how he could present his story somewhat different; maybe acquit this doctor fast and claim his reward.

'But surely the police matched this murder weapon to that of the victim,' Carl responded, trying to squeeze out all what David knew, 'and to the doctor?'

'Yes well, what I believe is that this prisoner, who obviously did not confess his crime, returned the weapon back to the greenhouse, after he killed the boy. See he must have had gloves on, but obviously the doctor has his prints upon the gardening tool. However, it wasn't the doctor's handkerchief that was bundled around the weapon.'

'Weapon?' Carl questioned, 'What was the weapon?'

'A small cultivator; like a steel fork used for weeding.'

'And this was used to do what?' Carl probed, sliding the documents around the coffee table.

'Gouge his bloody throat out, that's what!' David said, but stopped suddenly, staring at Carl to think. 'Surely, you heard about this murder; it was in your neighbourhood? It was in all the papers!'

'We did have a paper, but I was only young.'

'Then you may have gone to school with the boy that...' David paused, realising why he thought the doctor had been interested in Carl. Perhaps David was wrong not to have taken Carl; meeting the doctor may have brought out some history about Carl's father. It was certain that over many years these two men held a bitter grudge against each other.

'Probably a different school,' Carl said, gulping at his whisky. He coughed before continuing, 'We had bereavement in assembly one morning, but nothing else. What was his name; is it here?'

'It's somewhere in the case file on my computer. Those are just letters and photographs – old photographs; a class photograph and a scene of the murdered boy, some of the doctor and one of your father,' David explained looking at his watch. 'Blimey is that the time, I must press on. My parents are expecting me and I've got another early start tomorrow, but you can have another!'

Carl was dumbfounded by David's courtesy, especially as he poured more whisky into his glass. However, for some reason he was nervous, nearly spilling the whisky as his hand went shaky. Quickly, he slammed the bottle down on the coffee table and fidgeted around in his pockets before standing.

'Sorry, I can't give you everything, but a lot of material is explicit to the case and I've had written consent,' David said, turning towards the hallway. 'Maybe I could get you on the story; just don't tell the Editor that you have a personal interest.'

'Now that's too late,' Carl muttered.

'Sorry, what did you say?'

'See you later, mate,' Carl voiced aloud, whilst standing.

'Yes, see you tomorrow I guess; I'll see myself out,' David asserted.

Carl watched David turn to acknowledge him before shutting the door behind. He turned, looked at the coffee table and stood perplexed by his visitor's unusual pleasance; never mind the fact that he had bothered to bring him the folder of documents.

On his way through the front garden of Carl's flat, David stopped, turned upon the path and looked around. Lifting the object from his pocket, he held the chain aloft and released the pendant; watching the oval, black stone swing in the half-light. Suddenly, David felt a chill and turned to face the flat; it was as though someone was watching him. However, the curtains were drawn, the hallway dark, and the only light was from a street lamp some distance away. At his side he noticed a large stone ornament and realised that it rose into a bird bath. Clasping the pendant in the palm of his right hand, he turned and knelt down by the ornament. Stretching to hide the pendant in a nearby bush, he hesitated, remembering how the doctor asked for it to be hidden here; outside Carl's property, but why? Why take it from inside, only to hide it in the garden – not far from where it was originally? Maybe the doctor could easily retrieve it here; a hiding place that only they knew? But why not take it to him? Or even better, he could keep it as something to *bargain* with – as the doctor did say, it *was* old and precious. How much was it worth exactly? David knew a bit about antique jewellery, but this was something he had never seen before. He had never seen a stone like it before; so smooth and shiny, but black as night. After looking back once more at the flat, he swivelled the chain around his hand, released it into his coat pocket and strode towards his car.

It tasted almost neat after David had poured so much whisky in the glass. Feeling already woozy, Carl did not want to spill any water over the documents and so moved the jug aside. The handwriting of the letters proved hard to decipher, or was it the fact that his eyes were tired. Examining the old photographs, it was the class photograph that Carl noticed first. The image of the murdered boy was circled in pen and in the row below, several classmates along, was Carl; small, meek, sitting cross-legged and wearing those horrible, itchy shorts. Not having any pictures of Alex, it brought back a lot of memories, many of which were nice, but all were overshadowed by the one that was horrible.

He sifted through more photographs, feeling himself tearful, but suppressing his emotion, and then he noticed him, the Dark-man. It must be him; dressed in a light-coloured suit, contrasted to his black hair and dark piercing eyes. This was the man he had feared for most of his childhood, but he looked almost ordinary, as if he was just some middle-aged professor holding some sort of certificate. Amid the documents he appeared in another photograph, but this time he was older, amongst many others and dressed in black. Beside him was a woman, also dressed in black; a woman he had seen before and felt drawn to, but her identity escaped him. The shadows of the old, grey-shaded photograph made her face smooth and angelic, but somehow she looked fearful and oppressed.

As he rummaged through the documents, he found more copies of photographs. He found one of which was used in the newspapers to report the death of his father. It was a good photograph of his father; younger than to that of what he remembered, dressed in newly decorated garments, recently made for his commission as the parish priest. He must have been proud that day and his father's face showed it; Reverend Steven John Aston.

Around him were circled people. Most he did not recall, except one; his sister. His Aunt had died many years ago and so Carl could not question her. Maybe this obsessive pursuit to research his father was to come to a premature end; but there were many people, surely one person in the photograph was still alive today, and they would be able to enlighten him.

Placing the photograph down beside the others, he gulped once again at his whisky and noticed a similarity between two photographs. The angelic, but oppressed lady in the photograph with the Dark-man was indeed standing not far from his father in the other. Was this Carl's mother? To what vague memory he had of her, it could well be; maybe that is why he felt drawn to her. But why would she be standing by the Dark-man? Carl did not have any pictures of his mother to prove this identity, but Aunt Evelyn would; his mother's younger sister, and surely, unlike the eldest, she was still alive. Slowly, Carl's thoughts melted with a nauseous headache and he felt uncontrollably tired.

# SIXTEEN

AT FIRST IT WAS THE sound of distant hooves he could hear, but he could not see a thing; it was too dark. Again he felt petrified. He had heard this malicious sound before, but everything felt distrait. His fear increased as the gallop of hooves got louder and nearer, but then he could make out what lay beneath his outstretched hands.

Again he found himself on a woodland floor, the earth cold against his face. He pulled himself up, his vision clearing, noticing a frost beginning to cover the dead leaves below. He sat up and kneeling on one knee looked around, trying to deduce from where the sound was coming. Although weary, he could not wait for the sound to near and so ran in the opposite direction. But his feet were heavy, his mind blurred, and he sauntered clumsily through the bracken until he reached a gritted path. Stumbling out from the woodland, he realised what it was; where he was. Bordered with trees arching high above, was a railway line stretching straight into the distance each side of him.

It was not the cold air that made him shiver, but the sudden appearance of a glowing fog bank, becoming more visible, moving up towards him along the railway line. He turned and hearing the hooves from the woodland, started to run along the track; the sleepers frosted and slippery, the gravel heavy. He ran the best his legs would take him, but the mist was almost upon him, the hooves now resonating along the track. He was now plodding along, his muscles aching, his heart thumping, but the hooves were stridently near.

Glancing back, galloping ever nearer, he noticed the shadow of a black horse and rider within the mist. Two hellish, red eyes glowed in the mist as the beast powerfully exerted breath. Held by the cloaked rider and arching above, shone the reflection of a large scythe.

Looking in front to rectify his direction, he noticed how the earth each side of him cascaded away, revealing the overpass of a stone bridge. Quickly he made for one side and glanced down the slope, hesitant at its descent. He *had* been here before; how or when he could not recall, but nevertheless, somehow he knew it.

By now the mist was upon him, circling, glowing, and then came the deathly thud of hooves. Diving aside, he held on to the stone of the bridge and looked up. He saw only a short glimpse of the rider's skeletal face before the scythe swung and skimmed against the stone. The sound deafened his ears as he clambered about, struggling to hold on to the embankment. The scythe swung again, not far from his hands. Releasing his grip on the earth, suddenly he fell.

On the road below, he could hear the hooves stamping on the bridge above. He got up and stared about, thinking which way best to escape. But then it appeared; just a light mist at first and then a thick, glowing fog bank covering the road, flowing down from the embankment. Afraid of the shadows, he backed in to the tunnel slowly, thinking he could escape out the other side, but the mist followed him, forcing him deeper into the tunnel and into the dark.

The roadside had narrowed considerably, leaving only a little pavement, the gutter littered with puddles. The fog bank hovered outside the entrance as though it was toying with him. He looked into the tunnel, but could not understand it; the bridge above was only single track, yet he saw nothing but darkness.

Out of the shadows within the tunnel, he noticed something approach; a figure of a man. At first he was unrecognisable, but as he approached, the light from the glowing mist revealed his identity. It was David; bedraggled, exhausted, staggering as fast as he could toward him.

Suddenly, the sound of thunderous hooves echoed about the tunnel and out the darkness galloped the stallion, the rider poised with scythe in hand. Before Carl could shout, the scythe blade pierced David's back and appeared from out his chest. Abruptly, all went quiet. Blood exerted from his mouth as the blade was pulled free. As he dropped, the weighty animal circled before disappearing back into the darkness.

Carl ran toward him and knelt down. Quickly, he looked into the darkness, down at the body sprawled upon the road and then at the tunnel entrance. Along with the sound of hooves, the fog had gone. Pulling on his shoulder, he turned over David's lifeless body to see his face; surely he was dead? Suddenly David's eyes shot open as he hollered his last breath and within seconds his body burst into flames. The fire spread up Carl's arm, and he too, was on fire.

NERVES TREMBLING, HEAD POUNDING, CARL awoke. Again, he had been subjected to another terrible nightmare. As his body cooled and his heartbeat slowed, he felt sweat saturate his body. Blinking wildly, he looked about and realised that he was not in any tunnel, but at home and in his armchair. He massaged his face and neck with his hands, before gulping down the remnants in the glass before him.

In the bathroom, Carl washed cold water over his face to remove the images of the past nightmare. It was then that he realised what had happened to Sarah; surely David too would experience a similar bout. He never saw Sarah killed in his previous nightmare and maybe that was why she survived. But David, although he despised this work colleague, surely did not deserve to die, especially in such a manner; his life taken by the Angel of Death himself. But it was *Carl* that death was after, or was *he* the instrument causing all these murders? Suddenly, he remembered – the pendant. Surely, David was safe as long as it was under the sunlamp. But he had fallen asleep and forgot to switch it on.

With his face and hands still wet, he hurried to the bedroom, only to find that the pendant had gone! How long had he got before David would meet his fate? He barely got to Sarah in time and the bridge pictured in his dream was at least a couple of miles away. Being way over the drink drive limit the car was out of the question, but this was an emergency! Decisively, he grabbed his overcoat as outside, it was sure to be cold.

As Carl thought about the fastest route, he wrapped a scarf about his neck and pulled high the collar of his coat. A shortcut through the park was best; it would meet the railway line about a mile from the farm. But the farm was almost a mile away itself. Although feeling somewhat drunk, he shook his head and darted towards the end of his street where he could get across country.

It took ten minutes to reach the farm, so by the time he found the railway line, it must be at least half an hour. How daunting was it to follow the footsteps of his dream; to notice the sleepers glistening of frost, to see the shadowy woodland alongside. By the time he reached the bridge, his head was dizzy of alcohol, but the night air kept him alert. He could make out the overpass, the embankment, and half way down, he noticed the tunnel. All was quiet; the road empty, the tunnel dark until its exit on the other side, but then he noticed imprints. At first they meandered from side to side, but as he ran along the roadside, he could see them clearly in the grass. It was then that he realised from where they had come and to whom they belonged. These were surely hoof marks, and by the depth in the grass they were made by some large, weighty animal. He hesitated for a moment, apprehensive of the creature the prints would lead to, but time was short, it had been surely more than half an hour by now. Following the tracks he again began to run. After a minute or two he noticed a layer of mist retreat into the woodland and then up ahead, he noticed a light.

To anyone else, it was simply a crashed car; a receding fog bank, a dangerous snaking and slippery road and a man traveling too fast. But Carl knew different. As he approached, it was indeed the car David drove; he remembered it missing that morning. Was he too late, or was he still alive? Maybe, it *was* an accident, but there was only one way to find out.

The car had certainly hit the tree with speed. Steam was flowing out of gaps where the bonnet had buckled and the smell of fumes was overwhelming. Leaning against the car, he levered the passenger door open and looked inside. Lit by the inward turned headlights, Carl recognised David. However, he was not easy to identify. It was the frozen glare that proved he was scared stiff; that he had been killed by something other than the crash. Glass had pierced him in parts and blood was everywhere, but it was the garish hole in his chest that repulsed Carl. He backed away, stopping himself from vomiting; trying not to look at the gaping wound but to search the car instead. Directly in front of David and in the windscreen was a hole, slightly larger than the wound. Carl knew then what had killed him; he had seen the scythe in the tunnel; in his dream. Surely he was not responsible for this fatality, but surely he was now a witness.

From a distance, Carl heard sirens approach and looked along each stretch of the road. But what about the pendant, surely he could not allow another victim get hold of it? With one hand against the dashboard, Carl searched David's pockets, but could not find it. Carl coughed, finding it hard to breathe as smoke was pouring in from the engine. Carl attempted another search, feeling trouser pockets, coat pockets, and then the glove compartment of the car; surely it had to be here? He looked about the floor of the car, but the smoke was overpowering. But there was something between the seat and the handbrake; surely that was it! He stretched his fingers down into the gap and felt it, trying to pinch it between his fingers, but the smoke was choking him. Suddenly, he pulled it free and gasped the stone in the palm of his hand, before retreating from the car.

Placing the pendant inside his coat, Carl stood dazed for a second and then heard a voice as footsteps approached. The voice called again and Carl searched the darkness. Seeing the blue lights flicker against the tree tops, he realised that the sirens were nearby, but where had this voice come from.

'I've phoned an ambulance, but I think he's dead!'

Carl turned to notice a man running along the road.

'The nearest phone was by the old signal box, I ran as fast…' the man paused as he was clearly out of breath, 'Watch out! The engine's on fire!'

Carl turned back to look at the vehicle; flames were now coming from under the bonnet. He backed away as the man shouted something about the smell of petrol. As the ambulance approached its siren drenched any sound of panic as both men fled.

As the car burst into flame, Carl ran towards the woodland and the man scarpered back along from where he had come. Within seconds the darkness of the surrounding woodland lit up as the car exploded. Carl was thrown into the woodland and the man, of whom Carl could just make out, was running toward the ambulance. For a moment Carl sat up and witnessed the vehicle afire before looking at what he had retrieved. Wearily, he pulled himself up, placed the pendant into the breast pocket and began to amble back toward the railway line.

# SEVENTEEN

Although he had phoned Mike earlier about his doctor's appointment, Carl rushed through the doors of the office knowing he was late. As Mike did not know it was a lie, Carl hoped his friend would convince the Editor of his excuse. However, as he paced further into the office, the concerns about his absence were soon overshadowed.

Work colleagues were all standing, either grouped in small clusters or alone, peering at the Editor's office. Maybe it was the disorder that confused him, or was it the fact that he had hardly any sleep last night; but soon he realised what was happening. He had barely reached the Director's office when two police constables passed him; exiting the Editor's office. He stopped and turned to watch them leave the office and then heard someone call his name. Seeing Mike wave him over, he made his way to his friend. By now he had a good idea to what all the commotion was about, but tried to discount it.

'Did you mention my appointment, Mike?'

'Of course,' Mike answered, but quickly changed the subject. 'Have you not heard about David?'

'David?' Carl replied slowly, acting his naivety.

'Yes, he's been killed! They said he crashed his car!'

'Really, an accident?' Carl questioned, hoping his friend had more information.

'Most probably, but they're looking into it, asking whether he may have been drinking… with friends after work, that kind of stuff.'

'But he doesn't drink,' Carl stuttered, recalling David's words from last night. 'He never had any at parties, or night's out, did he?'

'That's what we all told them.'

'Them?' Carl asked.

'Those police constables. They've been taking statements from each of us. To get a description I guess. The main guy's still in with the Editor now. Suppose he'll take responsibility as the Director's on holiday again!'

'What main guy?' Carl was pretending to be naive.

'Detective Inspector, err… Campbell I think. Anyhow,' Mike paused, surprised at Carl's serenity, 'you talked to him, about *that* client. Could it be something to do with that case?'

'That's just work Mike, nothing to do with him crashing his car by accident!'

'Christ, you could be a little more concerned. I know he was obstinate, a stuck up brat, but bloody hell, poor guy.'

'Well, it's a shock, err… that's sure,' Carl said, placing his briefcase on his chair. 'As he didn't drink, it must have been slippery roads!'

'The girls say he always drove carefully, you know, when he's given them a lift.'

'Well, I don't know. What did happen to the car, did they say?'

'They think it exploded from a petrol leak. The car got torched; poor bastard didn't stand a chance!'

Carl turned away, trying to escape his vision of David before the car caught fire. He excused himself from Mike and headed for the toilet, distressed by his thoughts. He almost collided with a black policeman as the constable came out the Editor's office.

'Sorry,' Carl said, circling around him, 'I need a leak.'

'No problem, young man,' the Detective Inspector said, stepping aside.

'Hey, you've not had a statement off Mr Aston!' a voice shouted. As the Editor joined the Detective Inspector outside his office, he announced, 'Carl must have just come in, he's not given you a statement. He had recently talked to the deceased about a case.'

The Detective Inspector approached Carl who stood motionless, unprepared what to say.

'Mr Aston, err… Carl?' he paused, looking at his notebook. 'You worked recently with a Mr David Hedrick?'

Carl looked down, trying to conceal any indication of guilt. However, he noticed how stocky the Detective Inspector was; his hair shaved close to the head and how the sides were turning white, much like his moustache and goatee beard.

'No not really, he never got on with us,' Carl replied quietly.

'Us?' the Detective Inspector enquired.

'With Mr Mackenzie, Sir,' the Editor revealed, approaching. 'They work mainly in pairs; each pair work on different disciplines.'

'But you said he worked with the deceased?' the Detective Inspector stated.

'No,' Carl corrected, 'I wanted to, but he didn't permit it. David was working on the case alone.'

'Well, Mr Aston, if you could give a statement regarding your relationship with the deceased, I believe your Editor will forward it on to us.'

The Detective Inspector handed Carl a form and before heading for the exit, thanked the Editor for his cooperation. As he turned to watch the Detective Inspector disappear, Carl felt his heartbeat slow, but then looked up to see the Editor staring at him.

'So what's the doctor say, eh?' the Editor asked with the usual hint of sarcasm. 'Oh, well you'd better not tell me, probably more time off work. First one gets mugged, and now this, what bloody next?'

Carl found it necessary to warn the Editor in advance and so interrupted him.

'Well, I was advised to take some time off, and I,' he paused, noticing the Editor stop and turn, 'the doctor advised me to rest and, I… I would like to book some time off soon, if that's okay?'

'Yes, well, I suppose so given the circumstances, but fill out *that* form, and a holiday one too before you go swanning off anywhere, oh and yes,' the Editor paused before walking to the centre of the office. 'For everybody's attention, can I have your attention please?' He paused again, watching employees gather round. 'In light of recent events, and with regard to my conversation with the Director, the so arranged office building party for Halloween this weekend is cancelled. If you so wish, though I don't know why, want to celebrate this occasion, well you'll have to take it on yourselves and go elsewhere. As usual our office will close at nine. Thank you.'

After watching the Editor retreat into his office, he looked down at the statement form handed to him by the Detective Inspector and then made this way to his desk. On the way his thoughts were interrupted by two girls.

'They take ages to fill in; glad he took notes off me! Apparently, it's to get a recent character analysis to eliminate stuff like suicide,' Debbie declared, but eventually had her conversation interrupted by Lisa. 'Anyway, that's what the guy said who questioned–'

'The one who interviewed me was dashy. He had the looks of that old film star, you know the one in… what was the film?'

'I can't believe it, feels so surreal, an accident, I wonder if he…' Carl muttered, before being interrupted again.

'Bad isn't it, poor David, I can't believe it either. I know he was a bit of a…'

'A bit of a what, Deb?' Lisa said, facing her friend directly, 'a stuck up prick!'

'How can you say that? He's given you a lift many a time. Now you are being a bit two-faced if you ask me.'

'Yes, but now this *party's* been cancelled and I asked that guy from the ground floor out to it as well.'

'Now, that's definitely being dispassionate. Proves how much you think of your friends up here,' Debbie responded.

'Fallacious bitches.' Carl whispered, trying to pass them by.

'What? What did he say, Deb?'

'Attitude problem if you ask me,' Lisa replied aloud.

'He's not as innocent as he looks. Muggers my arse, probably got in a fight.'

After Carl pushed his way through them, he met Mike on his way down.

'Picking fights with girls now, eh?' Mike said, laughing.

'Well it's not with you, blonde,' Lisa replied, turning Debbie away.

Mike laughed as the two girls departed, but a look of concern stretched across his face as Carl walked alongside him and they returned to their seats.

'What is it, what's the matter?'

'Nothing,' Carl responded, 'it's just, it may have…'

'Has it got something to do with *that* case?' Mike said, trying to calm his voice.

'No, but,' Carl stopped as Mike had given him an idea, 'there maybe something on file, something that proves…'

'Proves what? A top earning employer, who is the only son of wealthy parents, having accomplishments as long as your arm, commits suicide by crashing his car!'

'No, of course not, that's *not* what happened!'

'Mind you, it's been known, the pressure of work. Surviving this place every day's enough, never mind chasing law suits and stuff like that. Maybe it was *that* case? Is that why…?'

As Mike stopped and stared at his friend, he suddenly realised Carl knew something. After years of knowing him, Mike knew when Carl was hiding something.

'It *has* got something to do with the case, hasn't it?' Mike claimed.

Carl got up and after looking around, made his way to David's computer where he sat to log in.

'What the fuck are you doing?' Mike whispered loudly. 'You can't log into that, you haven't the password. Besides, haven't you any consideration, the poor guy only died last night!'

'That's why I need to search more,' Carl demanded.

'More? Have you…' Mike stopped, as he saw David's files open up on the computer screen; obviously his friend had hacked into the computer before. 'If there's any files on there that prove it wasn't an accident, don't you think the police should handle it. They'll probably confiscate it tomorrow.'

'That's why I need to look now,' Carl stated.

'But you'll get into trouble, *proper* trouble, not just skipping a morning for a doctor's appointment.' Mike paused, realising the guilt in Carl's eyes. 'You didn't go did you, what the… Christ, what's got into you?'

Mike turned and waving his hands announced, 'It was an accident, everything shows it! You even said yourself that the roads were frosty.'

'But it wasn't the roads, it wasn't suicide, it was deliberate!'

'What?' Mike questioned, staring obvious at the floor.

'I saw him killed!' Carl whispered, but realised it *was* Mike he was talking to.

'Killed, what you were there?' Mike asked, stepping closer.

Carl realised he must somehow convince his friend that it was not just his dreams that were executing the people in them, but that he had witnessed David's death. Then there was the attack on Sarah, the police station, the man at the library. As Mike repeated the question, Carl realised using David's computer at this time was stupid and dangerous; surely like before, he could access it later as it would not be confiscated until morning.

After logging out the computer, Carl got up and guided Mike back to their chairs and sat him down; a look of sincerity in his eyes. He told him of what photographs David had on his computer and how David's client could be withholding information about his father. Mike argued, establishing the fact that Carl's search for information was selfish and that it had nothing to do with resolving David's death. Carl reiterated how his dreams had foretold people's fate; seeing their death before it happened and now they were getting so vivid – so real. He recollected their trip to the library and excused his reaction when seeing the victims face. Mike rejected his friend's explanation. How could he remember the face of a man in a dream, one that he had never seen before, and then identify him later when he was mutilated by blades of glass? Carl faltered; he wanted to tell of the unfortunate mugger, the dying policeman at the station, and most of all Sarah, the girl who witnessed an attack. But it would all sound ridiculous, especially to a cynic such as Mike. As he battled with his thoughts, Mike asked him how he saw David's death.

Slowly Carl began recreating his dream and how the hellish creature claimed David's life with his scythe; how it pierced right through his chest, how he yelled as fire shot up Carl's arm. At first Mike ridiculed the story, stating that Carl's mind was working overtime on David's case and that he was heavily influenced by personal interest. However, Mike could not disguise the fact that the car had been burned and that his friend had recalled the spread of fire. But why should a man get pursued by such evil? Mike did not learn of the pendant and how David had stolen it and for some reason why it now lay under a sun-lamp at Carl's house.

Carl's conversation turned to the photographs on David's computer and how these related to his father; somehow these two men confronted each another with opposing beliefs. Mike pried further but was getting no facts from his friend; it was as though he was making up stuff just to win him over. He thought of how a cause of events could have taken their toile on his friend; the mugging, his fit at the party; maybe he was besotted with Sarah and did not know how to handle it. Carl was now babbling on about strange dreams and how he thought past events had come back to haunt him. It was too much for Mike, he had problems too; especially as he and Rachael had been arguing a lot lately.

'Look mate, it all sounds difficult, but you can't just hack a colleague's file; especially one that has just, you know…' Mike paused, trying to control his anger. 'I know you've always had strange dreams, but everyone does, it's how your mind revives itself from stress and anxiety. For you it's probably fantasies as well. But you've got Sarah now, she seems to like you. Leave David's stuff alone and forget *that* client, if he's to you like he was your father, he's probably nothing but trouble.'

'But don't you see, I've got to find out now, I've got a lead to how my father died!'

'Well, if that's how you want it, sorry but leave me out of *that* bloody topic. I'm finishing off this draft,' Mike stated adamantly before continuing. 'Shit, now I've got to tell Rachael there's no Halloween party!'

Mike sat down as his friend went to speak, but he put his finger to his limps, indicating Carl to be quiet. Carl's temper flared and he spoke out.

'Well that's all well and good, nice that you understand, at least you've got your parents! Don't even want to help his friend research his father's *unusual* death,' he continued sarcastically as Mike stood up. 'Do it myself. I'll find out what happened, you'll see.'

'I'll tell you what's best to do,' Mike announced, pointing his finger at him. 'Take a break from here! Get away a bit. Go ask Sarah for a dirty weekend, maybe that'll take your mind of it!'

Carl's face turned red and was about to reply when Mike strode off saying, 'I'm getting a coffee. Fill in that form with the statement you just gave me. That'll go down a treat with that Inspector!'

# EIGHTEEN

ALTHOUGH HE OBEYED THE CUSTOMARY search, he could not help but feel that the routine was more strict than usual. He questioned the request to search his body all over, but joked with them to lighten the mood. Unfortunately, his attempt failed; the mention of a file hidden in the seam of his coat did not amuse them. One security man even commented on his wrist watch being the wrong time, but he explained that he often forgot to wind it up; that he wore this only item of jewellery in memory of a lost relative. As one security officer examined the newspaper he carried and rummaged through his coat pockets, the other scrutinised his packet of tobacco. He exclaimed that it was what he always bought; the same tobacco, an expensive cut, imported from the West Indies. The security man tapped the tobacco packet and looked questioningly at his accomplice until he nodded.

Once again he followed the security men along the white painted corridor to the usual meeting room. As he was nudged into the room, the elderly security man voiced his time allowance, but before he could turn to acknowledge his instruction, the door was slammed shut. Facing the door, he noticed the security guard peer through a small square window, but after a while he disappeared.

'Greetings, my friend,' a voice said aloud.

He turned toward the large glass partition, but could not see from where the voice had come.

'You'll have to forgive me today, I'm weak again,' the voice said, croaking. 'This place will be the death of me. If I don't get out soon, I'll…'

As the voice bellowed a cough, he found it an ideal opportunity to sit and observe his client.

'Mr Schroeck, err… doctor,' Daniel muttered, before being interrupted.

'Please, Daniel, its Joseph… how many times,' the doctor paused, looking around the small meeting room. 'I know I've been in here that long that your visits seem so formal, but we are one of the same, as so to speak.'

He nodded, looked to the floor and then reached into his coat pocket.

'Sir, I've managed to get more of what you ask,' he said, pulling out the packet of tobacco. 'Not that you'll get any more the way things are in here?'

The doctor laughed and told his client to ignore the security guards; to him they were nothing but men of limited intelligence; robotic slaves, trained dogs to obey whatever commands they are given. Daniel told of the stricter measures the institute now followed, but the doctor declared it was all to do with recent events. The doctor told his client to examine the morning paper of which he had asked him to bring. As he turned the pages, the doctor asked him to find an article regarding the death of a journalist. At first Daniel could not find it, but then stopped to fold a page. The doctor grinned, standing to view the newspaper through the glass.

'So he was killed in the early hours of this morning,' the doctor predicted, and then continued. 'Do the police say it was an accident?'

The doctor's client looked perplexed, staring at the photograph of a journalist pronounced dead by car crash.

'But, it's not the...' Daniel said quietly.

'What, it's not the boy... the journalist, I asked you to follow?' the doctor questioned.

'No,' Daniel said, placing the newspaper in the metal drawer, 'it's not the journalist on the photograph you *gave* me!'

The doctor pulled the drawer toward him, snatched the folded newspaper and glanced down at the picture. The victim claimed dead at the scene of the crash was indeed David Hedrick, the man who had been covering the doctor's court case; helping to get him acquitted. For a moment the doctor stood in silence, a look of disbelief on his face, but then read on. Although forensics would have to identify the body, the car was indeed registered to a David Hedrick, and that the man had not long left his parents' house.

'Shit,' the doctor whispered. 'Now my chances to get out of here have certainly gone.' He raised his voice somewhat and announced, 'What is it with young people today, don't they listen?'

Daniel looked blankly at the doctor and then pulled out a photograph.

'Do you still want me to track him?'

'Of course, you fool,' the doctor said angrily, 'he must still have the pendant!'

'Well I only asked,' Daniel said. 'Remember, I'm the only one who knows him, and of what the pendant looks like.'

'Yes, I'm sorry,' the doctor said, trying to compose himself, 'but I *need* that pendant!'

'I'm not having that *thing* on me at night… anytime at all come to that!'

'But you know it's harmless, unless…'

'Unless the evil is called,' Daniel stated. 'And *how* can you guarantee that?'

'You have my word my friend, no harm will come to you, just get me my pendant.'

'And this stuff; am I going to be rewarded for this?' Daniel asked, taking off his watch. With a hardened thumbnail he removed the back of his watch and tipped the contents on top of the packet of tobacco. Undeniably the watch was just a dummy; all the workings had been removed to ensure stuff could be enclosed. The doctor's eyes lit up, but the client pulled the tobacco packet towards him.

'You have more?' the doctor announced, pleased at the sight of the addictive substance, 'This means I can do more. Quickly put it in the packet; pass it through!'

The client noticed a face appear at the door window and so grabbed the packet of tobacco, placing inside the wafer of resin.

'I want you to help me avenge my brother's death,' Daniel announced.

'But that was year's ago,' the doctor declared, clearing his throat. 'Why now?'

Daniel described how he, his brother, and other henchmen like him, were receiving threats from villagers; people who once paid for protection, paid to join the dark circle, and now they wanted their money, their gifts, some return of wealth. The doctor stated that he did not want to avenge disbelievers, but that all of the circle will be rewarded on his release; when the circle is once again revived. For his loyalty, the doctor promised to reward Daniel and would consider his request, but Daniel also described of how followers of the circle had doubts, voicing that the power of the occult has diminished, that *he*, the master of the dark circle was powerless in jail and that he would never get acquitted for his crime; the murder of a small boy. The doctor became angry, proclaiming that all sceptics and disbelievers of the faith will, once he had reclaimed his mansion, incur his wrath. The client said he did not dispute the doctor, but that several items had already been stolen, that one of his fellow henchmen, like his brother, had been attacked whilst securing the property. The doctor became annoyed, pacing madly up and down the room, pulling at his neck-tie and collar, fingering his beard, questioning aloud his limitations. Suddenly he stopped, sat down and changed character.

'It is so good of you to get it, Daniel please push my tobacco through and don't worry,' the doctor paused, noticing a face appear again at the door window. 'Quickly, you don't have much time left.'

Daniel dropped the packet of tobacco in the drawer and pushed it forward.

'The newspapers say that your wealth is limited, doomed even; that by the time you've paid to get out of here, you won't even have anything to pay for that!'

'But we know that isn't true, don't we Daniel?' the doctor said slowly, examining the inside of the packet that he now held. After replacing the back of his watch, Daniel looked up to see the doctor run his nose along the opening of the packet and inhale. 'Nice to have some fresh, again,' he said, 'but not like the *real* cut when you're over there.'

The doctor's moment of ease was interrupted as the door of his client's room was briskly opened. Entering, the elderly security guard sharply announced that the client's allotted time was over and that he must be searched by his companion on the way out.

'Don't forget to get what's precious my dear Daniel,' the doctor said, 'no matter *how* you get it!' Daniel turned to be ushered out of the room, but looked back, hearing the doctor declare. 'You *will* be rewarded, my friend, I promise.'

The security guard pushed Daniel through the door and into the corridor. With a large grin across his face, the guard turned toward the doctor and said.

'Things are going to get a little more difficult around here, especially if your days here are to be few.'

The doctor gave the guard an intense stare and then grinned, a smile stretching the bristles on his chin.

'I'm sure your days here are *also* numbered my boy!'

# NINETEEN

IT HAD TRULY BEEN an exhausting day. With a lack of sleep following recent events, Carl felt drained. The fact that he had stopped late to examine David's computer again did not help, but he wanted to pry one more time; it may be his last chance to scrutinise the doctor's case file before the police intervened. Besides, after copying more old photographs, he had now become obsessed with research.

Now at home, Carl was compiling his own file; letters both handwritten and typed, photographs old and new, witness statements, invoices and listed appointments. He was quite proud of the visitor's agreement letter that he had altered; printing his own name over where David's had been erased. It looked quite genuine, but being unsure of when he may visit, left a space before the month of November. One thing he was sure of, he was going to use David's court attendance card, even if his attempt to modify it was not as admirable.

He sifted through documents spread across the coffee-table; placing modified documents in his briefcase and filing all others in a cardboard folder. The photographs however, he left aside and put them neatly on top of one another. Placing a photograph from David's case file in the centre of the table, Carl reached for an old photo album. Opening the album, he scanned his only collection of family photos, looking now and then at the one on the table. Somehow he recognised the man in the photograph; he was no relative but he stood close behind his father, holding a hat to his chest, a big onyx ring on his index finger. He studied the only photographs he had of his father, of the church, himself as a child, his school, college and then early days of work. There was nothing, not from his photo album, or anything from David's files to fit names to faces; surely the only person who may have answers now, would be his mother's sister Aunt Evelyn, but following arguments with his father, she had moved to Wales years ago and even so, would she *still* be alive?

Carl flinched at the sound of the doorbell and the photo album almost fell from his lap. It was not that it was quite late that evening, but he was not expecting anyone. Pondering on his thoughts, the doorbell resounded again. A shiver ran down his spine as he remembered it was only last night that David had called; not that anyone knew.

As he paced quickly through the hallway the doorbell rang again.

'Okay, okay, I'm coming, give me a minute!' Carl cried, opening the front door.

Stepping back in amazement, he noticed Sarah briskly bundle herself inside and close the door behind.

'Sorry, but I thought I saw a strange man outside, standing by his car!' Sarah announced, her handbag falling to the floor.

Carl opened the door slowly and peered out. From his apartment, the distant street lamp always played tricks with the shadows and being such a misty night, the darkness looked ever more eerie. After her experience last weekend, Carl thought of how it must have disturbed her, as he too had been agitated by the slightest sound. It was when he turned around from closing the door that his worries dissolved.

Seeing Sarah again was like a breath of fresh air; how her flowing blonde hair bounced as she lifted her handbag from the floor, her skirt tight against her thighs as she knelt, but most of all, again he was stunned by those beautiful, deep brown eyes. Dreamy, he missed the start of her conversation, but gathered that she had been unnerved by a man pacing around his car, some distance down the street. She proclaimed that he had been watching her, but Carl thought would not any man; her skin soft and tanned, her face unblemished apart from those cute small freckles around her nose. But this was his friend; a potential girlfriend and he came annoyed with himself – it was her welfare that he should be concerned with.

'It's okay, look your inside now, I've locked the door,' Carl reassured, his hands attempting to hug her. 'It's probably old Harold, he cleans his car at night – the poor guy has dementia.'

Sarah pulled away and sighed, but smiled as she removed her coat. With his arms outstretched Sarah placed her coat over one, but then wrapped her arms about his waist, before she kissed his cheek.

'Look, I'm sorry, I'm just a bit spooked today... Guess everyone's allowed one good scare for Halloween,' Sarah said, her dark eyebrows frowning as her face became serious. 'Oh my God, you must have heard; that guy from your work!' she said, covering her mouth with her hand. 'Killed in a car crash! Rachael said you worked with him!'

'David,' Carl announced, his throat going dry. 'He worked by us, Mike and me, but not with us.' He removed her hand from her mouth, trying to get her attention by looking deep into her eyes. 'Sarah, you're the only one I can trust, the only person that believes me…'

He began to explain, but by Carl's sincerity she construed what had happened.

'He was killed too wasn't he; murdered by that creature?' she cried, her eyes tearful, pausing before she set off for the living room. She turned and looked at Carl, noticing all the paperwork on his coffee-table. 'Did you dream this one? Could you have *saved* him like you did me?'

'Sarah,' he said softly, 'I'll explain everything… I know you understand, because I trust you, because…'

Although he wanted so much to tell her how much he loved her, he could not finish the sentence. It was irrelevant that he hardly knew her: horrific events triggering one night of passion, a romantic walk in the park, a loving Sunday night cuddled together. Sarah was the type of girl he had always wanted and although their meeting was bizarre, he did not want to lose her. However, his first impressions were certainly not virtuous; being crazed at her party, causing damage, endangering her and now discussing his weird past. But she was *here*; not running, not finishing the relationship before it started, or was that to come?

He approached her again and held his arm around one cheek, caressing her head until he slid it on to her neck. Although oppressed by recent events, whilst with Sarah he thought of nothing but love, hope, optimism; somehow her embrace, the sweet smell of her body made him buoyant.

Once the shadowy memories of the street dissolved and Sarah was comforted by Carl, her confidence returned and she felt a sense of resolution. Unlike his friend Mike and many other men she had befriended, Carl was not antagonistic, rude or vulgar; instead he had a dark secret, hidden away by years of neglect, only guided by his disciplinary father, and yet he had this deep compassion that she had never experienced. It was true that he was quite handsome as well; high cheekbones, dark and well groomed, silky brown hair, and eyes that twinkled bright like blue diamonds. His body was firm and lean too, but for Sarah, the exploits they had in bed that night were secondary; she wanted something more than physical pleasure, a man with character, depth and mystery. She looked up into his eyes, her shaggy hair sticking to the skin on his neck, and then noticed the pictures placed upon the coffee-table. As she started to enquire about recent events, Carl sat her down, massaging her neck and shoulders after pulling open the neck of her blouse.

'I'll do you a cup of tea, and then we'll talk', Carl said, his fingers kneading her shoulders. He stopped and pulled away, stepping towards the kitchen.

'Don't stop,' Sarah moaned. 'I like that!'

Carl called from the kitchen, elaborating on the other talents he had to offer, trying to lighten the mood, but mostly to calm his own nerves.

'What's with all the photos?' Sarah enquired, pushing the pictures about the coffee-table. 'Is this your family album?'

'No,' Carl shouted, turning to see her messing, 'well maybe, all my stuff is in that album; the one on the armchair'.

Sarah moved to the other chair, removing the album before placing it on her lap after sitting. Slowly she turned each page, looking closely to view smaller pictures.

'There's no photo of my mother, you know?' Carl announced, approaching with a cup of tea in each hand. 'But I think I may have found one.'

'Well, what are all *these* on here, then?' she asked.

'I got those from,' Carl hesitated, handing Sarah her tea. 'These are from the case file David was working on.'

'Is that the guy who was *killed* this morning?' Sarah said, 'It must have been hideous, what with being burned alive.'

Carl did not want to upset his guest with gruesome detail, but then again he gathered, she did not just visit him for tea either.

'I ask you to trust me and I think you do, but I need you to understand what really happened…'

As he had described his dream to Mike, he did the same to Sarah, but added attentive detail: firstly it was David that approached him, that he had boasted about having past information about his father and also of how David had promised to let him go with him that morning to see his client. Although Carl's act to retrieve the case file from David's computer was dishonest, Sarah thought that it was not as menacing as his voice projected. However, Carl turned his explanation to descriptions of his dream and how David had met his fate.

Smiling whilst paused at one photo of Carl in school uniform, Sarah continued flicking the pages of the photo album, but then stopped to look up at him as he told of discovering the car and David's body; that the horrible *accident* was no accident at all, but that he was murdered. Sarah's body turned cold as she asked about the creature; the one that came for her, asking if it was *that* which killed David. But Carl denied it, that he was there before it caught fire; that he had taken back the pendant after David had stolen it from his flat that night. After being attacked, and now that David had been murdered, Sarah professed that the police should know. Carl strongly rejected this idea, stating how ridiculous their story would sound; that an investigation would not only get him arrested, but probably get others killed too. He paced about the room sipping his tea, affirming that it was best to keep quiet until things were clear. Sarah stopped him in his tracks, asking to know the whereabouts of the pendant. Slowly, Carl announced that it was in his bedroom, back under the sun-lamp and safe with the light on. Sarah went quiet, her face bleached, her eyes glaring bitterly up at him. He deduced by her stare that she was annoyed with his act to reclaim the pendant; of how immoral it was to do *that* before saving David. Carl became emotional, reiterating aloud of how he was powerless to control these events; that should he dream again the owner would be murdered, so it was best to keep the pendant under the lamp as they both knew it expelled the creature.

As Carl sat down opposite her, he calmed down and told of his reason for leaving Rachael's house the one night; that consequences had to be dismissed and that the attack on the police station was foreseen. He explained how at first he did not understand his dreams and why they were so intense, that he awoke with headache, trembling, sweating, and sometime sick; but it was the outcome from the dreams that were truly monstrous.

Sarah felt nervous but sympathetic, her eyes visualising the creature again. Gripping the album tight Sarah raised the tone of her voice to proclaim that the creature had been destroyed by the light; the ultra-violet light from the lamp. Carl scorned her optimism, explaining that it was not *that* creature that killed David but something even more monstrous; that it was *death* itself. Sarah dropped the album and sat stunned as Carl slowly described the menacing figure; a rider on a hefty stallion cloaked body and head, a black veil hiding an evil face – a skull crowned in curling horns like that of a ram. Sarah went cold; goose dumps raising the hairs on her arms and legs, her eyes glazed and tearful. Suddenly Carl realised his words were frightening her and knelt down in front. He picked up the album and after placing it on the table, leant forward to comfort her. He heard her mutter some words, but was captivated by the sweet smell of her body, the soft touch of her cheek on his and her shiny blonde hair brushing against his forehead. She mumbled words again, but this time Carl heard her. In response to her question, Carl thought there was nothing they could do but keep the pendant safe and investigate the phenomenon together.

Carl turned and kissed her cheek, stroking his fingers through hers, finally holding her hands at palm with his. He assured that he would never let anything bad happen to her and that he *had* saved someone; Sarah, a girl more beautiful than in any dream he had had. She smiled in return and held his hands tight. He crouched forward to meet her lips with his, but she pulled away to talk about the photos on the table.

'Did you find anything from your poor friend's pictures?' she said, glancing at the table. 'Maybe, if its files stuff about your father, you might find a picture of your mother!'

'I've looked… there's not one there, or in my old album,' Carl stated, but frowned, thinking. 'There is one however, of that client of David's; there's a woman in a photo beside…'

Carl froze, obviously Sarah did not know that the client was indeed the Dark-man; the man he had discussed with her that Sunday morning. This was other information that he needed to clarify to Sarah before describing how this lady appeared in both pictures; one with his father and one with the Dark-man. Sarah disclosed the obvious; why would this woman appear with both men if they totally opposed each other? Carl sat bemused and silent. If it was indeed his mother, then why was she associated with *him*?

Sarah sorted through the photographs, picking at each of them to view them in their entirety. Carl pronounced how nice it would be for Sarah to come with him to help trace his family history; to visit his Aunt in Wales and maybe get some answers from the photographs she was examining. It would also be a nice break, as it was not far from the coast. Suddenly Sarah stopped and picked up one photograph.

'This is your father?' she questioned, turning the photograph toward him.

'Yes,' Carl replied, 'that's when he was made a priest of the communion.'

'Well, who's this behind?' she asked.

'I don't know, but he looks familiar, he…'

'I never forget an item of jewellery as it comes with the job,' she interrupted. 'I knew I had seen that ring before, it was on those library pictures!'

Carl looked dumfounded as Sarah stood up and throwing down the photograph declared. 'You talk of coincidence; how about *that* for coincidence?'

Carl also stood up, but looked at her perplexed.

'The guy in this photo is the one killed at the library,' she announced, raising her voice. 'I'm sure of it, he has the same ring; well at least it *looks* like the same ring!'

'And you've had these photos developed?' he asked.

'Yes, today… they're at the lab,' she announced, but then paused to think. 'No, they're in the car… in the boot I think.' Taking her handbag from the arm of the chair, Sarah took several steps towards the hallway before turning to announce, 'I'll have a look. I can always get others developed… besides only one was used for the story.'

After watching Sarah close the front door, Carl decided to fetch a half-full bottle of wine from the kitchen, before sitting down to look once more at the photos.

Outside, it was cold. Sarah hesitated, looking at her car parked down the street. Striding quickly to her car, she fumbled for her keys in her handbag, not noticing a shadow disappear from the pavement. She stopped and opened the nearside door, but realised that her camera case, equipment and satchel were in the boot. Poised at the rear of the car, she turned the key and the boot shot open. She looked inside, exhaling slow to take long breaths of cold air, trying to calm herself before reaching for the satchel. Slamming down the car boot, she turned and threw the satchel over one shoulder, but did not notice a face reflect in the car's rear window. She dithered, shivering; the cold now chilling her fingers and face, or was it that the shadows of the street unnerved her, thinking something behind was watching.

Quickly she strode toward Carl's apartment, her heels clinking against the pavement, her keys and handbag in hand, satchel hung over her shoulder. She stopped to look back at her car, thinking she noticed something. Taking another deep breath, she thought how stupid she was to let the silence and shadows of the street frighten her. However, she was certainly relieved to find that Carl had left the latch off the front door.

Inside, she shuddered as she stepped into the warmth of the lounge. Carl had already poured a generous quantity of wine in a glass on the table and his own was in hand. Usually she would not have much, but gulped at it to sooth her nerves. After noticing she stood trembling, Carl asked if she was okay, but to that she accused the cold. With another gulp of wine she smiled and sat down, pulling her satchel up beside her. Carl held the picture of the man, awaiting Sarah to sift through her satchel.

'Here's a good one,' she said, placing an enlarged photograph on the table. 'It shows his hand and face clearly.'

Carl turned the photograph around to view. Although the face was badly lacerated and he was obviously a lot older, it was indeed the man in David's picture. Carl could not help but look at the man's eyes; the stare revealing the evil that killed him, the vision of him in Carl's dream. It was not until Sarah pointed to the man's hand that he dismissed the memories. Carl reached underneath the coffee-table and pulled out a magnifying glass to examine closely the ring on his index finger. Sarah was impatient and wanted to see too, moving to sit on the arm of his chair. As she indicated from her experience of jewellery, this ring was not common and that she had seen nothing of its design; that it must be old. Carl deduced that this man must have known his father, that he too may have been a member of the church; but what use was it anyway if he was dead? As Sarah mumbled on about her friend Liz and how she may know about the symbol in the onyx ring, Carl suddenly realised that it was the library where he had found the pendant and how events had followed: the man researching the pendant, to discover its secret and power and that maybe why he got murdered. His dreams were undeniably orchestrating its owner's execution; certainly the girl talking in front of him was a witness to that. But Carl did not want to murder anyone, not even the mugger that put him in hospital; surely it was coincidence that this man was in his dream, or was it? Did he have a way to somehow control his dreams, maybe master them to only avenge bad deeds? Hearing Sarah stop, he looked up to notice her staring at him.

'You've not been listening again, have you?' she declared.

'I'm sorry, it's been a long day,' he said, rubbing his eyes. 'So much to investigate and think about, so much to…'

'And I'm boring you,' Sarah snapped, placing her glass of wine down firmly. 'Just thinking of friends that can help, especially if I'm not much use. Maybe I *should* go!'

'It's not that, my friend,' he asserted, moving his arm around her, 'you've already found one clue; this man… we know that *he* too got killed by the evil after the pendant; that he had it when trying to find out stuff.' He placed the magnifying glass down and pointed to the picture. 'If this man was researching the pendant to escape it's evil or even destroy it, maybe my father tried to stop this evil too. It may be why the Dark-man clashed with my father?'

'But this Dark-man, what has he to do with its power?' Sarah questioned and continued to elaborate. 'You've said, and we know, that it's *your* dreams that conjure this evil?'

'Indeed, and *he's* in jail,' Carl said slowly. 'Well the Wiltshire Rehabilitation Institute to be precise, and he can't do much in there now can he?'

He saw Sarah bemused and so changed the conversation.

'Look I'll explain everything… maybe we could take some time off and have a break?' he suggested, standing up to kiss her forehead. 'I've got just the place and know someone who might just have some answers.'

'A break… who… where?' she asked, standing to look in his eyes.

Carl explained that the only member of the family he had left, lived in Wales, in a cottage near the coast, not far from Tenby; the town his now deceased work colleague had visited. Of what he remembered, his Aunt Evelyn was the youngest of three sisters; Elizabeth being the eldest and his mother Eleanor being in-between. As the eldest had died before he was born and that his mother died giving birth to him, there was only this Aunt who may have answers.

At first Carl thought Sarah was captivated; a gleam of interest sparkling from her dark brown eyes, but she turned away and ridiculed the trip, saying that it may be a waste of time and he would end up even more distort. Carl announced he did not care, that he had been told to take some holiday. Besides, should their trip be unproductive, at least he had spent time with her. She was the one thing he wanted most of all; a beautiful girl on which to build a future. Sarah smiled, indeed she was very flattered, especially by Carl's authenticity, but there was something holding her back; it *was* something she could delay, but for how long? Gradually the passion in her heart overruled her mind and she agreed, but stated she needed time to arrange things.

Carl danced around her, emphatic like a small boy on Christmas morning and then stopped, standing face to face with her, grasping her hands, pulling them up to his lips. Powerfully he kissed her fingers and hugged her before holding her face in his hands. He promised her that she would not regret her decision and that they would have a great time. Sarah stood motionless and watched in bewilderment to how he reacted; she had never seen any man get so excited; just to spend a few days with her. Inside, she felt mixed feelings. Undeniably she felt drawn to this man and his mysterious past; a man like no other she had met, but she knew someday soon, she would have to tell him.

She smiled, gave Carl a powerful embrace and before walking to the hallway, grabbed her handbag. Half way she turned and pulling out a pen wrote a telephone number on the rear of a business card. As she handed it to him, she explained that it was her professional photography agent and that it was her own number on the back. Carl's heart raced with exhilaration as she turned to open the door, telling him to ring her tomorrow. Kissing the card, he turned and strode eagerly back to his glass of wine.

Outside, it was even colder than before, but her emotions to how she had pleased Carl comforted her. Her feelings of resolve were uninterrupted until reached the car, where whilst silent, she thought she heard a noise. Whether it was the effects of the wine, or that her affection for Carl was uplifting, she chose to ignore the darkness of the street and opened the car door. It was not until she got in and felt the cold of the upholstery, that she realised the door had been unlocked since she fetched the satchel. She paused before placing the key into the ignition and then looked in the rear view mirror. Reflected and behind her was a white, porcelain face; a mask, one of a clown with rosy cheeks, a large red nose and big eyes. She shuddered before trying to escape the car, but the mask behind moved forward, its green hair falling over broad shoulders. As she turned to view the evil face, she felt a cloth cover her mouth. She struggled, but found her body pinned back against the seat. Seconds passed as she fought, but gradually her vision blurred and all went black.

He was just about to pour another helping of wine when Carl heard the doorbell. For a second he sat perplexed, but then realised after looking at Sarah's satchel, that she had forgotten it. As he grabbed it and made his way to the hallway, the doorbell rang again. Thinking Sarah was unnerved by the shadows in the street, he opened the door without concern.

It was not Sarah that charged through the doorway, but a tall figure of a man, dressed in a long, black overcoat. As Carl was thrown back he could not help but notice a large face of a clown; a Halloween mask covering the man's face and a wig of frizzy, green hair. Shoved to the ground, Carl saw the man's figure pass him and as he turned, a fist struck his face.

Carl's vision returned as he crawled along trying to find his feet. At first he could only pull himself along on hands and knees, but staggered to his feet as he reached the end of the hallway. From the entrance to the kitchen he could hear a voice, swearing, shouting, and then noticed a torch light flickering about his bedroom. Steadying himself against the wall, Carl manoeuvred himself enough to peer into his bedroom.

At first he could see nothing but a torch light circling the room, but as it stopped and shone on his cabinet, he noticed the tall intruder; wearing a dark overcoat, collars pulled high and his face completely obscured by a mask. Knocking over the sun-lamp, a gloved hand snatched the pendant from the cabinet.

'How quaint, a sun-lamp,' the intruder's voice muttered, as he pulled out a wallet from his breast pocket.

Carl lunged forward, punching the man's face, cracking the mask and dislodging the wig, but the man merely flinched. However, it was enough to force the man to drop the pendant and the wallet he was placing it inside. Carl reached to grab the pendant, but felt a blow meet his stomach, sending him sprawled against the foot of the bed. In pain, he turned and noticed the intruder grasp the pendant from the floor before making his exit. With an outstretched leg, Carl tripped the intruder and saw him fall into the lounge. But this was not enough, as by the time he was on his feet, the intruder swung at him with a flick-knife. With fortune the blade missed Carl's face but entered the cuff of his woollen jumper, pinning his wrist to the architrave of the door. As he tugged and tore at his sleeve, the intruder, with pendant in hand, found time enough to vacate his flat. By the time Carl got out his front door, the intruder had disappeared down the street. Carl was furious and sped after him, but the cold froze his breath and he stopped in pain; he could do nothing but observe shadows. He leaned forward, his stomach in pain, looking back toward his flat. Yards away and still parked at the side of the street, was Sarah's sports car; the one he had seen at the library. Quickly, he ran over.

Sprawled across both front seats of the car was Sarah, unconscious but unharmed. After opening the car door, he pulled out her limp body. He grimaced in pain as he carried her toward his apartment and was certainly relieved to place her on his bed. He looked about his apartment; appalled that it had been invaded and that he too had been assaulted. But his concern was for Sarah and after realising she was unconscious but not hurt, he went to lock her car and collect her valuables.

On his return, he attended to Sarah, loosening the neck buttons of her blouse and removing her shoes. After placing a wetted flannel over her forehead, he began to tidy his bedroom. Picking up the toppled sun-lamp from the floor, he noticed the intruder's wallet and so retrieved it. Examining its contents, he folded open a drawing of the pendant, a picture of Carl and pulled out a visiting card for the Wiltshire Rehabilitation Institute. Looking over to ensure Sarah was okay, Carl returned to the lounge to nurse his bruising and to scrutinise his findings more closely.

# TWENTY

'Has it started?' Carl shouted, pushing his way through the crowd.

'Has what started?' the doorman asked.

'The court case for Doctor Schroeck; I think its court three?'

'Yes, but you've missed most of it; they're just waiting on the jury's decision,' the doorman replied, holding Carl back to request identification. 'If you want to go in I'll need to see some id?'

'Haigh and Reece, freelance journalists; I just need to report the outcome!' Carl announced holding out his revised visiting pass and his business card.

As the doorman waved him through two large double doors and pointed towards the press gallery, he was jostled by several people, all trying to enter the court room. Like the people in front, he was searched and again requested to show identification by security men, before making way to the press gallery. To his surprise there were only a small number of journalists, but the public gallery was full; some members who entered with him had to stand alongside security men.

It was all too chaotic; a man stumbling in front of him, obscuring his view as an announcement broadcast that they all stand. Obscured by the man in front and two security men, Carl could only make out members of the jury walking to their seats. Somewhere to his left he heard voices, followed by

241

more instructions. It was not until he sat that he saw the judge; a skinny, elderly man, his wig not far different in colour to his natural white hair. But then Carl looked to his right and then up, towards the dock. It was as though the man had just appeared.

There stood the doctor, the Dark-man as he had named him, and although quite tall, he stood just like any other man, except Carl now knew the face; his long and pale expression, those dark protruding eyebrows, but most of all his piercing dark eyes, black as night.

Carl leaned side to side, trying to observe him more clearly, but the doctor shuffled forward, his concentration focused on the judge and the words he was saying. Suddenly a voice bellowed out from the public gallery, calling for the doctor to be hung. It was when the doctor looked around, distracted by the commotion, that he looked straight at him. Carl went cold, his mind thumping, his heart racing; he had not seen those devilish eyes since he was a child. For a moment Carl thought that the doctor had recognised him, but looked back toward the judge, muttering words of disgust. The judge demanded silence and requested that order be resumed.

Gradually the court room went silent and after his proclamations, the judge looked toward the jury to request a verdict. After standing and removing his spectacles, an elderly black man announced that the jury's decision was not resolute; that without new evidence, the jury were undecided. The judge turned and facing the doctor, broadcast that with the necessity of fresh evidence, the case be postponed until further notice. From this, the court room burst with noise and activity.

Accompanied by two security guards, the doctor was led down from the dock and escorted along the aisle towards his defence lawyer. Suddenly from out the public gallery with bible held high, lunged a woman shouting words as she accosted the doctor. Carl noticed the evil in the doctor's eyes as he scowled whilst pushing the woman aside. The woman, although restrained by security guards, continued her words of hatred towards the doctor; asking how he could live after brutally murdering her son, but with such wealth, would undoubtedly walk free. Carl gathered that this woman was indeed Alex's mother but hardly recognised her; she had certainly neglected herself in years of mourning. He felt so pitiful that he wanted to approach her and maybe uplift her spirits, but Carl thought it may evoke past events and stir bad memories. As he watched his departed friend's mother get pulled away, the rest of the court room busied; people of the public gallery forcing open the double doors and rushing out, giving him no choice but to wait.

Eventually outside, Carl brushed down his coat from the bustle of the crowd and noticed an attractive woman up the corridor. Like Sarah, she was athletic but slightly slimmer, her black skirt tight above her knees as she stooped forward, holding a Dictaphone aloft, trying to record dialogue from the prosecution lawyer. Carl became intrigued; although he had witnessed the verdict, he had not learned enough about the doctor's case. Carl approached the crowd hoping to learn more, maybe this girl had heard something about the adjournment period; the date on which he could attend again. Suddenly, the crowd sprang backward, rendering the girl unstable, her high heels collapsing beneath her feet.

Carl was just in time to catch her as she tripped. Cushioning her back with one hand and holding her arm with the other, he noticed her eyes open wide with alarm, but looking straight up at him. He balanced his weight to counteract her fall and then steadied her.

'Thanks my friend,' the girl said, then raised her voice at the crowd. 'I'm glad someone's got some manners around here!'

Carl admired her glossy dark hair as her small, flushed face turned to him and smiled.

'I saw you struggling,' Carl pronounced, 'and that's quite a crowd!'

'Yes, indeed,' the girl said, replacing her shoe and straightening her clothes. 'I was just trying to get some more evidence, but this case has been going on years.' She paused to comb her hair with her fingers. 'Think I might give up on this one… try something else!'

'My name is Carl,' he said outstretching his hand. 'I work for Haigh and Reece, Bristol, you may have heard of them?'

'Oh well look at me,' she said, rolling her eyes, 'moaning at *them* for not having any manners… and here's me not introducing myself!'

Carl stood absorbed, not listening intently; but looked upon her pretty face. Like Sarah she had cute, small freckles round her nose, her eyes lighter brown, but her skin looked rough, her face long with prominent cheek bones. Although he found her quite sensual, she had not the quality of allure that he found irresistible with Sarah.

'I'm Amanda... Amanda Burley, I work for a local newspaper,' she announced shaking his hand, 'not that *this* story is of any interest around here.'

'You know a lot about this case?' Carl asked.

'Well enough just to satisfy the boss, you know… just collect enough to get by,' she said, pulling him away from the crowd toward a drinks machine. 'I'm having a coffee, do want one?'

Carl agreed and after receiving their drinks they moved to a quiet area and sat on a bench below an elongated window. Carl sipped at the hot liquid, quite taken in by the girl's interest in him as she asked about his work and where he lived. He smiled and to her questioning, replied mostly with one word answers, but again he became distracted.

'What do you know of the doctor?' Carl asked, taking the cup from her hand as she pulled a chocolate bar out from a flimsy handbag.

'Can't smoke in here,' the girl said, pulling a face, 'Guess this is the best other alternative, not that I have many… do you?'

'Do I what?'

'Smoke… then again I'm trying to cut down, so expensive nowadays.'

'Sometimes,' Carl said slowly, but was trying to dig for information, 'this case, how long have you been reporting it?'

'Not long really, I had to read up a lot about it,' she replied. 'The guy who previously followed the case took early retirement.'

'This doctor, Joseph Schroeck… how long he's been in an institution?'

'Well at least ten years or more, but has compassionate

leave to ensure his property is secure and that,' the girl explained, 'not that he should have any, after such a crime.'

The girl looked at him expectantly, thinking his next question regarded the doctor's crime, but Carl enquired differently.

'How long before he's acquitted?'

'Well apparently he's been on good behaviour, but has funny habits and erratic behaviour.' Chewing her chocolate bar and taking a gulp of coffee she continued. 'And unless the prosecution find new evidence that supports the doctor's original conviction, then soon he could walk free.'

'But the murder weapon had his prints all over it, didn't it?' Carl contested.

'Yes, but wouldn't any gardening tools of yours; have your prints on it that is and besides,' she paused to sip her coffee, 'the defence has found new methods that have analysed the wooden handle…'

'And…' Carl edged toward her, curious.

'Well leather particles have been sandwiched between the grains in the wood… particles that could well be originally from a glove. The defence lawyer suggests that these belonged to the murderer… the convict who escaped?' She looked questionably at Carl before he nodded. 'Well they say that *he* most likely planted it in the doctor's green house to frame him.'

'So they think it was this convict, after all?' Carl reflected.

'Well, the doctor has had many other disputes, but these were mainly with villagers who didn't like the meetings he held.

'Meetings?' Carl questioned, looking baffled.

'House gatherings, garden parties and social events for his society; apparently some people used to attend who were of substantial wealth or had social significance.'

'What do you mean... his society?'

'The doctor was infamous in his research... areas such as psychology, astrology, or was it astronomy?' the girl scratched her head, questioning herself. 'And in history, religion and so forth. Some, like that crazed woman in there, professed that he ran some spiritualistic society... dealings in the occult and all that crap!'

'You mean witchcraft and black magic?' Carl queried.

'Well it's not been confirmed and my investigations have been unsuccessful, but my colleague who retired stated that a group of villagers, years ago that is and before the doctor's arrest, found evidence of him practising the Black Art. However, the doctor proclaimed that his valued books were of what he attained through research both home and abroad; that certain rooms of his property were dedicated to astrology, clairvoyance and his late mother's interest in tarot cards and fortune-telling.'

'You seem to know your subject,' Carl urged.

'Well, it was my colleague who did most of the research and then left it to me,' she said and holding her hands aloft, declared, 'I'm just a puppet; pulled by the strings he made!'

Carl laughed and came quite aroused by her wit, not only was she determined and methodical, but assertive and enlightening. However, he could see by her erratic movements that she was quite nervous; either by being with him or in fact in need of her cigarette.

'Do you want to go outside for a cigarette?' Carl asked, standing up.

'Yes, okay,' she agreed, 'but I have another case to report on in less than an hour.'

'Blimey,' Carl asserted, 'they do like to work you hard!'

'Not really, I just pick the cases that coincide on the same day,' she stated, smiling, 'after you've reported one, well they all seem the same.'

She strode over to the staircase and before descending, turned to face him.

'Come on then, I'm not standing outside alone to have one!'

Carl followed, watching her slim figure bounce rigidly down the flight of stairs, her long black hair falling over her eyes.

Outside, it was not the fact that the daylight lightened her dark hair, bringing out a lovely tint of burgundy, or that her eyes shone bright brown in the sunlight, but the way she stood provocatively that aroused him; beckoning him to light up her cigarette. For some reason he felt guilty, but *what* was he guilty of; sharing a conversation with another journalist, discussing the doctor's case; trying to acquire information that Sarah would not know? Indeed, after the head rush of not having a cigarette for a while, he did feel drawn towards her, but he pictured Sarah's smile and how it was gorgeous and genuine, this girl however, smirked with mischievous exploitation.

With his mind busied with the court case and his recent female acquaintance, he did not notice people talking on the comfy chairs in the reception area. It was when he leaned over to see if Shirley was working in the back office that he heard his name called. Looking around, he did not see Mike until he approached.

Behind him, sitting and chatting on chairs were Rachael and Sarah. As Carl approached the girls, Sarah stood up, ran over to him and after wrapping her arms about him, kissed him firmly on the cheek. Although he had looked after her that morning after last night's attack, she had not seen him all day. Kissing him, Carl became embarrassed; it was the first time Sarah had shown affection to him in front of his friends.

Whilst Carl attended court, Sarah had found things to do and had completed most of her tasks, but the grimacing events of the previous night had frightened her and without Carl for company, she drove to Rachael's house. It was there that she revealed what had happened last night; that a man dressed in an evil clown mask had chloroformed her in her car, entered Carl's flat and assaulted him to steal the pendant. As Carl had requested, she concealed their secret about the pendant and the evil that it summoned. However with Rachael's rectitude, the two girls had, unknowingly to Carl, reported the incident to the police and completed a statement. The police had also photocopied the drawing of the pendant which Carl found in the intruder's wallet.

Mike joked at first, asking Sarah to leave him alone, but as Rachael joined her side Mike asked them both seriously if they were okay. As they agreed, Sarah saw Carl look at Rachael. She noticed how wide his eyes opened; excited at

249

seeing her legs in skimpy shorts that she had used recently for the gym. Mike cut her observations short, ridiculing the pendant, interpreting it as the opposite of a good luck charm and that they were best without it, but Sarah quickly interrupted him and guided Carl to the office window. To her request, he pointed to the desk of which was his and she smiled before complementing him.

Mike moved forward and interrupting them disclosed the news that he had heard; that Sarah had agreed on visiting Carl's Aunt in Wales, so the two could research Carl's past, to discover more about his father. Carl looked quickly at Sarah and then back at Mike, acknowledging that they had arranged to take the trip soon. At first Mike declared it as an excuse for a dirty weekend, but Rachael intervened, silencing him with a punch on the arm, stating they both deserved a break. Mike agreed that although the outcome of their endeavour may be disappointing, he thought that his friend could certainly do with a holiday. He thought of past events and how these had somehow oppressed Carl, inciting this obsession about his father and maybe some time with such a beautiful girl would benefit him. From his reaction and looking Sarah up and down, Rachael gathered that her fiancé was quite jealous. Mike confessed maybe he was, but that he was happy for his friend and after winking at Sarah, requested that she be gentle with him. Laughing and reaching up to snuggle her head in Carl's neck, Sarah turned to Mike announcing she would. In reply to Rachael's questions, Sarah revealed that she had finished her last assignment and booked several days off work in advance, but as far as Mike knew, Carl had not.

Quickly Carl excused himself from the group and opening the office doors walked briskly to the Editor's office, where after collecting a form, sat at his desk. As the girl's watched Carl, Mike faced Sarah and explained quietly of his friend's obsession with researching a client of their late colleague and that trying to uncover his father's past may prove futile. He also revealed, that should they go soon, Carl would not be able to attend David's funeral. Rachael snapped, declaring that it was Carl's decision and that at least Sarah was prepared to help him, whatever the outcome; indeed Mike had done nothing but ridicule his friend's wish.

Turning away from Sarah, Mike looked through the glass and watched Carl take his completed holiday form into the Editor's office. He then stepped towards the chairs and sitting in silence, looked at Rachael whilst brushing back his blonde hair.

# TWENTY – ONE

Up until now, Carl and Sarah had found their way with relative ease by passing major towns and cities and staying on main roads. It was not that they had exhausted their conversation, but Carl avoided discussion as the roads were snaking and narrow. At one point Sarah caught sight of the sea and annoyed Carl, shouting and jumping about like an excited school girl. But he ignored her as he did not want to argue; this trip seemed like their first date and it was the best chance he had to get to know her.

From sighting the coast, the road headed inland and the car got caught behind an agricultural vehicle. Carl became worried as the radiator started to overheat and kept trying to past the vehicle, but he knew that the winding roads were dangerous. After about a mile or two, Carl pulled in a lay by to check the radiator and to rectify directions. Surely his Aunt's residence was not far as it was positioned on the outskirts of a small town, several kilometres south of Bridgend. With help from a local map and Sarah's requests for directions, both were back on the road and within half an hour had entered his Aunt's village.

Following the name of the road indicated, Carl drove slowly up an incline until Sarah pointed out the cottage name; Celtic Mist. The first thing that Sarah loved about the property was its pebbledash walls, white as snow but enshrouded with the greenery of ivy. Small, square windows appeared like little eyes, decorated in black eye shadow and the dark slant between curtains resembling the pupil of each eye. Below the bedroom windows, stood a dark red narrow door that resembled a rosy, cold nose. This was obviously the front of the cottage as it was decked with a large, brass knocker that shone in the lowering sunlight. Leading up to the door from the road, fencing and trellis arched up and down, decorated by flowers of all types. This made the cottage shine out amongst its surroundings and providing it belonged to Carl's Aunt, Sarah could not wait to see inside.

Although eager to explore such an old-fashioned building, Sarah stepped apprehensively up the path behind Carl, but looked to admire the garden. She thought it unusual for such flowers to bloom so late in the year, but the air here was mild, although somewhat brisk and salty.

She almost stumbled over him as Carl stopped to ring the bell, but after no reply reached forward, keen to use the heavy brass knocker, now recognised as a lion's head. As she started to slam the knocker against its back plate, a yelp resounded on the other side of the door. Sarah jumped in surprise and grabbed Carl's shoulders, almost pulling him off balance. The barking stopped for a moment as a voice called the dog's name. Amongst the barking, Carl heard a voice and the sliding of a chain. Slowly the shiny red door opened inward and through the opening he could see the light blue eyes of an elderly woman, peering at him. Suddenly they disappeared, replaced by the bushy white hair of her head as she ordered the dog to be quiet. Carl called his Aunt's name and her eyes peered again, squinting as she asked who was there. Carl repeated again that it was her nephew; that he had phoned several times prior coming, but had no reply. After a safety chain was removed, the door opened but his Aunt retreated, trying to calm her dog. Carl stepped into the hallway but saw his Aunt near the back, shutting the kitchen door; preoccupied with restraining her dog. He could hardly hear her questions as he tried to introduce Sarah, but as she led them into the lounge, the dog silenced.

At first his Aunt looked at them strangely and asked several questions one after the other, but Carl reiterated that he had phoned both twice last night and the night before. His Aunt questioned the phone number and so he handed it to her; written on a letter of his father's. She agreed that the number was correct and removing her reading spectacles, assumed that she must have been at her social club where she goes practically every night to meet her friends, play bingo and have a port and lemon.

Sarah smiled, looking upon the old woman as endearing; a cute but fragile lady, lonely but happy in her beautiful little home, adorned with ornaments and antiquated furniture. As she had not seen one for a long time, Sarah looked admirably at the coal fire and its ornate surround, almost disregarding Carl's introduction. Sarah moved forward and whilst announcing herself, removed a bottle of wine from a bag and described it as a goodwill gesture. On thanking Sarah for her hospitality his Aunt told of how they should simply call her Eve; that it was nice to have visitors, as mostly she was home alone. She told of her friends who she socialised with and how the centre had its own mini-bus that brought her back home late. Carl and Sarah found it all comforting, especially when Evelyn presented them with home-made fruit cake and a cup of tea, but as his Aunt questioned the reason for their visit, Carl turned serious.

He told of how he and Sarah met, but left out the horrors that followed the pendant. He described how his work colleague had pictures of his father and maybe of his mother; that he had been perusing a client's case before he died, that this client had pictures of his father's past and that he wanted to know about his mother. Strangely, apart from the death of his work colleague, his Aunt did not waver or grimace at Carl's history of events, but in seeing her nephew knew he wanted answers about his past.

Whilst offering biscuits from a large ceramic jar, she revealed that after being the only sister left, she knew that one day her sister's son would want answers, especially as her sister had died giving him birth. For an hour she told of her two sisters; Elizabeth being the oldest, Eleanor being Carl's mother and of how they grew up. She declared that Elizabeth was the strongest and most intelligent and that Evelyn was stupid in comparison. Eleanor, Carl's mother however, was a very quiet woman and although she had been ill a good deal of her life, she had a strong mind and was known to have second sight. Carl and Sarah looked at one another but asked no questions. Evelyn presumed by their reaction that her nephew new nothing of Eleanor's gift; that she could predict the occurrence of events, often moved objects whilst asleep and talked to deceased family members. Sarah carefully probed, repeating stories and research that she had heard from Liz about psycho kinesis, extrasensory perception, fortune telling and séances, but discredited them as unproven and that many people were sceptical. Aunt Evelyn was absolute in her beliefs; her family had many séances in the past and it was Eleanor's way to ensure loved ones were at peace.

For a while Carl and Sarah sat quiet. Sarah did not want to enquire too much as she thought her questions may disturb her host. Carl was busy thinking of his mother; although he had never seen her, he pictured some fortune-telling gypsy, a mind bent, mystical old woman, like witches portrayed in books and films.

It was as though Evelyn had read Carl's mind, as adamantly she pronounced that her sister was nothing but the best sister she could have had; that she used her gift to contact people, to help them in time of grief, to comfort the bereaved. She asked Carl, not to think of his mother as some fabricated, money grabbing clairvoyant, but as a woman who loved him deeply, that his mother's love still lives within him, that her parting bought him into the world. Sarah was taken aback by Aunt Evelyn's words and found herself being drawn to Carl even more; this was the reason for his aptitude for kindness, his thoughtfulness and courteous manner. But how could his mother have any effect on Carl's temperament; it was his father that bought him up?

Carl and Sarah sat quiet, looking at one another whilst eating cake. As Evelyn got up and slowly made her way to a writing bureau, she commented on how Carl looked a little like Eleanor. She pulled out a photograph and returning to her armchair, held it close to her heart.

'Carl, this is your mother, my dear,' she said, her voice weakening as she handed him the photograph. 'This was taken a couple of years before you were born. I have some others but they're mainly of school, or of grandparents.'

'Yes, it is her,' he proclaimed, positioning the picture for Sarah to see. 'She's about the same age as in *that* picture… the one with the Dark-man'

'Yes, indeed it is,' Sarah said, seeing some resemblance to him, noticing Carl's eyes swell. Sarah turned to view Aunt Evelyn, noticing her eyes open wide and her body shiver.

'Dark... man?' Evelyn questioned slowly.

'Yes, Aunt, a doctor... I named him the Dark-man as he was horrible and disliked my father,' Carl explained and taking Sarah's bag, pulled out a folder to search for the picture. 'He appears in the only photograph I have of my mother.'

He placed the photograph he had got from David's case file down on the table.

Evelyn talked slowly, describing what she knew of the Dark-man, that although he was an intellectual and astute man, he was also corrupt, dealing deviously with antiquities and items of notable value; that he used cunning and blackmail to sway people of society, wealthy people, so that his circle would not only have thirteen members, but remain secret. Whilst Carl looked longingly at his Aunt's picture, Sarah wanted Evelyn to clarify the significance of thirteen members. Indeed, she had some idea from Liz why a society should have a particular number of members, but was terribly inquisitive. At first, Evelyn conveyed that the doctor had an astrological society, something she said that he was wrong to confuse with science; that spiritual things are not just black and white, that are indeed, difficult to understand. She then discussed the doctor's deceased mother and her prior interest in clairvoyance, but Sarah's question had not been answered.

Carl broke his silence and pushing the case file photograph towards her, asked for an explanation to why his mother would be standing by this man. Evelyn stared at Sarah, her piercing blue eyes showing anger, but suddenly changed character and began to smile. She disclosed that Carl's mother was so gifted and how the doctor wanted her to be part of his society, that he enticed her with jewellery, influenced her with his knowledge, even promising her land on which to build. At first she and Elizabeth did not know of Eleanor's secret; lying to them about her whereabouts when really she was under his influence, pretending he could relieve her sickness. Carl interrupted his Aunt, questioning her interpretation of the word, influence. Evelyn expressed that although Eleanor had a strong psychic mind, she was also easily influenced; to kind in trusting people, a little like the mind of a child. Evelyn described of how one night after Eleanor had pretended to go to bed, that she had been picked up later that night by a priest; her clothes soaking wet from rain, her shoes muddied and that Elizabeth had argued with her, pleading her not to visit the doctor again.

Holding up the picture of his father with his mother beside him, Carl ascertained that this is how they met. Evelyn frowned, looked sadly at the picture and then back at Carl. For a while all was quiet until Sarah encouraged the story to go forward, asking if both the priest and Eleanor were happy. Evelyn agreed, a smile brightening up her troubled face. It was under the priest's guidance that Eleanor came part of the church and that she and Elizabeth also joined the communion, enjoying happy days of good will, charity events and running school harvests. As his Aunt told of their harvest festivals, of lighting fires, dancing to live music and praising mother earth for her reaps of healthy crop, Carl realised this was the event he had seen as a child. He smiled and stood up; praising his Aunt's cottage and that Mother Nature was indeed looking after her healthy flowers.

His Aunt laughed, stating that it was hard work and careful nurturing that made her flowers look bright. Interrupting, Sarah was curious and asked of when Carl's mother married the priest and what became of their association with the Dark-man, but heard the dog bark and scratch at the door. Carl joked that maybe the dog was hungry, but changed the conversation, voicing that it was getting late and that they needed a place to stop the night.

Evelyn conveyed how nice it was to see them and that she enjoyed their company so much, she offered to put them up for the night. She announced that if Carl could clear some stuff out the spare room, that they could stay. However, Carl and Sarah smiled at one another when his Aunt stated that Carl would have to sleep downstairs. Carl thanked her for her kind offer but wanted a hotel, maybe somewhere to photocopy his Aunt's picture.

As Evelyn described some of the places they could try, she let in her dog, hearing it scratch at the door. The small, King Charles spaniel ran straight to Sarah, barking and whining, jumping up her khaki trousers, wanting her immediate attention. As she cupped its face and rubbed its ears, it sneezed, before scampering over to sniff Aunt Evelyn and Carl. It soon returned to Sarah, who after repeatedly fussing the animal asked his name. Evelyn stated how her dog had taken to Sarah and that his name was Sandy, as this was much his colour, along with white. Again Evelyn reiterated that they could stay and disclosed how nice it would be tomorrow, but Carl declined. As he heard his Aunt warn of evening rain, Carl held Evelyn's arm and promised to visit her before they went back; to discuss more about his parents and to return her photograph.

Sarah was baffled. By now they should have seen the public house that Aunt Evelyn had described. She looked again at the map, but it had nothing but major roads. Carl turned the car around to go back as this junction would take him back to the main road. It was not just Sarah's feeble attempt to find the place that annoyed Carl, but by now the sun had set and it would soon be dark. Not only that, but after noticing the car's temperature light blink, he definitely saw steam coming out from the engine. At first it was just mist, but as they drove slowly to find the Hangman's Tree, it got worse; steam started to pour out from engine, through bonnet vents, and up over the windscreen. Carl cursed as his control became awkward, the car jumping erratically, the engine wheezing and noisy. Decisively there was nothing else to do but pull over. Sarah looked aghast; it was not just the thought of being stuck in the middle of nowhere that troubled her, but that they must have passed the place not so long ago. Sarah got out and started moaning aloud. Her action provoked Carl and so he joined her, after which they soon began to squabble.

As a gentleman walked past, he heard the couple quarrel and mention the public house of which they were after. Luckily he knew the area and acknowledged that the public house was only some distance away. He asserted that indeed many strangers miss the entrance due to the high, ivy covered walls and overhanging willow trees. Sarah and Carl silenced, hearing the man suggest they push the vehicle to the car park and that he would help them. Carl agreed and thanking the man, wound down the window in order to steer the car while pushing. As the man declared that the landlord's brother was a mechanic, another man joined them, offering to help push the vehicle. Carl agreed and announced that on reaching the car park, he would by them both a drink.

Sarah released the car, stepping aside to allow the men to push the car faster. She heard Carl presume that the car had just a water leak of which he could probably fix in the morning. As she caught them up, they had entered the car park and Carl was guiding it to an open spot. Rather out of breath, Carl thanked the men and stated he would join them inside. Sarah, after gathering particular belongings from the car, locked the doors and followed Carl into the entrance of the old Georgian building.

Inside, as Sarah watched Carl order drinks at the bar, she heard one man refuse Carl's offer of an alcoholic drink; he proclaimed to be soon on duty, but Sarah saw no uniform or briefcase of clothing. However, as she heard the landlord regret not having any rooms vacant until tomorrow, her thoughts was of refuge and so searched for the public telephone, announcing that she would call Carl's Aunt. Again the landlord apologised but declared, although it was quite late for holiday season, how busy he was.

At first the little girl made Sarah jump, darting around the hallway, pretending to be on horseback, but then stopped in front of her. Sarah enquired to the location of the public telephone and as the little girl pointed, she noticed her small angelic, round face, obscured by long blonde hair, thick and straight, apart from where it stuck to her mouth. She thanked the young girl, presumed to be the landlord's daughter and dialled the number Carl had given her.

On her return to the bar, Sarah heard Carl engrossed in conversation. The landlord proposed that should Carl leave the keys with him, that his brother could check the vehicle next morning. Carl was unsure and went to assess the car's damage himself. Watching Carl walk out the room, Sarah sat at the bar and looked upon his unfinished pint of lager. As they had no transport to drive to Aunt Evelyn's cottage, Sarah thought it an apt time to order a glass of wine. She messed inside her handbag to note the amount of cash in her purse and reviewed her appearance in a cosmetic mirror. Thanking her for Carl's hospitality, the first man had politely said his goodbyes before leaving, but the other man, who had refused a drink, sat looking at her from behind, reflected in her handheld mirror. It was not that he unnerved her, as he looked quite astute, well dressed and conservative, but his large green eyes kept prying at her as if he wanted to ask something.

Carl returned and interrupting Sarah's observation, told her about the car; that it was more than just a split hose that leaked water, but it was something else more serious and would indeed require a mechanic. Sarah frowned and asked the landlord about a room again, but he denied having any until his attic room would come available tomorrow. Forgetting their luggage in the boot, Carl and Sarah requested the services of the landlord's brother and handed him the car keys. Realising they must soon make a move to get to his Aunt before she went out, they quickly finished their drinks.

Carl asked for directions to his Aunt's cottage and the landlord looked pensively down his long, roman nose and through his spectacles at the address, but denied the whereabouts of the property. As he retreated to a back room in order to ask a barmaid, the man whom Sarah had watched, moved closer to them along the bar. He asked them of the address to where they wanted to go, but was interrupted by the barmaid who knew of the street. As she gabbled on in her Welsh accent, Sarah tried to note down directions, but failed. Sarah handed her a pen and paper and to their request the girl drew a map; arrows directing them from an old church to a shortcut she knew through woodland and on over fields to a main road. Carl looked up with concern, but the girl smiled, stating she had used it many a time. But it was already dark, Sarah proclaimed. The girl shrugged her shoulders, suggesting they take a torch, stick close to the path and watch out for low mist.

It was not that the dark looked menacing, but after seeing the shadows of the old church and its graveyard, Sarah was spooked, gripping on to Carl's coat, following the torch light beam down from his hand. As the barmaid's map instructed, they had followed the stone wall alongside the graveyard, out an arched gate and on to a small field. The next move was to follow a path that meandered through the woodland and as the girl indicated, stick close to it or they could easily lose their way. In the flickering torch light Sarah stared at the crude drawing of Aunt Evelyn's cottage and wished soon that they would be there.

Walking across the field, Carl dropped the torch into long grass. With its light obscured, the landscape surrounding them darkened and Sarah panicked, hurrying to pick it up. It was when she turned to hand it back to Carl that she noticed he was quite distraught. As he covered his ears and closed his eyes tight, she could see he was in pain. Answering her concern, he told of nausea; that he felt like vomiting and that a high-pitch noise resound his ears. But all was quiet Sarah asserted, in fact it was too quiet, nothing but daunt silence. Carl fell to his knees, his vision of the field and distant woodland nothing but unsteady shadows, his mind aching, his ears deafened by the same unearthly sound he had heard at the superstore and in hospital. Sarah's concerns were now increasing; she could not steady him and hold on to the torch. With strength strained from her emotion she pulled Carl to his feet and walked him along, holding the torch with the arm that supported him. After a while she stopped to rest and trying her best to ignore the dark of the trees, comforted Carl, wiping his face with her soft handkerchief.

After a minute or two, Carl revealed that he was feeling better and holding Sarah's face in his hands, managed to kiss her forehead before hugging her tight. She whinged at being squeezed tight, but smiled, feeling overwhelming affection. He looked at her again, noticing the light of her hair dance in the torch light, looking upon her beautiful face; concerned but smiling. He turned and grasped Sarah tight, pacing slowly at first but announced he was becoming strong again and that he felt fine. Sarah was glad, thankful that her partner now encouraged her on, for when they reached the woodland, the pathway in looked ominous.

After a while Sarah's nerves settled, thinking that in the torch light, the woodland floor looked the same everywhere, but she kept her head down, evading the gloom between the trees. For some time they sauntered their way through the woodland, Sarah holding on to Carl's arm, following the torch light flicker along the path below. Suddenly as Carl's foot snagged on bracken below, he tripped and Sarah almost tumbled with him. He felt a cold wetness around his legs and realised he had fallen into a large muddy puddle. As he cursed and beckoned Sarah to help him up, she laughed, finding his predicament somewhat amusing. Picking up the torch and shining it towards him it was then that she noticed his face turn white.

'No, no… it can't be, surely…' Carl whimpered, holding on to Sarah to pull himself up.

Sarah looked back over her shoulder to what Carl was staring at. Between the trees and in the distance to where the torch beam reached, was a mist. At first it meandered softly with a slight breeze that they both felt, but soon it began to glow colours of deep blue and olive green. Carl panicked and stumbled along the path, holding the torch outstretched in one hand and pulling Sarah along with the other. She begged him to calm down, explaining of how the girl said low mist was expected in this area, but he pulled her onward, away from the mist and along the path. Suddenly Sarah lost grip of Carl's hand and fell upon the muddied woodland floor. Carl stopped for her to pull herself up, but she was moaning at the state of her clothes. Gradually the mist entwined in to a large fog bank and ahead of it the landscape was clear, but behind, even the darkness became obscured. She turned and noticed it hang there like an animal, waiting to pounce on them, but unlike Carl, she had no idea of what it brought. As it weaved itself around them, from the floor and up to their chest, neither could move; somehow they were frozen, confined by invisible shackles. Carl held Sarah tight before pulling them both away, unsure of where the torch would now take them as all around them was a thick, strange glowing fog.

Suddenly they stopped, hearing a distant cry. Sarah drew closer to Carl, snuggling up as the mist was freezing and her heart was pounding. As the sound cried again, Sarah hid her head in Carl's coat, asking what creature it could be. Carl was frightened too but his words scared Sarah more.

'That's no animal… It's a man!' Carl whispered.

They heard a noise like that of flapping wings and a screeching sound. Suddenly, another cry bellowed out but then was silenced, until all they heard was a horrible gurgling noise.

'It came from over there!' Carl announced, pulling Sarah in that direction.

'No Carl, please don't go… stick to the path!' Sarah begged.

'What path… I can't see anything, but I know where that came from!' he asserted, pulling her slowly along, carefully avoiding the bramble and low trees.

The couple held each other close but scurried through the woodland, waving away the thick mist, trying to see beyond the torch light. They stopped for Carl to hit the torch, annoyed that the light was dimming; that the batteries were indeed dying.

'Over there Carl!' Sarah shouted, pointing in the direction of a small light, shining in depths of fog.

By the time they had located the source of the light, strangely the fog was clearing; its malignant folds of mist withdrawing, dissipating as it retreated from the trees and out the woodland. Sarah scampered over to find a small torch in the undergrowth and announced her discovery. As she awaited Carl's company, she shone the torch about her feet. A short distance away and unnaturally twisted in the undergrowth was a corpse; a man with his throat gouged out, his eyes staring, his mouth wide open, stiffened by the horror that killed him. Sarah turned in disgust, holding her mouth, trying best not to vomit. It was not the fresh smell of blood splattered everywhere that repulsed her but the fact that although his face was distraught, he was in fact the man from the Hangman's Tree; the man that had studied her from behind. Noticing her grimace at the sight, Carl pulled her to him. He could not believe it either; the man had helped only hours ago. Sarah squealed as Carl approached the body, but he turned and demanded to know the victim's identity.

Sarah turned and walked away to catch back her breath. Carl leaned over the body and grimaced at the sight of the man. It was not the gaping wound that horrified him but the fact that the fatality was similar to his friend Alex. It was as though some kind of spear had impaled the throat only to be pulled back out; a hook pulling out the trachea. Ignoring the bloodied sight, Carl searched his pockets for identification. He tugged at something in the breast pocket of his coat and pulling out a large wallet, called Sarah over to shine the light on it, as the other torch had now died. She grasped the wallet quickly from his hand and walking aside, began to shine the small torch upon it.

'He's a policeman… some kind of investigator. He was the man…'

'I know… the man at the pub,' Carl interrupted, watching her look close at the badge inside. 'I'd better put it back. We don't want to get involved!'

'But we're the only witnesses,' Sarah stated.

'Of what?' Carl declared, looking back at the body, 'We didn't see a thing... nothing but that fog!'

From the pocket where he had pulled the wallet, was a chain. Carl peered at Sarah and noticing her examine the wallet, pulled the chain. It was the pendant; the one he had found but his intruder had stolen. He rose to his feet more puzzled than horrified, knowing indefinitely that the fog and some evil within it had tracked him down.

'His from the Bristol constabulary,' Sarah said, questioningly. 'You'd think he'd be from this area, you'd you?'

'Yes you would indeed,' Carl said, taking the wallet from her hand.

After cleaning it with his handkerchief, he placed it back in the man's coat and stepped toward her.

'We can't leave him like that!' she cried.

'Well, there's nothing we can do for him now,' Carl said. 'He's not going to get cold now, is he?'

Sarah thumped his arm, annoyed at his dispassionate response, but realised he was right.

'Or mind if he's going to get wet either.' Carl announced, feeling rain start to fall on his forehead. Sarah started questioning Carl about the policeman; that after the pub, he must have followed them, but why? She asked him to search the man again, but Carl pulled her away from the scene, stating he would report the incident once they were safe and dry.

Lit by the small torch, they followed the path through the woodland until they reached a clearing. It was then that they realised how much shelter the trees were giving them, as parked not far down a slope was a car; rain noisily hitting its body. Sarah pulled away from Carl and taking the torch inspected the dark inside to look for evidence.

'Come away from there!' Carl demanded, worried that her footprints may leave clues. 'For God's sake don't touch it!'

'It's locked!' she shouted, her hair now flattened by the rain and water beginning to stream down her face. 'But it definitely is *his* car… it's got a police radio and other stuff like that!'

'Leave it!' Carl shouted. 'The keys are probably in his pocket; we just need to find Evelyn's place.'

Sarah was curious, but ran back up to Carl. He turned her in the direction of the track across the field, but she stopped him, telling of how she thought the man had followed them, that after helping with the car had been listening to their conversation. But Sarah could not understand why? Carl snapped at her, demanding that they move on and quick as the rain was getting heavy. Hand in hand they ran across the field, muddied puddles splashing their feet and legs, their clothes gradually becoming soaked.

At the corner of the field they eventually found a gully that led to a side street. At first they seemed lost, the barmaid's illustration was wet and crumpled and the light from street lamps scarce, but briskly they marched on through the pelting rain until they reached a main road. Carl was lost, but Sarah recognised a small petrol garage that she had seen on their way.

'Come on,' she shouted, 'it's less than several streets away, up this hill and left.'

'Are you sure?' he asked.

'Quite sure,' she responded, winking at him. 'A photographer's always got to have an eye for detail.'

She stepped to run, but Carl pulled her back. For a moment he looked longingly at her flushed, wet face and then kissed her lips powerfully. At first she surrendered to his outburst, but pulled away.

'What's the matter?' Carl asked, thinking her emotions uneasy by the policeman's death.

'Some bloody rain has gone down my neck and back!' she responded, frowning, but managed a smile as she grabbed his hand to pull him up the street.

'My God, you look like two drowned rats, come in, come in!' Evelyn shouted, seeing Carl and Sarah dripping wet under her front door canopy. As Carl repeated the story of his car breaking down, Evelyn requested they leave coats on the banister and their shoes by the stairs. Fetching a towel to dry their hair, Evelyn told of how she had moved some of the stuff in the spare room, but needed Carl to move some heavy boxes. Suddenly she stopped chatting and noticed Sarah shivering. Sarah declared that after running through the rain she was tense, but Evelyn avowed that she have a hot bath; the boiler was still hot from her preparations to go out.

It had not been long after welcoming in her guests that they heard a horn from the street. Grabbing an umbrella from a hat stand and buttoning her own coat, Evelyn turned to them to announce that her lift had arrived and that they had come just in time. She told of how she would wash their clothes next morning, but did not realise her guests spare clothes were in the car. She declared how stupid it was of them to leave their luggage behind, but was sympathetic due to the weather. As the horn sounded again, she affirmed of how they could use spare clothes left for jumble sales; that they were in the spare room along with bath towels. As Evelyn turned again to tell them to look after Sandy and to feed him light, the horn sounded again. As she scampered out the front door, she turned and chatting away, waved to them as she descended the path. Carl shut the door and watched his Aunt enter the mini-bus from the side window. He looked back and saw Sarah padding her face and hair with a towel. For a while they looked sternly at one another, noticing how muddied they were, but laughed simultaneously. Sarah declared how relieved she was to have made it; before Evelyn had gone out that is. Carl agreed and offered her the bathroom, as he would clean up in the back room first, before checking out the spare room for clothes.

Dressed in a cardigan and baggy shorts, Carl had freshened up and had sorted out the spare room whilst Sarah soaked herself in a hot bath. The dog had settled from his excitement in seeing Carl after he had fed him a little food. As he had promised Sarah, Carl phoned to report the policeman's death and booked a room at the Hangman's Tree for the following night. Confirming that the attic room was fine, Carl turned to see Sarah come down the stairs, wrapped only in a bath towel, moaning at the nightdress he had left for her.

'I can't wear this old thing,' she professed, pacing down the stairs. 'It's hideous and too big'.

'Tell me about it,' Carl said, pointing at what he wore, 'think I'd wear *these* if had the choice!'

'Is there nothing else?' Sarah asked, walking about the kitchen, searching about before noticing the dog. 'Hello beauty... my boy'.

'Don't fuss him; I've just got him settled.'

'Maybe he needs a walk?' Sarah proclaimed, kneeling down to stroke the dog.

'What this weather?'

'Maybe in the morning then; Evelyn said it's going to be nice tomorrow!'

'Well after tonight, it can't get any worse,' Carl said, following Sarah into the living room. 'I've put more logs on the fire and opened the wine.'

'But that's for your Aunt, isn't it?'

'Well we both need something to warm us up,' Carl said slowly, turning her to face him.

'Argh, so that's why only one lamp is on...'

'Well it does make it, you know, more...' Carl interrupted.

'Romantic?' Sarah announced, hypnotised by how the fire light flickered about the room. Suddenly she felt Carl stroke his hand along her thigh. At first his gentle touch moved slowly up and underneath the bath towel, feeling her buttock, but then reached the warmth between her legs.

'Carl, we can't do anything here, it's not right?' she stated, pulling the towel tight around her.

'I can't help it, I'm still nervous, and this helps,' he said slowly. 'And you're so beautiful in the fire light.'

As Carl pulled her close to kiss her, Sarah felt something tickle her foot. Licking around her toes was Sandy, panting and screeching a bark. Sarah pulled away from Carl, her passions for him disconnecting. Carl grabbed Sandy in his arms and rushing for the kitchen, closed the door behind after placing him in his basket.

Carl paced toward Sarah, her concern now upon the nightdress she thought of changing into upstairs.

'Where are you going… please stay,' he asked. 'I think tonight's unnerved us both and we deserve a bit of fun, something to help us forget, don't you think?'

'Yes, I know, I'd like to, but…' she admitted, looking at the clock on the fireplace, realising it was still quite early.

'She won't leave until eleven.' Carl affirmed, following her eyes to read the time.

Suddenly feeling him kiss her neck and grope her thighs, she released the nightdress. As it dropped to the floor he teased her, feeling the round of her breasts below the bath towel, the other hand clenching her thigh. Surrendering to his passionate advance, she reached for him behind her and the towel fell to the floor. She closed her eyes, the warmth of the naked flame and his touch released all tension. She felt one hand release her, but the other continued, sliding up and down her stomach. Suddenly she felt a cold liquid run from her shoulder, down over her breast and enter her belly button.

'No, Carl, it's sticky,' she said, kneeling down for the towel. 'I've just bathed.'

'Well, I'll get it off another way,' he said replacing the wine glass on a table before moving his head down towards her waist.

From where the wine had run in and out her belly button, he licked and followed its route up her body, stopping at her breast. At first he revolved his tongue around her nipple, but then grasping hard her buttocks, took the nipple of her breast in his mouth, sucking slowly to produce a smacking sound. She tried to reach down for the towel, announcing her concern for split wine, but Carl had unleashed the cord of his shorts and with them over his knees, knelt down with her, enticing her to sit back on him. It was then that all else did not matter. As she felt him penetrate the moisture between her legs, the fire warmed her, her body now dry except for perspiration on her forehead. The more she leaned back, the more he entered her and the more he played; moving his fingers down below. Gently they rolled over together and on their sides Carl's movements were slow but rhythmic, the fire light flickering upon their bodies.

Following their climax, they hugged each other for some time, bodies sweating, mouths panting, until Sarah reached for the bath towel. After taking a gulp of wine from the glass, she placed the bath towel upon them and wiped Carl's face.

'Yes your right, it does help,' Sarah whispered. 'But that's not the only reason I want you. You are different to other men, your more… you know, gentle?'

Carl looked at how the fire light flickered against her dark eyes and stroking her cheek, declared, 'I can't say how much I've wanted someone like you.' He paused to stroke her hair, but then continued. 'In all this dismay at least something good… great has come out of it. I don't care what others think, only that you believe in me.'

'Of course I do you fool, I think I'm falling for you; no-one has ever touched me like that,' she said, dismissing the one important thing that she wanted to tell him. 'I want us to spend some time close together you know… before we go back; maybe get a pub lunch, visit the seaside tomorrow and grab some new clothes.'

'But it's almost November… and the car's broke,' Carl declared.

'We'll ask your Aunt if there's a bus… and while the car gets fixed, well go… surely the coast's not far.'

'But it'll be cold.'

'Where's your sense of adventure?' Sarah gestured, sipping again at the wine glass.

'I've shown you some tonight!' Carl laughed, groping her body again, tickling her under the towel.

Carl looked up after finishing off the glass of wine. The fireplace clock read half-past eleven and he became somewhat concerned. The fire had died down over the past hour and he was not sure whether to put on more logs. He looked at the fireside rug and recalling their guilty pleasure, wondered if his Aunt would notice the little wine stain on the rug. Suddenly he heard Sarah's voice shout from upstairs.

Half way up the staircase, Sarah announced from the top of the landing that she had found a nightdress, knickers and socks, and although they were uncomfortable, fitted her better. Carl followed her to the spare room and retrieved some pillows he had left out earlier. Noticing the bedclothes pile, Sarah sorted out a blanket for him and bedclothes for her. Suddenly they both froze, hearing the front door open and the voice of his Aunt. Sarah grabbed Carl's hand and placed it under her nightdress; on her thigh.

'Going to have to wait a while for some more my boy, but love you!' Sarah whispered, kissing him on the cheek, 'Tell her I've gone to bed early!'

After winking at him she quickly retreated to the spare room and closed the door.

'Are you here?' Evelyn announced. 'Where are you my friends?'

'Up here Aunt,' Carl called from the top of the stairs and putting his finger to his lips whispered. 'Sarah's gone to bed, but we've sorted stuff out for tonight and tomorrow.'

Carl joined Evelyn in the kitchen where she fussed a sleepy dog.

'I've put all muddy clothes in that washing basket, got stuff ready for tomorrow, but I'm afraid we were a bit weary, so we've drunk some wine, hope that's okay.'

'It's yours anyway,' she said smiling and pulled out a tombola prize. 'Besides I've won some more, well port actually... and some chocolates!'

'Don't let Sarah see those, or they'll all disappear,' Carl whispered. 'But she's had a long day, well both of us have, and...'

Carl stopped and thought of the policeman, of how he was killed, but why he was killed? He went cold, but faked a smile, hiding his anxieties from his Aunt.

'Don't worry, I take a cup up to bed,' his Aunt said. 'You get your head down; I see you've found bedclothes alright, but you must be exhausted.'

'Yes Aunt,' he said, 'I must say again how grateful we are, what with the car breaking down and everything, but we've booked a room at the pub for tomorrow night. Sarah felt a bit awkward imposing on you like this... well actually, we both did.'

'She's a pretty one my boy, just hope her heart is as lovely as her looks. Don't want my sister's only boy heartbroken now do we?'

# TWENTY – TWO

RUMMAGING THROUGH AN OLD SHOE BOX for memorabilia about his father, Carl's attention soon came distracted. At first it was a small, flowery patterned pair of knickers that lay on the floor of the spare room, but as he picked them up, he noticed Sarah outside the window, walking with the dog. He could not help but notice how short her skirt was and how it swung side to side, exposing her thighs as her athletic legs stepped down the path. For a moment he was transfixed, thinking how she looked like a sexy schoolgirl; the pleats of the dark blue skirt stretching, an old dark cardigan unfastened, revealing a white blouse tight against her breasts. She turned to pick a wild rose from the hedge that ran alongside the garden fence. Hastily, he bundled all which lay on the bed back into the shoe box, ran downstairs through the back door and on to the path.

Catching up with Sarah, he noticed her pull at her skirt as she strode toward the garden gate. Opening it slightly, the dog bolted through the gap and toward the back garden. She stepped her right foot up to the top of three steps to leverage the gate open and noticed Evelyn hanging out their newly washed clothes. Leaning forward she could just see Evelyn just enough to wave. As the dog approached Evelyn, she saw Sarah waving and acknowledged her before pulling along the clothes line.

As Carl approached and held her waist, Sarah flinched, retracting her hand from waving. Telling her not too move,

Carl asked if his Aunt could see them. Sarah disclosed that she could hardly see her now, but kept wriggling and pulling at her skirt.

'I couldn't help but notice how great your legs look in that skirt,' Carl whispered, sliding one hand upon her breast and the other along her leg.

'As nice as Rachael's,' she asked, looking at him from the corner of her eye.

'Nicer of course, yours are more… athletic,' he replied, but came agitated. 'Why do you keep wriggling, what's the matter?'

'It's this skirt, it itches,' she said. 'I know it's good of your Aunt to lend us this stuff, but it's also too tight… it's like wearing stuff from lost property at school!'

'Maybe it's the knickers she's leant you,' Carl suggested. 'I've got old baggy pants and they're itchy too… just like these bloody shorts.'

'I'm not wearing any underwear,' Sarah whispered, continuing to fidget.

Carl slid his hand up her thigh and felt about her buttocks.

'Indeed you haven't,' Carl said, pulling her hand from the fence and directing it to his groin. 'Someone else has been irritated by the lost property, but is excited and is really big today.'

Sarah probed around Carl's baggy shorts and felt something firm. As he guided her hand inside his underwear, he pushed closer, the palm of her hand now pressing against his testicles and wrist feeling warmth from his penis. Sarah whimpered, fearful of his Aunt seeing them, but after brushing his face alongside hers, Carl reassured her that they were out of sight.

Holding her chest with one hand, the other moved his erection up and down, pressing against the opening between her legs, tickling her hair as he brushed past. She groaned as a wind lifted her skirt; the skin of her legs and buttocks going dry from the cold, but between her legs she was wet. Indeed, she had felt the tingling sensation, but felt numbed by the outside air and was not sure if she had come or whether Carl had. But he was still hard and was entering her a little, rubbing himself around her opening. She felt guilty for her pleasure, but could not help herself. Ignoring the fact that his Aunt was but a small distance away, she pressed backward to feel him enter her completely. She tried to control her breath, but groaned as she used her arms to push him back, stooping down with outstretched arms; hands clenching the gate. It was not just the fact that their act was daring, but in the stir of the open air she had never felt such eroticism and now he was motioning, his groin smacking against her buttocks. Holding her waist, he motioned faster for a while but then started to slow, his breath heavy. By the sensation inside her she knew he was about to come, and she too felt a climax.

She turned after feeling him go limp and pull out, but started messing with him as she kissed his panting mouth. A moment passed as they caressed each other, but was interrupted as his Aunt called.

'Sarah, Sarah, have you seen Carl?'

'Better put *him* away now, hadn't we,' she whispered before shouting aloud. 'He... he was in the house, the last I knew!'

Giggling and holding his hand, Sarah pulled Carl toward the cottage door and then they both ran inside.

Upstairs, Carl quickly washed and then entered the spare room. Passing Sarah on the landing, he noticed her rush in the bathroom to wash. After tidying the bedclothes, Carl sat on the bed and looked again through the shoe box, hearing his Aunt pace slowly up the stairs.

'Carl, are you up here?' Evelyn called.

'Yes Aunt, in the spare room,' he replied. 'But what's that music you've got on downstairs; singing about climbing wooden stairs and a land of dreams?'

'Oh my boy, amongst others, that's one of my favourites,' Evelyn announced. 'You wouldn't know the singer I guess, but a lot of service men did!'

'Service men?' Carl questioned.

'Yes, she sang to the hearts of those at war and kept their spirits high in times of despair and adversity,' she exclaimed, looking at her feet, thinking. 'They were great dance tunes too. Your grandfather would know of her as he was in fact a pilot; used to fly hurricane fighters or some plane like that. Then we had the telegram when I was young and we didn't see him again.' Evelyn looked again to her feet, her face solemn and eyes watery. 'But where's Sarah?' she asked, avoiding past memories. 'She brought back Sandy from a walk, but haven't seen her since?'

'She's cleaning up in the bathroom and trying on different clothes,' Carl replied, pointing at the bathroom door.

'Well don't mess them all up, I've washed some to take to our church jumble sale this weekend,' she exclaimed. 'But I suppose if any fit, she might as well have them. There's more in there!' she said, pointing at a cupboard in the spare room.

'She's got some from there, but is thinking of getting some in town as we need to see the landlord anyway,' he explained. 'We need to check the room, get our luggage and ask about the car.'

'The Hangman's Tree isn't it, you're staying at?'

'Yes Aunty, the landlord's brother is going to fix my car, I hope.'

'Well, he has a daughter, a young girl that takes jumble to her school. This is where the vicar collects it. Could you take what you don't want and give it to her?'

'Yes, we'll take what we can; I can always come back for other stuff once the car is fixed.'

'You're a good boy; it'll save my legs,' she said, about to descend the stairs. 'Shopping is not so much fun now, especially when my friends aren't there; there's not many at church these days either.'

'Talking of town, Aunt,' Carl said lowering his voice. 'Is there a bus service to the coast? Sarah liked to go and I thought…'

'A day out, yes that would be nice, even this time of year; it's supposed to be clear and sunny all day! There's a bus-stop not far from the pub. It goes through Bridgend and circles the coast, before heading back. I go in summer sometimes with my friends from town,' she proclaimed before whispering. 'Give the girl at treat eh, buy her something nice. I think you go well together, but who am I to say?'

'What goes well together?' Sarah questioned, opening the bathroom door.

'Some of the clothes my dear,' Evelyn said, winking at Carl. 'Your stuff should be dry to iron by tea-time; if you can pass by to collect them later?'

'We'll make sure we do before going back, won't we Carl!' Sarah said, stepping into the spare room. 'Providing the car is fixed, that is!'

Evelyn paced carefully downstairs, the dog waiting at the bottom and looking up at her.

Sarah danced about the spare room like a little girl. After finding comfortable underwear, she was now picking out other clothes, trying them on and playing around. At first Carl found Sarah's performance annoying, as his Aunt wanted the clothes folded and tidy for the jumble, but they would no doubt be washed again. Anyway she was happy and he found her irresistible, dancing half-naked in garments, even if they were baggy, tight or old fashioned. She threw some at him and wrapping an old tie around his neck, pulled him near.

'Calm down for God's sake,' Carl whispered strongly, 'my Aunt's just down stairs!'

'That didn't stop you earlier did it and besides, look at these; you'll look gorgeous in these,' Sarah said laughing; pushing another pair of shorts into the ones he wore. 'And this, argh what a great top… looks French, or is it Spanish?' she said kneeling on the bed, throwing the shirt upon his face, 'Please wear it, please; it'll look good on you, I promise!'

'If you fancy me in it, I'll wear it, and the shorts, just for you!' Carl announced, blowing her a kiss before declaring, 'Besides it'll be just the thing for the *seaside*!'

With his announcement, Sarah skipped forward and kissing him powerfully, placed a large hat on his head. Giggling, she pulled him on top of her and together they fell on the bed.

It had been quite an exhausting walk to the Hangman's Tree; following his Aunt's directions had not only taken longer, but carrying clothes for the jumble sale had weighted them down. Inside the hallway of the pub, Sarah explained to the landlord's daughter, Aunt Evelyn's jumble sale donation, but wanted back the large canvass shoulder bag. The girl frowned as Sarah put the clothes in plastic bags, but quickly explained how she wanted the bag for the seaside. Hearing of their daytrip, the little girl begged to go with them, but the landlord dismissed her plea.

Following the landlord into the lounge and seeing Carl not there, Sarah abruptly stopped her conversation with the girl. Standing a while, looking at the empty bar, Sarah disregarded the girl as she walked sadly out the front door.

'He's checking on his car,' the landlord announced, 'something about ditching your damp coats and getting your luggage,'

Sarah walked quietly to the bar and before she could ask, the landlord disclosed his earlier conversation with Carl. The car did indeed require attention, as not only had a radiator pipe leaked, but the water pump had ceased. According to his brother, who had examined the car that morning, they were lucky that the engine was not damaged. As his brother could not get car parts locally, he was to visit Bridgend to get what was needed and so the car may not be fixed until late afternoon. Additionally should they require a room to stay an extra night, they would need to find other accommodation. Sarah asked for a lunch menu, but on seeing the tariff declined to order; explaining that they could get something by the sea.

Hearing voices, Sarah turned towards the front door and noticed Carl carrying their luggage, accompanied by the landlord's daughter. She heard Carl tell the little girl that he could not take her as her father said she could not go, but said he would bring her something nice back. Sarah smiled and patting the girl on the head, joined him by the hallway to help take their luggage upstairs.

Being an attic room, it was quite small; the bed although not full size, took up most of the room. However, Sarah was happy to stop the night with Carl, as although she had made love with him last night, alone in the spare bedroom her sleep was distraught with dreams; images of the dead policeman. Her thoughts were interrupted as Carl handed her a suitcase; it was her own and he did not know where she wanted her clothes. Carl was quick and bundled what clothes he had in a wardrobe and the bottom draw of a chest. Sarah was slow and although she looked forward to visiting the seaside, had other thoughts; apart from discovering the policeman last night, everything was great and did not want their trip to end.

Sarah stood silent; admiring the view from the highest room after putting away the last of her clothes, but was interrupted.

'Come on, the bus leaves soon and it's only every so many hours,' Carl announced, seeing her blank expression as she looked at the bed. 'I thought you were okay to go, or don't you want to stay here tonight with me?'

'I am, sorry, just thinking,' she replied slowly, but perked up, her face smiling. 'That's the lot, now where's my bucket and spade!'

'Get what you need; I'll just pop my car keys down to the landlord so his brother can fix the car.'

Carl was relieved to get off the bus as it had been a bumpy ride and his backside was numb. Sarah squinted as she joined him; she had been asleep most of the trip and although low in the sky, the sun was powerful. Rubbing her eyes, she ran across the road, ignited with excitement, almost dropping the canvass bag to view the beach. Carl followed, but trailed behind until he strode across a boardwalk to enter the beach. Already she was dancing, kicking the sand in the air and taking deep breaths. He hardly had chance to keep up with her as she scampered across the sand dunes and down to the flat beach, running toward the sea. As he caught up with her, he had too taken off his sneakers and felt the sand melt between his toes, but Sarah stood silent, backing away from the oncoming wave. He noticed her standing silent, her eyes closed and the sunlight revealing darkness in her hair.

'Sarah, are you okay?' he asked.

'Yes my dear, perfectly okay. Don't you just love the simplicity of it all,' she replied, turning to face him. 'Here, please take my bag, the first wave is always the coldest; like swimming really, then you get used to it!'

He grabbed the bag off her and placing it safely down felt Sarah pulling him towards her. He watched as she stood barefooted, eyes shut.

'Now, close your eyes and feel it; the cold that wakes you up as quick as the flash of a camera,' she said aloud.

Carl felt the sudden coldness of the water as a wave moved across his feet. Indeed, numbing his toes, it woke him up; the second was not so cold, the third he kicked. He looked toward Sarah, her eyes still closed, taking in large breaths, braving the cold waves. Suddenly parts of her body were sprinkled wet as Carl kicked water over her. She squealed but soon returned the favour, kicking madly at the sea, trying to soak him. He laughed, but tried to stop her, saying that they got soaked enough last night. She shouted at him, telling him that he started it, but Carl raced up and lifting her, walked further into the sea. She begged him not to drop her and he almost did, but placed her down safe, feet first. At first she thumped his arm but smiling, wrapped her arms around him and looked along the beach, wishing things could be like this always; the beauty of the coast, the wind brisk and rather cold, but feeling powerful warmth from the low sun.

It was on the way back from their dip in the sea that Sarah noticed that her left plimsoll had split and the other was splitting too. Crossing the dunes, a distance on their way back to the road, she noticed how small valleys were sheltered and secluded, that they made nice, little picnic areas. Carl's concern was more with Sarah's footwear, as on the beach they could walk barefooted, but the roads were different. Following the road that snaked alongside the beach, they reached a small, local store that resembled a beach shack. Inside, Carl treated Sarah in buying similar footwear along with some sunglasses. Outside, he directed her to a wooden bench, where he disposed of her old plimsolls and put on her new footwear. She had not had a man replace her footwear since her father changed shoes as a child and what a gentleman he was.

Together they confessed their hunger to the shop owner and were directed to a small cafeteria further along the road. Carl ordered meals and coffee, but twice had to ask Sarah her choice as she stared at the interior, admiring the walls and ceiling. Above were hung old fishing nets, paddles and sailing equipment and on the walls were pictures of sailors, sailing ships, contraband and fish.

As they ate, they talked of his Aunt and her sisters, his mother and that he must ask Evelyn about how his father died. Carl noticed how the conversation began to upset Sarah and asked of her family, trying to help forget the events of last night. Like Carl, she was the only child and that her parents had gone to America to visit premises abroad, in the hope that as her father's company expands, he would be offered promotion. She ridiculed the idea, but told of how it would benefit her mother; that her mother had come quite fed up of Bristol and after her operation, wanted a change; a new start. She admitted that her own job was not the best, but it paid her lodgings and helped finance her sports car. Should her parents sell the house to go abroad, she told that with the money she would get her own place; especially now that Carl had trashed it. He came concerned, apologising for his irresponsible behaviour, but she laughed and admitted that she was only jesting. However, with thoughts of her parents abroad as she looked out to sea, her face saddened and turning back, looked down to pick the sand beneath her fingernails. Feeling guilty about the consequences of his accident, Carl offered to buy her more clothes from a small town up the coast road.

For an hour or so they shopped around the little town, visiting novelty and antique shops. Sarah had brought amongst other things, a beach blanket of which she insisted on using to watch the sun set; from the dunes she claimed the experience would be wonderful and so dragged Carl back there.

Once on the blanket and in the shelter of the dunes Carl felt happy, especially watching the girl with him, brush away fine sand caught in her wavy blonde hair. He noticed how the roots of her hair were darker than when they first met, but was afraid to ask. He deduced that it must have been dark originally, as certainly her eyes were a gorgeous dark brown. Watching her mess with purchases in the canvass bag, she turned and requested he fetch ice-creams, but Carl declined, claiming it was the wrong time of year. Sarah insisted; the shop was only by the road and it may be their last chance to buy some. Reluctantly, Carl got to his feet and with her handing him a note, strode off over the dunes towards the shop.

On his return, Carl noticed Sarah lying on the blanket and silently crept up to her. Suddenly she jumped, feeling a bitter cold freeze her nose.

'You wanted ice-cream my love?' he announced.

'Yes, but not on my nose, I wondered what the bloody hell it was!' she replied, about to wipe it off with her hand.

'Hold it,' Carl said. 'Allow me.'

Sarah giggled as he licked the ice-cream from her nose.

'It tickles,' she laughed, removing her sunglasses. 'Give us a kiss instead.'

Carl laughed and after kissing her sweet lips, lay down beside her, finishing the cold sweet. For a moment, Sarah let the ice-cream melt in her mouth, feeling the last of the low sun warm her body. Stretching his arms above his head, she heard Carl sigh and noticed he had finished his ice-cream. Feeling mischievous, Sarah slid her hand down his shorts. Suddenly Carl panicked, sensing a freezing cold on the tip of his penis. As he sat up, he saw Sarah arch over him, fingers messing and mouth around his erection.

'Stop it,' he insisted. 'You can't do it here; there may be people about!'

'About where?' she said, looking up at him, ice-cream melting down her chin. 'Besides, like *you* said, there's another way to get it off!'

As she resumed teasing him, he groaned pleasurably but was afraid of passers-by.

'What if someone sees you?' he said, checking the long grass in the sand dunes.

'We'll have to find another way then, won't we?'

After her announcement, Carl noticed Sarah pull up her newly brought dress, but was blinded by the sunlight that shimmered behind her. Suddenly, he could see her again; her body obscuring the sun, her legs open and buttocks sitting on top of him. He tried to sit up properly but Sarah reached over him to pin back his arms with her hands and with her knees anchored in the sand, wriggled to find his erection.

'Have I aroused *big* boy again?' she asked, provocatively.

'He's not that big,' Carl said, feeling her push down on him.

'Maybe not, but hard,' she replied, her hips writhing in a circular motion, feeling him inside her.

'Someone will see us?' Carl said, trying to control his pleasure.

'This dress is long enough; just looks like I'm playing. Besides my dear, you didn't mind this morning,' she contested, starting to breath hard. 'You seduced me last night, teased me this morning, and now,' she cried, her blonde hair falling on to his face, 'it's *my* turn to tease!'

Carl lay back on the sand; he could not resist her seduction anymore. Feeling the heat, the moisture, the sense of climax, Sarah thrust forward and backward, gripping his hands with hers until she felt dizzy. Suddenly she yelped and falling on top of him, gasped for air. He too was sweating, but felt the cold sea breeze as her lips found his. She arched backward and looking about the dunes, proclaimed.

'See, there's no-one about!'

Pulling away from him, she stared about the dunes again before replacing her knickers and after dusting the sand from her knees, looked mischievously at him.

'I'm afraid playtime is over,' she said. 'You'd better put him away!'

It was not until they reached the road from the dunes that they realised how quickly it was getting dark. Although it had not taken long to collect their belongings, by the time they reached the pick-up point, the bus had its lights on and was indicating to leave. Carl raced along the road, waving at the bus, trying to attract the driver's attention. Sarah followed but was burdened with the canvass bag. Luckily, seeing Carl slump against the door and shout, the driver stopped to accelerate from the roadside. Once Sarah had caught up with him and boarded the bus, they thanked the driver and sat laughing.

'That was a close one!' Sarah shouted, her breathing heavy. 'But worth it; that sunset was amazing!'

As the bus pulled away and they settled into their seats, Sarah realised that their little seaside trip was over.

After snaking its way through the streets of the town, the bus stopped at a junction beside the harbour and Sarah looked longingly across the bay. Although she had seen the harbour on arrival, in the twilight and calm of dusk she noticed how still the bay was; like an oil painting with strokes of vibrant colours used to reproduce reflections on the sea, as dancing waves broke and crashed upon the shore. In the distant bay the harbour lights shimmered and above in the sky, the first sight of stars appeared. As she thought how tranquil and beautiful it was, a tear escape her eye; was it the sadness in leaving or was it the realisation that she had to reveal her secret soon. She glanced at Carl, seeing him tired, his head tilted back, his face flushed, but looked back to admire the scene. As another tear ran down her cheek, she smiled and before shutting her eyes, pictured the harbour.

# TWENTY – THREE

'Have you tried her out yet?' a voice said from behind.

'Excuse me?' Carl replied, looking around after putting down the bags of jumble.

'Your car, the Peugeot 205?' the landlord announced walking towards him. 'My brother's just finished fixing her!'

'No, I'm sorry, I didn't know, see we've only just got back,' Carl confessed. 'But we want to visit my Aunt later, so I could test her out then. Would you give this to your daughter?' Carl said, pulling out a rag-doll from the canvass bag. 'I promised I'd bring her something back from the beach!'

'But you shouldn't have; she gets spoilt enough when her Gran comes over from the coast, but it's good of you,' the landlord stated, examining the doll in his hand.

'Well, actually, it's only from one of those novelty shops, but it's…'

'I would prefer you to settle my brother's bill, if you don't mind?' the landlord interrupted. 'I'd like it paid separate to your lodgings if that's okay?'

'No problem,' Carl replied, opening out his wallet. 'I'll give you cash for our stay and put your brother's bill on my cheque guarantee card, if that's alright?'

The landlord nodded and processed the transaction, giving Carl back receipts.

'Where's your partner?' he asked, handing Carl back his card.

'She's freshening up in the attic room,' Carl replied, 'well probably sorting out the place; you know what women are like; can't leave things alone.'

'Well, it's just that we had a phone call from some Detective Inspector while you were out; asking about some murder last night. Apparently he traced the call to a relative, but they directed him here... something about stolen property?'

Carl froze for a second, but started to explain the situation; of how after following the barmaid's directions, had discovered a body in the woods and that he reported it later to the police from his Aunt's house.

'Must have been grotesque, being the first to find him?' he proclaimed.

'Sorry, but how do you ...'

'The evening newspaper,' the landlord interrupted, holding the paper aloft, showing the front page. 'Not much happens around here, so a policeman's murder is big news!'

Carl took the newspaper and reading it a little abruptly handed it back after seeing Sarah in the hallway, talking to the landlord's daughter.

'Keep it handy, I'll read later!' Carl requested.

'Why, what's the matter?' he asked.

'Don't mention this to Sarah, please,' Carl pleaded, rolling his eyes. 'It was a bit of a shock for her!'

'I'm not surprised; finding anyone in that state certainly would come as a shock,' the landlord admitted.

'Shock, what's a shock?' Sarah questioned, approaching them from behind, holding the little girl's hand.

'The price for fixing my car,' Carl said, winking at the landlord.

'Well exactly how much is it?' she asked.

'It's okay really; it's done now and he did have to get the parts out of town.' Carl explained, again rolling his eyes in view of the landlord. Quickly Carl changed the subject and bent down to talk to the landlord's daughter. 'But have looks at what your Daddy has; what we got from the seaside for you!'

The landlord handed the rag-doll to Carl, insisting that he give it her, as he had indeed bought it. The little girl's face shone with excitement and thanking them ran into the hallway. After confirming the settlement of both bills Carl thanked the landlord, stated that they would have an evening meal and quickly pulled Sarah away.

'Let's say our goodbyes to Aunt Evelyn, I want to leave her my address and phone number.'

It had not been long after his Aunt had let them in that she remarked on the phone call she had earlier that day. Sarah was curious about the police phoning, but calming down his Aunt Carl told Sarah not to upset Evelyn about last night's incident. Instead he changed the conversation and guided his Aunt to the comfort of a fireside chair. Evelyn talked of ironing of their clothes, but Sarah intervened and stepped into the kitchen to finish the task. Carl spoke of how later both he and Sarah would take all the bagged clothes ready for the jumble and give them to the landlord's daughter, and now that he had the car back, he could take the lot. Evelyn confessed how good it was to use the spare room again and should they visit again, said it was always at their disposal.

She asked about their seaside visit and thought of the day as unusually beautiful; the weather especially warm and sunny for late October. She asked too of their accommodation at the Hangman's Tree, but whilst Sarah was busy in the kitchen, Carl's concerns were more of his father's past.

Evelyn reiterated of how his father stopped the Dark-man of controlling Eleanor; of how this doctor promised to make her well, that he knew how to cure her life long illness. But it was all lies; he was nothing but a mischievous sorcerer that wanted to use her gift for his own devious prosperity. However, although Evelyn conveyed how loving and protective his father was, for a man of the cloth to get Eleanor pregnant, he was ridiculed by many members of the church. He denied taking advantage of her, but she lived with him, took comfort in him and stated convincingly that she was happy living under his roof. Evelyn disclosed that not long after Carl was born, that many political and lawful people harassed his father; that a man to be priest should not have a son, but as Eleanor had wished in her last words, she wanted him to take care of her son, and indeed he did. After losing Eleanor, she and Elizabeth visited Carl and helped him through early days of school, but then disaster struck. His father, not long after receiving his commendation for service to the church, was killed; trapped within his church whilst it burned down on top of him. Carl asked if she knew of any misconduct, but all she knew was of the many arguments that followed and that Carl was sent to boarding school shortly after Elizabeth died.

Evelyn's eyes began to swell and Carl apologised, but stated that she may be the only one who could provide answers.

Evelyn looked down and into the fire, hearing the wood snap under heat. Reluctantly, she confessed that indeed there may only be two others that could have answers. The first was the man they all hated, the doctor; that he did have many encounters with his father, but also did one of his friends, a member of his circle. In the past this man had been close to Elizabeth, but his commitment to the doctor was absolute. Carl asked of how she knew this and so she explained of a ring that Elizabeth had stolen from this man; arguing that he should not wear it as it was his commitment to the doctor and not her.

Carl thought for a second, but ridiculed the idea; surely it was coincidence that the man killed at the library was indeed a past friend of the doctor and maybe a lover of his deceased, eldest Aunt. There was only one way to find out and so again Carl dug out his folder to show Evelyn the picture of the man with the onyx ring. Evelyn was uncertain; in those days she was only a young girl, that she hardly knew him and that by that picture, she could hardly make it out. Carl thought, but realising he did not have Sarah's library photographs; he too looked anxiously into the fire.

Carl's thoughts were severed by barking as Sandy bounced into the room, looking up, awaiting Sarah. As she placed the newly ironed clothes in the canvass bag, she looked upon Evelyn and Carl, who were quiet.

'I'll take these to the car,' she exclaimed, moving over to wrap her arms around Evelyn to kiss her on the cheek. 'We had better get going, but I loved every minute here, with you… and you!' she announced, hearing the dog bark again. 'I'll miss my lovable little friend the most won't I, my floppy-eared boy!'

From that she took the canvass bag and waited in the hall, looking up the stairs.

'Carl, have we all the jumble here… in these bags?'

'Yes my dear, they've just got to go in the boot!' Carl shouted, getting up from the armchair. He hugged and kissed his Aunt and passed her a note of paper. 'Here's my address and number; should you remember *anything* please let me know. Sorry we can't stay any longer but we've asked for an evening meal at the pub. However, you've been a great help Aunt, it's nice to know that my parents were good people, if not a little weird.'

'Guess it runs in the family, my friends tend to think I'm a bit crazy too.' Evelyn chuckled, turning to follow Carl to the hallway. 'Doubt you'll become a vicar, like your father though,' she said winking and pointed at Sarah, watching her step down the little path with Sandy barking behind her. 'But then again, stranger things do happen!'

'Go back my dear, go back!' Sarah shouted, turning to face the front door.

Evelyn called back her dog and reluctantly Sandy retreated inside. Carl kissed his Aunt again and together they waved at her whilst descending the path.

It had been a hearty meal and Carl felt full. Sarah had picked at her food but eventually finished most of it, along with the last of the wine. Carl reached for the bottle and groaned at discovering it was almost empty.

'That man was reported about today,' Carl announced, tipping the last drops of wine in his glass.

'What man?' Sarah asked, picking at the last bits of food on her plate.

'The policeman... the man we found dead in the woods,' he replied.

Sarah went cold and looked at Carl staring at the bottle.

'So is that why you didn't want to talk about it at Evelyn's; poor girl, they must of traced the call. We didn't think about that, did we?' Sarah announced, pushing her plate aside. 'You didn't predict that one happening, did you?' she exclaimed. 'Not like the one with me, or your work colleague.'

'How could I?' he replied, turning the bottle on the table. 'I wasn't asleep to dream about it, but that dizzy spell, maybe something was trying to make me sleep, but what? Why would I want that policeman dead? Even if...'

'Even if what?' Sarah asked.

'Nothing, things just don't make sense. I don't want to hurt anyone, but now this has happened and *without* a dream causing it,' Carl said, sitting back in his chair. 'Now we've reported this, guess the police will be asking questions; questions I can't answer; stuff I don't understand yet myself!'

'Well maybe it's just coincidence that these deaths are somehow related.'

'Related, related,' Carl said angrily. 'What if I could have *saved* David, what if I hadn't *come* to you in time?'

Sarah went quiet. Obviously he had struck a nerve, seeing her eyes recollect the image of the creature; the scaly hands lifting her before Carl intervened.

'Look, I'm sorry,' Carl said softly. 'We've had a lovely day, I don't want to spoil it... it's just that I wish I could get answers, but all I know now, is a little more history.'

301

'Well forget about it now, let's get another drink, we haven't got to leave until late tomorrow morning,' Sarah said, moving her way to a comfortable velvet sofa. 'Besides, I was thinking of asking Liz to help, she knows all about weird stuff like séances, witchcraft, clairvoyance and…'

'She'll think I'm a crack-pot, or at least someone with a crack-pot history!' he interrupted.

'No she won't! On the contrary, Liz has had to put up with lots of abuse herself; people think she's some geek, a weird loner, but really she's well intelligent, just doesn't study the things that most people regard important or necessary.' Sarah exclaimed, defending her long-time school friend. 'She understands people better than you know!'

'Sounds a bit like what Evelyn said about my mother,' Carl said slowly.

'Well if you want to know what I think,' Sarah commanded with sympathy in her voice, 'I think that your family, or at least your father, battled this doctor, this evil man, maybe because he did evil deeds, blackmailed people and things like that. Your Aunt did say he was into magic and stuff; that he could be the cause of all this, members of an occult circle, or something like that.'

'That's just an astrology group; nothing reckless or malicious, just an innocent members club of some kind.'

'God, you sound like Mike,' Sarah said, curling her legs under her. 'He ridicules everything without evidence, without wanting to hear you out!'

'Yes, and he's beginning to think I'm daft also.'

'No he's not, he just cares for you. He wanted you to come on this break,' Sarah exclaimed, squeezing Carl's hand.

'I've seen some changes in you, and I've done stuff I don't usually do; guess we've both been a bit nervous, you know, with what's happened.'

'A bit nervous; discovering a dead copper, people killed in burned out cars?'

Sarah tried her best to evade thoughts of oppression and recalled their passion.

'Yes, but look at what it's made you do, how its brought you out, and believe me you're no way boring; making me have it in broad daylight, tipping wine all over me!'

Carl smiled and placed his hand on hers.

'I'm glad you understand. I was right about you, you're not just gorgeous, but an angel... one that listens and understands,' Carl said, sincerity in his voice. 'Besides, how can any man, even as dark and learned as that doctor, do anything from a prison cell?'

'Exactly, things always look different in the morning. Now Carl, let's have any early night!' Sarah suggested, her expression exposing a little naughtiness.

Upstairs, Sarah lay on the bed, expectant that Carl would want her again; that they would play around like before and that he would again tease her. As she lay on the bed, half naked in a short and skimpy nightdress, Carl was half undressed too, but looked out the window at his car on the car park. Sarah, seeing him sad, confessed that she too regretted that their little trip was coming to an end. Putting his car keys down on a dresser, Carl declared that it was not just that. Sarah assumed that his worries were with driving back next day and so asserted that his car would be fine as they had tested it out to and from his Aunt's house. She continued, expressing how much of a lovely time she had had, but whispered that the night was still young and that they were alone in the same room. Carl turned and smiled. Once he saw the beautiful girl lying willingly on the bed, his worries dissolved. Snuggling up to her, he turned off the light.

# TWENTY - FOUR

'I TOLD YOU TO HURRY up; your breakfast's gone cold by now!' Sarah exclaimed, dipping a piece of toast into her fried egg. 'I like my eggs runny, but yours will be hard by now.'

Carl sat down opposite Sarah, blurry eyed and still very tired. As Sarah nattered on about having cereals and fruit juice first, he reached for a slice of toast and spread butter on it. Making a cup of coffee, he bit at the toast.

'This toast's cold,' he said frowning and then sipped at his coffee. 'The coffee's not warm either?'

'Well having a lie-in, you can't expect breakfast to wait for you,' Sarah said sipping her tea and finishing off her eggs. 'You're lucky I persuaded the landlord to postpone yours 'til last.'

'What an angel, what would I do without you?' he replied, finishing off the triangular piece of toast. 'It must be having you beside me; I felt so at ease. As you can see, I'm rapt by your beauty.' Continuing to talk, the landlord placed a fried breakfast on the table before him. 'No, seriously, apart from your kicks in the night, that's the best sleep I've had in ages,' he whispered, winking his eye at her.

'Kicks?' Sarah questioned, also whispering.

'Yes, my dear, I'll tell you later,' Carl said, noticing the landlord return with more toast.

'Good morning my friends, I'm glad that you find the room okay,' the landlord announced, renewing the pot of hot water, 'but we don't wait for everyone you know!'

'Yes, I'm sorry, but we drive back later and…'

'We'd like to talk alone, if you don't mind,' Sarah said interrupting Carl, looking up irritably at the landlord.

'Well, I was just wondering,' the landlord murmured, but then announced aloud. 'But about what time can I expect you to be leaving then?'

'As soon as we get our stuff packed,' Carl said, swinging a sausage aloft on his fork. 'It'll be about another hour after we finish here!'

'But I thought we had 'til mid-day to vacate?' Sarah questioned firmly, pouring another cup of tea.

'Yes miss, it's okay, it's just…' he paused to tidy the table, then continued. 'Never mind, it's nothing to do with me.'

Carl and Sarah looked at each other and frowned.

'What's his problem?' Carl muttered.

'Has he been paid?' Sarah questioned.

'Yes, I paid for everything yesterday!' Carl replied, watching the landlord retreat to the kitchen.

For half an hour Carl and Sarah sat, ate and drank, discussing their trip and how they had enjoyed visiting Aunt Evelyn. It was all well, laughing about their exploits, especially their mischief in the dunes, blaming each other for being naughty. Sarah looked at an old clock sitting on the mantelpiece opposite and then at her watch. With her breakfast finished, Sarah was waiting for Carl and so broadcast of how she would make a start on packing, as they needed to get a move on. As she stood, she noticed the landlord talking with two men and point in their direction. She started to move but was blocked before she could leave the table.

'Excuse me, sir, miss,' a deep voice announced. Sarah sat down again after realising who they were. 'I'm Detective Inspector Lawrence Campbell and this is my partner Mr Thompson.'

The broad shouldered, black man looked down at each of them in turn, but stopped to stare at Carl.

'Excuse me sir, but have we not met before?' the Detective Inspector asked, fumbling with his goatee beard.

'Well, err, I don't think so, maybe,' Carl said, realising he had questioned him at work but wanted to evade a recollection. 'What's it you want Detective Inspector? See we've got to be out by noon and we've not yet packed.'

'Just a few questions, if you're the guys who reported last night's murder?' he enquired.

'Murder?' Sarah said fearfully.

'You are a relative of a Miss Evelyn Jones, are you not?' he queried.

'Carl is, she's his Aunt,' Sarah said, suddenly becoming concerned. 'Is she okay, nothing's happen to her as it?'

'No my dear, she's fine,' the other policeman reassured, 'it's just that the call came from her phone number as we had it traced you see.'

'And she said that her nephew had made the call, that you are indeed a Mr Carl Aston who resides at 63, Gate Street, Bristol?' the Detective Inspector enquired and with a nod from Carl he continued. 'We just need you to describe to us quickly what happened.'

'But we need to get moving soon!' Carl professed, moving back his chair.

'It won't take long,' he declared, 'there's no need for a statement, but if you can just quickly talk through what happened, my colleague will note it down.'

Carl agreed to the policeman's request and described quickly the story; of their car breaking down, the barmaid directing them to his Aunt's house and the discovery of the body in the woods as they got lost in the fog. He told of how he recognised the body as the man who helped push their car, but stated that they were sickened by his death, and that in the pouring rain, they just wanted to reach his Aunt's house.

'And you didn't touch the body, move it in anyway?' he asked.

'No,' Carl said, staring at Sarah, 'it was horrible, as if he had been mutilated.'

'Why do you ask?' Sarah questioned timidly.

'Well, apparently an item of jewellery is missing from the policeman's body; he was following up a report of theft… and according to his report,' the detective paused to read some notes, 'another claimant professes that it was originally his.'

'Another claimant?' Carl asked.

'Well son, it's really not your concern.'

'But what if the jewellery was mine and the policeman was to return it to me?'

Sarah stared at Carl and she went cold, thinking surely he didn't have it.

'But according to our records, the theft was reported by a woman; a young woman,' Mr Thompson said.

Carl stared at Sarah and she looked away at the clock and then at her watch.

'I must get packing Carl,' Sarah demanded, rolling her eyes at him. 'I'll get started, if you don't mind helping these gentlemen with their enquiries?'

'That's okay miss,' the Detective Inspector said, interrupting Carl's reply, 'if Mr Aston can just finalise some details for us, we won't detain you any longer.'

'Sorry to pry, but the jewellery,' Carl said, watching Sarah walk from the table. 'But who else claims it?'

'Well, after it was reported stolen, a piece of jewellery fitting its description was retrieved from a man visiting the Wiltshire Rehabilitation Institute, but...' the Detective Inspector was interrupted by his partner. 'The man was restrained, but said he was returning it to its rightful owner... one of the patients, a doctor convicted of a murder years ago.'

'But *that* man can't have the pendant, it isn't his!' Carl announced, forgetting himself.

'But how do you know it's a pendant?' Mr Thompson enquired.

Carl fumbled with his words, but after realising that Sarah must have reported the theft from his flat, pretended that it was his.

'It is mine. I kept it safe until that intruder stole it from my flat!'

The policemen turned away to talk amongst themselves, but Carl heard them mention the dead policeman, stating that he was an indecisive character, nervous in interrogating people and that he was just to follow and report. The Detective Inspector asked if the car had been searched and his partner confirmed it had; that no pendant was found either on the body or in the police vehicle. Carl was becoming anxious and asked if he could be excused, stating that he had to vacate the room by noon. The policemen turned and facing him requested other details. They asked the time he and Sarah had discovered the body, of what time the man had helped push their car and the last time they saw him at the Hangman's Tree.

Outside, Sarah stopped in the middle of the car-park and looked angrily at the car keys she had got from the attic room. Although it was late morning she felt a chill, but it was not the cold air that made her shiver, it was what she had to do. With the canvas bag hung over one shoulder, she dragged her small suitcase to the car boot. Opening the boot, she placed both items inside before slamming shut the boot in temper. She approached the passenger door and after opening it, pulled back the seat. Tears swelled in her eyes as she paused momentarily before reaching in side to take the damp coats. She pushed her coat back into the plastic bag, but laid Carl's coat flat on the back seat, hesitant to perform the search.

'Already to move on,' a voice shouted, making her jump. 'You should be okay, my brother does a good job!'

Sarah retreated from the back seat to see the landlord looking at her by the open door. As her heart stopped racing and nerves calmed, she managed a smile.

'Yes, thank you, we had a run yesterday and it was fine.'

The landlord wished her a safe trip and asked her to say her goodbyes to her daughter; declaring that she had not thanked them properly for the rag-doll. Sarah agreed and once he had gone, regretfully went back to examine Carl's coat. Fumbling around in the outside pockets, at first she found nothing, but from the inside pocket she pulled on a chain and at the end was the pendant; undeniably the same one she first saw at the night of her party.

Sarah had been quiet most of the journey back. Apart from short questions about the policemen's enquiries, she restricted conversation to a minimum. As she had enjoyed their little break so much, it was not just that it was coming to an end that upset her. Indeed, she was annoyed in letting Rachael influence her to go to the police, but the fact that Carl had kept the pendant secret from her was infuriating. Looking out the window, watching the streets of Bristol fly by, she wanted to avoid confrontation, but knew sooner or later she would have to get stuff out into the open.

Carl was also quiet, but this was his attention to driving. He kept glancing at Sarah, wondering why she had hardly spoken throughout the journey, but assumed she was saddened by coming back home. It was not until he requested road directions that she spoke, advising the best way to her house.

He stopped the car alongside the kerb and looked past Sarah. Although his thoughts were more of the back garden and the woodland that lay beyond it, her house was as he remembered. He had only just switched off the engine when he heard the boot open. Soon after, Sarah had collected her things and was stepping clumsily up the driveway, burdened by her suitcase, her handbag and the plastic bag of coats. Carl dashed to the rear of his car and retrieved the canvass bag, calling Sarah as he closed the boot. She did not look back, but stopped, listening to him mention the canvass bag; that she had forgot to take her favourite souvenir.

'Bring it then, will you, I've too much to carry!' she snapped.

'What's the hurry?' Carl shouted, running to catch her up. 'Here, let me, I'll take some of this stuff!'

'It's okay, I've got it!' she announced, turning to face him, her hair obscuring one eye. 'Just bring *that* will you!'

Carl could not help but sense tension between them; for some reason the girl that he adored was fiery. At first he thought it was her realisation of their return to normality, but saw a change in her character as the front door opened. Dropping everything, Sarah ran up the driveway and into the arms of her friend Liz. Carl followed and hearing them talk on their way inside, picked up the luggage.

Entering the lounge, he kicked off his shoes and placed down the luggage. He stood for a moment, looking out at his car, hearing the girls chat in the dining room. Their conversation at first was of the trip and the seaside, but changed as Sarah asked about the patio door repairs; maybe this was the reason for her mood and why she seemed distant from him. Although the incident was accidental, it was he who had caused the damage and the new set of reinforced patio doors he heard, were quite expensive. As Sarah walked in, thanking Liz for looking after the house, Carl sat and apologised, disclosing that he would help pay for the damage, as and when he could.

'It's not that which has annoyed me,' Sarah announced approaching Carl and turning to Liz. 'I'd hoped you could stay a little, but I've not yet said anything.'

'Have you said that I can help?' Liz stated.

'Yes, but with the circumstances…'

'Circumstances, what circumstances?' Carl demanded.

Sarah walked slowly over to the luggage on the floor and pulled her damp coat from the plastic bag. Watching Carl's reaction, she placed it down, pulled out his and reached down into the inside pocket.

'Care to tell me how *this* got in your coat?' she said, pulling out the chain and pendant.

'I didn't want to worry you about that,' he explained, feeling somewhat nauseated. 'I was simply going to put it back under the sunlamp.'

'So, there I was, lying to those policemen, covering up the fact that I messed with the man's wallet, when you stole this *thing* off him and didn't tell me!'

Liz looked at Carl and sat some distance away; feeling uncomfortable, her face serious.

'Yes, but they wouldn't have come asking questions if you hadn't reported it missing,' Carl indicated with hands open.

'But your flat was burgled, didn't you think it important to tell the police?' she responded.

'Until this,' Carl paused to look at Liz, not knowing how much Sarah had told her. 'Until this *drama* is resolved and I have answers, I didn't want to involve anyone else, I thought you understood that!'

'Well, I only mentioned to Rachael that you were burgled and so she persuaded me to –'

'Oh, so I'm not the only one who's dishonest here, then am I?' he exclaimed, rolling his eyes. 'What else does Rachael know?'

'And Mike?' Sarah scoffed.

'I've told him nothing… not that he wants to understand anyway!' Carl said and then paused to look at Sarah with sincerity, 'That's why I trusted you, because I love you!'

'But don't you see, you put everyone in danger… me, you, poor old Aunt Evelyn,' Sarah shouted. 'If you truly loved me, you would have left that *thing* back with the dead man that it murdered!'

'But there was no dream, I couldn't have caused it so…'

'Isn't it obvious,' Sarah interrupted. 'It's not your dreams that cause these things to happen, but something else!'

'What, then?' he demanded. 'You've not had the dreams and seen people's fate acted before you, only to discover moments after it's happened!'

'Well I'm not sure,' Sarah replied angrily, 'but going on what your Aunt said, it's got something to do with that doctor!'

'But he's in jail, some institute for the criminally insane, or something like that!' Carl replied.

'Well I give up, maybe Liz might know,' Sarah whined, feeling exhausted. 'She knows a lot about these things. Besides she might be only one who can help you soon.'

'Liz, the only one to help me,' Carl said slowly. 'Won't you help me anymore?'

'Can I look at it?' Liz said timidly, trying to avoid another argument.

'Why not; be my guest?' Carl said sarcastically.

Sarah handed her the pendant and at first Liz examined the chain, sliding her hands along it. However, it was not long before she was drawn to the stone; a black oval like pebble encased in a silvery metal, engraved with patterns and ancient symbols. As it must have been so old, the thing that fascinated Liz was how shiny and unblemished it was.

'So, you mean to say, this thing causes people to die?' Liz enquired.

'Pretty much,' Carl whispered, leaning forward. 'Well who ever has it on them when I dream; something comes after them.'

Liz went cold, but was comforted by Sarah as they sat together.

'Shall I tell her about what happened?' Sarah asked, looking at Carl with concern. He agreed and listened to Sarah's explanation of the night the snake creature attacked her; of its ghostly accomplices and how the blue demon-like figure picked her up, almost strangling her before Carl intervened. At first her eyes opened wide as Liz could not believe the story her best friend told, but Sarah continued without breath, as if it was believable – that it did indeed happen. She explained how Carl had tackled the creature, but how together they would have died if not for the ultraviolet rays of her sunbed. She told of the policeman whilst they were away, that he had followed them to trace the true owner of the pendant. But this policeman was murdered, killed by something out of the fog that night; something evil, probably a demon like the snake creature.

Carl listened as Sarah explained more about his dreams and its connection with the pendant. However, by the look on Liz's face, she was to take some convincing, probably ridicule Carl as some freak that had found influence over her best friend. But as Sarah stopped, unable to continue, recalling the terror on the dead policeman's face, he looked at Liz. To his amazement she was absorbed, fascinated by the jewellery in her hand and the stories linked to it. Carl realised Sarah was right about her friend; although Sarah described the horror in Carl's dreams and the events that followed, Liz did not falter in attention or deride any of what Sarah said.

As Sarah retreated to the kitchen to make tea, Carl described the history disclosed by his Aunt. It was then that he saw Liz become anxious, wanting to ask a question like a school girl holding up her hand. He paused and in doing so saw Liz fidget and finger her long, straight, black hair. Timidly her sharp blue eyes peered at him through the lenses of her spectacles, but he noticed a positivity of character he had not seen from her before. She excused herself from imposing on their experience, but as Sarah entered bringing cups of tea, she revealed her thoughts. She declared that Carl was being negative about his dreams; that he was blaming them on causing death. Carl and Sarah sat bemused, but eager to listen to her ideas. Slowly she recalled what his Aunt Evelyn had said, that his mother was a great woman, but set back with illness; that maybe his dreams were not a source to cause death, but a premonition to prevent it.

For a while Carl and Sarah sat quiet, subjecting the idea upon their own thoughts and experience. Carl was courteous, but discredited the idea; the deaths were too vivid and had unprecedented authenticity in their outcome. Sarah, although sceptical could not disprove the idea; indeed Carl had not dreamed the policeman's death, but it all happened too fast and there was not chance to prevent it. However, he did save her and to that, Sarah should be indebted. Taking a big gulp of tea, she realised that she must reveal the news she had kept for so long; as it was not just virtuous, but if he loved her, Carl would understand.

As Sarah moved to sit alongside Carl on the sofa, she nodded at Liz, gesturing her to leave. Unfortunately, Liz was captivated by their story and at the jewellery in her hand.

'Carl, my dear, I've got something to tell you,' Sarah announced, holding his hand, 'and if you love me, you'll understand…'

'Haven't you told him yet?' Liz muttered.

'Told me what?' Carl enquired.

'Well I'm going to miss you too!' Liz said sheepishly, looking down at the carpet, her face sad.

'What does she mean; she's going to miss you?' Carl questioned, turning to face Sarah.

Quickly, Liz stood and bursting into tears, ran to the dining room.

'Why is she so upset, where are you going?' Carl asked his voice heavy.

'Well, you know that I told you about my parents being in America –' she said.

'Looking for property… part of your father's promotion… some kind of business opportunity.' Carl interrupted, recollecting their conversation in the shoreline cafeteria.

'Yes,' Sarah said, finding it hard to explain, 'well another opportunity has come… for me that is.'

'In America?' Carl cried.

'Yes, in Boston to be precise,' she revealed. 'It's to do with fashion photography and marketing; stuff like that.'

'It's a great opportunity, isn't it Sarah?' Liz muttered, peering from the dining room door.

'You knew of this?' Carl shouted, standing up to approach Liz.

'Don't shout at Liz, she knew little of it. It was Rachael who helped me get it, well, along with my father's contacts,' Sarah indicated.

'How long for?' Carl questioned, turning to face Sarah.

'I don't know,' she answered, 'well not until I get over there. It could be indefinitely, but its –'

'But what about what's happened? What about helping to fathom all *this* stuff out?' Carl shouted, his eyes swelling with tears. 'What about us... me... so there's no future for us then?'

'I don't know,' she snapped back, her eyes also tearful. 'It may be just for a contract... six months... a year. Liz said she'll help you, she knows a lot about –'

'Six months, a year!' Carl interrupted aggressively, 'In that time someone like you will find another guy; some bloke who don't give a fuck about you!'

Sarah sat quiet. She had hoped Carl would not take the news badly; but she was wrong.

'Ah so, like some newspaper article; beautiful woman is black widow spider who entices her mate and once used, kills him off to make nest elsewhere...'

'It's not like that Carl,' Liz muttered. 'It's a great opportunity I hear.'

But Carl carried on, not listening to Liz, not noticing Sarah's eyes stream with tears.

'No, oh no, it's like she's baked her cake of seduction; mixed up *all* the right ingredients, added a hint of passion and flavourings of love, slowly heated up the expectations and after tasting a piece, wants to let the relationship go stale. And most likely it'll all get thrown away!'

'Calm down!' Sarah shouted, standing up. 'Don't you think your over reacting somewhat, it may be only for a few months, it may even fall apart... besides I do have a thing called a telephone!'

'Yes and when those American guys sweet talk you with all their money and big cars, you'll find it hard to answer any of *my* calls.'

'It's not going to be like that Carl,' Sarah said sincerely walking towards him. 'I'll probably be with my parents and you haven't met them... Dad's well protective of me; it'll be all work I promise you!'

'Oh, yes but of course!' Carl said sarcastically, but noticed Liz approach.

'Her father *is* very protective you know, but a nice man; he thinks a lot of me,' Liz said quietly. 'He helped me a lot at school, with bullies and that, although Sarah took most of the flack.'

Carl sat down with resentment and mixed feelings; not sure what to do. Slowly Liz walked over and standing by him, stared at Sarah.

'I promised Sarah I'd help you Carl,' Liz muttered, 'and I want to, not just because I owe Sarah big time, but I can.'

Sarah moved to accompany Carl on the sofa and held his hand as he looked to the floor.

'Anyhow, you could always come over when I'm sorted,' Sarah announced, sliding her fingers through his. 'Maybe they don't have ghosts and ghouls in America?'

Carl looked up, his eyes swollen with tears, but smiled.

'You promise to keep in touch,' he asked, 'and that you'll think of me.'

'Well, unless there's some handsome millionaire!' Sarah laughed, winking her eye, nudging his shoulder with hers.

# PART THREE

# TWENTY – FIVE

'WATCH WHERE YOU'RE PUTTING YOUR DIRTY paws you filthy dog!' Amanda shouted, pushing away the security guard. 'I shall write a letter of complaint about your conduct.'

'Sorry Miss but we have orders to search you and your belongings,' the security guard affirmed. 'Since one of the doctor's visitors was caught trying to sneak something in; we've had to be thorough.'

'I've heard about that, but that's no excuse to grope my chest,' Amanda asserted. 'I wouldn't mind if you were cute, but two ugly guys like you pair; well I would never.'

Once released from the grip of the security men, Amanda pulled straight her skirt and stormed through the large white door.

Inside, the room was small but bright white; the lamp hanging high above giving powerful light. Amanda stepped forward and noticed a small chair before her as a muffled voice announced.

'So, are you the replacement journalist?'

She turned to face from where the voice had come and noticed a thick window of glass separating two rooms. Above the glass were air holes through which the sound had travelled and below was a metal drawer, fixed rigid in the wall.

'What's your name my dear?' the deep voice asked slowly.

'Are you the doctor?' she questioned. 'I can't see you. How can I help if I can't see you?'

'Patience my dear, patience,' the voice replied calmly.

From within the shadows of the room and on the other side of the glass, moved a tall, slim figure, dressed in a dark suit. As the doctor came into view, the thing that unsettled Amanda were his piercing dark eyes that looked her up and down with discontent.

'Yes, err... sir,' she hesitated before her confidence returned. 'I am Amanda Burley. Since the arrest of your colleague, a Mr, err...'

'Daniel, my grounds keeper,' the doctor paused, scratching his chin. 'House keeper as well come to think.'

'Yes, well, since his arrest and the death of another journalist who was pursuing your case,' she said clearing her throat. 'A Mr Hedrick–'

'David, his name was David,' he doctor asserted, pausing momentarily. 'A quite resolute and intelligent boy, but like most, selfish and greedy.'

'Yes, well Mr Hedrick–' Amanda was interrupted again.

'David, I prefer to know people by their first name, don't you?' the doctor stated.

'Well, David,' Amanda announced, feeling that her nerves were being tested, 'I hear his employers have dropped the case and no others are interested and so on behalf of my company,' she said holding up her business card. 'I've come to pursue your case.'

'So young lady; looks as though I'm at the mercy of *your* ability,' the doctor responded sarcastically.

'Well, yes, if you want to get out of here and not piss about trying to smuggle in stolen property!'

'I take it you know of *my* pendant. Being stuck in here, Daniel wanted to bribe me.'

'Indeed,' Amanda said. 'And so a man who after all these years has surely looked after your property, of which I believe, is of some wealth, would suddenly turn against you?'

'It's complicated,' the doctor snapped angrily. 'A young, impassionate girl like you would not understand. That pendant is worth more than simply value in money!'

'More like something your life depends on,' she said slowly and assertively.

The doctor squinted angrily at her as he stood close to the glass; thinking surely she did not know the history of the pendant.

'Well, I have been doing some extensive research and know a little of your background.'

'Indeed,' the doctor replied.

'But firstly, this pendant, being that it is so dear to you, it must be retrieved, but apparently has gone missing again. The last to have it was a policeman in Bridgend who was tracking the one who reported it stolen – its owner.'

'Tracking its owner? But I am its owner!' the doctor flared, raising his voice. 'Will I never have it in my possession?'

Suddenly one of the security guards entered to see the doctor smack his fist against the glass. He warned the doctor that such behaviour would enforce him to remove his visitor and asked Amanda if she was okay. She responded that she was and that his anger was in response to bad news. Slowly the security man closed the door behind whilst looking desirously at Amanda's thighs, exposed as seated in her short skirt.

'Sorry, young lady,' the doctor said quietly, 'but I am at a loss without the assistance of Daniel. He's not the brightest young man, but a faithful and reliable one.'

'Well, he may be restrained for a while, but there are others that can get this pendant for you,' Amanda replied. 'There are other commendable services that I offer at a reasonable price, but it's not money that interests me.'

'Not money,' the doctor chuckled. 'I thought it was all about the money with *you* lot.'

'Not always,' Amanda asserted, stroking her thighs and watching the doctor look at her as she crossed her legs and pulled straight her skirt, 'but I guess you've seen all that before; being a wealthy and astute gentleman like yourself, entertaining many a young lady.'

The doctor smiled but turned away, thinking of Amanda as another upstart.

Amanda cleared her throat again and after stating that indeed money was useful, she confessed to her more dominant love of power and excitement, such as indulging in naughty sacraments. At first the doctor neglected her talk, looking at this sexy, little girl with contempt, but as she voiced her knowledge of his practice in the occult and recollected past ceremonies held with governmental figures, he realised her worth. He listened carefully as she recited her research into his past, but conveyed that his indulgence in the Black Art was but research.

'As you can see, I am restrained by the walls of this institute,' the doctor interrupted, 'that the crime I was convicted for is an injustice, as somewhere out there is the *real* criminal and when I find out who set me up they–'

'But surely the practice of witchcraft has been condemned for centuries,' Amanda snapped, flicking through images connected to her research. 'Science has prevailed in discrediting such acts of treachery and blasphemy?'

The doctor looked at Amanda angrily, before reminiscing.

'Don't be shadowed by what you don't understand my girl. Centuries ago the use of an invisible power would have had a man burned at the stake or left to rot in shackles, but today we use it as electricity. It took me years to research grey areas between science and the paranormal, trying to decipher literature after literature, book after book, meeting fellows who thought me mad. But many a scientist has been ridiculed in the past until they fall on some ingenious discovery.'

'So what made *your* research so significant?' Amanda questioned.

The doctor, although bewildered by her interest in the subject, quickly reviewed his travels to the West Indies and his studies of voodoo practiced on a certain island. Indeed at one point his life was threatened, but before fleeing the area he visited different islands and became convinced that the ceremonies, although primitive and barbaric, had a great connection with blood sacrifices, amongst other things. He turned his head to face Amanda and was astonished that she was absorbed by his commentary. The doctor sat and looked at her through the glass, thinking that her interest was genuine, but also realised, that now David could never visit again, she must help. Amanda beckoned the doctor to continue, but declaimed voodoo as primordial. The doctor sat back and looked at a map on the wall that displayed the British Isles. He continued his narrative on his history of research and how it took him to remote parts of Ireland, where Gaelic rituals were practiced by folk of simple upbringing; where he learned from their ancient writings and rituals of how to summon evil. Although the doctor wondered off on tangents and grumbled somewhat, Amanda learned of the doctor's exploration to several areas of the world and how his research connected different rituals and ceremonies that were practiced there. As the doctor again muttered off on a tangent, discussing how warlocks were known to retain summoned evil within objects, Amanda asked a question she had declined to ask for some time.

'What do you claim was the pinnacle of your research?'

For a moment the doctor sat quiet, but stood to pace back and forth.

'Blood my dear, amongst other things that without a life's work you would never understand, but a blood-letting ritual.'

'Surely stuff like that is just a gimmick to drink, dance and have raunchy sex,' Amanda smiled and realising what she had just said continued. 'Well in that case, if think I may become an exclusive club member.'

'Like I said,' the doctor announced, 'secrets you would never understand.'

'Secrets?' Amanda voiced. 'If you don't think I know of secrets, well you'd better look at these!'

She placed a number of documents in the metal drawer and slid it towards the doctor. As he pondered through the documents, squinting and turning them towards the light, he groaned and wheezed. He asked to how she had got them and Amanda responded whilst brushing her legs provocatively, by her personal and effective methods of research. The doctor asked her if she knew the gentlemen of which the documents listed, but she simply recollected her persuasive visits and that many other antiquities saleable from his property had recently been established as forgeries.

The doctor groaned and excused the sales to keep his property, to pay extortionate bills and keep Daniel in pocket.

Amanda smiled and reassured the doctor that his little endeavour would be kept secret, along with his recent contact with some political and wealthy people of whom he used to associate. The doctor confessed that the sales and recent contacts were part of his desperate measures to get out of the institute; that in the first time in his life he was afraid and had to get free before it was too late. Amanda became puzzled.

'Too late for what?' she asked.

'To reimburse the services I've abused,' the doctor muttered, but realised he was disclosing too much. 'I just need some assistance and should you keep things quiet my dear, rewards may come your way; you may even have an exclusive membership to the club.'

'Plus the exclusive ownership to your story?' she requested.

Resentfully the doctor agreed to Amanda's tenure of his case and to her fee and dropped an unsigned cheque in the metal drawer. Before he pushed the drawer forward, he wrote on a drawing he had made and retold of their agreement; that the cheque would be signed once Daniel had confirmed by telephone that he had the pendant. As she pulled the drawer towards her, the doctor told of how Daniel had been given a photograph of the journalist; the one he believed still had the pendant.

The doctor leaned forward, baffled by Amanda's ignorance. Tapping the drawing vigorously upon her thigh, she kept repeating the name he had wrote on the drawing.

'Mr Carl Aston,' she whispered slowly and then repeated, 'Carl... Carl?'

The doctor paused; realising she was thinking, but then his curiosities become the better of him.

'Do you know of the boy?' he asked.

Seductively crossing her legs again, confident she had the doctor's attention, Amanda winked and undoing her blouse, placed the drawing inside the cup of her bra.

'You underestimate the efficiency of my methods,' she said slowly and whilst buttoning up her blouse continued, 'but I suppose they wouldn't work on an elderly gentleman like yourself; not that you haven't seen any action, but been stuck between these four walls must be a drag.'

The doctor reacted by turning away in disgust, resenting her comment and voicing his concern of being in the hands of a headstrong prostitute.

'I heard your comment doctor,' she snapped, her dark brown eyes staring him out, but calmed herself as she fingered with her dark, long hair. 'I thought by now you would've gathered that I'm not just a pretty face.'

'Is that so?' the doctor laughed.

Amanda voiced her defence, telling of how the doctor's knowledge was restricted by his confinement and that he needed someone like herself to do duties on the outside. She continued to tease the doctor; stating that the figure they had agreed was too low and that her future services may come at a higher price. The doctor ridiculed her as a novice, but as she had evidence and knew a lot about his case, it was time to play her trump card. As she leant forward and straightened her jacket, Amanda glared at him and raising her eyebrows, disclosed.

'I'm surprised you've not thought of my idea to get you out, but then again, your information is somewhat restricted in here isn't it. What is it... one newspaper a day?'

'Well my dear,' the doctor said, leaning forward attentively, 'what kind of an idea have you in mind that *I've* not thought of ?'

Amanda recollected the policeman's death near Bridgend and that the incident was not far from the doctor's manor. The doctor poised, his hands outspread on the desk, beckoning her to continue. With a hint of sarcasm, she voiced her concern to how the policeman had got his throat torn out. The doctor interrupted, but spoke softly, talking of how certain events may be unfortunate, but asked to how this information incurred such an expensive service. Slowly Amanda disclosed that the policeman's death was closely related to how the boy died; the one he was accused of murdering so many years ago. But the doctor turned his face away and groaned.

'Don't you see,' she announced, 'if I work my magic in *broadcasting* that after all these years, the escaped convict is still at large; and with you inside...'

She paused, watching the doctor's eyes grow wide as he realised her intention. A cheeky smile stretched across his face as he agreed that new evidence like this, drafted in his favour, could get him acquitted.

Amanda stood and pushing her bra straight, winked again at the doctor before knocking on the door.

'As I told you, I'm not just a pretty face!'

It was her long, dark hair and sensual walk that captured Carl's eye as he walked slowly in to the reception area. As the girl stopped at the coffee machine, he noticed more of her face and pondered to where he had seen her before. He glanced at her again, but needed to concentrate as he was almost at the reception desk. Averted by her anger with the vending machine, he glanced at her again.

'Can I help you sir?' a voice asked, but noticing him distracted by the girl, the voice repeated. 'Sir, can I help you?'

Quickly Carl turned to face the receptionist and after apologising, introduced himself and the company he represented. Placing his business card on the desk, he reached inside his jacket for his appointment letter. Nervously unfolding it, he flattened it on the desk, trying not to look at the parts he had changed. After rummaging about her desk and glancing at the letter, the receptionist found her pen and pointed through a diary of appointments.

'I'm sorry sir, but I don't have any more appointments for Dr Schroeck today,' she said clearly, looking at him above the rim of her spectacles. 'Appointments must be agreed by phone first. Did you book prior to coming?'

'Yes the appointment was booked some time ago,' Carl lied convincingly. 'Maybe it's not been registered or has been overlooked somehow.'

'Believe me young man after recent events we don't *overlook* appointments,' she said sternly. 'What was the name again?' she asked, fingering with his business card.

'Mr Carl Aston,' he announced, 'a journalist to see Dr Schroeck on behalf of Haigh and Reece, Bristol.' He continued after viewing the waiting area. 'I can wait if need be; whilst you sort out an appointment.'

As he spoke, Carl did not see the dark-haired girl approach and listen in on their conversation, but saw a nurse appear to give the receptionist instructions. After a short discussion the nurse disappeared in the back room and the receptionist spoke.

'I'm sorry sir, but due to the request of our patient, the doctor refuses to see any other journalist apart from one he has specified.'

'And that is?' Carl asked.

'Unfortunately sir,' the receptionist said firmly, 'we are not allowed to give out that information.'

'Is that so,' Carl said angrily, grabbing his suitcase from the desk. 'Great, that's just great!'

Swinging around eagerly to storm away from the desk, Carl brushed past the girl.

'You stupid idiot,' the girl shouted. 'You should watch where you're going!'

'I'm sorry,' Carl voiced sympathetically. 'I'm sure I didn't knock you?'

'Of course you did,' she declared. 'Why else would I be drenched in coffee?'

Carl placed his briefcase down and fumbled around his pockets for his handkerchief.

'It's ruined that's sure,' she continued, 'and my jacket!'

Carl apologised again and swabbed the coffee from her blouse. As she took his handkerchief and walked into the light from the window, she looked at him strangely.

'Sorry, a bit of a fuss, but it was hot,' she said checking her jacket. 'But haven't we met before somewhere?'

'Maybe,' Carl said sheepishly, but then realised, 'isn't your name Amanda?'

'Yes, that's it, your Carl,' she said, moving aside to remove her jacket. 'It's stained my blouse as well – right down the front.'

'I'll get it cleaned for you I promise; properly at a dry cleaner,' Carl announced removing his sweater. 'Here, use this… I believe the ladies are over…'

Carl stopped, amazed as she removed her blouse. Looking away in embarrassment, he noticed an elderly man staring from the waiting area. Reaching high to pull the sweater over her, a grunt of disgust was voiced from the receptionist. As she pulled down the sweater, she rolled her eyes at Carl and told him to ignore the receptionist. Suddenly a piece of folded paper dropped from her body and hit the floor. Before Carl could reach to retrieve it, briskly she snatched it.

'It's just telephone numbers and that,' she said smiling, 'but important ones.'

For a moment Carl stood quiet, but followed her as she folded her clothes.

'That certainly was a good attempt to get an appointment,' she stated, a mischievous smile stretching across her face, 'but I'm afraid security has gone super tight since a man was caught sneaking in stolen property.'

She paused to think, her face showing concern.

'Of course, yes I remember now,' and continued with whispering, 'we met at the retrial. You're following the doctor's case, but not having much luck by the look of it.'

'Yes, I need to get answers,' Carl muttered, his face glum. 'Personal stuff.'

'I wouldn't worry too much about the doctor's case, if it's a top story you're after, you're barking up the wrong tree. It's not worth much anyhow; I've done cases like this before.'

'Today I thought I'd get at least some answers,' Carl muttered, pacing gently beside her. 'Guess it's just another bad day gone worse.'

'I don't think so,' Amanda announced and then muttered quietly to herself. 'It's turning out to be an easier task than I thought'.

'What did you say?' Carl asked.

'It's easier to clean than I thought,' she replied.

'What is?'

'This sweater of yours!'

'Look, I am sorry about that,' he said taking her clothes from her. 'I promise to get them dry cleaned by the weekend. But how shall I return them?'

'Look, how about me coming round,' she said brilliant with charm. 'Once I've washed your sweater, I can collect my stuff at the same time.'

Carl paused somewhat embarrassed, but noticed Amanda's eyes shine beautifully brown in the sunlight.

'How about we discuss the case,' she said convincingly. 'There's stuff I might be able to help you with.'

Carl nodded and pulled from his pocket his business card. After writing on the back of it his address, he handed it to her.

'Well at least it's come to some use,' he said, regretfully not getting an appointment.

# TWENTY – SIX

ON HIS WAY UP THE office staircase, Carl's mind was cluttered by mixed feelings. Largely he was annoyed by the failure of his attempt to visit the doctor, but otherwise pleased with meeting Amanda again. Although she did not have that powerful attraction that Sarah had, it was as though she hid some dirty little secret of which he wanted to be part of. As he approached the reception desk of Haigh and Reece, he was quite looking forward in meeting her again, but what was to become of Sarah if she left for America.

At first he thought Rachael was just visiting Mike and that they were using the reception area to talk, but suddenly he realised that David's funeral was that afternoon. Seeing them sat and engaged in conversation, slowly he walked toward them, waiting to announce his presence.

'What's this? Aren't we paying our respects today?' Carl asked, finding their clothes not dressed for a funeral. 'I must admit I forgot about it being at two.'

'I'm sorry pal, but I haven't had chance to tell you,' Mike said, standing from the couch. 'Due to complications, David's funeral has been set back.'

'Complications, 'Carl asked. 'What complications?'

'Well, I don't know all the gory details,' Mike said, ushering Carl to one side, 'but apparently after the coroner examined the body, or at least what was left of it, he's not convinced it was an accident. Actually, a primary autopsy has suggested that his death could lead to a murder investigation.'

'An investigation,' Carl croaked, frowning. 'A *murder* investigation?'

'Well, apparently a pointed instrument, of which at first they thought was a tree branch, broke the windscreen and punched a hole through his chest,' Mike whispered, 'and although the tree was burned a little, there was no charred branch at the scene.'

'Why should this set back his funeral?' Carl questioned.

'Well they think something else killed him; not just the crash. So another autopsy has to be done.'

'Well what's with all the secrecy?' Carl asked, as Mike whispered and escorted him away from Rachael.

'Well, it's not my business to pry, but it's a bit weird to how you mentioned his death a few days ago,' Mike replied, looking at him sincerely. 'You said he was pierced through his chest, killed by some instrument; a scythe I think you said?'

'That was all from my dream,' Carl stated, trying to cover up the fact that he had seen the accident.

'But you said you were there?' Mike declared, raising his voice.

'No, he was killed in my dream,' Carl repeated. 'What are you suggesting?'

'Look pal, I just think you've not been yourself since that mugger and...'

'What, you think that I–?'

'No,' Mike said, pausing to correct his words, 'it's just weird how you said he died and now, with this examination of his body, how he *actually* did.'

'How could you even contemplate me doing such a thing?' Carl snapped angrily.

'Well you've certainly not been yourself since…' he paused, watching Rachael approach. 'And with your vendetta against this doctor that David saw; and then there's this stuff about your father.'

'Can't fucking believe it,' Carl snapped, turning to enter the office.

'Watch your language,' Rachael shouted, parting the two and staring at Carl. 'What's with all this secrecy?'

'I'm just angry about not paying my respects,' Carl pretended.

'According to Mike, the both of you *hated* the guy anyhow,' Rachael declared.

'It's not that we hated him, just…' Mike asserted, but changed the subject. 'He'll be angry when he finds out what else has happened!'

'Finds out what?' Carl asked.

'The other news,' Mike said quietly. 'Rachael, I think you'd better tell.'

'Tell me what for God's sake!' Carl demanded.

'I was hoping to say goodbye too, but the only person who's seen her is Liz and…' Rachael paused, leading Carl to the couch. 'Well according to Liz, due to her father's request, Sarah left for America early this morning.'

Carl sat perplexed, thinking at least he could have waved his goodbyes at the airport or something.

'He couldn't have satisfied her enough by the looks of it!' Mike said sarcastically.

Suddenly with a rage Mike had never seen before, Carl went to hit him but was blocked by Rachael.

'What the *hell's* got into you two?' Rachael shouted.

'I told you he wouldn't take it well,' Mike asserted, 'but blimey, what resentment!'

'Stop winding him up then, God dam it!' Rachael beckoned, turning to face Mike after Carl. 'You *deserve* a sock in the jaw for comments like that!'

'Well he might as well frighten us *all* off,' Mike proclaimed, pulling Rachael aside, 'as his obsession with this doctor has obviously scared Sarah away. I was hoping their little trip might take his mind off things; maybe knock some sense into him, but looks like Sarah's had enough too.'

'She went to her father's wish –' Rachael said, but was interrupted by Carl as he brushed past her.

'If he keeps talking like that, I'll fucking deck that deceitful boyfriend of yours.' And before leaving, Carl muttered, 'I've got time off, I don't need to hang around *here*; funeral or no funeral.'

At first he thought it was the television, but waking from a nap, Carl realised it was the sound of his doorbell. As he struggled to get up and almost knocked his whiskey glass flying, the sound rang again.

Opening his front door, he was amazed to see Liz; that she had remembered where he lived or was it that Sarah had told her where he lived? He couldn't remember; guess drinking early evening certainly took its toile. Nervously Liz asked if she could enter and after nodding, Carl watched her gingerly make her way along the hallway. Eyes glancing around his front room, Liz forgot her manners and apologised as he entered after her.

'I'm sorry for disturbing you,' she said, her eyes wide with disconcert, 'but have you heard about Sarah?'

'What, that she's gone without saying goodbye; that some of us don't mean anything to her anymore?' he responded.

'That's not so, it's not like that,' she said nervously, 'Sarah said she couldn't face parting with you or Rachael and that she was hurried to get a flight.'

'Yes, Rachael told me she'd gone early this morning,' he muttered, returning to his armchair, gulping down the remains of whiskey and soda. 'Why's it she had to leave so quick? Does her father not like me already, although he's never met me?'

Liz could see that Carl was distraught and that he had been drinking to reduce tension; that indeed his voice slumbered with the intoxication of alcohol.

'Her father has found property that he wants her to approve and –'

'What he can't decide for himself and her mother?' Carl interrupted.

'Well, if I can continue,' Liz said sternly, finding Carl's manners impertinent, 'he's confirmed the job she was hoping to get, but she needs to start quickly; something about other competition.'

'We get a lot of that in journalism,' he slurred, standing to pick up his glass. 'Cut throat business you know – and that's just *our* place.'

He laughed and approached Liz, waving his glass.

'Fancy a shot?' he croaked.

'No sorry, I don't drink,' she said firmly, 'but I would love to see that pendant again, if you still have it, and…' she paused to follow Carl into the kitchen to hand him an envelope. 'I have some photographs Sarah said may help you in your research.'

'The pendant is in the bedroom,' he announced pouring more whiskey in his glass, 'but don't get taking it with you, I'll have to kill you first – joking of course.'

After adding a dash of soda to his whiskey, Carl walked to the bedroom but saw Liz hesitant to enter the room.

'Go on, it's okay, it's only a bedroom and I don't bite; well not friends anyway,' Carl slurred and muttered on, 'she might be gone but any friend of Sarah is a good friend of mine – especially after our lovely little time together; no matter how short it was.'

Carl paused, leaning on the wall for support and noticed Liz examine closely the pendant.

'It gets people killed that thing does you know,' he announced. 'That's why I keep it under that light.'

'Why,' she asked, 'why a sun-lamp?'

'Ask Sarah, she'll tell you why,' he replied. 'As if it wasn't for those ultraviolet rays, both of us would be six foot under now.'

'It's as black as night, but shiny like glass,' she said slowly. 'It's like a pebble.'

'That's what I thought when I first found it.'

'Where did you get it?'

'It was at a library, where some man got killed,' Carl said, but did not disclose to her the man's face in his dream.

'So this is what Sarah wants me to help you research?' she said looking at him keenly though her thick spectacles.

'Does she now?' he chuckled. 'Some sort of peace offering for leaving me sad and blue.'

'No, she was adamant that I help you, and that's what I'll do,' she said determinedly. 'Besides this things fascinating, don't you agree?'

'Yes it is,' he said slowly, turning back to sit in his armchair. 'I certainly need some answers, about that, this doctor and my father.'

Liz moved from the light of the sun-lamp to follow him into the lounge.

'Put it back,' Carl shouted, sitting up. 'Put it under the lamp!'

'Sorry,' Liz said, anxiously placing the pendant under the sun-lamp. 'Sorry I don't mean to; it's not mine and I shouldn't brood.'

'No, it's me that should be courteous,' Carl said sympathetically, 'it's just that things have happened; unexplainable things and I'd hate…'

Carl paused and turned to face Liz, seeing that his words were scaring her.

'I know that you had a dream about Sarah,' she said awkwardly, 'a nightmare of her getting attacked by some creature.'

'Yes, it was what made her realise,' he stated, 'that we survived together, but I guess you think it mad.'

Carl put down his glass and tried to focus on Liz from his armchair. To his surprise, she was serious with no gesture of disdain, but thinking.

'So you were Sarah in this dream?' she asked and then continued. 'You saw yourself from her vision.'

'Yes,' Carl said slowly.

'Unusual don't you agree; to see yourself as another person? Usually in dreams it's you and you alone that experience what you see.'

'Yes, that is weird,' Carl agreed.

'So this creature attacked you; you as Sarah that is?'

'Yes, it came up out from the mist below the window.'

'But Sarah wasn't killed,' Liz asked, 'in the dream that is?'

'No, I woke up and so thought that she was in danger.'

'That's weird,' she paused, fingering her lips, her hair and then her glasses. 'Just think, if you could master dreams like that, you could govern who gets killed or not.'

Carl leaned forward, looking at the whiskey mix in front of him.

'I can't believe that you don't say I'm crazy,' he proclaimed.

'At first when she told me, I thought Sarah a bit crazy,' she said, 'but I have a knowledgeable past about stuff like this; my mother, my grandmother – something about a second sight.'

'Like séances and psychic readings?' Carl asked, recalling the visit to his Aunt.

'Yes, but I've traced my past back to witchcraft practiced in the southern counties,' Liz revealed, 'and so I find this stuff enthralling.'

'You wouldn't find the evil that follows that thing enthralling,' Carl whispered, thinking Liz would not hear him.

'That pendant is amazing,' she said excitedly. 'We've got books down at the polytechnic that cover this stuff; plus there's my stuff at home.'

Carl looked again at her and followed her as she moved to sit opposite.

'We could look stuff up there this weekend; I'll get you a pass,' she said assertively. 'There are volumes on historical jewellery and witchcraft; being daylight, we could also try and match the pendant up with something.

# TWENTY – SEVEN

HE COULD SEE BY HER face that his tea was not to her liking, but Liz drank what she could, as it was only polite. Carl paused to watch her drink as she sat on his sofa, wriggling and glancing repetitively at her watch; it was obvious she had not visited many men before, especially being alone with one in his house. As she placed her cup down to look up, he turned to enter his kitchen.

'Can we go now?' Liz asked tensely. 'I got here early so we can catch my friend before she leaves the library.' She looked down again at her cup, her spectacles shimmering from the light between the curtains. 'Only she'll get you a pass before Mrs Jenkins gets in and–'

'It'll be easier without your boss there you mean,' Carl interrupted.

Liz nodded and got to her feet.

'Did you read the note?' she enquired, stepping timidly towards him. 'Sarah said something about telling you why she left and…' Liz paused, seeing Carl's face become stern. 'Research she did into some man at a library.' She turned and folding her arms asked, 'what's all *that* about?'

Carl collected her cup from the coffee table and stood silent for a moment.

'What man?' Liz questioned, her curiosity getting the better of her. 'Sarah said something about a ring as well?'

'Well the photos she had enhanced show a ring that all members had,' Carl replied, entering the kitchen.

'What members?' Liz shouted her eyes wide with excitement.

'Members of some astrological society they called it,' Carl pronounced from a distance, 'but anyway, what intrigues me is the research Sarah managed to get about this man.'

'What did she have on him?'

'It's a bit complex,' Carl quietened, stopping by the kitchen door and noticing her near, 'but somehow, after wanting no more to do with this society, he had threatening letters that would reveal his handling of art forgeries, but hid them after agreeing to pay an arrangement of fees.'

'It sounds like blackmail to me,' Liz said quietly.

'Exactly, but I guess he knew more about stuff than so called forgeries,' Carl declared.

'What's this got to do with–?'

'The man with this ring?' Carl intruded. 'He appears in photos of both my father and a Doctor Schroeck–'

'A doctor who?' Liz questioned.

'An evil man who hated my father and opposed his religious work,' Carl said, moving close to her, 'a man sent down for killing a young boy – my friend!'

Liz froze, startled by Carl's anger as he stood staring down at her.

Look,' she said nervously, 'we'd better get a move on, it's–'

Suddenly, the door-bell rang and both Carl and Liz looked towards the hallway. Quickly it rang again.

'You're not expecting anyone are you?' Liz whispered, moving swiftly to peer through the gap between the front window curtains.

'No,' Carl croaked, 'it's not a policeman is it?'

'Why no,' Liz said slowly, 'it's a girl – a dark-haired girl.'

Carl hesitated before opening the front door, but as he did the girl swung around from facing a postman retreating up the path.

'Oh hello,' she said, 'didn't think you were in for a second, I was just going to push these through.'

'Amanda,' Carl said surprised but relieved, taking the letters that the postman had handed her, 'I totally forgot about you coming around.'

'You mean you haven't had my stuff cleaned yet?' she asked, handing him his sweater.

'Yes I have,' he said retreating in the hallway, 'they're just in the bedroom somewhere.'

'Carl, please can we leave now, it's–'

Liz stopped by the hallway, noticing the doorway blocked by Amanda.

'Oh, I'm sorry, I didn't know you had company,' Amanda announced, stepping along the hallway. 'If I knew your girlfriend was here, I would have called later.'

'I'm *not* his girlfriend,' Liz slurred, backing into the kitchen entrance, 'she's in America and being her best friend, she asked me to help out with things.'

'Like what?' Amanda said sarcastically looking Liz up and down. 'Can't be the ravishing company and thrilling nights out, surely?'

'Actually we're off to the library,' Liz croaked, watching Amanda find her way to the lounge, 'and we've got to hurry.'

'Is that so,' Amanda said softly. 'Nice little place you got here Carl.' She paused taking in a good view. 'But a bit dingy for my liking,' she said quietly leaning towards Liz and then said aloud, 'more room than you first think.'

Her first impressions held firm as Liz was suspicious about this provocative and curvaceous young woman; noticing her eyes search the lounge and then step aside to examine the kitchen.

'We've really got to be going Carl,' Liz broadcast, backing into the bedroom, 'as my friend leaves within the hour.'

'It's okay, I've found them,' Carl announced, brushing past Liz to hand Amanda the clothes. 'They're in this bag.'

It was at this point that Liz noticed Amanda's disinterest for her clothes, but saw her glance over his shoulder, at the sun-lamp in the bedroom.

'That's unusual,' Amanda declared, 'a man having a sun-lamp in his bedroom?'

'It's Sarah's, my girlfriend's,' he fabricated, turning to see Liz step back towards it, 'she left it here by mistake.'

It was then that Liz noticed Amanda become agitated as Carl blocked her view once more.

'Why so interested,' Carl questioned obstructing her view, 'your clothes are here, in this bag?'

'I don't know... guess I'd like one,' she said shrugging her shoulders. 'But you can't be sure they're safe. I use professional sun-beds, down the gym that is; can't you tell?' she said, turning to show Carl her bronzed legs and lifting her skirt a little.

Suddenly, Liz snatched the pendant and placing it in her cardigan, paced forcibly across the hallway and outside.

'We haven't got time for *those* antics,' Liz shouted from outside the door, 'we need to get a move on!'

'I'm sorry, but who made *her* the boss?' Amanda asked

cynically, but then realised Carl was anxious too, 'Look, where is it you work again – I could call in.'

Holding his briefcase open on his knee, Carl handed Amanda another business card after dropping in the letters she had handed him. At first Amanda's face was stern, annoyed by Liz's demands as she tried to scrutinise Carl's briefcase, but then smiled mischievously.

'Look we can't possibly discuss the doctor's case here *or* at your work,' she said winking, 'so why not come round my place, but make sure you ring me first.'

Vindictively she slowly wrote her name and number on the back of the business card knowing Liz was stamping her feet with impatience.

'You never know, maybe we can sneak you that appointment with the doctor,' she said looking once again over his shoulder and into the bedroom.

'We'll see,' Carl said, ushering Amanda along the hallway and out the door, 'got other things planned for now, so if you don't mind.'

'Well aren't you the forceful type all of a sudden,' Amanda said, holding his arm before sauntering away. 'Maybe sometime later then darling?'

Passing Liz by, Amanda stared her up and down and whispered.

'Leave the exciting work to the professional my dear; personally, I don't think he'd be interested, even with his girlfriend out of the country.'

Liz smirked as Amanda strolled down the path, but once her back was turned, Liz stuck out her tongue.

'Come on, there's no time for that,' Carl said, pushing Liz toward his car, 'I don't know what type of journalist she is, but it pays for a nice car!'

Liz was mostly quiet on the drive to the polytechnic, but fretted somewhat with the gate security before they reached the library. On their short walk to the entrance, Liz stopped Carl by the arm and having a troublesome frown, announced her unease about Amanda; that she had a funny sensation and there was something wrong about her. Carl smiled and ushered her aside, saying she should have more concern about her friend leaving soon. Liz glanced at her watch and suddenly sped off towards the entrance.

Inside, the library was quite vast, with high arched windows that was much a contrast to the modern polytechnic buildings Carl had previously seen. He observed the high collections of books that circled him and ones on the ground which ran along parallel shelving. However, his surveillance was severed by calls from Liz; that her friend had already finished, but had waited to print him a weekly pass. Unusually the formalities were quick; only some evidence of his permanent address, his driving licence and a signature were required. However, as Liz reiterated from her friend, the pass would only be valid for a week, but hopefully that would be enough time for Carl to complete his research.

Before he had time to examine his new pass, Liz was escorting him about the building and pointing to areas of interest; books that could help with research and computers he could use as a visitor. Eventually, after his quick but delightful tour of the building, Carl found an empty desk where as a visitor, he could use a computer. As she assisted Carl to log on to the computer and briefed him on how to search for books, she noticed the business card he had in his briefcase. Impatiently Liz waited and tapping her feet glanced at Carl's briefcase whilst helping with a book search. In an attempt to distract him from tending his belongings, Liz asked if he needed the toilet or directions to the book he had searched, but he was busy writing. As he pulled out some drawings of the pendant, she felt the object in her cardigan pocket and pondered on the jewellery.

'Looks like you don't need the pendant,' she stated, pointing to his drawings, 'those should be enough to do the research, shouldn't they?'

'Yes, that thing needs to stop where it's safe,' he replied, 'under that sun-lamp at home.'

Liz froze; although she had picked it up to hide it from Amanda's prying eyes, she could not reveal that it was indeed in her pocket. Carl looked up at her, seeing her nervous but inquisitive.

'What's wrong?' he asked. 'You look flustered.'

'Can I look at Sarah's photos,' she asked timidly, 'those of that man's ring? I may be able to research that stuff for you?'

'Yes, help yourself,' Carl announced typing away at the keyboard, 'they're in the large brown envelope.'

With his permission, she rummaged about his briefcase and whilst retrieving the envelope with one hand, snatched the business card with the other.

'I'll be by the reception desk, if you need help that is,' Liz said, sneaking the business card into her other pocket, 'you know; if you need to find stuff and that.'

Carl groaned his acknowledgement and undistracted, continued to flicker through pages on the computer screen.

As she propped open the parting in the desk, she smiled at another girl serving a gentleman and then sneaked behind the cabinets to the staff computer. Quickly she turned over the business card and after scrutinising Amanda's handwriting, entered her name into a customer search. Unfortunately, nothing was returned; the only two surnames of Burley were male clients. She tried again with a national library search, but no match. Again she tried by typing Amanda's first name with a key search on her telephone number, but again, nothing.

'You are Liz, right?' a voice barked from behind.

Liz jumped and felt her head go dizzy, before turning to notice the girl she had seen at the desk.

'Yes, sorry,' Liz said, her hand against her chest, 'you startled me for a second.'

'I'm sorry,' the girl said softly, 'but I didn't think you were working today; you're not on the rota?'

'Well, I'm not but,' Liz stopped, pausing to place her words, 'I'm helping a friend with his research, but he doesn't know the place, if you know what I mean.'

'What's he like?' the girl asked with a look of excitement in her eyes.

'Okay, I guess, but his going out with my best friend,' Liz replied and getting rather anxious to do her task in secret, tried to persuade her to leave. 'Carl's in the research lab, near the journals, if you want to take a look?

'Well I might just have a nosey over there later,' the girl said slowly, but snapped suddenly. 'What's it you're trying to do?'

Liz did not want to disclose her task, but was desperate to find out about Amanda.

'These records only list *current* clients, don't they?' Liz asked, pushing her spectacles right. 'You can't search other records, can you?'

'I don't think so,' she replied, 'but have you tried a national library search?'

'Yes, but nothing,' Liz said, and exhaled in frustration, 'the client's address will be a start!'

'Why not try the phone book,' the girl said, turning to serve another client, 'it's how I find addresses to mail lost cards.'

Liz's eyes grew wide as a smile of certainty stretched across her face. Quickly she raced to snatch the telephone book from the service desk and scuttled back to the computer, to be hidden amongst the cabinets. After looking up Burley, she matched a telephone number by the initial A.

'Got you!' Liz shouted, but realising her excitement may attract the girl again, quickly wrote down Amanda's full address beneath her name and telephone number before hiding the card back in her cardigan pocket. Slowly she whispered, 'I'll see what else I can get on you later.'

By the time Liz returned, Carl was standing to stretch his arms aloft.

'Get a bit cramped sitting here,' he declared, releasing a sigh, 'but I've managed to compile some sort of a list. Don't know if it has everything, but could you find this stuff for me; maybe I could take some out?'

'Sorry, you can't take out books as a visitor,' she remarked, brushing her hair from her face to take his list, 'but if some *are* important, I'll issue them on my card if you like.'

Carl smiled in agreement and thanking her, watched her skip off to her undertaking. Whilst fingering the coins in his pocket, he yawned and noticed in his briefcase the letters Amanda had handed him from the postman. Suddenly his curiosity overwhelmed his thirst for a hot drink and so sat to read the letters. As he ciphered through the first few and dropped them back into the briefcase, he stopped at one letter; noticing that the handwriting was careful and neat, the envelope old, but rigid. After placing down the others, he hesitated before opening the envelope with his pen. Pulling out a folded letter, he noticed something fall to the ground. Dragging back his chair, he saw on the ground, a key; somewhat tarnished, but shiny in the dim of the floor. Slowly he reached down to pick up the key and after placing it in his briefcase, began to read the letter.

> *My dearest nephew Carl,*
>
> *It was great to meet you and your lovely friend Sarah over those few days, but your questions have left me somewhat troubled. As I promised our late Steven Aston, it is not my duty to explain in full, past family events, but realise you must find peace of mind. You must appreciate that recollecting some past events may be quite disconcerting, but I too must have closure, if only brief.*

*A friend of Reverend Aston, a Mr Carrington, who was previously involved with the man you call the Darkman, later feared this doctor, as he told of his capabilities even whilst confined. Before I moved to Bridgend, this man made his own memorial to our Reverend as his poor grave was vandalised after he died in the church fire. I don't know if this man can help you, but after the doctor betrayed him, he became close friends to our Reverend and buried a metal box about this memorial. The key was sent to me by Mr Carrington as he said I was the only relative, but also wrote of being in fear of his life.*

*I believe this box contains a diary, of which I hope provides the answers you want, but you must contemplate; learning of past events may incur some displeasure. I apologise for being brief, but you must appreciate, recalling Eleanor's past may bring back fond memories, but it also brings some sorrow.*

*I don't know what was made from the ashes of the church, but believe the memorial lies somewhere near an old, disused wall fountain.*

*With love and God's blessing,*
*Evelyn Jones.*

Liz had been a while before returning with a pile of books, but it had been enough time for Carl to drink a coffee. As she placed them on the desk before him, Carl started browsing the book titles along each of them.

'Most of these are about the occult, witchcraft, supernatural powers – stuff like that,' Liz declared, removing one held under her arm, 'but the small, dirty green one maybe of interest; it's to do with séances, dreams and having premonitions like you say you have.'

'They're dreams, powerful and vivid I admit, but not premonitions,' Carl said quietly.

'I disagree,' she retorted. 'According to what Sarah said–'

'So I *have* been part of your discussion,' he interrupted, looking up at her, 'and hope you have nice things to say about me?'

'Mostly,' Liz replied, awkwardly trying to smile and changing the subject, 'but this is the book I want to show you!'

'It looks an old one,' Carl acknowledged, opening the page to which Liz had bookmarked, 'and you've found it; well something like it?'

'This book is from our restricted section, so I'm afraid that even *I* cannot take it out,' she specified, pointing to an image on the page Carl had turned to, 'but that looks like the stone in your pendant, don't you agree?'

'You have a good memory to what things looks like,' Carl said, taking the drawing from his left. 'It just looks like a dark pebble to me?'

'Well I do have a good eye for detail,' she said, hiding the fact she had the pendant in her pocket.

'That's exactly what Sarah said about jewellery.'

'Well, that's probably one of the things we have in common.'

'One of the things,' Carl repeated with a hint of sarcasm.

'But anyway,' Liz said disregarding his comment, 'this book describes that before the stone was cast as an item of jewellery, it was used centuries before to lure evil spirits using alchemy mixtures of mainly sulphur and mercury.' She paused to pick up the book and after reading a sentence, described: 'The stone was later used by warlocks to capture evil spirits or as witches have been known to cast the evil spirit upon an enemy.'

'Go on,' Carl signalled, a sudden interest appearing on his face, 'what's that about witches casting spells?'

'Well, it doesn't say exactly,' she revealed, handing him the book carefully, 'as it goes on mainly about casting metal to make the stone an item of jewellery.'

'But how can we be certain that it's the same stone?' Carl questioned.

'I'm not sure,' Liz remarked, 'but according to another book; a very old book that this book references, it glows when evil is summoned.'

'What glows?'

'The stone,' Liz announced. 'And it states that its then that it can be broken.'

'Broken – with what?'

'I don't know, but in other books that I've read about stuff like this,' Liz indicated, 'should the spell be broken, the conjurer becomes the invocation. I guess that's what witches were in fear of; becoming the victim of their own spells.'

'This book,' Carl stated, 'the old one that says that the stone glows – where is it?'

'I thought you may ask that. I too was fascinated by the fact that a stone, probably only made of black onyx could glow, and that it being quite ancient–'

'Where is it?' Carl demanded.

'Well after doing a quick reference,' Liz said, pausing to remove a piece of paper from up her sleeve, 'it's at… Centridge House.' She paused again to think. 'That's near Shipham I think. It's not *that* far from here.'

'It's no good to us now,' Carl professed, looking to the floor in disappointment, 'it's been destroyed.'

'How do you know?' Liz asked frowning. 'How was it destroyed?'

'Because my dear, it's a journalists job to find out these things and besides,' Carl paused to look up at her, 'that's the old library where I found the blasted thing; it's there where I saw *that* book burned, and it's there I–'

Suddenly Carl felt a shiver shoot up his spine, realising what his Aunt had just told about a Mr Carrington. Leaning forward and seeing that he had gone quite pale, Liz became concerned.

'Are you okay, Carl,' she asked softly, 'you're as white as a sheet?'

However, Liz's words went unheard, as Carl's mind busied itself with connecting pieces of information; the man at the library was undoubtedly Mr Carrington, the friend of his father that his Aunt had just described; the ring Sarah had photographed on his hand proved that surely.

'Sorry Liz,' Carl said slowly, still thinking, 'maybe with these books, something will come up.'

'You say a man got *killed* at Centridge House,' Liz queried.

'Yes.'

'When did this happen?'

'A month ago,' Carl said rubbing his eyes. 'No; probably more than that.'

At first his eyes were blurred after rubbing them, but noticed Liz scuttle away.

It was several minutes later, whilst Carl was browsing the books more closely, that Liz returned to open a newspaper.

'It's in this one, I think.'

'Where did you get that?' he questioned.

'With the journals,' she replied. 'We keep backdated copies for certain cliental.'

Walking slowly towards him, sifting through the pages of the newspaper, Liz suddenly stopped.

'Here it is,' she announced, starting to read aloud the reported article from the newspaper. Slowly she described of how a man was found dead after lightening had hit the observatory dome of the building, when Carl interrupted.

'Carrington,' he pronounced, 'the man's name is Carrington!'

Squinting at him after lowering the newspaper, Liz mumbled her curiosity to how he knew the man's name before she had chance to announce it.

'Oh, but of course,' she remarked, realising he had been assigned to report the incident, 'you found it out as part of your job!'

'Actually Liz,' he stated resolutely, 'it's the first I've heard of it!'

Liz frowned at him for a while before continuing to read the article aloud. He listened to her narrate some of the man's past; that he had got caught up with art and antique forgeries, but later accused an astrological society of blackmailing him to sell them. As Liz read the rest of the article, Carl became disinterested, feeling a bitter resentment against the doctor; surely it was Carrington's word against the *whole* of this doctor's society and after being blackmailed, the pendant was planted on him to shut him up. But as he had discussed with Sarah, if it was not his dreams conjuring the evil, then how could it be timely summoned to kill Carrington? Whilst he was in solitary, maybe it was this society that was doing all of the doctor's dirty work; indeed the burglar who stole the pendant could be a member of this society. Suddenly his thoughts were disturbed.

'How does the evil get drawn to the stone?' Liz asked.

'I'm not sure,' Carl replied quietly, 'but I certainly know my dreams come true; that they make horrible things happen.'

'From what Sarah said after meeting your Aunt,' she muttered, 'I think your wrong.'

'What?' he said in disagreement, 'I don't think so – if you'd had the dreams.'

'But you have the dreams before anything happens, right?'

'Yes, but–'

'Well, can't you see,' she stated convincingly, 'Sarah said that your Aunt, and your mother, were righteous people; they used séances to stop bad things from happening. Maybe that's what been bred into you.'

'Don't be so stupid, how can–'

'If you don't believe me,' Liz interrupted, 'read some of the accounts in *those* books, you'll be surprised what powers people have; stuff we don't understand, just because science can't explain it!'

'Man, the only thing I've inherited,' he laughed, but then coughed, 'hopefully is my immunity to a number of diseases.'

'Fine, go ahead, ridicule me,' she said stamping her feet like a little school girl, before scampering off. 'At least *Sarah* would listen to me!'

Carl looked quickly at the books and realised, indeed Liz had gone out of her way to help and that both of them were missing their friend. Speedily he ran and caught up with her near the service desk.

'Look I'm sorry,' he said sincerely, 'I miss Sarah too, and it's come to be difficult without her. I'll have a look at the books and maybe they'll convince this *fact only* journalist. After the things that have happened over the past few months, I shouldn't ridicule anything.'

The time had passed faster than Carl had thought when Liz announced she wanted to go. Fascinated by the books of which Liz had got him, he asked her to take out one for him on her card. It was not until she got into his car, she remembered his business card in her pocket, along with the pendant. As she buttoned up her cardigan, she recalled the girl she had met that morning.

'I don't trust that girl,' Liz said quietly.

'What girl?' Carl asked.

'That girl: Amanda.'

'She's a bit potent, I'll agree; but she might be my only way to interview this doctor.'

'She wants more than just your help; those girls always do.'

'I feel a hint of animosity from the noble girl beside me,' Carl said turning to smile at her. 'Didn't think you had feelings like that.'

'We all have feelings Mr Aston; it's just that some have to learn to hide them.'

Carl could see by her words that Liz was somewhat upset by his statement and that something else was troubling her.

'How do you fancy a trip to my home town,' he said, rectifying his road directions, 'if you have the day off tomorrow, that is?'

'Yes, yes, I have,' she said baffled, 'but what for?'

'I need to find a metal box, somewhere in a churchyard.'

At first Liz looked even more puzzled, but became excited.

'Like a treasure hunt?'

'Not exactly, but not far wrong,' he said, turning the car about a corner, 'but first I must book some extra days off work.'


It was late by the time Carl came out the office with Mike and Liz was concerned he had been so long.

'What's with the new girl?' Mike said sarcastically.

'Who?' Carl asked.

'She's a nice piece, but a little timid, don't you think?' Mike sneered. 'Then again maybe she is *your* type.'

'What *are* you on about?' Carl questioned, as they neared his car. 'Oh, you're on about–'

'Isn't that…?'

'Yes Mike,' Carl announced, 'it's Liz, and before you say anything more, she's just helping me out.'

'Oh right, what with, *exactly?*' Mike said, winking his eye.

'Well, she's helping with research; a favour she said she'd do for Sarah.'

'Not much of a substitute for Sarah though if you ask me; she's not got, you know?' Mike said gesturing a woman's figure with his hands.

'What is it with you – is everything about sex?'

'Well, it takes your mind off *this* place,' Mike shouted, pointing at the office building whilst backing away.

'Don't much care for him, either,' Liz said as Carl entered the car.

'What Mike?' Carl clarified. 'Don't worry about him, his harmless; it's just his ego controls his head.'

Liz frowned for a moment and then laughed, a sniggering sound reverberating her nose. Carl settled into the driver's seat, trying best to ignore the grunts coming from the girl beside him. After requesting her address, she silenced to tentatively state where she lived.

Although it had taken him an extra hour to drop Liz off at her house, he could not help but stop at his favourite café to browse the book she had lent him. Again the coffee was only warm as he sipped at the mug to browse pages of interest. As the bacon sandwich went down a treat, he became fascinated by a number of pages regarding fortune telling and psychic readings; that people could describe future events or identify a card someone held in secret. As he read on, the following chapters described more of psychic powers and provided examples of gifted people who unwillingly have predicted danger.

He paused to drink the remains of his now cold coffee. Over the page he learned of a mother's call to a movie theatre after knowing that her daughter was in danger. Indeed, on her way to meet her father and brothers the little girl had been hit by a car. Carl read on, fascinated by the number of accounts; some told of clairvoyants who helped police with their enquiries and when asked about their power, they disclosed that it is simply inherited. Suddenly Carl went cold; maybe his dreams were related to what he had read. He felt a shiver come over him and his ears burning. Maybe Liz was talking about him to her friends he thought, but now it was him that was becoming superstitious.

It was a short drive to his flat, but after being accosted in that alleyway, Carl would probably never walk it again at night. However, for some reason, he could not help but continue to feel uneasy. As he reached his front door, he noticed a blue light shine dimly from the kitchen window.

Inside, Carl could see that the lounge had been tampered with. Lying on the floor, upturned and facing the door, the sun-lamp shone blue upon the ceiling. He turned on the bedroom light to gasp at the open window and his bedroom turned upside down. He looked desperately about him thinking of what was stolen, but there was his watch, the small portable television and other things of value.

He looked to the lounge to scrutinise the room. Definitively it had been ransacked, but still, nothing was stolen. He raced to the telephone, but hesitated, realising what Mike had said about the police wanting to question him. Looking back to the bedroom, suddenly he noticed the pendant missing. As he searched the floor and under the bed, he realised of course; the place ransacked, the sun-lamp on the floor – this was probably the same burglar as before, or at least, another accessory from the doctor's notorious society.

# TWENTY – EIGHT

IT HAD TAKEN LONGER THAN he thought to find a parking space by the churchyard, as the town had changed somewhat to how he remembered it. Turning off the car engine, Carl rubbed his eyes and thought of the letter his Aunt had sent him. Although it had been an hour's journey, he had not spoken to Liz about his flat being ransacked last night. Undoubtedly like Sarah, she would want to get the police involved and that was the last thing he needed. He had been late picking up Liz as after trying to fix the broken window, found it difficult to secure.

Liz looked at Carl as he squinted out the windscreen. Awkwardly she fidgeted about the passenger seat, trying to release the seat belt without catching her clothes. It was not that her clothes were expensive, but the fact that she had left both his business card and the pendant in each cardigan pocket. In her mind she kept thinking of reasons to visit his flat that evening, as surely an opportune moment would come for her to return both the card and pendant; maybe pretend that she found the pendant under his bed or cabinet. But why not put it back under the sun-lamp? Carl had obviously not seen that it was missing or he would have said something.

'If I remember, the main gate to the churchyard is long that road,' Carl said pointing down a narrow road. 'But it'll be easier to park here I think.'

Liz looked at him warily and although she was not an expert, she did best to hide her guilt. As she slammed shut the car door, she felt the cold of the outside air. She huddled her clothes around her body; not listening to Carl moan about her action.

'Why is it that girls slam car doors so bloody hard?' he said, locking his door. 'Sarah was the same; total disregard for the old girl!'

Liz stepped around the front of the car, still ignorant of his words as her mind was curious to her whereabouts. Slowly she wandered down the road to where Carl had pointed and so he stepped after her.

After following a high bricked wall for a minute or two they approached a concrete archway leading to a metal gate. Approaching behind Liz, Carl could see her test the rigidity of a large padlocked gate.

'It's locked tight Carl,' she announced in dismay, 'it won't budge!'

'Here,' Carl said taking her hands away from the lock, 'let me have a go.'

Disappointedly however, his forceful tug proved ineffective and the padlock held firm.

'My father never had to lock his churchyard when I was a kid,' he said with disdain. 'Bloody vandals – why don't they leave the dead in peace?'

'Why is *your* father in there?' Liz questioned, a look of concern in her eyes.

'Yes, according to my Aunt,' he paused to think, 'he's still buried in there, although some bastards vandalised his grave.'

'Isn't that so –?'

'Thoughtless!' Carl interrupted angrily. 'But what am I to do *now*?'

'Don't you know anyone down here?' Liz enquired.

'No, not really,' he said, looking into the churchyard, 'I left this place, years ago; I haven't seen it since going to boarding school.'

'Well why didn't you make arrangements before you came?' Liz queried, but noticed Carl become annoyed at her declaration.

'Cause I didn't have *time* to drill out people from my past,' he said pacing about angrily, 'besides, there's probably no-one left that knew my father!'

'Well if he was the local clergyman,' Liz indicated looking around the street, 'someone around here must know of him and how to get in here?'

Carl tested the gate again and thought of climbing over but his actions were stopped as Liz blocked his way to point.

'Try the pub!' she announced. 'There's a pub down the road; maybe the landlord knows who locks this place?'

'Guess it's worth a try?' he said stepping off in that direction.


The doors were open but after entering a lounge, Carl and Liz heard a voice shout.

'I'm sorry, but we're not open just yet!'

Carl and Liz turned to face a figure approach from beyond the bar.

'We don't want a drink,' Liz muttered, somewhat uncomfortable with the strange surroundings.

'What then,' the voice shouted, 'we don't do rooms, if that's what you couple want?'

'No, we don't want that,' Carl rectified, smiling at Liz as to what the man assumed, 'I just want to know about the churchyard down the road; of who looks after it and has a key to get in?'

'What's it got to do with you?' the man said.

'My father's grave is in there and we…' Carl revealed but stopped, wanting not to disclose too much.

'Mr Collins,' the voice shouted, moving a barrel around from under the bar, 'the farmer up at Hillside Gardens; about half a mile west of here.'

'Which way is that exactly?' Carl asked.

'What?' the voice said. 'Ask Mr Collins and stop bothering me.'

'Come on,' Liz growled, pulling Carl from out of the entrance of the pub, 'west is this way as the sun is low over there.'

After walking several minutes, the incline of the road increased and they found that it had narrowed into a country lane. Bordered by naked woodland and surrounded by fields, the uneven and gravelled lane led to open land where stood an old cottage, covered in lifeless ivy and other dead foliage.

'Hillside Gardens,' Liz announced excitedly, 'that's the name we passed; it must be *that* cottage.'

'We'll see,' Carl stated, pacing quick to beat her to the door, 'leave the talking to me, will you? This farmer may have known my father.'

They waited sometime before an elderly gentleman answered the door; a predominantly white-haired man, although most hair adorned his face and his moustache was discoloured yellow. As he peered through the half open gap, he asked to what was their business.

'Sorry to bother you sir but,' Carl searched words to make his request more compelling, 'I need access to the old Saint Bartholomew's churchyard in order to see my father's grave.'

'Why you want visit that place for?' the farmer requested. 'No-one visits graves there anymore, besides the ruins of the old church are dangerous – that's why it's locked.' He paused to take breath, removing the rolled cigarette from his mouth. 'And because of those pesky vandals.'

'Well I need to visit my father's grave to assert renovation costs.' Carl fabricated.

'Most are in a right state, but actually,' the old man thought aloud, 'the only grave damaged is the old clergy's.'

'Yes,' Carl affirmed, 'that's my father – Reverend Aston; a Reverend Steven Aston.'

'So you must be?' the man paused, scratching his head.

'Mr Carl Aston, his son from Bristol,' Carl revealed. 'Please we've come a long way and–'

'Come on in,' the man announced, his grim face turning into a smile, 'got to be sure about these things now-a-days, but have you got any–'

'Yes, here!' Carl said, opening up his driving licence. 'This will do as id won't it?'

'I suppose,' the man muttered, shutting the door behind him to stare closely at Carl's picture, 'mind you, you don't look much like the old clergy; he had a larger nose?' he said, pointing to Carl's driving licence. 'As for the churchyard, I only keep the key 'til they know what to do with it.'

The old man stubbed out his cigarette after licking his finger and ushered them to the kitchen, where he retrieved a key from a nearby shelf.

'Coz I'm sorry about the way he died,' the farmer said slowly, swivelling the key in sight of them, 'must have been dreadful being caught in that church, fire blazing and all. But I never understood how he couldn't get out, or how it started for that matter.' He paused again, feeling his breast pocket for tobacco. 'A bit of split candle wax couldn't be that bad, surely?'

'Well I was told it was an accident,' Carl said looking at Liz, who staring, was captivated by the story, 'but now, I believe differently.'

'Best to leave the past alone,' the farmer said, placing the key into Carl's hand, 'but at least someone cares about the old clergy. I have tried to patch the place up but, well, don't get the time like I used to, what with my legs; that hill gets harder to climb every visit.'

'We shouldn't be too long Mr Collins,' Carl stated, bouncing the key in the palm of his hand. 'We'll try and get it back before it gets dark.'

'Well it gets dark earlier now you know,' he said searching for his matches, 'and with some rain due, you've only got a couple of hours.'

'We'd better get a move on then, hadn't we Liz?'

Not only was the padlock hard to open, but the gate too. As Carl used his body weight to force open the left gate, it screeched on its hinges. Liz hated the sound and hurried past into the churchyard to evade it. At first he did not see Liz wonder off and was talking alone; describing how the place had not been visited in ages, but as he turned, noticed her scurrying down to what was a path.

'Watch your footing,' Carl shouted, walking briskly after her, 'the old man said the ground is dangerous!'

Liz looked back to see Carl approach, but was captivated by the task.

'Most of these are untouched,' she said, tip-toing about the graves, 'but the poor things haven't been cared for in years.' Stopping, she turned to ask. 'What was your father's full name again?'

'Steven Aston, but I think it was engraved Reverend Steven Aston.'

Trying best to watch his foothold as well as keep up with Liz, he stepped across between graves until he heard Liz announce.

'This might be it,' she shouted, but quietened as she saw Carl standing near. 'This one's over grown alright and its stone is cracked.'

Suddenly Carl saw Liz stumble as she tried to lean over it, but caught her by the arm just in time to prevent her from falling. As she looked up in to Carl's eyes, strands of hair escaped her ponytail and fell over her face. Although his grip hurt her arm, she became entranced by his strength and the concern on his face. Fingering her hair back and steadying her balance, she felt drawn to the man now holding her waist. She had never experienced such a sense of attraction to a man and stood mesmerised by his words of kindness and support. Releasing her, she saw Carl's face grow stern as he looked to the ground. Behind her he noticed a grave; one that uncannily matched an image he had in a dream, or was he in fact recollecting childhood memories. The earth was dug about the edges and although the headstone was cracked and covered in foliage, he could make out the wording. Before he could read it and capture past memories, Liz read aloud the inscription.

'Reverend Steven John Aston, devoted partner to Eleanor and servant of God.'

Liz stopped for a second, trying to make out the dates below, but Carl intervened.

'Please Liz,' he said calmly, 'could you look for the metal box whilst I tidy up this place?'

Seeing his eyes tearful, she walked away slowly, but needed to know where to look for the box.

'Sorry Carl,' she said softly, 'but where is this box?'

'It's buried around some old water fountain,' he said staring at the grave stone, 'near the churchyard wall.'

As Liz gingerly stepped through the undergrowth, trying to observe the walls of the churchyard, Carl tried best to tidy the grave.

It had been a while before Liz announced her find. Carl sped off towards her, weaving carefully through the graves, but on reaching her, heard her scream. As he approached, she tumbled back in fright; seeing a large spider run along her arm from where she had probed. Quickly Carl brushed it off and she stood to back away.

'What is it?' he asked.

'A bloody big spider,' she exclaimed, 'you saw the size of it!'

'No, you fool,' he said laughing, 'did you find the box; where is it?'

'In there!' Liz shouted, pointing; looking at her arm and then around her feet.

Between the churchyard wall and a crumbling stone fountain, Carl could see an object pushed down into a gap. Like Liz had already tried, he pushed his arm into the cavity and probed about with his hand. At first he could not reach it but fingering the box, moved it inches towards him. Suddenly, grasping it and pulling hard, he fell back with the force of which had pulled. Liz laughed and started to irritate Carl again with her bursts of sniggering, but soon found it quite amusing himself; relieved to see the metal box clenched in his hand.

Sitting on the ground, Carl retrieved a key from his pocket and tested the lock of the metal box. At first it would not open, but after turning the key at different angles, the box opened. Inside it was rusty, dirty, but from within a cloth, Carl pulled out a small black book – a diary. As Liz leaned overhead watching, he pulled out a large crucifix; a silver crucifix, and then a square shaped bottle on which was engraved a cross. He moved the cloth from the box to find folded sheets of paper but nothing else. Placing all items except the diary in his pocket, he closed the box with the cloth inside and pushed it back into the small cavity. Inquisitive, Carl thumbed the diary, flicking through the pages and noticed a folded newspaper cutting in between pages. Reading the inset page, Carl noticed the name of his father scribbled, along with a number of dates.

'Can't you read it later Carl?' Liz said looking up to the dark sky, feelings heavy droplets of rain on her face, 'it's beginning to rain and looks heavy.

Although he was compelled to read the diary, his interest was interrupted by the start of heavy rainfall.

'Come on then,' he shouted, searching his trouser pocket for the padlock key, 'we'll get back to the old man by car,' and whilst escorting Liz through the graveyard announced, 'I'll have a read of this later!'

Back at his cottage, the old man saw that Carl and Liz were quite wet, even though they had parked the car only at the end of his driveway. As he invited them both in and offered to make tea, Liz looked apprehensively at the state of his cups. However, Carl visually directed that she should help make tea as he wanted information from the old man.

'If you could please Mr Collins,' Carl braved to take command of the conversation, 'what can you tell me of my father's past?'

'Well, where do I start?' he replied.

'My Aunt told of good times about these parts,' Carl said, but coughed to clear his throat, 'before a doctor moved into Arlington Manor.'

'Yes, before *that* man arrived, things were different. The clergy had a large communion and we had great harvests those days and celebrated good Mother Nature for her kindness. Indeed many good festivals were celebrated on

Fiddler's Mound; drinking the fresh rain water collected by the great rock was thought to bring health and prosperity, but then he came and claimed the old manor from the previous squire.'

'I believe my father had difficult times with this doctor,' Carl enquired, gesturing the farmer to continue.

'Yes, shortly after *he* arrived, our crops started to fail and some of the community left the area; unwilling to struggle on. But I would not. That man would never drive me off my land although I had…'

'Had what, Mr Collins?' Carl asked as the farmer wavered.

'It was not just my land, the crops and that you see. But my livestock was dying; I was losing them one way or another. I questioned your father to why our crops and livestock should perish, but he did nothing but say it was *that* doctor's fault; that he had evil ways. But this doctor found wealth and so did others that joined him. Indeed, I could have become his gamekeeper when my wife was alive. My hard work, like many friends of mine around these parts, was failing to reap rewards.'

'What livestock did you lose?' Carl interrogated further.

'Well at first lambs and goats. I thought it was bad weather you see, and with foxes and other beasts about these parts, I guess they disappeared. But it never explained my prize cockerel going missing. I reckon it was some competitor that found out where I kept him. I know my livestock stray, but that idiot at the manor ordered me off his land.'

'What the doctor?'

'No,' the farmer corrected, 'that gangly fellow who's a bit short of a brain – the doctor's gamekeeper.'

'Oh yes, but of course,' Carl realised, 'your land must back onto his?'

'Yes, the manor is about–'

'I can't keep him from barking!' Liz interrupted, running into the lounge.

'Must be cats around the back again,' the old man announced.

Following the farmer into the kitchen, Liz revealed that she was simply fussing the dog when he continued to bark at the back door. Soon the farmer opened the back door and the Alsatian sped off into the backyard.

Hearing Liz talk to the old man in the kitchen, Carl grasped an opportunity to examine his father's diary. Flicking through the pages, he stopped at the page bookmarked by a newspaper cutting. Although he could not make out some of the handwriting, Carl learned from those pages of a Councillor Raymond, who after sermon, confided in his father as he feared the doctor. At first Carl could not understand some wording, but the councillor's declarations revealed a conspiracy to promote the doctor in the community; that he tried to convince people to believe in his ways, but in fact, individuals were being bribed or scared into submission. The councillor confessed to his faithful clergyman that to become a wealthy member of the doctor's society, he had indeed sold fake jewellery, but when realised the doctor's intentions, wanted no part of the secret coven. Carl read on, deciphering best he could the handwriting.

The following pages told of several meetings between his father and the councillor; describing his admissions to the doctor's blackmail, his recommendations of the doctor to governing bodies and specially arranged meetings with influential people. Carl read on, but the entries became short and sketchy. His father's last meeting with the councillor recorded a concern for him; stating how the councillor feared for his own life as some dark evil followed him, that his mind was disturbed and he heard strange voices.

Carl turned the page, but saw only dates etched with arrows on the other side. He turned back the page and began to unfold the newspaper cutting as Liz steadily walked in with a tray. She looked at Carl as she placed the tray down, but noticed how preoccupied he was with his new discovery. Accompanied with a small facial picture, the clipping reported of how Councillor Raymond was brutally killed in a car crash, but told that his death was in fact caused by some spear like object entering his chest. Suddenly, Carl went cold, but looked up to see both Liz and the old man looking at him.

Carl swallowed his tea without thought and only nibbled at one biscuit. He could see that Liz found the tea even more distasteful than his, or was it the state of the farmer's crockery. Carl stood to thank the old man for his hospitality, but announced of how he needed to get back to Bristol. Fumbling with the diary, Carl told of how he tried to tidy his father's grave before the rain came.

'Yes, its pesky weather isn't it?' the old man groaned. 'It won't do my crops any good either having too much rain. Not that I cultivate much now. It's mainly all pasture for gazing.'

'Well it's very nice of you to help us out Mr Collins,' Carl said, ushering Liz out into the hallway. 'It's very much appreciated.'

'Yes, thank you Mr Collins,' Liz murmured, walking out the front door.

Considering a dash to the car, they had just got to the path, when they heard the old man calling about the key to the churchyard. Giving Liz his coat to shelter her from the rain, he turned to return the old man his key. After watching Carl go back to the cottage, Liz ran to the car but stood for a second, thinking she had seen someone. With the coat above her head, Liz circled around to the passenger door and stopped to grasp Carl's car keys from his coat pocket. It was then that her senses grew fearful.

Opening the passenger door, Liz turned to notice a hooded figure approach. Suddenly the hooded figure grasped at her, but she managed to push at the offender's face. The figure backed off and stopped to replace the hood that had dropped, but was soon upon her again. Recognising the angry face of Amanda, Liz grasped the pendant out of her cardigan pocket and after placing it in Carl's coat, threw his coat on the passenger seat. Quickly pushing down the door lock, Liz then slammed shut the car door. Annoyed, Amanda shouted at Liz, declaring that she must have the stone on her as it was not at Carl's flat. Realising she had dropped it in the coat pocket; Amanda demanded she hand over the keys.

She commanded Liz to give her the pendant as it was not her property, but Liz pushed her away and scrabbled around the bonnet to the driver's side. She tested the driver's door and grasped tightly at the car keys, but Amanda assailed her again to try and steal the keys.

Liz screamed and called to Carl at the top of her voice, but suddenly felt a blow to her forehead. Within seconds her sight went blurred and she fell beside the car. Throwing away the branch that hit Liz, Amanda pulled forward her hood and tried to grasp the keys, but realised Carl was almost upon her. Empty handed, but unknown to Carl, Amanda ran into the darkness of the nearby woodland.

Carl froze as he glanced upon Liz's unconscious body. He considered chasing the offender but realised Liz lay hurt in the pouring rain. He grasped the keys from her hand and opening the driver's door, lay open his coat on the passenger seat before opening the other door. As swiftly as he could, he pulled Liz's body from the drenched floor and carried her to the passenger seat. After carefully laying back her head and folding the coat about her, he closed the door and returned to the driver's seat. For a moment Carl looked anxiously at Liz and considered whether to call an ambulance, but thought it best to find the hospital himself.

Carl was fatigued after carrying Liz through to the emergency unit, but was relieved to see her stretchered through the corridors to an inspection room. Although he wanted to stay, Carl was later escorted to a waiting area to be questioned by a nurse. He described how he had found her knocked unconscious after scaring away someone trying to steal the car and that he got to the hospital as fast as he could.

Nervous and pacing about the waiting area, Carl decided to fetch a coffee from a nearby vending machine, but after taking a few sips was approached by a doctor.

'Are you Carl,' the doctor asked holding several sheets of paper, 'the guy who brought in Miss Elizabeth Woodall?'

'Yes, yes I am,' he responded eagerly, 'is she going to be okay?'

'She'll be fine, but needs to have more tests tomorrow,' he indicated, reading the sheets he carried. 'She's lucky that the blow hit the back of head and not her temple.' He stopped to inspect the sheet more thoroughly. 'But we believe she also banged her head when she fell and then there's a small chance of hypothermia… but you did well to wrap that coat–'

'Can I see her?' Carl interrupted, pacing down the corridor. 'Is she awake?'

'No, she not unconscious yet but,' the doctor advised, trying to walk alongside, 'you can see her, but don't bother her too much; she's had a sedative and maybe a little delirious.'

As he poked his head around the corner he could see Liz, her head wrapped in a bandage, her eyes flickering and she was groaning. Quickly he walked in to lean over her.

'It's okay now,' Carl reassured stroking her face, 'you took a knock but you're in the hospital now and in good hands.'

'She wants it… but don't trust her…' Liz mumbled, her eyes unfocused, 'throw it away… in the river!'

Carl tried his best to console her, telling her that she was under sedative, but she came restless and irrational, 'Sarah's stuff… in my locker…' she continued but looked at Carl as if she saw him, 'Sarah… our research… my locker…'

'What stuff Liz?' Carl asked.

'You know it… my birthday of course…' Liz wriggled, smiling peculiarly.

'What research?' he said raising his voice. 'Sarah did research, but whom for?'

'Please, you must leave her alone,' a voice shouted from behind, 'you must sort things out tomorrow; after she's had rest.'

Carl felt a firm hand on his shoulder that eventually pulled him away.

'But she must know stuff,' he proclaimed, 'Sarah's research, or something?'

'Please sir, she needs rest,' the nurse said and with more conviction advised, 'sir, it is best that you leave. Call on her tomorrow; normal visiting hours.'

The nurse forcibly led Carl away from Liz's bedside to the doorway.

'I presume you know where the exit is my good man,' she announced staring, 'left after the waiting area and out the main doors.'

She turned away but then stared back at him to say, 'Don't worry, we'll look after her.'

# TWENTY – NINE

'A LITTLE LATE FOR A visit, is it not Miss, err...' the doctor paused, trying to recall Amanda's surname.

'Burley,' she announced, tidying her clothes after being pawed again by the security guards, 'Amanda Burley; you remember from–'

'Yes of course I remember,' the doctor said aloud, but calmed somewhat to continue, 'must be important news you bring to permit such a late visit?'

'Well, it's only near eight,' she joked. 'I wouldn't call *that* late!'

'Most visitors have to leave here by seven my dear,' the doctor said slow and deep, stepping forward from out the shadows. 'Hope you have good news?' he questioned, noticing a slight cut on her face. 'Struggled to get my pendant, I deduce?'

'Yes doctor,' she admitted, 'some bitch stopped me from getting it... some book freak friend of that journalist!'

'You mean you come here empty handed?' he said angrily.

'Not exactly,' Amanda sighed, feeling the soreness of the scratch on her cheek, 'but I *will* get it, mark my words and when I get hold of that bitch –'

'Just an occupational hazard my dear,' the doctor interrupted, staring hard at her through the glass. 'You shouldn't let your emotions get the best of you; they cloud a rational mind you know.'

'But I don't know who has it now, do I?' she confessed. 'But I will get it, I promise you that.'

'Tracing it isn't a hurdle hard to jump,' the doctor said slowly, 'but maybe an exhaustive one?'

'But how can you trace it,' she enquired, 'stuck in *this* place?'

'No, I admit, I can't myself, but you can,' he professed.

'How can I,' she argued, 'either of them could have it?'

'I do regret to have to do this…' the doctor said quietly whilst turning slowly away, 'especially to the young man… but if it's not them, it could well be me…'

'What did you say?' Amanda requested. 'How can I trace your pendant?'

'Follow the reports of death, my dear,' he said quietly, but raising his voice to face her, changed the subject. 'But my dear, surely the failure of *that* quest is not your only news as you wouldn't be sitting in here?'

'No, of course,' she replied, pulling a folder from her bag, 'putting forward the story we discussed previous, along with convincing a number of important clients, well,' she paused to take breath, 'a re-trial will be held within a week.'

'A re-trial?' the doctor shouted, 'Is that all?'

'Yes, but –'

'Don't you think I've had enough already; that trials lead to nothing?'

'Well, at least you could have a look,' she said angrily, throwing the folder into the drawer. 'Oh, and for my services so far, you can *sign* that!'

The doctor pulled out the folder and examined the contents under brighter light. Inside he saw the cheque that he had previously wrote, plus several documents.

'You hand me a few letters and names of the jury and expect payment,' the doctor sniggered.

'Yes, but with *my* new evidence, this is also a *new* jury,' she pronounced, 'clean and fresh to convince in your favour.'

'How can you be sure they won't favour the prosecution?'

'Well, you see sir,' she announced smiling mischievously, 'a small number of them; certain people that is, maybe persuaded to vote in favour of your defence.'

'Is that so?' the doctor murmured, fingering the documents.

'You may even know *some* of the names listed,' she declared, 'surely some enlightenment to get you acquitted?'

'Yes my dear, yes,' he muttered sitting, 'at least a positive note.'

The doctor sat reading for a several minutes as Amanda checked her cheek with her hand mirror. After standing and turning towards the drawer, he threw in the folder and pushed it forward. Quickly Amanda retrieved the folder from the drawer and sat to inspect the contents.

'Where is the cheque – my payment?' she asked.

'Did you meet with Daniel?' the doctor enquired, wanting to be sure she had the right man. 'Are you sure that journalist is the one on *his* photograph?'

'I don't need *that* photograph!' she said forcefully. 'My intuition gets faster results than that!'

'But results that yield no pendant?' he said sarcastically.

'But it was at his house, under a sun-lamp in his bedroom; I'm sure of it!' she affirmed, 'and that bitch must have taken it, knowing that I saw it.'

'A sun-lamp,' the doctor said slowly, 'how quaint, but effective no doubt.'

'Effective,' Amanda questioned laughing, 'to give a pendant a sun tan?'

'It's not just an item of jewellery my dear,' the doctor grunted, wanting more information. 'You've spoken to Daniel then,' the doctor said annoyed, 'surely he's told you what to do once you have the pendant?'

'No not quite,' Amanda barked back at him. 'He said *something* about gathering thirteen people, but some are missing… but missing for what?'

'Tell Daniel that you *must* become a member of our society,' he declared, 'as he can visit me no longer, you must be my messenger. He may be slow witted, but he knows what to do; how to prepare for things once I'm out of here.'

The doctor took a small piece of paper and after writing on it a list of names, threw it in the drawer with the cheque.

'Give that list to Daniel,' the doctor asked politely, 'and you may cash the cheque.'

Amanda looked at the signed cheque and with the list, pushed them into her bra.

'Remember my dear,' the doctor said in a deep voice, 'that's a down payment on getting me acquitted, plus you *must* give Daniel that list.'

'But what about your precious pendant; how do I–?'

Amanda's questioning was interrupted by the entrance of the security guards.

'Sorry Miss, but we said half an hour and you've had that time.'

'Yes okay,' she said, but stalled to ask one last thing, 'but what about the –?'

'Hand my friend *that* which you tried to get before,' the doctor asserted, 'and you'll have another like payment.'

# THIRTY

HE COULD NOT HELP BUT think of Liz as he walked up to the reception desk of the library. Indeed, if it was not for her, he would not have such research facilities at his disposal. Yet in contradiction, as she lay hurt in hospital, he wanted to raid her locker for what she said was in there; to see if her research had anything. How many more people had to suffer because he wanted to know the truth about his past? It was not his fault that some bastard had floored Liz just to try and steal his car; that Sarah had been scared by some creature and that his father's friend had died so horribly at Centridge House. But why had so many bad things happened of late? He could not deny that since he came in touch with the pendant, lots of shit had happened.

'You've only had this card issued recently Mr Aston,' a stern lady said from the reception desk, 'so do you require assistance,' she gestured opening her hands, 'finding resources and alike?'

'No, a friend of mine showed me around before,' he said placing his briefcase on the counter, 'but I could do with a favour to show her my gratitude.'

'And what would that be?' the receptionist asked, her eyes opening wide through her spectacles.

'Well, I think that it's her birthday soon and I'd like to get her something, but I can't remember exactly the—'

'I'm sorry Mr Aston, but we can't give out employee's personal information.'

'Not even for me to get my friend a present?'

'I'm sorry, no,' the receptionist stated, 'besides I wouldn't know it off hand anyhow.'

'Well, I hope I have more luck in my research than I've had here so far,' Carl groaned, 'just a simple birthday,' he muttered pushing his way through the turnstiles, 'didn't even want to know her name!'

After passing the rear of the reception desk, Carl strode ahead, but was interrupted by a young girl whispering.

'Sir, Mr, who's your friend?' she said leaning over the desk. 'Whose birthday did you want to know?'

'Well, that lady,' Carl said quietly, pointing, 'the one in her high chair won't give out *that* information.'

'We're not supposed to but,' the girl said giggling, 'if it's a friend – who is it?'

'Her name is Elizabeth Woodall, but I call her Liz,' Carl said quietly, moving nearer the girl.

'But her birthday's not until June the eighteenth next year?' the girl said scratching her head.

'Thanks a lot!' Carl said smiling and walked briskly away to find the desk he had sat at before.

Suddenly the girl's face changed from being perplexed to her realisation of stupidity.

Pretending to look at books, Carl had deciphered the combination of the door after watching staff pass in and out. Although his belongings were spread out on a desk and out of sight, he was determined to retrieve the research of which Liz had described.

Hastily and whilst the area was quiet, Carl entered the code he had observed and slipped through the staff door into a corridor of paraphernalia. Gently he stepped along until he noticed a line of lockers, each with four digit code locks. Not knowing how to identify her locker, Carl thought that his task had come to an abrupt end, but then saw abbreviations on the front of each. Thinking back, Carl recalled that Liz had shown her badge and that it had read Elizabeth A. Woodall. Quickly he scanned the lockers until he stopped. Slowly Carl began to grin. Half way down and on the end row, he saw a locker initialled E.A.W.

With the date that the girl had inadvertently given, he soon had Liz's locker open. It was then that a sudden realisation came over him. Surely he was not deceitful; rummaging through a friend's possessions in exploit of their misfortune. He thought to how wrong it was, but knew Liz was adamant in helping Sarah. So if she was to help Sarah, then she was to help him. Indeed, Liz was ecstatic whilst conducting research for him. From amongst her belongings, he pulled out a folder on which Sarah's name was sketched, and after closing the locker door, escaped back to his desk.

As the contents of the folder spilled over the desk, he could see that most of it was photographs. Some photos of the late Mr Carrington he recognised from what Sarah had replicated, but some he had not seen before. One of which showed the doctor attending court and upon his finger, like in old photos, was a ring like Mr Carrington's. To ensure a likeness, Sarah replicated another photograph of which enhanced the ring in more detail. Convincingly both black onyx rings matched as too did one from another photograph. This was of a gangly man, dressed in black and pictured recently inside a courtroom. Written on the back, Carl noticed Sarah's handwriting to which noted the date and a court case of a Dr J. K. Schroeck.

Held together with an elastic band, Carl noticed photocopied sheets with notes circled and arrows pointing to sections underlined. As Carl read her confessions to not knowing the date and manufacturer of the ring, he deduced that this was work Liz had done for Sarah. Reading her admission that the ring related to nothing she had seen before, her later notes referenced books about occult groups; that the symbol etched into the ring represented devil worship. Carl scanned the pages, quickly reading Liz's notes and the illustrations they referenced, but most were confusing. After skipping several drawings of old woodcuts and sketches of witchcraft practice, Carl noticed Liz's reply to a question written by Sarah. After describing how the pendant glowed in the dark on the night she was attacked, Liz listed many references, but conveyed no answer. Instead he read on, discovering what Liz had found in books.

Although persecuted throughout history, he read how warlocks trapped evil spirits in reflective objects; where after being besotted by its own reflection, evil spirits would become entrapped. However, she confessed to not being sure that if the object breaks, whether the evil is released. Glancing away, Carl thought that no wonder breaking a mirror brought a superstition of seven years bad luck. He focused back to reading; learning of how to prevent spirits from entering this world and how to destroy them once their detention was broken, but grew disinterested.

Instead, after fingering the other findings held in his briefcase, again Carl reached for his father's diary. He flicked through pages until he noticed small illustrations that referenced the sheets discovered in the metal box. Of what Carl could make out, these sketches was research that his father had made to help protect his friend from evil. Not only that, but after what Mr Carrington had observed during his time with the doctor's society, his father had investigated ways to destroy this evil. He had just started to read a diary discussion between his father and Mr Carrington, when he heard a stern voice behind.

'Sorry sir, but the library is now closing,' the receptionist announced, pushing chairs under desks, 'as our late nights close at nine.'

'That's okay,' Carl said turning to face her, 'I'm nearly done here.' He paused, leaning forward to hide Liz's folder within his briefcase. 'I think I can do the rest at home this evening.'

Driving home, Carl's thoughts were busied reflecting the entries of the diary. First of all he deduced that Mr Carrington, after his disparity with joining the doctor's society, exposed him not only to blackmail but to the evil that the doctor could summon. But his experience proved invaluable to his father; the etchings made on the banqueting hall, the rituals practiced by society members, his description of devil worship proceedings. Recalling the last entry he had read from the diary, the Reverend had told his friend of how his observations closely tied in with the book Carl had stolen as a child. His father's theory to keep a bible, crucifix and holy water close at hand for protection was hindered by the flood of childhood memories. However, by this time, he was almost home.

After finishing off some hardened cheese on toasted bread, Carl was pouring another shot of whiskey when the telephone rang. It had taken some time to fix the bedroom window and did not realise it was almost ten.

'Hey Carl,' the voice called, 'did you say you're in tomorrow?'

'No I'm not,' he replied, 'as I'm visiting the hospital.'

'Hospital, why the hospital?' the voice asked.

Carl suddenly realised that Mike had not heard of what had happened and told of how some thug attacked Liz and tried to steal the car. Mike became openly concerned and asked how Liz was. Carl described of what the doctor had said, but because she was sedated, avowed to visit her next day. After Mike noted down the ward number, he promised that both he and Rachael would also visit tomorrow. However, forgetting that his friend had become somewhat more belligerent since the mugging, Mike asked the wrong question.

'Tell me mate,' he paused, trying to suppress his anger, 'why is it lately that everyone who hangs around you either gets scared off, attacked or even killed?'

Carl went silent for a moment, but his temper got the better of him.

'What the fuck do you care!' Carl shouted. 'You don't want to know about stuff; Sarah's got an excuse not to help, but at least she *tried* to help and now has Liz to help instead.' He paused to take a sharp intake of air. 'What the hell have you done apart from bicker or take the piss?'

Mike groaned words under his breath as Carl continued.

'No wonder you've stayed out of the way,' he declared, 'scared that *something* might happen to you, eh?' Carl awaited his reply, but heard nothing but silence. 'At least *some* people care about helping me find out about my father and not screwing around all the time. I don't know why Rachael –'

'Look pal,' Mike's voice snapped back angrily, 'you're not in tomorrow; that's all I want to know!' But before the receiver buzzed, he heard him announce, 'I'll see you down the hospital tomorrow – we'll both be there!'

Annoyed, Carl threw down the receiver and after taking a gulp from his whiskey glass, sat down to read again his father's diary. Hoping to forget Mike's antagonism, he turned to the page he had bookmarked with folded drawings.

The next entry in the diary conveyed Mr Carrington's impression that the ring he and all members wore protected the bearer against evil, but his father discredited the idea, stating it was only ceremonial. On the next page his father wrote of a blood-letting ritual that Mr Carrington had witnessed, and along with what he had learned from the doctor's book, realised the doctor had found some connection between voodoo practice and pagan rites; that this ritual was used to summon evil.

Carl paused to think and gulped again at his whiskey. Was it the stone that called the evil or was it just a lure? By now he was adamant that whoever had this warlock's stone after such a ritual, would be in peril; Mr Carrington killed at the library, the mugger beheaded, David's car crash – who next?

He read on. A sketchy account from Mr Carrington described to his father the blood-letting ceremony; that blood was burned and drugs taken to enhance a trance like state. On one account the doctor admitted his fear in doing the ritual; that he was indeed at risk by summoning such deadly forces and that young animals had to be sacrificed as compensation. Depicted as a selected and powerful beast, Mr Carrington described the doctor's slaughter of a black cockerel as a ritual to the Black Art.

Suddenly Carl realised that shortly after the doctor arrived at Arlington Manor, Mr Collins' livestock were being taken; but surely the poor farmer did not know what came of them.

In the last entry of discussion with Mr Carrington, his father noted how oppressed his friend was; that he feared for his life, but described how soon he would get away. Although sketchy, Carl read that the doctor's practice was getting dangerous and putting him in jeopardy; just to satisfy his greed for power. Mr Carrington also questioned the doctor's sanity, that he was deranged enough to even contemplate sacrificing a coven member; especially should his own life be in peril.

Carl's eyes grew tired as again he gulped at the whiskey glass, returning only to read about Mr Carrington's promise to expose the doctor through police investigation. As he looked at the blurred hands on the mantelpiece clock, he noticed it was near eleven. Listening to its melodic ticking of the clock, he fell asleep.

# THIRTY – ONE

CARL LOOKED DOWN INTO THE puddle beneath him. Strangely he could see himself as a child again; wearing those horrible shorts he and Alex wore to school. But this was not school. It was no place he had seen before, as he never went to playgrounds when he was small. He looked up from seeing his feet in water to notice he was holding a key. He frowned and then looked up to the grey sky above. With a low lying cover of rain cloud, it was also beginning to get dark; that cold and uncanny twilight, gradually choked by darkness.

Suddenly he looked around after hearing a call from the playground. Standing on a roundabout not far away, was a girl about his age or maybe younger; dressed in school uniform and wearing large spectacles. Holding a black, metal box before her, she called his name again. Approaching, for some reason he recognised her.

'Liz?' he verified.

'Carl it will not open?' the girl said, stamping her feet in temper.

'Here, I have a key!' he announced but became tenuous to use it, as from behind her he noticed a fog bank, poised on the edge of the park.

'Why Carl, you're shaking,' she declared, 'here let me try.'

Unsteady upon the movement of the roundabout, Liz grabbed from him the key and turned it in the lock. Slowly she opened the lid of the box and peered in.

'Carl, there's nothing inside?' she whined in disappointment.

Carl stepped forward and was about to take a look when the roundabout started to move. Within seconds the roundabout rotated at increasing speed and the girl clenched at the bars, struggling to hold on.

'Help me Carl!' she shouted, her voice muffled by the movement. 'Help me!'

But Carl could do nothing to board the object; it was turning too fast. He called for her to throw away the box and use both hands to hold on, but by this time a dense, black mist rose from out of the box. As the roundabout circled, the mist entwined upward, gathering high above Liz into a cloaked figure. Carl stepped back in horror as he observed the assemblage of a face.

At first it resembled a human skull, but as he looked on, a pale, powdery skin shone in the darkness; revealing black nostrils, eye sockets, lips in a crescent moon shape hiding razor sharp teeth. The eyes were like death; glaring pupils, black against the white of the eyeball. As its eyes looked at Liz below, its mouth opened and elongated to unnatural proportion.

Carl shouted, cursing the evil to leave her alone, but from its mouth flew dark shadows which turned and twisted about her. She screamed as the dark spectres writhed and carped about her, telling her of hell and its wonders, but she shut her eyes, covered her ears and prayed. As each phantom flew past her, Carl saw her body turn, her limbs crack, until her screams were silenced by the twist of her neck.

Trembling and body frenzied with sweat, Carl awoke to realise that again he had been subjected to his nightmares. Rubbing his eyes, he sat up but knew it was not just a nightmare, but some premonition. He had seen David killed in his dream and had got there too late. Surely now, Liz was in mortal danger, but thinking of the stolen pendant, how could she be? If aides to the doctor had performed a ritual to call forth some evil, surely Liz did not have the call stone. However, he could not chance it. Should something happen to Liz, he would never forgive himself. Having whiskey on his breath, driving would be a chance he would have to take and not having time to prevent David's death, he knew he had to be fast. Besides, the hospital was miles away.

After gulping down some tap water, Carl reached for his coat, but realised he had covered Liz with it at the hospital. Decisively, there was no time to waste; he must get to the hospital and as quick as he could.

It had taken some time to find the lavatories in the hospital. Although still dazed, Liz was disappointed that her single room had no toilet. She turned a corner, trying best to trace her steps back to her room, but her eyes could not focus on the signage above. Although unattended, she recognised the nursing desk to the end of her ward and entered the corridor from where she had come. Uneasy, she steadied herself against the hospital wall as she ambled down the corridor. Near her room she suddenly felt a chill, but thought it a side-effect from her sedation. But the corridor was cold; in fact her breath exhaled into freezing air. She began to shiver and then turned, sensing something wrong. She looked down the long, empty corridor, blinking wildly and trying to focus, but saw nothing unusual.

Suddenly, at the far end of the corridor she saw the ceiling florescent light flicker and go out. Still trying to focus through weary eyes, she stood poised not far from her door to look down the corridor. Consecutively, closer and closer the lights flickered for a few seconds and then went out. As each light faltered, she noticed a black figure appear and move behind in the darkness before disappearing. Soon she realised that half of the lights down the corridor had now gone out and behind, in the darkness, something sinister loomed. She ambled along the corridor wall, but panicked trying to open the door. As she fumbled with the handle, the failure of lighting increased towards her and in the darkness that followed, a mist assembled into a dark figure. Pushing open the door and falling into the room the figure was almost upon her, but she crawled to her feet to shut the door.

After pushing it, the door slammed shut, but she noticed the lock flick inward and hold. Slowly the door swung back open and beyond it was blackness; nothing but a swirling mass of dark mist until a cloaked figure emerged. At first she was petrified; her eyes horrified by the presence of the black figure, but then looked about to notice a mist at the window. Noticing Carl's coat, she grasped it and fumbled through the pockets. Clasping the pendant she withdrew it from a pocket and dropped the coat. Strangely the dark of the stone glowed deep red. Stepping backward, suddenly she slipped upon the coat and hurtled to the floor. For a second he was dazed, but quickly turned her head to see the cloaked figure stand tall above her.

Below and hidden in the depths of its hood was a powdery white face, its crescent mouth bordered by black lips that revealed dagger-like teeth. At first she saw its mouth and dark nostrils, but then as its head lifted, deathly black pupils glared down upon her, enhanced by the white of its glistening eyeballs. Its mouth opened wide and quivered whilst the whole darkness of the body shimmered. Hearing unearthly voices, like that of a reversed played record, she could not look at the fiendish glare and covered her ears. She tried to scream, but her voice was muffled by evil laughter.

She crawled along the floor to the bed, but felt a hand crush her foot. She looked again upon the figure; it's one hand clasping her foot, the other holding high its cloak. From beneath its arm she saw faces of people: twisted, contorted and plagued by evil torment; phantoms that eventually sprung out at her. She screamed in agony as the spectral bodies pulled at her hair, disjointed her limbs, choked her breath and crooked her neck until her spectacles fell. Not sure whether it was laughter or cries of agony that she heard, but as she dropped, she felt her soul escape her.

Carl ran into the lobby of the hospital. By now he knew the place rather well. As he rushed past reception and down a corridor he heard a voice call, telling him to wait as visiting hours were over. However his concern was stout as he had seen the movement of a fog bank approach the hospital.

He stopped to take notice of the ward number and then climbed a nearby stairway. As he pushed open the fire door, he recognised a reception desk and quickly made his way to the ward where Liz was.

He had just turned the corner and ran fast down the corridor, when he heard a nearby scream. Rushing toward Liz's room, Carl noticed a nurse step backward and out from the room; her face white, her eyes glazed with fright. He glanced in the room as the nurse backed against a wall in shock. Carl walked slowly towards Liz's body, noticing her lying at the foot of the bed.

The first thing that disturbed him was how her limbs were at unnatural positions; that somehow her bones had been dislodged and her body contorted. He crept slowly toward her from behind and saw her spectacles on the floor. Glancing at her reflected face upon the one intact lens, he perceived the true horror of her fate; but it was not until he leaned over to see her face for real, that his heart almost stopped.

With her head stretched from her shoulders, her face was a glossy white and elongated like melted wax; the mouth extended downward capturing the terror of her scream, her eyes fixed and glazed. Perturbed by the fate of the girl he had only been with that morning, Carl could not move, but a sense of apprehension came over him. Quickly he looked at his coat on the floor and retrieved it to search its pockets; but there was no pendant. He looked about the floor until he saw Liz's outstretched hand clasping the object. Trying his best to compose his feelings, he prised open her fingers until he could pull it free. Suddenly, he thought of Sarah and then again of Liz that morning; her face content and smiling. As he sat back behind her, he felt his heart ache and breath difficult. He started to whimper, tears escaping his eyes, his voice hoarse whilst questioning Liz's involvement and why she took the pendant. He heard voices approach and brushing away his tears knew he had to be strong. Carl stood and put the pendant into this coat. He muttered words to Liz aloud; saying how he regretted getting her involved.

As two nurses ran past him into the room, Carl stumbled out; questioning of how a terrible death could ever occur and what kind of thing could do such a vicious murder. Running down the corridor and wrapping his coat around him, Carl could hear a nurse call after him, asking him to stop, but on he ran.

He could not remember his journey home as his thoughts were of Liz and to how Sarah would react. Apart from one near miss, he was lucky that the roads were relatively clear. But soon he was in his flat and drinking whiskey, apprehensive to telephone Mike and tell him the horrible news.

'Mike is that you,' Carl muttered, taking another sip from the whiskey glass. 'I'm afraid I've got some terrible news.'

For a moment, Carl heard nothing but groans from the receiver, but then a voice replied.

'Sorry, is that you Carl?' Mike questioned, somewhat distracted by Rachael. 'Mate, its bloody late, isn't it? What was it you said?'

'Mike,' he paused, trying to swallow, 'I'm afraid there's some bad news about Liz.' He clenched the receiver hard, 'I'm afraid she's been attacked… by some thug trying to steal my car… and then at the hospital… well…'

'But she's alright isn't she?' Mike questioned loudly.

'No,' Carl hesitated, 'she's dead… something killed her.'

'What?' Mike questioned in disbelief, 'What happened? What did this thug do?'

'That's what hurt her and why she went to hospital,' Carl described slowly, 'but not what killed her.'

'Was she knifed? Knocked unconscious… What?'

'Some thug trying to steal my car, he hit her head, but…' Carl stuttered again trying to reveal that the thug was not the murderer, 'she has just died at the hospital. I've just come from –'

'She's dead… killed by some thug?'

'Well that's what happened, but not how she died.'

'What did she die of then?' Mike questioned angrily.

'Something visited her… something evil.'

'Well I didn't think it was her fucking fairy god-mother!' Mike said sarcastically. 'But then what did kill her?'

Carl hesitated, knowing the evil would be ridiculed by his friend.

'I don't know,' Carl waned, 'but could Rachael tell Sarah about poor Liz as I can't do it!'

'Why not,' Mike questioned, 'she's your girlfriend? Besides you were with Liz only this morning, weren't you?'

'Yes, but –'

'Well do it then,' Mike said, but heard his friend whimpering. 'I'll ask her but…'

For a moment silence came between them until Mike again became curious and asked seriously.

'Carl, what was it that killed her?'

'Something evil,' Carl said, his feelings for Liz overwhelming any ridicule his friend could throw at him, 'I saw it in my dream, I wasn't there, but I know…'

Carl awaited Mike to snap back, but the receiver went silent.

'Not all this fucking stuff again about that doctor and your father,' Mike replied angrily. 'Liz gets killed by some thug and you think it's about you?'

'But if you saw her face,' Carl stated in tears, 'it was terrible.'

'Sort yourself out!' Mike reassured. 'It's an accident!' But Mike thought of David and of how strange deaths trailed Carl. 'I don't want to hear about your stupid dreams again, especially after what's happened tonight, if it is indeed true? Why is it people you know get killed? Is there something else I should know?'

'If you're stating that I've lost it, then you can piss off!' Carl shouted. 'I've tried to prevent Liz's murder… and David's!'

'Wasn't very successful though were you?' Mike declared sarcastically. 'It'll take more than a stupid dream to save you from Sarah when she finds out! You know how close a friend Liz was to her!'

'Sarah will understand,' Carl muttered.

'What, after this?' he barked. 'Don't think you'll be seeing Sarah again after this, do you chum?'

Carl slammed down the receiver and grasped for the whiskey glass, gulping madly at the liquid. He snatched his father's diary and pacing about the room flickered through the pages. He muttered to himself, talking of answers being somewhere in the diary; that people were being killed somehow by this doctor and his society, and on top of that, he was suspicious that Aunt Evelyn was hiding something from him. Was he losing his sanity? And now his friend was suspicious of him; that it was indeed because of him that Liz had got killed. But what would become of Sarah?

With rage he launched the diary at the wall, followed shortly by the whiskey tumbler. He paced about his lounge, trying to piece things together and going over the research; the photographs, his Aunt's letter, the diary entries – all that he had learned.

Somewhat calmer, Carl stepped over to where he had thrown the diary. Bending down to pick it up, he noticed the leather binding split at the rear and revealing something white sandwiched in a slit. Slowly he pinched his fingers at the paper, trying to prise it from its tight opening and eventually found it to be an old envelope. Curious he frowned, before pulling it free.

Inside, accompanied by an adoption certificate, was a formal letter dated six months after his birthday. In disbelief Carl read a letter signed by his father – Steven John Aston. The letter described of how the Reverend had agreed to adopt the boy and to be named Carl Edward. This was in request of Eleanor's two sisters Evelyn and Elizabeth Jones; that due to death whilst giving birth, the Reverend would adopt her son as his own.

Carl scanned the page again and looked up. He glanced at the back and about the envelope but unfortunately nothing in the letter described Eleanor's partner. All that was typed to describe his real father was the word, *Anonymous*.

# THIRTY – TWO

CARL MUST HAVE COMBED THROUGH every bit of research he had in his flat. It was not just the library books and Liz's notes he read, or the letters and all entries in the diary, but he checked family photographs and ones Sarah had collated.

He picked up the diary from the armchair, crumpled from where he had slept the night, again glancing over the adoption certificate and letter. But this diary did not belong to his father; his true father remained unknown and he loathed the thought of now not knowing who he was. But at least he knew that the Reverend had cared for him, that he had indeed been a better father than his real one could ever be; that although he missed having sisters and brothers, the Reverend found time for him and helped with school.

It was when that doctor sunk his venomous claws into his church communion that things started going wrong. Staring at the photograph of the Reverend, Carl recalled memories of which had previously evaded him. Some, like the harvest festivals of which his Aunt had described, were happy times; but some confrontations with the doctor, he now remembered and realised how times turned hard for the church. It was not just the bricks thrown, or that the church grounds got vandalised, but that the communion was dwindling.

Carl stood motionless, staring at the picture and then at the one of his mother. If this was his mother, then why was she pictured with that doctor he came to despise? Maybe he

411

was a medical man back then, as Evelyn had said her sister was weak and that he had unusual cures. But she also despised the doctor; he remembered that from visiting his Aunt and of course reading her letter.

Suddenly Carl heard a knock at the door. It was a double knock that he should have recognised but was apprehensive. He had been visited by two policemen that morning and got to the window just in time to see them go. Cautiously, he had also parked his car some distance down the street to make it look as he was out. The next knock on the door was louder and he heard two voices; one being a girl. He looked through the slit in the curtains to notice Mike glaring back at him.

Nervously, Carl opened the door and peered behind Mike and Rachael before bundling them into the hallway.

'What's with the secrecy, Carl?' Rachael asked, not liking being pushed.

'I don't want to be bothered by those pesky police, do I?' he said pushing the door firmly shut and holding the handle. 'I got things to sort out before they start interfering.'

'But they're only doing their job,' Rachael signalled.

'Yes, but Carl was at the hospital last night, weren't you?' Mike stated. 'And so what *did* happen to Liz exactly?'

Mike and Rachael followed Carl slowly into the lounge.

'Blimey Carl, what have you being doing?' Rachael asked. 'Had a party or something?'

'No, I haven't,' Carl said quietly, 'just trying to find out stuff about my past and that you know.' He paused, but then realised the purpose of their visit. 'Did you visit the hospital to see what happened?'

'Yes, we did but –'

'The place was crawling with police, forensics and that,' Mike interrupted. 'Police have been into work again and asking about you, but I said you were on leave.'

'Did you not see Liz then?' Carl continued quietly.

'No we did not,' Mike replied, 'but we heard that the death was...' He stopped to think before Rachael intervened.

'Abnormal,' she said moving about the room, 'irregular symptoms to the cause of death, I heard one forensic say.'

Carl removed a pile of paperwork to sit in his armchair.

'Poor Liz,' Carl sighed, his eyes tearful, 'she had such passion for research and determination... it hardly means anything now.' He paused to see Mike and Rachael stare at one another. 'How was I to know she had it on her?'

'Mate, are you alright?' Mike asked, looking at his friend's appearance and the state of his lounge. 'Your usually a bit tidier–'

Mike stopped, a nudge coming from Rachael's elbow.

'I wanted to go out,' Carl said looking at each of them, 'I wanted to find out about... never mind.' He paused before telling them of his investigation about the doctor, but realised how Mike resented it. Instead, he asked about someone dear to him. 'Did you manage to tell Sarah?' He stopped, finding it difficult to swallow. 'Has she been informed about Liz?'

'Yes, I do believe that my dear fiancé here,' Mike scorned, 'has done *that* dirty work for you!'

'Well, I left a message with her parents,' Rachael corrected, 'and they said she'll probably come back over,' Rachael started stuttering, her voice breaking, 'for the funeral that is, after they've done tests and stuff.'

'I don't know why you're so obsessed with this *doctor* story; the one that David gave you,' Mike commanded, 'but along with those dreams you've been having, I can't deny that something unusual is happening.'

'Then you believe me,' Carl replied quietly, 'that something killed Liz, David and other –'

'Maybe you should take a look in the mirror!' Mike stated, gesturing to Carl's clothing. 'You look as much as a mess as this place?'

'Mike, don't!' Rachael said trying to stop another argument.

'You still don't believe me, do you,' Carl questioned whilst standing, 'that it wasn't her injury that killed her, but that something evil came for her…'

'Sorry pal, but it sounds ridiculous!' Mike retorted, 'It could well be that you've been taking something.'

'You're not serious?' Carl reacted, his eyes searching Rachael's.

'But you were at both…' Mike paused to correct his words, 'accidents?'

'Stop it, both of you!' Rachael demanded, coming between them. 'I've had enough! You're supposed to be *best* friends? Girls don't tear claws into each other like you two do!'

For a minute there was silence as Mike circled the room, looking at some of the photographs.

'I'm sorry,' Carl said, 'I've not even offered you tea, or coffee?'

'It's okay, I think we're going now,' Rachael said, staring at Mike, 'we've got things to do ourselves.'

'I see,' Carl replied, 'don't worry about this place; I'll fix it up, eventually.'

'I'll phone tomorrow,' Mike announced, following Rachael to the door, handing Carl the morning paper, 'but there's a story in there that may be of interest to you, not that I should encourage you.'

'But the phone keeps ringing,' Carl declared, 'and it's probably the police, but I need time to –'

'Don't worry,' Mike assured, winking, 'I'll ring twice and stop, before ringing immediately after and then you'll know it's me.'

After seeing his friends shut the front door and say their goodbyes, Carl looked down at the newspaper and browsed the pages.

Inside, after turning a number of pages, he noticed an article about a retrial; that in fact the doctor was to appear in court tomorrow following new evidence that may get him acquitted. Carl froze; surely this doctor would not be freed from that institute. Carl could not comprehend what evil he could be capable of doing or what he might find out about him. With his mind troubled, again Carl reached for the whiskey.

The room was relatively dark when he awoke to the ring of the doorbell. About him he could see only shadows and so reached for the reading lamp. It had silenced for a while, but as the lamp lit the room he heard the doorbell again. Suddenly he forgot; maybe the police had called again and this time, surely he could not pretend he was out. Again he peered through the slit in the curtains, only to observe the dark figure of a woman; her hair long and black, her short skirt revealing long, slim legs.

Unsteady, Carl opened the door and looked upon Amanda; her face chilled by the cold of dusk, but wrapped by a silk scarf.

'It soon gets chilly, doesn't it?' she announced, stamping her high heels. 'Guess I'm not dressed for it; it's been a long day at the office, if you know what I mean?'

Carl stood oblivious to Amanda's chatter, his head still giddy from alcohol.

'Well, don't leave a poor girl standing out here in the cold; can I come in then, or what?' she asked.

Carl opened the door wide and sneaked behind to allow her brush past. As she strolled slowly down the hallway, he watched her bare, athletic thighs stretch tight her black skirt. It could well be the effects of alcohol, and although she was leaner than Sarah, he observed with desire the movement of her buttocks. Following her into the lounge, he noticed her remove her black, furry jacket, her scarf and undo the top buttons of her blouse. Placing her scarf and jacket on the back of the settee, he saw her kick off her shoes, before turning to him.

'Now then, where do you want me?' she gestured, her raised eyebrows revealing some sexual connotation, her brown eyes glistening as she looked him up and down. 'Not for that mind,' she corrected, 'but what do you want to know about this doctor?'

For a moment Carl stood perplexed; he did not know whether it was the alcohol that slurred his movement, or the fact that he thought her sensual. Attempting to remove his coat from his favourite armchair, Carl stopped her.

'Sorry, no,' he said, contesting for the seat, 'I prefer to sit there!'

Amanda looked in surprise, but backed away to sit on the settee.

'But have a drink,' Carl said slurring, 'and make yourself at home. Would you like something to eat?'

'No, nothing to eat my boy, but I would like a smoke, would you?'

After lighting cigarettes and offering Carl one, she observed her surroundings and looked down to see him pour another glass of whiskey. Noticing his hand shake she deduced that he was either nervous or already somewhat intoxicated; or could it be that he had not had a cigarette for a while.

'You look a bit stressed out my boy,' she announced, a hint of sympathy exaggerated in her voice, 'is everything alright?'

'Things have been a bit weird lately,' he explained sluggishly, 'things have happened that I can't explain.'

'Like what?' she asked.

'People have been killed,' he said sadly, 'people I know; people I've come across in work and that.'

'Well we all do that, don't we?' Amanda proclaimed, 'especially working for piss-pot journalist companies who pay shit wages.'

Carl was taken aback by Amanda's direct approach and noted she was somewhat restless; smiling in short bursts while he looked at her searching the room continually.

'And today,' Carl announced, 'I've found out that I was adopted; that my father wasn't really my father at all.'

Noticing that Amanda was uninterested, Carl continued. 'Neat?' Carl saw a frown develop on Amanda's face, 'do you want it neat?'

'Oh, the whiskey,' she laughed, 'no thanks, oh no, please have you any soda water… lemonade?'

Carl strolled to the kitchen to fetch a small bottle of tonic water that he knew he had in the fridge.

On his return, Amanda had poured the last remains of the bottle into his glass and beckoned him to sit beside her. However, Carl chose to slump in his favourite armchair. After pouring equal amounts of tonic water into each glass, Amanda handed Carl his glass.

'I've probably had too much already you know,' he said, raising his glass, 'but cheers anyway. Here's to that bastard of a doctor and his stupid little case.'

Amanda sipped at the whiskey as she watched Carl gulp at his.

'This tastes slightly odd,' Carl declared.

'Maybe it's the tonic water,' she professed, 'maybe it's off a little, but mine takes okay, have you ever had it with tonic before?'

'No,' he said, taking another swig, 'I can't say I have, but what about this doctor then?'

'What about him?' she contested.

'How come is it that you've got the case and no one else has?'

'I have contacts my dear,' she declared, 'and I do believe the doctor has great faith in me.'

'Probably have something else of interest, as well.'

'Excuse me,' she said, pulling down her short skirt.

'Well, you are very nice looking that is,' he slurred, but realised the alcohol had reduced his inhibitions too much, 'and intelligent,' he paused. 'You were awfully kind that day at the institute, what after I plastered you in coffee, of which of course I am very sorry, but we covered that, haven't we?'

Whilst smoking, Amanda laughed and sipped again at her drink, before moving over to the armchair. As she perched herself on one arm, she looked down to see Carl place his glass and cigarette on the coffee table. As he sat back, she curled one leg over the other and as she had expected, Carl glanced longingly at her legs. Carl felt the tender touch of fingers caress his hair and work their way down his neck to undo his collar.

'Like what you see Carl, do you,' she said provocatively, 'a girl with slender, long legs; bronzed and smooth?'

Carl felt her hand take his and guide it to her thigh.

'Had them specially shaved for you today my dear,' she said, guiding his hand with hers upon her leg, 'know how to turn a girl on do we, Carl?' she said, sliding his hand up between her legs as she uncrossed them.

'You are nice, you know Amanda,' he slurred, his eyes rolling to see her blurred face, feeling the warm of her knickers.

'Or do you like my other assets?' she teased; now guiding his hand in between the buttons of her blouse. 'But have another sip first before we talk business,' she enticed, handing him his glass with her other hand.

Talk business, eh? Is that another word for it?' Carl

slurred, taking a gulp. 'But I did want to know about the doctor's case... do you know his retrial is tomorrow... he could get out!'

'But of course I do,' Amanda said smiling, watching Carl's eyes transfixed on his hand, now groping at her bra, 'I'm the one helping him to get out... I've got him new evidence and great rewards await me.'

'What like?' Carl said sluggishly, his mind drowsy. 'A nice flashy car, no,' he paused, 'you got one of them, so it must be money... or is it sex... you don't need money for that, coz I would love to make love to a slender girl like you, you've got...'

Suddenly Carl's head dropped and Amanda knew the drug that Daniel had got for her had affected him. Slowly she removed his hand from between her blouse and placed it down beside him. As he slouched back, his eyes closed and Amanda doused the cigarettes in the ashtray before she got to her feet.

She searched high and low the bedroom after not finding the pendant underneath the sun-lamp, but continued to rummage through cabinets, wardrobes, and Carl's chest of drawers; even under the bed. As her search become more unsuccessful, her rage increased until she was stripping the bedroom, pulling out drawers, knocking over ornaments as well as the sun-lamp. She bounced into the lounge and stood, her angry face flustered as she watched Carl groan. Obsessed, she examined the room; looking everywhere she thought he may have hid the pendant.

Eventually, she glared down at him and the things he had scattered about. But, of course, his briefcase she thought.

Quickly, she leaned over him and pulled the briefcase from the floor and up to the settee. Fortunately the combination sequences were engaged and so she flipped up the locks. However, finding no pendant in the briefcase, she thumped the armchair and cursed, raising her fist to the sky.

'Where is it, my dear?' she said satirically, looking down at him, her rage gradually calming. 'Where could it be... please, just this one thing?'

Suddenly, she heard Carl snigger; his nose reverberating a snore, his hand instinctively reaching for his nose. It was then that she thought of the handkerchief she still had of his; the one he used to wipe the split coffee from her blouse.

After moving his body aside, Amanda pulled slowly the coat from underneath him and he groaned, muttering nonsensical words. Although the coat was caught beneath Carl, with most of it free, Amanda searched the pockets before feeling something round and hard.

With the ecstasy of a child in a candy shop, she pulled out the pendant and danced about. Hearing a strange voice from Carl's mouth, she stopped, but then realised he was sedated and delirious. As she swung the pendant above her in the light, she muttered to herself that the jackpot bingo had come and mocked the job to be easy money.

Replacing her shoes, scarf and jacket, Amanda zipped the pendant into her jacket pocket and made her way to the front door. For a moment she paused to look at Carl, her face exposing an expression of guilt, but looked him up and down.

'Never mind my boy, it's a pity business comes before pleasure... as it would've been nice to have fucked you!'

*Colin Martin*

# THIRTY – THREE

CARL WAS AWOKE BY TWO shrills from the telephone. With his head still nauseous from what Amanda had put in his drink, it took some time to realise he had been in the armchair all night. The phone rang again, but this time it continued. He then realised that Mike used two rings to indicate that he was phoning. Unsteady, Carl eventually made his way to the telephone in the hallway.

'Carl is that you?' Mike asked, rather apprehensive. 'I didn't think you were ever going to answer.'

'Yes, it's me alright,' he replied somewhat queasy, 'I'm not feeling too well mate; must be the effects of some sleeping powder, or something that bitch gave me.'

Ignoring Carl's remarks, Mike continued, although fairly apologetic.

'Look mate, I'm sorry for arguing yesterday, but Rachael's had it in the neck off Sarah about what's happened to Liz, and you know what happens then, I get it in the neck too.'

'What about Sarah?' Carl enquired. 'Is she okay?'

'What do you think?' he replied cynically. 'She devastated of course!'

'Well maybe I should ring her,' Carl muttered, 'you know, explain things; maybe give her my support. Has Rachael got her number in America?'

'Mate, I don't think that would be wise, not after how bad she took it.'

'But she didn't give it to me before she went?'

423

'Look if you'd take my advice, I'd stay clear for a while.'

'But she's supposed to be my –'

'Stay away from Rachael,' Mike stated, 'they blame you for Liz's death; for not looking out for her and that.'

'But she wanted to help – I didn't ask her!'

'Look I've been told she's coming back over, but I think its best you wait until she calms down.' Mike paused to take breath. 'I too want you to get a grip on yourself.'

'So even *you* think I'm losing it,' Carl said. 'I guess there's no chance of hiding from the police at Rachael's then, until I sort myself out?'

'No way mate, there's no way she'd –'

'What just for a while?'

'No, God dam it!' Mike shouted. 'Something is definitely wrong about how you knew about David's death; his true cause of death. Besides,' his voice alleviated, 'I'm sick of lying for you at work or to that Detective Inspector. They have an identification of you being the person who took Liz to hospital.'

'So you are going to abandon your best mate, when he needs you most?'

'I can't keep covering up for you.'

'Oh, I thought it me who was the scaredy-cat,' Carl decreed, 'and getting myself seduced by some –'

'I won't risk getting involved.'

Expecting a reply, Mike heard nothing from the receiver.

'Carl? Carl, are you still there?'

'She took it,' Carl announced fumbling in the pockets of his coat. 'That's what that bitch wanted; not to seduce me!'

'Seduced? What are you on about?'

'That bitch who calls herself Amanda,' Carl revealed, 'she drugged me with some sleeping pill; pretending that she was interested in me.'

'Two women in such a short time,' Mike chuckled, 'count your blessings, I don't get *that* lucky.'

'It's no fucking joke!' Carl exclaimed. 'It's not here.'

'Calm down. What's not there?'

'The pendant… she's stole it out my coat… for that doctor no doubt.'

'Oh no, not that *doctor* again,' Mike sighed, 'that bastard is sending you –'

Abruptly Mike stopped in middle of his sentence, realising Carl had not seen the morning newspaper.

'But there's a connection between that pendant and the doctor,' Carl stated, 'Liz was researching it until…'

Carl silenced, guilty of what had happened.

Before hanging up, Carl heard Mike disclose, 'I've got to go mate, but I think you'd better read the local newspaper. I think that doctor of yours was released this morning.'

Carl had never realised how difficult it was to conceal his identity. Not only had he put on an old beanie hat, but he had his coat collars high and a scarf over his mouth. At first it seemed like desperate measures, but after finding it cold outside, he had good reason to cover up. Intentionally, he had gone out just to get the morning newspaper, but after noticing a police car in his street, retreated to the warmth of his favourite café.

After refreshing sips of coffee, he sifted through the pages of the newspaper until he noticed the doctor's article. It was the figure of Amanda that first caught his eye; pictured slightly behind the doctor, accompanying him out of the court house.

Reading the article, Carl learned of how, after almost a decade, the doctor was acquitted from an early morning retrial; where a new appointed jury had found the doctor innocent of his alleged crime due to recent events and compelling new evidence. Annoyed at the doctor's statement, Carl read of how the doctor ridiculed the justice system and condemned all his days in solitary confinement, but would celebrate his freedom by reuniting people of his astrological society. Despising the doctor's liberty, Carl read on and learned of how Miss Amanda Burley, his new accomplice and journalist, had linked the recent death of a policeman to the boy that the doctor was originally accused of murdering. It was the approval that the recent murder had replications of the past which swayed the jury in favour of the doctor's innocence. Under his breath Carl swore and rolled the paper in his hand before downing the cup of coffee.

Angrily, he made his way to a nearby telephone box, where after looking about him, bundled himself inside and dialled Mike's number at work.

'Mike, Mike, that is you, isn't it?'

'Yes, is that you again, Carl?' Mike asked. 'Where are you?'

'A phone-box, outside… well never mind,' he paused to look about him, 'but I've read the newspaper and the doctor's out.'

'A telephone box,' Mike questioned, 'but why?'

'I looked earlier and there's a police car in my street. I think they've been knocking on doors; asking where I am.'

'I know,' Mike asserted, 'that Detective Inspector has been in again this morning, asking about the leave you booked.'

'Nosy bastard,' Carl voiced, 'what's it got to do with him; all I did was take Liz to hospital.'

'But this is to do with David as well,' Mike revealed, 'they believe your prints were on his car.'

'But it burst into flames... it was burnt out, wasn't it?'

'Yes, but they have your fingerprints, or something like that.'

'It's probably when he gave me a lift,' Carl pretended, 'the stupid bastards.'

'Well I don't know what to tell them anymore,' Mike argued, 'I can't keep lying, even if I am good at it.'

'Mike, just tell them that all you know is that I've gone away... Wales again or something, but please I need you to do me a favour.'

'No Carl,' Mike protested, 'I'm not getting any more involved.'

'But I can't get about, if coppers are looking for me.'

'Well, what... what is it you want?' Mike sighed before defining his conditions. 'This is the last thing mind. No more shit after this!'

'Yes, okay,' Carl groaned, 'all I want is to know is where the doctor goes and who he visits; stuff like that. I'll pretend I'm not at home, but ring twice first before –'

Carl was interrupted by a tap on his shoulder.

'Excuse me sir,' a voice said from behind, 'but aren't you a Mr Carl Aston of sixty-three, Gate Street, a couple of blocks from here?'

Carl turned to see a policeman opening the door of the phone-box and slowly put down the receiver.

'What's it to you, constable?' Carl replied, determined to protest his rights.

'Well, I have cause for you to accompany me to the station,' the constable stated assertively, 'with regard to the murder of a…' the constable flipped open his notepad, 'a Miss Elizabeth Woodall, who was brutally murdered.'

As the constable spoke, Carl stepped outside the phone booth and followed him as he described the requests made by a Detective Inspector Campbell.

'Apparently, Mr Aston you were seen by a nurse, and by doctors, to have brought Miss Woodall in hospital due to head injuries, and that later you were seen leaving her room shortly after her death. We will need a statement.'

Carl kept silent. Not because he knew it stupid to reveal the impact of his dreams, but he was calculating his chances of escape; somehow to stop this doctor before any other murders occurred. But what if he could persuade the police to investigate the doctor; trace his steps and monitor his actions. As they passed the alleyway to where he was previously attacked, Carl thought it best to chance it alone and escaped the grip of the constable.

He could hear the sound of loud footsteps behind him as he disappeared into the depths of the alleyway, but knew of a concealed passage between the back of houses. Using his rolled newspaper between the gaps, he lifted the latch on a gate, allowing just enough room for him to squeeze through. By the time the sound of running feet slowed to walking pace and circled around, he had shut the gate firm and secured the latch. He shuddered as he heard the tall gate rattle; the constable testing its rigidity and others further down. Quietly, he raced through back gardens, opening other gates and closing them behind, until he reached another street. Precariously, he stepped about the back streets, his body close to each wall as he studied the nearby houses. For a while he reclined into a gulley between buildings, listening out for the stomp of heavy feet, but heard nothing but vehicles pass.

Again by the time he sneaked his way home, a police car was parked outside his door. But his venture through back gardens reminded him of the weak fencing that Amanda must have removed to enter his bedroom. In addition, with the bedroom window not secure, not only could he get in but he could escape the same way, should police come snooping.

He was quite right about the fencing and indeed the bedroom window. As he had only sandwiched a piece of plywood in between, a large screwdriver from his car, levered it open. Inside, he peered at the police car outside and kept quiet while collecting things. For a while he sat, reading parts of the diary and glossing over the drawings, studying notes of Liz's research and skimming through Sarah's photos. Hearing sounds from the road outside, Carl looked up and then noticed the half dowsed cigarettes in ashtray upon the coffee table. Remembering these were ones he and Amanda had half smoked, he picked up one and nervously lit it with a fireside match. After he inhaled the mild taste a number of times, his eyes began to tire, his mind lay dreary and so he put it out.

Again Carl awoke to the shrill of the telephone. As it had ceased after two rings, Carl awaited for it to ring again. Again it rang and continued until he picked up the receiver.

'Carl, are you there?'

'Yes, it's me,' Carl replied quietly, 'but I'll have to whisper; there's coppers outside… but what do you have, anything?'

'That doctor friend of yours is a well shifty character; he's so hard to track.'

'Why, what's he been doing?'

'Well luckily I caught him back at that institute, gathering some belongings and stuff before making his way with some fit, young, dark-haired girl. And when I mean fit, I mean well –'

'That's the bitch who seduced me!' Carl exclaimed.

'Well I wouldn't mind been seduced by that,' Mike pronounced, the tone of his voice excited.

'Don't believe it mate,' Carl disputed, 'she's certainly beautiful but a deadly venomous poison, I can tell you… took my pendant right from under my nose, literally… she uses people like puppets.'

'Pity, she's one hell of a puppet master,' Mike affirmed. 'I can see her now from this phone-box. She's talking with a gentleman outside some gentleman's club… you know the type that does –'

'Yes, I gather the type,' Carl interrupted, 'but where else have they been? Have you heard anything said?'

'Not really, just visiting different people. Councillors mainly, you know, people of some affluence and wealth. I guess guys like that can afford it here.'

'Get what where?'

'You know, a bit on the side; without the wife knowing.' Mike stated before changing his conversation. 'She's leaving now, with a basket and black clothes of some kind… bloody nice sports car… what's she do?'

'Never mind her; it said that the doctor is going to give a reunion for his society tonight.'

'Well he has just got out after nearly ten years,' Mike asserted, 'guess he's got a right to celebrate.'

'Not to what I believe he's going to do!' Carl confirmed.

'What's that?'

'Nothing, please I just need another favour.'

'No, I've done enough, I'm sick of coppers asking where –'

'Look,' Carl snapped, 'please just delay him from getting to Arlington Manor!'

'Getting to where?'

'Arlington Manor,' Carl repeated, 'it's not far from where I used to live.'

'No, sorry Carl, it's crazy; you're crazy,' Mike asserted. 'I'm not getting involved anymore. I've done this favour, so don't expect anymore!'

At the point that Carl heard Mike hang up, there was a loud knock on the door. Hidden behind the armchair, Carl peered again through the gap between the curtains. This time he could see two policemen, accompanied by the Detective Inspector, who again knocked loudly on the door.

Hastily Carl grabbed his coat, some belongings he had prepared in a bag and made his way through the bedroom window. By the time he had sneaked through the back garden and to the top of his street, from a distance he could see the policemen talking by their car.

Gingerly he ran to his car and opening the door, bundled his bag inside. As he sat in the driver's seat, he glanced in the rear view mirror and then down at the open bag. He looked at each item, thinking if all was necessary; his father's diary and drawings, Sarah's photos, Liz's research, but most importantly, the large silver crucifix and square bottle of holy water.

Within seconds on starting up the car engine, he raced his car up the incline and turned a corner; out of view of the policemen. As Carl sped about the streets to reach the main road, his thoughts were of the doctor; that tonight he must prevent his society practicing witchcraft, but more importantly for him, the doctor must not find out about what he did with Alex as a child.

# THIRTY – FOUR

THE ROOM WAS JUST AS Carl remembered it; collections of old paintings, ornaments, furniture and wood-carvings, all covered with dust cloths and untouched in years. This storage room was indeed the route he and Alex had took all those years ago, but he was a lot smaller then and the squeeze through the sashed window proved somewhat difficult.

With partial light from the window, gingerly he stepped about the room trying best not to knock over antiquities or creak any of the wooden floor boards. He knew the car was safe; parked down the lane, behind some trees and out of view, but did not know if anyone was at home. As he crept towards the room's only door, he stopped and realised what the farmer had said about the doctor's henchman; some tall and burly delinquent, who looked after the manor and its grounds.

Exiting the room, Carl tip-toed along a lengthy corridor of which he recollected was a hallway to downstairs bedrooms. Forgetting he was heading in the wrong direction, he turned, realising the large banqueting hall, dining room, library and study were on the north side of the building. It was the study that he required, as this was where he and Alex had found the book before. Surely if Carl could steal the book again, the doctor would be helpless; as without all his years of research into the occult and the incantations he had devised he could not conjure evil.

Changing direction, Carl looked about him, remembering the large pictures hanging above him; ones of which scared him as a child. He passed a number of portraits; most of gentries' horse riding in the countryside, but some of older artists – religious etchings and paintings depicting confrontations with evil. By now he knew he was close to the study, as above him hung an enormous painting; one that scared him the most. Accentuated by the dark of the wall, the eyes of three angels followed Carl wherever he stood, as if their enlarged pupils observed him from any angle. Covering one hand above his eyes so not to be perturbed by their unearthly stare, Carl continued down the hallway and towards the study. Suddenly, he saw a hooded figure race quickly across the hallway and rest against a wall.

Slowly Carl strode toward the figure but stopped, thinking it may well be the doctor's accomplice; but it was small and now sneaking along like him, towards the study. Examining behind, the figure abruptly turned to face him, but luckily he hid behind a large clothed table, covered with an old tapestry embroiled with a coat of arms. Noticing the figure disappear into the room, he stood up to pursue it, but selected a large silver candlestick to protect himself.

Precariously he peered into the study, holding still the half open door. Through the gap, Carl could see the hooded figure examine a large central desk, rifling through draws and scouring through documents. With his candlestick poised overhead to protect him, silently he entered and approached the figure. Suddenly, Carl's next step squeaked the floor and the figure turned to face him. As his hand swung the candlestick, he noticed the long blonde hair of a woman fall from the hooded face. As the girl shot back in fright, Carl pulled away his weapon and withdrew the candlestick. In amazement he watched as the girl removed her hood, and after her long blonde hair had parted, Carl could see the startled face of Sarah.

'What the…' Carl shouted before realising he needed to be quiet. 'Sarah? What the hell are you going here; here in the doctor's house?'

Carl could not gather whether it was guilt or relief that made her grin, but grasped that Sarah had purpose to search the house.

'I could have knocked you to tomorrow,' he whispered aloud. 'What the hell are you doing here?'

'Carl, thank God it's you!' she reassured. 'I thought it was that bitch; the one I followed here!'

'What, Amanda,' he enquired moving close to her, 'a dark-haired girl, slim build, athletic type? She's visited here?'

'Yes, she had black cloaks of some kind; gowns with red lettering that she took from her car. Also a cane basket with –'

'A black cockerel inside,' Carl deduced.

'Yes, but how did you know?' she asked.

'Been doing my research, or at least…'

Carl could not mention Liz's name; recollecting that in fact she had been killed whilst helping him.

'But what are you doing here?' he questioned to avoid the subject. 'Why follow Amanda here?'

'That bitch killed Liz, I'm sure of it,' she said angrily, 'I saw her address on your business card and stuff Liz wrote about that bitch before she…' Sarah's face changed with anger. 'She offered to help, but *you* were supposed to look after her. You shouldn't have let that bitch anywhere near her!'

'No it's not like that,' he exclaimed. 'You've got it wrong!'

But Sarah was not listening, infuriated by the loss of her friend.

'No, everyone thinks I'm still over there, so when I get hold of the bitch…'

'No Sarah please, calm down,' he said, grasping her hands, noticing her eyes fill with tears. 'I'm telling you that it wasn't Amanda, but something like what attacked you; what we fought off together.'

'And you were there?'

'No,' he sighed, 'by the time I got to the hospital, she was…'

'But how did you know?' she wailed. 'Why did you not stop with her?'

'I went to her as soon as I woke from the dream,' he replied.

'You dreamt about her dying; like you did of me?'

'Yes, but I didn't get there in time, she –'

'So you could've saved her?'

'I tried; believe me, I so tried, but…'

Sarah sprang forward and punched at Carl continually until he could grasp her fists.

'Sarah, please, I can't control the dreams I have, they just happen,' he tutored. 'If I could've saved her I would've; I was *just* in time to save you.'

He paused to look around, realising it wasn't the place to argue differences.

'Liz believed what my Aunt said about my mother's physic power; that they used her gift to predict future events and that maybe somehow, I've inherited my mother's gift to prevent –'

'Well you didn't do a very good job of it, did you… to save Liz that is?'

'But I can't control my dreams. I don't have powers to change things,' Carl pronounced. 'Don't you think I'd contest the doctor's evil if I could?'

'Is that why your here,' she asked, 'to find answers?'

'But why only of the doctor?' Carl questioned himself, searching about the study. 'Why dream *only* the evil he does?'

'Maybe your mother hated him so much,' Sarah sobbed, wiping the tears from her eyes. 'Maybe she wanted to help your father and his church; to stop the doctor's power?'

Carl looked curiously at Sarah and then smiled, thankful to see her beautiful face once more.

'I've missed you Sarah,' he said sincerely, 'believe me, I've missed you.'

Sarah smiled and stroked his cheek with her hand, but frowned.

'Why *are* you here, Carl?' she reiterated, holding his arm. 'Have you a plan to stop him… the doctor that is?'

'I'm going to steal that book back,' he instructed, 'the one that Alex and I stole when we were kids. That should stop him and his society conjuring evil.'

'But what if the doctor is the chief officiator?'

'Is what?' Carl queried.

'The adjudicator,' Sarah stated, 'a high-priest of the Black Art?'

'What if he is?'

'Then surely he hasn't had the book in that institute; to conjure the evil from inside?' Sarah disputed.

'Well maybe, I hadn't thought about that, but,' he paused, knowing that the doctor's work was precious to him; that the book could be kept as a bargaining tool, should the doctor find out the truth, 'but, I need it in case he finds out.'

'Finds out what?' she asked.

Carl took Sarah by the hand and led her nearer the door.

'Sarah, you're the one person I can trust, aren't you?'

'Yes but of course, after all that has happened.'

'And for you I'll do anything.'

'Anything?' she asked, frowning.

'Well you remember that morning in the park, after our first night together?'

'After that thing attacked us, the night before?'

'Yes, well I told you, as kids, Alex and I stole the book from here,' he said, pointing his finger at the study, 'that we escaped across the grounds, someone after us.'

'Or, something?' she interrupted.

'That's not the point,' Carl said quietly, looking at the door. 'When Alex was found dead next day, he had on him that pendant, but then of course, I didn't realise...' Carl paused as a chill overwhelmed his body, thinking someone else was listening, 'but I blamed the doctor and now I know I was right.'

'And so...' Sarah said slowly, somewhat confused.

'Well the garden trowel that Alex fell on,' Carl disclosed, 'and the handkerchief that I tied around his knee, I... I went back after hearing of his death and hid them in the doctor's glasshouse.'

'So he'd get –'

'Get blamed for Alex's death, yes.'

'I was going to say framed,' Sarah said with a tone of displeasure.

'But he *was* to blame,' he ascertained, 'well something he had conjured.'

'But you set him up!' she contested, raising her voice and stepping back towards the door. 'So the doctor and that escaped criminal were innocent? You set him up to avenge Alex's death?'

'Yes but, wouldn't you do the same for your friend – for Liz?' he justified.

Suddenly behind Sarah, the door burst open and a tall figure in black assailed her. Before Carl could do anything with his weighty candlestick, he noticed the doctor's accomplice pointing a shotgun at him with one hand and a cloth covering Sarah's mouth with the other. As he pulled her back to the door, at first Sarah struggled and almost got free, but as she inhaled the chloroform, her eyes circled and she fell.

'Interesting story that,' Daniel shouted, watching Sarah drop to the floor, 'I'm sure the doctor will want to hear it. Not that you'll be alive to regret it.'

As Daniel raised the double-barrel shotgun and squeezed the trigger, Carl flew forward with the candlestick. Fortunately the shotgun fired just as the candlestick struck it from aim and a shot blistered the wall. As Daniel swore and readjusted his aim, Carl assailed him again, throwing the candlestick at his legs. Although he heard Daniel cry in pain, he had no time to rescue Sarah; he had to get away, survive and devise some other plan to return.

As he raced along the hallway, he knew the storeroom window would be difficult to exit and changed direction to the open doors of the main hall. Inevitably, after Daniel staggered out from the study, he was after Carl, his gun at hand. Without concern Carl bashed against the main doors, but took quite a bruising as they were tall and heavy. Nevertheless he knew the shadow of Daniel was close behind and so stumbled out upon the gritted driveway that circled a large statue. He searched the grounds and in the distance recognised the location of his car.

Stumbling over the long grass, Carl could hear the doctor's accomplice shouting, threatening to shoot again, but he ran on, closer and closer to his car. Turning a corner to see his parked car, Carl glanced back at the manor. Along the narrow drive from the house, he could see Daniel racing toward him, his shotgun held high.

Quickly Carl raced inside his car and started the engine. Revving it up, he placed the gear into reverse and pulled his foot up off the clutch. At first the front wheels span in the wet grass, but once embedded, the tyres took grip and the car reversed back into the cloud of smoke it discharged. Seeing the car now upon the grit of the drive, Carl's foot hit the brake and the wheels held firm, skidding the tyres. Changing into first gear, Carl glanced into the rear view mirror to see Daniel stop to load his shotgun. As the front wheels span and belted grit backward, Carl heard the sound of the shotgun hit the car. Suddenly finding grip upon the earth below, the car screeched forward and Carl bounced in his seat as it meandered off course. Again Carl heard the sound of the shotgun, but this time against the back bumper.

Watching the figure of Daniel disappear in the rear view mirror, Carl steadied the car along the narrow road, but something was wrong; the steering difficult, the car veering to leave the road.

Distraught, Carl glanced to see if Daniel was following behind, but suddenly the car hit a tree. Sprung forward, Carl felt his head hit the steering wheel and then all went black.

# THIRTY – FIVE

AT FIRST CARL THOUGHT HE was reliving his experience with Liz, but how could he; she was dead? As he turned the corner of the hospital ward, he could hear commotion coming from a nearby inspection room. Approaching a half open door, the sounds of shouting grew louder. Opening the door, Carl could see the rear of a doctor trying to hold Sarah upon the bed, but she was frenetic; yelling to be let go, trying to pull free her arms whilst kicking her legs. Suddenly she saw Carl enter the room and eagerly called to him.

'Carl, please,' she pleaded, her eyes looking wildly at her stomach, 'tell them to stop the pain… it's killing me!'

'Where my dear,' he shouted, reaching forward for her hand, 'where's the pain?'

'My stomach,' she signalled, 'please, what's wrong with me?' Frantically Carl undid the buttons of her hospital gown and looked upon her bare stomach. At first there seemed nothing wrong; her navel, waist and legs untouched, her underwear clean and normal, but then noticed something bizarre. As a wound appeared just above her navel, blood started to pour out and spill in several streams across her stomach; one which reached her crotch, stained her knickers.

'Carl, please… the pain,' she cried. 'What's happening to me?'

Carl placed his hand over the wound to stop the bleeding and turned to the doctor for help. As the doctor's head spun to face him, Carl glanced in horror, as it was no other than that of Doctor Schroeck – the Dark-man. As he hollered in amusement, Carl saw his face mutate into that of a skull; it's once empty, black eye sockets now revealing blazing red eyes that glared at him, its jaw bouncing with laughter and then it shot towards him in a burst of flame.

Heart pounding and body fevered, Carl again awoke from a vivid nightmare, and this time his neck was stiff and his head sore. As his eyes focused upon the steering wheel of the car, he realised that the crash must have knocked him out.

Scrambling out from his vehicle, he noticed the front of the car slammed against a tree. But it was driveable; only the headlight, right wing and bumper dented. However, stepping back to view the car boot, he noticed one of the rear tyres flat; splintered by the shrapnel from Daniel's shotgun.

As his mind cleared with the cold of dusk, he suddenly realised what was about to happen. Surely with what his nightmare forecast and the fact that Sarah had most likely been kidnapped, he knew she was now at the mercy of the doctor; but without his vehicle operational, he could not go far to save her. With the dark of night rapidly swallowing up the remaining daylight, Carl also knew he had limited time.

Tightening the last bolt to fix firm the spare wheel, Carl heard vehicles approach. Luckily he was a distance from the driveway and in darkness of the trees he noticed headlights appear from the main road. Crouching behind the rear of his car, he saw several pairs of headlights move down the driveway and towards the manor. Hiding, but peering to observe them, he noted many expensive vehicles; one of which he thought was Amanda's.

Shortly after removing the scissor jack and rolling the car back from the tree, Carl noticed more headlights turn from the main road and head towards the manor. As the red of the rear lights faded, once again he was alone in the darkness of the manor grounds. With the convoy of vehicles he had just witnessed, he knew the doctor's society was about to meet. He walked a distance toward the manor; enough to view car lights flicker off and hear the sound of voices diminish into the manor. Knowing for certain that the parked sports car he has passed belonged to Amanda, he rushed toward the manor. However, with the doctor's henchman wondering the grounds in vengeance, again he secretly squeezed through the storeroom window.

Carefully stepping between the familiar antiquities, he paused to realise he had not brought anything from his car; that he may indeed need what was in the metal box. But it was too late to go back now; Sarah could be in danger and he must go on. Reaching the door Carl paused again, cautious to open it, but heard strange chanting and laughter.

Looking to the floor, so to not observe their intimidating gaze, Carl passed the painting of the three angels and stepped closer to the sounds of chanting. He paused to define his location in the manor, but then heard the shrill of a wind instrument, accompanied by unusual drumming. At first the drum beat was slow and melodic, but after more chanting and laughter, a faster drumming echoed the corridor. As he crept toward the sound, he noticed a small stairway and turned to climb it. Kneeling with his face peering between heavy curtains, Carl could see that he was on a balcony that circled above a large banqueting room. Curious to see from where the chanting was coming, he crept to the edge of the balcony and held tight two vertical balustrades.

Below, Carl could see a capacious floor, decorated by large tiles and bordered with ornate cabinets and tables. Although obscured by people dancing upon it, drawn upon the floor, he noticed two large circles enclosing a pentagram with symbols between. At points where the pentagram touched the inner most circle, he noticed copper bowls burning a pungent liquid, each of which were supported by large metal stands. Featured between the circles were also many tall, black candles of which colour matched the floor markings. As he observed the assembly of people dance and make merry, he noticed their strange gowns; trimmed in red, each of which was decorated with an inverted cross, scarlet against the black of the cloth. Looking to his right and towards the far end below him, he saw two musicians, their heads covered in animal masks; one a serpent and one a goat. On a stage above and behind them was a long table decorated in black cloth, with similar markings imprinted to that on the gowns, but this had more complex decoration.

He looked again at the people prancing about. Most were drinking red wine and were joyous from the alcohol, or was it the odour of scented candles and burning oils that made them euphoric. At first sight Carl thought it nothing but some erotic party, but soon grasped the concept of what was really happening. Resting from their antics in one corner, he recognised two local governmental figures groping a woman underneath her robe. Further down and beside a cabinet, one man was knelt in front of another and holding his robe aloft, was performing oral sex.

Scanning the hall in hope to save Sarah, Carl recognised no one but the local councillors frisking the woman. Indeed most were still masked; passing and groping one another without guilt, spilling wine and licking it off. But then he saw a young, dark-haired girl crouched forward, her stomach resting on furniture as her robe was lifted from behind. At first he noticed her naked legs and buttocks, but as she removed her mask, he could see that it was Amanda. Holding firmly her mask and grasping the edge of the table, she glanced at the man from behind as he probed to enter her. From his forceful penetration she squealed, but after moving steadily, she moaned pleasurably and looked back to observe him. Suddenly Carl heard Amanda squeal again, but this time it was from hard slaps on her thigh.

With the aroma that rose from the hall and his aching mind Carl become faint, but had to stop and witness the revelry; maybe somehow prevent this ceremony, but more importantly, save Sarah. As he sneaked closer around the balcony and towards the large clothed table, he noticed long, heavy curtains stretch down to the stage. Testing the strength of the material and its rigidity, Carl's attention was diverted to a large figure appear carrying something wrapped in a white sheet. Leaning forward, he watched the hooded figure place the wrapped object upon the long table, before retreating to collect a square basket.

As the light of the room dimmed, the crowd dismissed their pleasures, replaced their masks and applauded the entrance of a cloaked figure. As the chanting amplified along with the vigour of the music, the figure approached the table. At first, all that Carl could see was the body of a man covered head to foot in a dark purple robe, etched in scarlet symbols. Slowly the figure raised its hands and once the crowd silenced, the only sound was that of a cockerel, cackling from the basket.

From the hood of the cloaked figure strange words were announced and ends of sentences repeated by the onlooking crowd. Carl found the language hard to decipher; it was not foreign or Latin, but something he had never heard before. Again many sentences were announced and the congregation echoed last words. For several minutes Carl witnessed the crowd repeat the words until the first figure approached the table; holding the cockerel by its legs to hang it upside down.

Slowly the crowd removed their masks, as too did the figure holding the cockerel. Unveiled, and holding the cockerel, was Daniel. Carl therefore deduced that the figure dressed in purple was that of the doctor, and as he pulled back his hood, indeed he was right.

Daniel approached the table and with the cockerel held aloft, also produced a copper bowl. Suddenly the doctor produced a curved dagger and shouting strange words, slit the throat of the cockerel; its blood pouring into the copper bowl below. As the crowd watched with exhilaration, Carl turned his head away, disgusted that they showed no remorse. Turning back to examine the doctor, he watched as each crowd member stepped up to him and had their forehead blooded with a sign of an inverted cross. To the slow beat of a drum, each member returned to the centre of the pentagram and constructing a circle, faced the doctor. Cleaning the blood from his dagger, the doctor signalled Daniel to uncover the body that lay upon the table. It was then that Carl held his breath.

Staring in horror, Carl gazed at Sarah's naked, unconscious body lying upon the table. He grew cold, his nerves trembling; surely the doctor would not sacrifice an innocent human just for his occult gathering. But then he remembered about what he had learned and the power of the pendant that now hung around Sarah's neck.

In desperation Carl searched the balcony but saw nothing that would help him stop this witchcraft. Hearing him shout aloud another set of strange words and smudge blood about Sarah's navel, Carl fears grew worse. Seeing Daniel move directly beneath him, Carl recognised the shotgun placed in one corner and leapt at his best opportunity. Sliding down the curtain and hitting Daniel with both feet, the doctor held high the dagger, but stopped his words in surprise. Pelted against the wall, Daniel was rendered unconscious but the doctor carried on his ceremony, his words hurried.

Turning back to the crowd the doctor signalled his audience to stay as they were, but his left hand still held high the dagger. He spun back his head to observe Carl, who now moved toward him, pointing the shotgun.

'I'll shoot!' Carl exclaimed, his face grim with menace. 'Put down the dagger and let her go, or I'll shoot you where you stand!'

'You have no idea do you son?' the doctor proclaimed. 'Interfering on this sacrificial repayment; the need to repay my debts!'

'What, in killing an innocent woman?' Carl asked, motioning the shotgun with aim. 'She has nothing to do with your sick society!'

'But she holds the gift of new life, my son,' the doctor said lowering the dagger, 'and her youth will honour me to that of the highest!'

'Put down the dagger,' Carl demanded again, 'or I'll shoot – anyone of you!'

'You've certainly chosen a beauty,' the doctor said, looking upon Sarah's body and then his audience, 'but my friends here don't know *who* you are, do they my son?'

'Stop calling me son,' Carl growled angrily, 'or I'll fucking shoot!'

'But you are my son, are you not?' the doctor proclaimed, turning to face him. 'The Aston boy adopted by the clergyman… from the feeblest sister of three… the spiritual girl who asked for my assistance… my help to heal her illness, after *your* God abandoned her?'

'No you can't be,' Carl shouted, shaking his head, 'Father Stephen Aston was my father… not a corrupt bastard like you!'

'What do you know of the past?' the doctor questioned, his temper rising. 'That weak excuse of a child coming to me after all else failed her… wanting my help… but she was a temptation I could not resist and one–'

'What, my mother?' Carl shouted. 'Another poor innocent girl you can rape or dispose of at *your* will?'

'Argh, but my demand is necessary to honour the great evil, or–'

'Or what,' Carl shouted, pointing the shotgun to the crowd whilst moving towards them, 'you'll get mutilated by some *great* evil… an evil you cannot control should I have the same blood as,' he paused before saying sarcastically, 'my father?'

'You have no knowledge of the Black Art,' the doctor professed, 'it is beyond your means. I, however, will have compensation… once this sacrifice is…'

The doctor turned back to face Sarah's naked body and raising the dagger again said aloud words unknown to Carl.

As the doctor drew down the dagger, Carl caught his left arm with the shotgun barrel and stopped the blade above Sarah's stomach. In the seconds of a struggle, the barrel raised and fired; a blast hitting the support of the other curtain. With the discharge, Carl jolted back and the doctor's grip was released. Uncontrollably the doctor's dagger hit downward and pierced his right hand, pinning it to the table. The doctor wailed in agony, but found breath to curse Carl; saying this was no way to treat his father and that his son will soon regret ever interfering.

Seeing the doctor restrained and in pain, Carl leapt to help Sarah, but paused to watch the curtain and its supporting pole tumble upon the crowd. As the gathering threw down their masks and ran to avoid the fall, the poles bounced upon the floor, knocking over candles and the bowls of burning liquid. Quickly the liquid spread across the floor and along with the curtains, burst into flame. Carl watched as the doctor's congregation ran for the door and after lifting Sarah, he followed too.

'There is only one that gives true power!' the doctor shouted, pulling the dagger from his hand, and holding aloft his wound. 'You've started the blood-letting yourself my son… and so now… let evil prevail!'

Wrapped tightly by the sheet, Carl rushed Sarah's body to the door, but turned back in anger.

'You're no one to me!' Carl shouted before slamming shut the door. 'You'll never be the father the Reverend was… you're just some corrupt, evil bastard!'

Seeing the key in the lock, Carl put Sarah down along with the shotgun and after locking the door, rushed her quickly to a couch in the study.

Staring angrily to see his hall ablaze, the doctor stumbled toward the door to find Daniel trying the lock. Turning to view the doctor, Daniel grimaced at the blocked exit and glanced fearfully at the spreading fire. Returning to the clothed table, the doctor commanded him to break down the door, but Daniel's attempts proved unless. The doctor started chanting words that Daniel knew summoned the evil and so leapt upon a chair and crashed through a nearby window.

Finding a gown in the study, Carl dressed Sarah and also put his coat around her. It was when he placed her on the couch, that he again noticed the pendant around her neck and snapping it free, placed it in his trouser pocket.

'Haven't you forgotten something?' Daniel announced entering the study with the shotgun, 'can't carry everything can we?'

'I had to save her,' Carl shouted, 'surely you wouldn't let the doctor murder an innocent girl like that?'

'That's not my concern,' Daniel replied, pointing the shotgun, 'but I tell you what is; that pendant, the one around her neck!'

'This one you mean?' Carl stated, pulling the pendant from his pocket and swinging it in the light.

'Yes, that one *indeed*,' Daniel said indicating that Carl should move aside. 'Now move and take it with you before it comes!'

'Before what comes?'

'The evil of course,' Daniel shouted sarcastically, 'the doctor has voiced the summoning words... and now it will come for you!'

'Not if I stay here,' Carl threatened, 'then we all get it!'

'And not save your beloved?' Daniel said with cynicism. 'Move while you still have a chance... quickly, before I get trigger happy!'

Carl glanced longingly at Sarah, but was motioned swiftly to the door; the barrels of the shotgun pushing into his back. Giving him a final shove with the shotgun, Daniel pushed Carl upon the hallway floor, but heard Daniel lock the door.

'She'll be trapped in there!' Carl shouted.

'But safe from the evil,' Daniel growled, 'now get moving before I shoot!'

Crawling to his feet, Carl wrapped the pendant about his hand and raced for the main exit. Outside, he stared about the car park, watching individuals disperse in their cars, but it was not the people that now concerned him.

Left of the manor and from the depths of distant woodland, Carl noticed a mist emerge. At first it thickened in separate clouds, but then assembled to swirl into a large fog bank. Stunned and curious, he stood to watch it glow green and blue, but then realised it was this that killed the policeman; or something from it. Although it was a distance to his car, decisively Carl ran.

Staggering along the gritted driveway with his heart pounding, Carl's legs felt like jelly, but seeing the mist almost upon him, he ran on. Reaching the car and unlocking the door, Carl felt something tug his shirt and pull him backward. Sprawled upon the grass and watching the car door swing open, he felt the pendant ice cold and saw it glow deep red before hearing shrieks above him.

Transparent as if part of the mist, Carl saw phantoms writhing and circling above him, but these had dirty green faces that resembled bat-like masks with pointed ears and mouths that reformed without a lower jaw. Black eyes glared at him as their deep purple, spectral bodies flew in and out of the mist. Horrified by the apparitions, Carl crawled to his feet and managed to grasp the car door as one flew past. As if a knife had slashed his arm, he felt the phantom cut his skin and turn upward; its mouth a gaping blackness. He grimaced as another slashed his shoulder, but dragged himself further into the car. In sight of the metal box, he pulled open the lid and in hope of its blessing, grabbed the bottle of holy water. He squealed in pain as another slashed his back, but opening the bottle, turned and sprayed the liquid about him. As the jets of liquid sprinkled into the surrounding mist, Carl heard the phantoms screech and perish, before dissipating.

Replacing the cork to the bottle, Carl sighed and sat in the car to nurse his wounds. However, it was not long before his fear returned. With the car door open he could hear the sound of distant drumming, but was mistaken; it was indeed the gallop of hooves. He slammed the door shut and turned the ignition key, but the car groaned; the working headlight flickering upon the mist. He tried the ignition again, but nothing. Turning off the lights, and turning the key, Carl looked aghast through the window of the car door.

Shadowed within the mist and galloping straight toward him was a weighty stallion; deathly black like the rider upon top. All at once Carl truly feared for his life as surely this was the Angel of Death; the evil that killed David, and now it was coming for him. Quickly he tried the ignition again and pumped at the accelerator pedal until suddenly, the engine roared into action. Hearing an almighty bang, Carl thought the engine had blown, but saw a scythe scrape across the bonnet.

Flooring the accelerator pedal, at first the car slid upon the wet grass, but turning the steering wheel side to side, the car tyres found grip. As the car bellowed out exhaust fumes, Carl switched on his one only headlight and looking anxiously into the rear view mirror, sped toward the driveway.

Reaching the main road he screeched the car left about a corner and sped to Fiddler's Mound; the only place holy enough to protect him. But more importantly, on top was the consecrated rock; the one carved and blessed at harvest. Recollecting passages in the diary, along with Liz's research, he had one chance to turn away this evil and send it back to the one who summoned it. But what was the wording he had to recite, the phrase to break the curse?

Driving one handed, Carl grabbed the diary, holy water and the crucifix and put them in his trouser pockets. He fumbled with the pendant, but found it cold, almost freezing as the dark stone glowed intermittent red. Steering with his arms, Carl slowed down the car to test the stone; it was firm, but from the blackness within, a deep scarlet light shone repeatedly.

Suddenly Carl lost control of his vehicle as something bashed against the car boot. Dropping the pendant, he grasped the steering wheel to take control, as through the mirror he could see his adversary behind, galloping ever closer. Snaking the car from side to side, he hoped to stop the evil reaching alongside, but found speed was best. Driving straight, he pushed down on the accelerator pedal and the car bellowed through the night air. He glanced again into the mirror but saw nothing behind but mist, and by now he was pulling free from that. A quick glimpse was all he needed to recognise the road sign to Fiddler's Mound and after veering right, sped to the foot of it. If he remembered correctly, the fastest way to the hilltop was a path through the woodland until reaching a steep, grassy ascent.

Scrabbling to find the pendant about his feet, Carl did not see the headlights of an oncoming car and at the last minute swerved to miss it. In the skid that followed he turned back the steering wheel hoping to regain control, but the car swerved, sliding backward until the rear hit a tree. Conscious but dazed, he pushed open the door and returned to search about his feet, rummaging until he found the pendant. Sliding it into his back pocket he exited his vehicle and pondered on directions. In the distance he noticed the fog bank move unnaturally toward him and so ran to the woodland.

Tearing through undergrowth, Carl saw the mist develop about him, but it was the resonance of galloping hooves that struck fear in his heart. He ran as fast as his legs would carry him to the opening beneath the hill and gasped to take a breath. Suddenly, hearing the respire of horse nostrils, a scythe missed his head and sliced a nearby tree. He looked up and through the swirling mist, saw his mounted assailant; its skeletal face identical to that in his dreams.

Hurriedly he escaped its gaze and scrambled up the incline, but found the grass wet and slippery. He dug in his boots and with hands clenching the clumps of grass, crawled high up the embankment until he reached the top. Wheezing and his heart pounding, Carl knew he had no time to stop; abnormally the mist had climbed the hill and the canter of hooves was not far distant. Staring through the clouds of mist, hastily he ran toward the great rock and pulling free the pendant from his back pocket, wound the chain around his wrist. Leaning against the consecrated rock, he recognised its bowl-like shape from childhood and between the carved circular inscriptions poured the remains of holy water. He probed his pocket for the diary but found it wedged in his trouser pocket.

Through the mist above the great scythe swung again at him but scored the rock; the evil retracting its weapon for another attempt. With his fingers cupped, Carl scooped the holy water and flung the liquid at the evil. It thundered in dismay as the stallion reared and kicked out its fore legs.

Arched low, he pulled free the diary and the silver

crucifix from his pocket and squinted to locate his adversary. Holding high the crucifix in sight of the evil, it withdrew; the hefty stallion trotting backward, the cloaked figure on top thrashing in the mist. He pulled a page from the diary and remembering his research read aloud the words of Latin; the words devised from holy gospel that the priest hoped would rid the evil. But it was only the crucifix the creature feared; the large blazing eyes of the stallion loathing the sight of the object.

Remembering Liz's theory to reverse the spell, Carl drowned the warlock's stone in holy water and hit it with the crucifix. At first it did not break and again, another hit proved useless. Frantic, he kissed the silver crucifix and turning to the sky, prayed for all people to avenge their deaths; to break the spell and summon the evil upon its conjuror. With abnormal strength Carl's hand brought down the butt of the crucifix and smashed the stone in two. In amazement, he watched as the glowing centre dispersed and bubbled beneath the water, leaving a cold and pungent vapour.

As all went quiet, Carl looked to the sky and then about him. Gradually above him the mist cleared and nearby, strangely his adversary had disappeared. He looked down into the trough of the great rock and pulling out the pendant saw that the stone was nothing but a half hollow shell.

Overwhelmed and relieved, he stood and leaned against the great rock, but felt his task was not quite over. Watching the mist retreat to the land below and pass his crashed car, he suddenly realised to where the evil now headed. According to Liz, the evil would now claim the life of its conjuror - the doctor, and with his manor ablaze, he remembered Sarah locked in the study.

# THIRTY – SIX

Unable to start his car, it had taken Carl some time to reach the grounds of the manor. Scrambling over undulating grassland, his heart pounded and legs were heavy, but he ran on as fast as he could to save Sarah.

Approaching the manor, at first he thought it fire smoke, but strangely a mist had expanded to the depths of distant woodland. Walking to calm his breathing, he noticed afar brilliant white sparks that shot together to form a large ball of fire. He squinted to focus on the hovering, fiery mass, but was obscured by mist; as it now swirled towards him. Glancing repeatedly at the distant fireball Carl trudged on, but stumbled upon the grit of the driveway. Falling a distance from the manor entrance, he winced at the sharp gravel that score his hands, but looked again to the woodland.

As the assemblage of smoke and fire sped towards him, flames from the centre spread out and twisted to form arms and hands with talon-ended fingers. The core flared and expanded to reveal a demonic face crowned with twisted ram's horns; below fiery eyes glared as a mouth opened wide to reveal razor sharp teeth. Speeding through the night air, the fiery demon distorted but reformed, growing ever bigger as it flew towards him.

Carl tried to pull himself up from the cold gravel, but lay aghast; surely if this hellish creature was to strike him down, Sarah would perish in the fire. But he had broken the warlock's stone and reversed the spell, so why was this malicious nightmare hurtling towards him? Was it that he had the same blood as the doctor – his real, biological father?

Hearing voices shout from the entrance, Carl witnessed Daniel turn back into the mansion, but saw the doctor run out and see him. Clenching his dagger with pretence, at first the doctor smirked, but Carl pulled free the pendant from his pocket and swung it above his head. Seeing the stone nothing but a cracked hollow shell, the doctor scowled. However, it was when he turned to face the fiery mass towering above him, that the doctor showed true fear. Amazed at the size of the demon, the doctor stepped back and in desperation shouted strange words.

Carl scrambled to his feet to be at any second ready to run, but the doctor pointed at him and bellowed out orders. As the doctor stood pointing and turned to face Carl, one of the demon's fiery hands protracted from its nebulous body and clasped the doctor like a rag-doll, smothering him in flame and burning him instantly. Turning his head so not to look, Carl also dismissed the doctor's bellowing cries of agonising pain. Whether it was to see the doctor turned to cinder or to truly witness the creature from his nightmares, Carl could not help but glance back as he ran for the study. The last he saw was the demon's hand throw the doctor's charred body upon the driveway.

Inside the manor, Carl was overwhelmed by the extent of the fire. Not only had it engulfed the banqueting hall from where it had begun, but it was burning quickly the timeworn wood of the building. He raced to the study door, but through a cloud of smoke saw a figure standing by it and pointing a shotgun. Daniel told him to halt and declared that now all riches of the manor were to be lost, he had no interest but to avenge his master. Grabbing a nearby candlestick, Carl ran at him but heard the shotgun fire. Luckily the shot only splintered a cabinet to where he fell for protection.

Peering to see Daniel reload the gun, Carl knew he had limited time to save Sarah and so assailed him again. Hitting Daniel's hand with the candlestick, both weapons fell to the floor, as did both men; but in the struggle it was Daniel who retrieved the shotgun first. In pain and with eyes stinging from clouds of smoke, Daniel got to his feet and stumbled towards Carl, arching over him to aim the shotgun. As he announced his dislike for Carl and that he considered saving the girl for himself, a piece of burning timber swung down and pelted Daniel against the wall.

Watching Daniel's unconscious body fall to the ground, Carl crawled to grab the shotgun and scrambled through the fire and smoke to the study door. He tried the door, but realising Daniel had the key, glared angrily at his still body. But scorched lumber was falling about him; wooden panels burned, floor boards were smouldering and smoke filled the room. Suddenly Carl realised to what he was holding and aimed the shotgun at the lock. The first shot hardly penetrated the thick door, but the second shell blasted away at the lock. Nevertheless the door remained tightly shut and so he kicked repeatedly the lock and threw his body weight against the door until suddenly he stumbled through.

Inside, Carl noticed the study had also succumbed to fire, but fortunately most smoke had rose to the ceiling. Quickly he staggered over to retrieve Sarah from the couch, but carrying her in his arms felt uncontrollably weak. He plodded on, readjusting his hands to balance her weight, but had to rest against the doorway. By now most of the hallway and stairs were ablaze and thinking Daniel was amongst it, Carl gazed wearily through the smoke. Through what he could see, Daniel's once unconscious body had now disappeared.

Lowering Sarah's body to the ground to wrap his coat more tightly around her, Carl heard sirens through the sound of fire and splintering wood. He shouted at Sarah to wake, telling her that help was coming and soon she would be safe, but as he lifted her again, a hefty joist crashed to the ground and broke the floor. With the only exit now hindered and trapped by infernal heat and smoke, Carl knew he had to do something fast. With all his strength he ran towards the entrance and with Sarah grasped tight, jumped the opening. Amazingly his feet made the other side and although he stumbled in trying to balance, he stepped to move forward. Suddenly beneath them the floorboards splintered and the area on which Carl stood collapsed, toppling him back into the cellar below.

As she awoke, the first thing Sarah felt was heat on her face. Gradually as her eyes focused upon the collapsed ceiling, a pungent smoke scathed her throat and she coughed. Trying to gasp at what air she could, she noticed Carl's coat wrapped about her and fidgeted until she saw a hand. She looked to one side and then glanced back to see Carl's face; realising he was unconscious and beneath her. She wriggled free of the coat but held it around her to shield her from the heat. Sliding herself from his grasp, she grimaced at the fire about her, before looking back at him. For a moment she laid perplexed, but realised she was in some basement; that both of them were trapped with the building burning around them.

Senses aroused, Sarah started to panic and slid to face Carl.

'Carl… Carl?' She called, slapping this cheek with her hand. 'Please wake up, I don't know where we are but this place is coming down any second!'

She looked again to observe the ceiling and noticed the only stairs to the cellar door had been crushed by falling joists. Distraught by her circumstances, Sarah pulled on Carl's shoulders but his unconscious body would not move. She pulled on him again, her soiled hair sticking to cascading tears that ran down her face.

'Carl, please, Carl?' She shouted, turning quick to watch another joist collapse.

Wriggling her foot free, she noticed that she had no shoe and underneath the coat she was dressed in a strange black robe. But it was when she pulled herself up that she grimaced in horror. As she dragged away the coat from Carl's chest, she noticed a metal rod spearing out; the blood already congealed by dust and debris.

'Carl, please, you've got to wake up!' Sarah exclaimed, hopeful that he was still alive. 'We've got to get out of here!'

Sobbing, she kissed his lips before lying down her head by his neck. She fingered with his mouth, feeling for his breath and listened for his heartbeat, but the noise of the fire was intense. Suddenly as she lay crying, a hand clenched her hair and fell upon her shoulder. Trying desperately to revive him, Sarah kissed his face and saw her tears fall on him.

'Carl, you're alive,' she bellowed, her smile showing relief but anxiety, 'got to get you off that thing,' she said trying to lift his shoulders, 'before the whole place comes down.'

Gradually Carl's eyes fluttered open but Sarah realised he could not see her.

'I feel your hair,' Carl said, his voice hoarse and weak whilst reaching to touch her face, 'and your tears… but I cannot see you?'

'I can't move you,' Sarah announced, desperation in her voice, 'but we've got to get out of here!'

'I can't feel my legs,' Carl groaned, 'but all is not dark now.'

'What, can you see me?' Sarah said, looking desperately into Carl's glazed eyes. 'Can you see where we are? Is this the mansion's basement?

'That is of no concern now,' Carl muttered, fingering Sarah's long hair, 'the doctor has been avenged for his doing… mother told them to adopt me, but looked over me… there is no more fear.'

'No Carl, my fear is that I lose you,' Sarah sobbed emotionally. 'Remember our time together; the beach, the harbour lights… I want more,' she bellowed, her voice croaking, 'so don't you get giving up on me now,' she continued in a determined tone, 'you saved me, so I'm going to save you!'

'So bright, isn't it my dear?' Carl said his voice fading.

Suddenly Carl's head dropped slowly back, his breathing slow but rhythmic, his eyes still glazed.

'Carl… Carl, hang in there!' Sarah called, her voice desperate, 'I haven't told you about,' Sarah's throat choked

464

with smoke, 'how much I love you… that's really why I came back!' She coughed again before announcing. 'We'll be safe soon, you'll see!'

Strangely from Carl's mouth a voice of a woman muttered words to her.

'Do not weep my child,' the voice instructed, 'he has avenged the good and commanded justice… and now he's finally with me.'

'But Carl,' Sarah stuttered, 'but, Carl that isn't you,' she said, tears flooding her eyes. 'What will I do without you?'

As Carl's face shone a bright pale, Sarah noticed his hand cover her navel. Suddenly, feeling a strange sensation within her stomach, Sarah heard the voice again.

'Look after those who you will love, as in return they will love you.'

Perplexed by the strange voice, Sarah watched Carl's body grow limp and his head turn to one side.

'No, I can't lose you,' Sarah hollered, 'come back Carl, please…'


Noticing the manor ablaze, the Detective Inspector informed the station that firemen were required at the scene. Stopping the police car alongside the entrance, the driving policeman turned and instructed Mike to stay seated, but Mike argued that his friend may be caught in the fire. Once stationary, Mike leapt from the police car back seat and ran toward the entrance; the policeman shouting for him to stop.

Running after him, the policemen stopped to glance down to see the cindered body of what had been the doctor.

'What the hell's happened here?' the constable questioned, kneeling over the charred corpse.

'Whoever that is,' deduced the Detective Inspector, 'looks like they escaped the building, but not the fire!'

'Inspector Campbell,' the constable enquired, 'to whom does this place belong again?'

'It is supposed to belong to *that* doctor,' he answered, 'the one just out of that institute; the one the Governor knew.'

'The one locked up for killing that kid?'

'Yes,' the Detective Inspector acknowledged, 'and was only released the other day.'

'Well if that's him,' the constable asserted, 'I think he would've been better staying where he was!'


From above and through the noise of fire and cracking wood, Sarah heard a voice calling. Feeling no breath or pulse from his wrist, she thought Carl dead but could not leave him.

'Sarah,' the voice shouted, 'is that you?'

Sarah turned to face the hole in the ceiling, her eyes glistening with tears. Through the smoke, all that she could see was a shadowed figure, crouching to look down.

'Is Carl down there with you?' the voice shouted.

'Yes,' Sarah cried, her voice muffled with sorrow, 'Yes, but I think he's dead.' She crawled, moving close to the on looking figure. 'I think Carl is dead. Is that you Mike? Please can you get us out? Maybe he's still alive!'

'I can't get down, but the fire brigade is on its way!'

'I can't leave him but,' Sarah started to choke profusely, 'it's getting too much, the fire and smoke…'

466

Mike noticed how much the floor had weakened and that the whole area was being eaten away by flame.

'You've got to get up here quick,' Mike asserted, holding out his hand for Sarah to reach, 'it's all going to crumble before the firemen get here!'

'No, I won't leave Carl,' Sarah cried, stumbling back to his body. 'There's a chance his still–'

Suddenly, taking Sarah by surprise, a large beam of timber splintered and fell to the floor, missing Carl's body by inches. She screamed, but noticed how his body never flinched; surely he was dead and she could do nothing for him now.

'Come on you stupid girl,' Mike shouted, edging close to the top of the beam, 'climb up and catch my hand!'

Hesitantly, Sarah looked at Carl before running towards the beam that stretched overhead. Clasping unburned parts of the beam, she climbed as much as she could, before reaching for Mike's hand. Just as the floor behind collapsed and engulfed Carl's body, Sarah grasped Mike's wrist and he pivoted his weight to lift her. Together they fell backward but to the safety of the hallway. Nevertheless, the whole building around them was on fire and impatiently Mike picked himself up and helped Sarah to stand. At first Sarah held back, but seeing nothing but smoke rise from the collapsed floor, trailed behind Mike, tears flooding her eyes.

Together they ran outside and rested near the entrance; Sarah now coughing uncontrollably. As she cried about losing Carl, Mike steered her down the steps and then lifted her head to offer her his handkerchief. She looked at Mike and sobbed that now all she had was memories of her short time with Carl. She thanked Mike for saving her, but realising all what must have happened, asserted that it was Carl that truly saved her. However, frowning at Mike, she stopped in mid-sentence.

'How come you knew?' she asked. 'How did you know we were here?'

'Carl told me he was coming here,' Mike revealed, 'and asked me to prevent the doctor from getting here, but I thought him deluded. But maybe he was right; someone certainly must have followed me to knock me out!'

He paused before ushering Sarah to the police car where the Detective Inspector looked on.

'When I eventually woke, I became anxious and had to go to the police. Even if Carl got arrested, at least things would get sorted.'

Hearing other sirens approach, Sarah looked back at the burning manor.

'I should have listened to him,' Mike stuttered, his eyes stinging with tears. 'I guess it doesn't matter now, I just hope my poor friend is at peace from his nightmares.'

# EPILOGUE

'STEADY MY GIRL,' A VOICE said, 'been having those bad dreams again?'

Sarah woke to feel a damp cloth touch her forehead and saw the round face of a nurse looking down at her.

'There are friends waiting to see you,' she announced. 'Shall I ask them to come in?'

Sarah nodded whilst trying to focus her eyes; it was as though some liquid was blurring her vision. As she pulled herself up from the hospital bed, she realised of how she was advised to stay in overnight; that she had been sedated for tests. As she turned to face the door, her eyesight cleared enough to recognise Mike and Rachael.

'Some episode that was last night my dear,' Mike proclaimed, his voice sympathetic. 'Carl did well saving you from that devil worshipping maniac!'

'Don't be so blunt,' Rachael snapped, hitting his arm with her fist. 'Poor girl doesn't even know what happened.'

'She did,' Mike replied, 'because I got her out. It was a good job I –'

'Did they find Carl?' Sarah croaked, her eyes now flooded with tears. 'Did he survive?'

Watching the couple glance at one another, Sarah deduced he must have been lost in the fire, as indeed she had seen the hallway collapse on him herself.

'I'm sorry Sarah, but –'

'It's okay Rachael,' Sarah said, turning her head away, 'I guessed as much. I have truly lost him haven't I?'

'Yes my dear,' Rachael said quietly, 'it's true you have, but he was such a good guy; a sincere and righteous boy, his Aunt said.'

'Not all righteous, you know,' Sarah said. 'He set up that doctor to avenge his school friend's death; putting his bloody handkerchief around the doctor's gardening tool – mind you, he did fall on it, and apparently…' Sarah paused, frowning at both of them in turn, 'Carl's Aunt?' she questioned, 'you've spoken to his Aunt?'

'Yes Sarah,' Rachael disclosed, 'we found a letter addressed to him and traced her number.' Rachael paused for a moment to look at Mike. 'Besides, she is the only relative we know for the funeral.'

'Carl's funeral,' Sarah said slowly, looking down at her bed, 'but when is it, as I must go?'

'Not at the moment my dear,' the nurse announced looking at her chart and then at Mike and Rachael, 'not in your condition.'

'But surely I'm just cut and bruised?' Sarah declared, but saw the nurse look at her visitors, 'I'll be out soon, won't I?'

'She doesn't know?' the nurse enquired, looking expectantly at Mike and Rachael. 'Obviously, it's the first she's come round since the test results.'

Sarah sat up and became agitated by their discussion.

'What is it?' she demanded. 'Is it bad; internal bleeding or something?'

'You've not told her yet I take it?' the nurse asked.

'No,' Rachael replied, 'it's the first we've spoke to her, she's been –'

'Will someone tell me what's wrong with me for God's sake?' Sarah shouted.

For a moment all went quiet and the nurse nodded to Rachael as she brushed past her.

'You see Sarah,' Rachael said slowly, 'you've got to take it easy because…'

'Because, what?'

'Because you are pregnant, that's why!' Rachael said, looking awkwardly at Mike. 'Is it Carl's?'

'Of course it's got to be,' she snapped trying to disguise her surprise, 'who else do you think I've been with?'

'Then its okay Sarah,' Mike reassured, 'don't you think this is great? At least you have something of his and not just memories.'

Sarah looked at Mike, her angry face changing to a smile.

'Will you name it after the father?' Rachael asked, stepping toward her to hold her hand.

'If it's a boy, that is!' Mike asserted, smiling.

For a moment Sarah sat quiet and looked at Rachael's engagement ring.

'No, it's going to be a girl,' Sarah said confidently, 'and her name will be Emily.'

At that point the nurse brushed past Mike and Rachel and looked at Sarah.

'From the scan you had this morning,' the nurse disclosed, 'you'd better think of two other girl's names.'

Lightning Source UK Ltd.
Milton Keynes UK
UKHW020635050922
408358UK00009B/1100